ALL FIRED UP

ALL FIRED UP
SONGS OF THE ASCENDANT - VOLUME II

DARIN KENNEDY

64 SQUARE
PUBLISHING

To Keith Nelson,
my immortal friend and other hemisphere
The corpus callosum is still strong after all these years

Stand strong, my heart; through even worse pain you have suffered.

— HOMER, THE ODYSSEY

CHAPTER 1

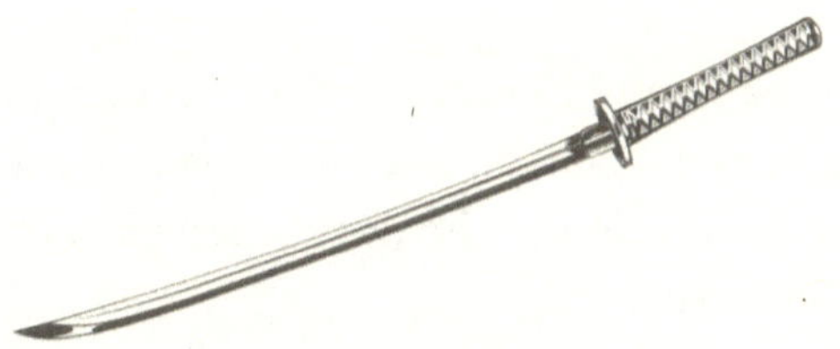

THE GLAMOROUS LIFE

The woman shot me a practiced smile from beneath jet-black bangs as she studied me from across the draped table laden with every torture implement imaginable.

Mother always taught me to meet force with force, but those tactics, unfortunately, won't serve me here. Grinning and bearing it, as Ethan likes to call it, is not my strong suit. Never has been. But I'm here for Seph, and regardless of the pain or consequences, I will maintain my composure.

"Whoa, Rosemary," Seph laughed. "You're, like, hyperventilating." Her expression went pensive, and then the proverbial lightbulb from the books Mother read me as a child went off over her head. "Wait," she whispered, "you didn't tell me the truth before."

Caught in a lie. Shamed, I turned away from her accusatory stare.

"This *is* your first pedicure, isn't it?"

Abashed, I glanced back in Seph's direction. "And what if it is?"

"For starters, we could have gone a little more basic for your first time. I've sprung for the whole shebang."

"Do you two ladies need a moment, Miss Snow?" asked the middle-aged Asian lady who'd served us hot tea moments before and now planned to dig into my toes with her tray of stainless-steel scissors, hooks, and other tools the purpose of which I didn't care to imagine. "I can bring a cool washcloth for your friend if that would help."

"That would be lovely." Seph waited for the outwardly pleasant—suspiciously so, in fact—pedicurist to disappear into the back before raising one lone brow the way she does when she's about to call you on your...well, whatever.

"What the hell, Rosemary? I spring for mani-pedis and you act like she's about to shove bamboo under your toenails to get you to spill your guts." At my wide-eyed surprise, she added, "Sorry, it was in one of Ethan's old war movies."

Ethan. In the month since the disaster in L.A. resulted in the European leg of Seph's Sparkle Tour getting postponed indefinitely, he and I had been training daily, getting Ethan up to speed as a so-called Agent of Neith. Fortunately, the remainder of August and the first half of September had passed without event and we'd made significant progress. Seph showed up from time to time to, as she playfully liked to call it, supervise, though her presence, however delightful, usually proved nothing but a distraction for a red-blooded male like Ethan. Other times we trained alone, which I much preferred.

When focused on what he's doing instead of making eyes at our favorite pop star, Ethan learns fast, and it's not simply Mother's Light shining through him. He's bright, brighter in fact than a lot of people give him credit for. He has a strong work ethic, he's willing to put in the hours, and he's not afraid to take criticism. It was going to take some time before I could pass on even a tenth of all I'd learned from Mother and Father, but I couldn't have asked for a better student or partner.

"Rosemary?" Seph asked. "Are you listening to me?"

"Yes."

Funny. My mind wandered. My mind never wanders.

"Sorry." I glanced Seph's way. "I was deep in thought."

About your boyfriend, to be more specific.

Persephone Snow, reigning Princess of Pop, was the first person to ever designate me their BFF. Still, though everything with me and Ethan was totally platonic, that didn't change the fact I wasn't saying a word about where my mind had wandered, much less with whom.

"I guess I'm trying to avoid thinking about what this woman is going to be doing to my feet." I continued to deep breathe, focusing my thoughts on what lay before me, both physically and metaphorically. "I mean, people pay handsomely for such service every day, right?"

Seph shook her head as she stared at me incredulous from the corner of her vision. "You understand she isn't going to hurt you, right?"

"I will be fine." I took a sip of my hot tea. "Like you said, she's not going to hurt me." The woman returned from the back holding a wet washcloth in her hand. "Thank you, Ms. Lee." I held out my hand, my fingers steady despite my trepidation. "I'll take that." I leaned back in my chair, positioned the washcloth across my eyes, and forced my mind a thousand miles away from anything resembling a cuticle remover, muttering under my breath a barely audible, "Do your worst."

Ms. Lee started with a chemical assault, the sharp smell of acetone burning my nostrils as she scrubbed my toenails with a cotton ball to remove the bismuth pink Seph left there three days ago when this nightmare started.

"What do you mean your mom never let you paint your nails?" Seph had asked me that evening as the movie we were watching went to commercial.

"I never said she didn't *let* me paint my nails," I'd answered. "All I said was I never painted my nails growing up. It all seemed a bit girly at the time, I guess, when I was starting every day with a five-mile run." A chuckle bubbled up from within. "She did drill a tiny hole in my right big toenail with a knife one time to let out the blood after she stepped on my foot in training." In that moment, I had missed my mother very much and said so, despite my efforts to keep such emotion to myself. Seph swooped in, and the next thing I knew, my toenails were the color of the medicine dad takes when he gets an upset stomach on the road.

"Ow!" A pinch at my left pinky toe brought me back to the present.

"Sorry," Ms. Lee apologized before turning to speak in Chinese to the lady who worked on Seph's feet.

My Mandarin was rusty at best, but I was pretty sure she said something about "the talons of an eagle."

I forced a smile. For Seph. All of this was for her.

With Dad still recuperating from his various injuries, the role of personal bodyguard for pop sensation Persephone Snow had fallen to me. Ethan, for all his obvious personal involvement, couldn't be with her 24-7. Between training with me, continuing to build his budding relationship with one of the most famous women in the world, and eating and sleeping occasionally, it was a wonder he got anything else done.

Neko kept an eye on her when Ethan and I were busy training, but that almost ended when our favorite tiger theriodan accidentally dropped the B-word.

No, not that one.

"*Babysitting?*" Seph had fumed. "You think you're all *babysitting* me?"

That discussion went about as well as expected. Neko managed to dig himself out of the mess, but it was only because he and Seph had far more in common than a world-famous pop star and I ever would.

For instance, he would be eating up this whole mani-pedi experience.

Me, on the other hand? If she jabbed my toe—still sore, by the way, from Ethan blocking a kick the day before—with that cuticle stick one more time, I was considering introducing her to one of my own sharp metal implements.

Trim, file, cuticle goo, and remover done, I got to stick my feet in the little whirlpool bath which, I had to admit, felt pretty good. Same with the buffing of the nails and the pumice stone to get the callus off my feet, though Mother would be aghast knowing I let someone erode away my soles' well-earned protection.

She'd never made me walk a bed of hot coals, but barefoot across a room of Legos in the dark apparently was a tried-and-true method to teach a young woman how to move silently under difficult circumstances.

Another soak was soon followed by a scrub of my feet and ankles with some stuff that smelled like strawberries only to be followed by yet another soak.

Once you got past the initial torture, apparently, the rest wasn't so bad.

Ms. Lee dried my feet with a fluffy towel, used a little alcohol to disinfect all the little cuts—yes, that stung a bit—and then it was time for the main event.

"What color?" Ms. Lee directed my eye to a veritable rainbow of polish suggestions. "Did you finally make up your mind?"

I'd scanned the entire selection multiple times, but the one that kept drawing my eye was never in doubt.

"The dark red." I pointed to a circle of deep burgundy the color of half-dried blood. "I want the dark red."

"Somehow, I knew that would be your answer," Seph said, one of her feet already done with the first coat, a bright shade of turquoise. "The red will go well with your skin tone."

I admired Seph's perfect calves, perfect ankles, perfect skin, perfect everything.

"Does anything *not* go with yours?" I asked.

"You'd be surprised." She rolled her eyes. "The year after *Teen Spies* went off the air and before I really started with the singing, I went through a bit of a goth phase." She raised a blonde eyebrow beneath her platinum locks, her smile making it all the way to those crystal blue eyes. "Black? Not exactly my shade."

"Don't forget," I laughed. "I've seen you in black."

"You've seen me in black and blue, that's for sure."

If only Mother could see me. Best friends with the biggest pop star in the world, or at least that's what the pop star in question kept telling me.

I've never said it out loud, but I think of her more like the sister I never had.

And then there's Ethan.

It's interesting, watching Seph and Ethan together. They make it look so easy. Back when it was me trying to make it work with a...boy, things were anything but. On the other hand, Ethan doesn't have a ravening canine lurking behind those big blue eyes guiding his every thought and move, at least no more than any other American male walking around.

Okay, Rosemary. No dredging up the past while you're supposed to be enjoying a day off with Seph.

Funny. Something so basic as a pedicure seems almost like a rite of passage for womanhood. Over there, two sisters; next to us, college roommates; and right across the way, a mother and her daughter commemorating the girl's thirteenth birthday.

Mother and I had never entertained such a moment. Five a.m. workouts five days a week? No problem. Weapons drills, synchronized kata, gymnastics training? Standard fare. But we never went to have our hair done, never shopped for clothes other than what was absolutely necessary for school, work, or training, and certainly never engaged in anything as luxurious as having someone else trim our nails.

All of the above and more, I've done with Seph in the four short weeks since Los Angeles. The moment Seph found out she was Ascendant, everything changed, and yet, as much as her discovering her true nature took her from simply a megastar to something even rarer, her status as Ascendant and separate from the rest of the world was what fueled the bond between us.

Not to mention her connection with Ethan.

In the annals of history, Daughters of Neith have dallied with Ascendant, sometimes out of true emotion or attraction and other times simply as a means to an end. Never, to my knowledge, has one of my line and one among the Ascendant forged a union such as theirs.

To hear Ethan tell it, Seph totally hated his guts the first time they ever spoke, but Seph remembers it more like she was exhausted and "hangry"—one of her favorite words and one I've actually started to use myself—that night in Albuquerque, and even as she was berating him in front of his supervisor, Mr. Reid, she thought he was "cute." And that was before he leaped into the breach with me, Mother, and Father and rescued her from a skiomancer attack.

After that, she's proclaimed to me half a dozen times, "I never had a chance."

And I get it. I mean, how could I not?

Ethan and I were developing our own sort of bond. Training several hours a day will do that. And my eyes? They worked just fine. Already a superb specimen, a month of training had left both his pecs and arms more defined than they were when his main exercise was simply moving equipment from truck to stage and back day in and day out.

Like the other day, when he whipped off his shirt and thought I wasn't looking—

"Whatcha thinking about?" Seph asked as her pedicurist finished the top coat on her turquoise nails and brought over the dryer to finish the job. My squirming had slowed my own nail expert down a bit, and she was still applying my second coat of "Once Bitten" polish. "You've been even more quiet than usual."

"Just relaxing." I covered my tiny pang of guilt with a laugh. "Mother taught me all about meditation, mindfulness, and being in the moment. Letting my brain slip out of gear and relaxing feels almost...naughty. Does that make sense?"

"That's okay, right?"

"It's more than okay." My lips pulled wide into a genuine smile. "It's positively luxurious."

"One of the many perks of this life." Seph returned a devilish grin of her own. "When I'm busy, I'm really busy." She swung her arms wide, indicating our posh surroundings. "And when I'm not..."

"You say that," I let out a chuckle, "but I know your workout schedule and the hours you spend keeping your voice in shape. In your own way, you train as hard as me, and your nutritional regimen is way more intense than mine."

"After my first tour, I took it seriously easy for a few weeks. Truly let myself go for the first time in years. Gained a whopping five pounds." She shook her head. "From the way the tabloids spun it, you'd have thought I'd grown a third eye."

"Speaking of the press, I'm still amazed the rest of the world still doesn't seem to know what happened in Los Angeles last month."

Seph shook her head. "It would be funny if it wasn't so unfair. I put on five pounds and people along the Amazon who have never seen a television in their entire life hear about it. But shadow-dealing assassins, element-controlling mercenaries, and three individuals who are effectively demigods show up to the last show of my tour and tear the place apart? That's 'a publicity stunt' or something similar."

"Father keeps scrubbing the internet for anything regarding the actual events of that night, but all he keeps finding is 'technical difficulties' and 'unfortunate equipment malfunctions' as explanation. Not even the conspiracy websites have anything up about the various Ascendant present and the fact they nearly tore the place to the ground."

"All I can say is the 'technomancer' or whatever you call the internet wizard working for El Ángel del Alba must be working overtime to keep up with the people at TMZ."

My pedicurist finally finished putting the clear top coat on my last nail and brought over her dryer to complete the new suit of blood-red armor on my ten little piggies, as Mother used to call them when I was a child. The pungent odor of the place continued to burn my nostrils as it had since we arrived, but I'd grown used to it. Ten minutes into the drying phase, however, the venti Frappuccino Seph had bought me finally kicked in, and I needed to relieve myself.

"Excuse me," I asked the woman I'd put in charge of my toes for fifty-eight minutes of my life, "is it okay if I go to the restroom?"

"Of course, dear." She looked across the room and her amicable expression shifted to one of regret. "Sorry. Sign's up again." She sighed. "Our toilet has been having issues. Trust me, you don't want to go in there right now."

"Okay." I shot Seph a frantic look. "I can hold on for a bit, but..."

"Don't worry, Rosemary." Seph pointed out the salon's big entrance into the mall proper. "The public restrooms are right outside. No need to sit here doing the pee-pee dance when salvation is right across the way."

Sometimes Seph puts things in such a way that arguing becomes pointless.

In seconds, I'd been fitted with the flimsiest, ugliest, least comfortable pair of flip-flops imaginable and headed for the exit, walking like a television zombie as I tried to keep the polish from my very first pedicure in reasonable shape. The relatively fresh air of the mall corridor was a welcome relief after the hour-long barrage on my nostrils by the chemical stink of the salon.

There was no time for lollygagging, as Father called it, though. I was a woman on a mission.

The bathroom across the way only boasted three stalls, and as I entered, a quick inspection revealed all were occupied. Mother had taught me how to control my bodily functions to a degree most would never master, so Seph's so-called "pee-pee dance" never came to pass. I must admit, however, that my foot was tapping to a tune only I could hear.

When one of the stalls finally opened, releasing a mother and a three-year-old who clearly wanted to be anywhere but the mall, I rushed in to claim my territory, doing my best not to kill myself in the salon's ridiculous excuse for footwear. Finishing my business as quickly as possible, I handed the toilet off to the next desperate woman, washed my hands, and stepped back out into the mall proper, one ungainly step after the other.

No sooner had I opened the door, however, than a scent that hadn't lit up my senses in two years wafted through the air. The potent combination of earthy sandalwood and musk brought with it danger, excitement, and passion, not to mention, unbridled anger.

Maddox's cologne.

And then, as if the scent wasn't enough, a voice I'd hoped to never hear again and yet had never stopped listening for hit my ears.

"Hey there, Rosemary." I turned to find a smile that always used to make my heart race and now sent a shard of ice straight through my chest. "Been a while."

CHAPTER 2

OUT OF THE BLUE

"Maddox." I spun around, the flimsy flip-flops off in an instant, nail polish be damned. "What the hell are you doing here?"

"Whoa, whoa, whoa." His hands were up before his chest in joking surrender before I could so much as throw the first kick. "I didn't come here to start a fight."

"You're seriously going to show up and say, 'Been a while'?" I stepped closer, not only so he could hear my whisper, but also to put myself within suitable range to launch a throat strike if I needed to. "Do you remember the last words you said to me?"

"I told you I loved you."

"Right after we..." Memories I'd pushed away, locked down, and buried beneath a mile of rage sprung to life anew: the touch of his strong hands, the smell of his hair, the taste of his skin on my tongue. "Imagine my surprise waking the next morning to find you gone."

If I expected to find shame in those dusky grey eyes, I was sorely disappointed. His hand went to his neck as he tipped his head forward, the only sign of remorse I was likely going to get. "Things were getting complicated. I—"

"Things were 'getting complicated' you say?" I shifted my weight onto my back leg instinctively, my every muscle fiber aching to throw the roundhouse kick Mother taught me on my seventh birthday. "So complicated you had to disappear for *two years*?"

His smug smile diminished a bit. "I guess I deserve that."

"You guess?" A quickly growing ball of rage-fueled hate transformed the ice at my core to a burning inferno. "Listen very carefully, Maddox. You let fly one more stupid break-up cliché and I will drop you where you stand." My body dropped instinctively into a Krav Maga tactical stance ingrained in my muscle memory since I was a child. "Do you hear me, *coyote*?"

That last word made him wince. Good.

"I hear you." Maddox pulled in a deep breath, his mischievous grin evaporating altogether. "Look. Can we start over?"

"Start over? Now? After two years? You've got to be—"

"Not *us*, Rosemary," he interrupted, "this conversation."

"Oh." My cheeks burned. I'd been preparing for this moment for two straight years, and less than five minutes in, I'd already come across like I was pining. Perfect. "Say what you've got to say, Maddox, and then get going." I relaxed from my combat pose and crossed my arms. "You've got thirty seconds."

"Here?" He gestured to the crowd surrounding us in the packed corridor. Most ignored us, but a few of them stopped to stare at what must have appeared a lover's quarrel. "In front of everybody?"

"You're the one in full stalker mode in the middle of a shopping mall after two years of no contact." One of Seph's favorite expressions popped into my head. "Your circus, your monkeys." My head tilted to one side as my patience began to grow thin. "Now, talk or walk."

"Wow," Maddox laughed despite himself. "And I thought you were assertive before."

"You have no idea." I checked the little watch Seph had given me as a thank you present after Los Angeles. "Fifteen seconds."

"This is how you're going to be?"

"Ten."

"Fine." He growled, the coyote within coming to the surface as his fists clenched at his sides. "You're in danger, Rosemary. You and your father, not to mention this Harkreader person you're hanging around with." His eyes stole to one side. "You've already lost your mother in the first wave of what's coming—my condolences, by the way—and I don't want to see you lose anyone or anything else."

"Huh." I cocked my head to one side in a move Seph had helped me perfect over the preceding weeks. "Funny how you know so much about my life when I haven't heard a word from you in two years. And your big revelation is that we're all in danger? What else is new?" I glanced left and right, my body reassuming its fighting stance. "Who is it this time?"

Nearly a dozen faces flitted across my imagination before the question had even passed my lips. I could think of four skiomancers, a quartet of elementalists, and a couple of Angels who likely were still icing their bruised egos a month after Los Angeles, not to mention two of Maddox's own buddies who we'd left limping in Vegas.

And that didn't take into account the hundreds of Ascendant Mother had crossed in one way or another over her years as the latest and possibly last Daughter of Neith, a role that had been destined for me and that remained, for the time being at least, postponed.

"You really don't want me to go into that out here in the open." Maddox's eyes wandered over the crowd, half of which had whipped out their phones to document what could possibly be the next viral video if Maddox and I were to get into it. "Can we go somewhere and talk?"

"Still using that line, eh?"

"Rosemary, please." His eyes shifted from their usual grey to the yellow of the coyote that lived within. "I'm just trying to help."

"Please?" I chuckled. "Now, that's a first."

"Look, I came here today because no matter what went down between us, I still care enough to make sure you're okay."

"What happened between us is you pursued me for six straight months, finally seduced me into your bed, and vanished the next day." My cheeks went white-hot. "Did I miss anything important?"

"Daaamn!" came a comment from a trio of young black women watching from the sidelines.

"You tell him, girlfriend!" came another shout-out from the opposite direction, a freckled girl with shoulder-length red hair and round glasses.

I shook my head. "As you can see, despite the fact that I'm standing barefoot in the middle of a mall surrounded by gawking strangers, I'm doing just fine."

"You won't be, if you don't listen to what I have to say."

My entire body tensed. "Is that a threat?"

The crowd surrounding us grew quiet, awaiting his answer.

With a swallow and a crack of his neck, he answered. "Not from me."

"Rosemary?" came Seph's voice. "Everything okay?" Her platinum locks concealed again under her ball cap and those crystal blue eyes that decorated literally millions of CDs, posters, and television screens across the world hidden behind dark shades covering a third of her face, she pulled up on my flank.

"I'm fine."

"Who is this man?" Something in her demeanor, her stance, even her breathing shifted almost imperceptibly. "Wait. Is this—"

I raised a hand. "Don't say his name."

"Miss Snow." Maddox leaned forward in a polite bow. "Wow, Rosemary. I'd *heard* you've been keeping some interesting company these days."

The crowd around us began to whisper, the repeated five syllables of Seph's name in varying shades of excitement and disbelief hitting my ears like an ancient mantra. In one fell swoop, Maddox had proven dashingly charming and simultaneously shown utter disdain for the needs of the woman standing directly in front of him, namely Seph's desire for the two of us to be able to walk into and out of a shopping center without being mobbed by fans.

As far as I was concerned, he was running true to form.

But now, not only was Seph's day irrevocably screwed up, but mine as well, as I downshifted from friend mode into bodyguard.

"Come with me, Seph," I took her arm and gently tugged her in the direction of the door. "Let's get you to your car before this spirals out of control."

Something had told me sneaking out was a bad idea, at least that particular morning. We'd headed out together, just the two of us, more than once over the preceding month, but this time, I'd ignored my gut. Hopefully Seph wouldn't have to pay for my mistake, though how I was supposed to predict Maddox showing up out of the blue was beyond me.

I sensed a lecture from Father in my near future, a lecture I at least half-deserved if for no other reason than the fact both my parents had taught me countless times to trust my instincts.

"Miss Snow," came a ten-year-old girl with her mother, "can I take a picture with you?"

"Hey," came a rush of preteen girls from the opposite direction, "we saw her first."

Voice after voice, each louder than the one before, added to the hubbub as the crowd converged on our position. Seph, Maddox, and I pulled close together, each of us facing outward against the oncoming fame-seekers.

"Thanks a lot," I grunted in Maddox's direction.

"I recommended we go somewhere quiet and talk," he answered. "You're the one who insisted on grandstanding in the middle of a Montecito shopping mall."

Though it felt like gaslighting, a part of me recognized the truth in his statement.

"Fine. Help us get out of this, and I'll listen to what you have to say."

"That's all I ask," he answered. "And without further ado..."

As Maddox turned to face the crowd, something in his overall demeanor changed. His back arched, his arm pulled slightly out to each side, and he let out a loud growl that cut through the cacophony of the crowd.

"Move on," he barked at no one in particular. "Nothing to see here."

"I wanna know what this fine lady has to say about that." The lead teen in a trio of Latino boys stepped forward. "I hear she's single these days, so I'll keep it to hello. She don't like what she sees, I'll step."

"I said," Maddox's voice dropped an octave to the point you felt his words as much as heard them, "move on."

With his back turned, I couldn't see his eyes, but I had the distinct suspicion Maddox had let *el guapo* see the beast within, as every bit of swagger left the teen's features and his own eyes grew wide along with those of both his friends.

"All right, *ese*, chill." The kid—funny calling him kid, I'm at most three years older—ran his fingers through a shock of pomade-laden dark locks and kicked his head to one side. "Come on, boys."

As the most aggressive trio in the crowd sauntered away with barely a look back, Maddox turned his attention on the remainder of the approaching mob. I let him handle the masculine side of the equation while I turned away the various women and girls. The division of labor wasn't made out of fear; past experience with men had taught me that the Y-chromosome set simply doesn't take a five-foot-eight young woman that society deems attractive seriously until she's broken their nose.

A few minutes later, we'd defused the situation with Seph actually acquiescing to a few photo ops with the youngest among the crowd and the rest moving on from their all-too-brief brush with fame. If there was one thing I'd learned over the preceding month, it's that Seph always has time for her fans, especially the young ones. I suspected it had everything to do with something she felt she missed in her own childhood, but we'd never really talked about it.

"Come with me." Maddox motioned for Seph and me to follow as he headed for the end of the mall that housed the food court and chain restaurants. I slid back into my sandals—Seph had slid them into her bag—and wondered at the miracle that the deep crimson polish of my inaugural pedicure had somehow survived both an ex-boyfriend ambush and a mob of Persephone Snow fans. A quick visual sweep of the area revealed nothing more dangerous than a gaggle of tweens staring from a store across the way.

"Come on, Seph," I muttered. "Let's get this over with."

Following Maddox, we wandered past a busy department store advertising a clearance sale for the fall season still a few weeks away, a couple of boutiques, a pharmacy, and then, the tight courtyard opened up on a large food court. Father and I both typically steered Seph clear of such areas, something she never fought us on, but on this particular day, it appeared the perfect place to get lost in a crowd.

Maddox sat at a circular table. "We should be good here for a few minutes as long as all the people posting their pictures to the internet don't bring the rest of the city down about our ears."

"One good thing, I suppose." I shot Seph a sidelong glance. "We can see if our friend, the mysterious technomancer, is still keeping tabs on you while making sure no one else does."

"What's that?" Maddox asked.

"Nothing." I sat across the table from the coyote with Seph, purposefully nondescript in her ball cap and shades, at my side. "So, you came all this way, tracked me down in public, all to tell me I'm in danger?" I leaned forward on my elbows, arms crossed. "What, coyotes don't know how to email?"

"Rosemary..."

"Or maybe you lost all my contact information leaving out so early. That would explain why I've not heard a peep out of you in two years."

"Look, I'm—"

"I didn't even know if you were still alive. Linus and the others assured me that you were most likely fine, but you didn't even tell *them* where you went, and they were your best friends. Who does that?"

"*Rosemary*," Maddox growled, "if you'll stop talking for half a second, I'll try to explain."

I inhaled to continue my rant, but curiosity finally got the better of me. "Fine, but first, it's lunchtime. If you want my undivided attention, go get Seph and me some fish tacos."

He leaned back in his chair. "Fish tacos?"

"Yeah." Seph and I shared a knowing smile. "Seph likes hers blackened a bit, if they can do that here, and I like mine with a little extra lime and cilantro." I considered a moment. "And two Diet Cokes. Not too much ice."

An annoyed half-smile blossomed across his face. "You're going to ride this wave as long as you can, aren't you, Rosemary?"

"You say I'm in danger, but no one seems to be attacking us at the moment, and I can't defend anyone on an empty stomach." I motioned him away. "Feel free to get yourself a snack as well." I answered his weak excuse for a grin with a beaming smile of my own. "We'll be right here."

As Maddox wandered off like a whipped puppy—or maybe that was simply my imagination—Seph pulled close and squeezed my knee.

"So?"

"Yes," I sighed. "That, Persephone Snow, is Maddox Trainor."

"You said he was attractive." She stared after him as he stalked through the crowd in his black jeans and leather jacket, his full head of prematurely salt-and-pepper hair styled immaculately above those prominent cheekbones, square jaw, and two days of stubble. "But you never said anything about those eyes."

Yes. I failed to mention the eyes. Those eyes that had melted me a hundred times, the stare that bored holes through my soul, the steel grey adoration that still haunted my dreams despite the 724 days since Maddox vanished from my life.

I'm sorry, Seph, but that was on purpose.

"You're telling me you used to kiss *that* on a regular basis?"

"Can we talk about this later?" I asked, already knowing the response I'd get from Persephone Snow, pop star extraordinaire and totally-missed-her-calling interrogator. "I'm trying to keep up a brave front here—"

"But seeing him again with those smoldering thundercloud eyes, broad shoulders, and exactly the right amount of facial hair makes you a little weak in the knees?"

"Something. Like. That." The fire that had burned in my cheeks back in the mall proper returned with a vengeance. "Now, listen. All I want to do is hear what he has to say, determine whether or not what he's talking about poses a credible threat to me, my family, you, or Ethan, and then get out of here and try to forget he exists."

"You're going to try to forget that ass?" Seph crinkled her nose. "Good luck."

As Seph continued to wax poetic about the various physical attributes of the first and only man to break my heart, I tuned her out as much as I could while still maintaining situational awareness. With one eye on Maddox and the other on every other person in the food court, I kept tabs on the space as a whole the way Mother taught me.

And not just Mother.

I sat across the table from Father, the sixty-four black-and-white squares of the chessboard between us. I was twelve, and had developed enough skill to defeat him at the game we played when my intense training schedule allowed such frivolity.

Or so I thought.

That day, after I'd defeated him three times in a row, he forced me to play for the first time blindfolded. At the time, I thought it punishment for becoming too skilled for him to defeat anymore, but I now know better.

It wasn't a punishment, and chess wasn't something to simply fill the time when Mother was too tired or busy to continue my physical inculcation. Chess was part of my training, as much as the five-mile runs and the hours spent on gymnastics, martial arts, and the like.

Those trained my body.

Chess trained my mind.

And if you can keep track of all the pieces even when you can't see them, then you can monitor a room full of cranky children, stressed-out mothers, and bored fathers as they wait in line for chicken sandwiches, gyros, or even—

"Fish tacos," Maddox said, "as ordered." He set a paper plate before Seph. "Blackened, Miss Snow, but still moist and tender." He turned to me. "And for you, Rosemary, an extra squeeze of lime and all the cilantro you can handle." He rested my own plate before me, and then placed napkins and drinks before each of us.

"Where's yours?" Seph asked.

"I ate a big breakfast," Maddox answered. "Won't be hungry until dinner."

"You could at least get a drink." Seph studied his muscular forearms. "Surely you worked up a thirst dealing with all those people in the mall."

Maddox laughed. "That's very kind, but if I know Rosemary—and trust me, I know her very well—she wants nothing more than for me to relay what I know and then get the hell out of here." He turned his attention on me. "Isn't that right, Miss Delacroix?"

"Against my better judgment, I agreed to hear you out." I scooped up my fish taco and took a bite, the refreshing spritz of lime hitting my palate like a summer breeze. "Now, talk."

CHAPTER 3

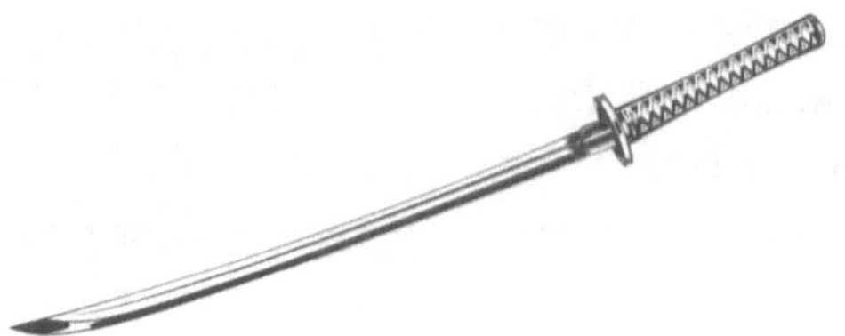

CRUEL TO BE KIND

"Where should I begin?" Maddox leaned forward on his elbows, his biceps bulging against the sleeves of a T-shirt a couple sizes too small. Nice to know his fashion sense hadn't changed, though he'd clearly stepped up his workouts as he was somehow more buff than I remembered.

And it wasn't like he wasn't buff before.

"I don't know." I mirrored his position across the table. "Maybe start with where you've been the last two years and follow up with why I should believe a single word you say."

"The first is a long story..."

I smiled. "I like long stories."

He cleared his throat. "And as for the second, if you don't listen to what I have to say, the consequences could be disastrous."

"That's pretty vague." Seph looked my way. "Don't you think that's vague, Rosemary?"

"Quite." I returned my attention to Maddox. "Down to brass tacks, then. Where have you been since...well...you know?"

"Honestly, I've had to stop myself from calling you a thousand times. If you had any idea how many times I've stood there with my finger on the dial button—"

"Dance around the subject one more second and Seph and I are leaving."

"Fine." His chin dropped ever so slightly. "So, you know more than pretty much anyone else on the planet the business of the Ascendant." He glanced in Seph's direction and dropped his voice briefly to a whisper. "As I understand it, I owe you a congratulations of sorts, Miss Snow, on joining our ranks." His eyes returned to me. "But there are things you don't know. Arrangements that keep the peace among the various Ascendant factions. Deals brokered centuries before any of us were born. Aspects of Ascendance not even the oldest of us truly understand."

He had my attention. "Go on."

"The Daughters of Neith and the Delacroix line have policed the Ascendant for two millennia, but regardless of what your mother may have taught you, Rosemary, the majority of the policing remains and always has been an internal matter."

"Could have used some of that policing a month ago," Seph muttered.

Maddox fixed her with a stern gaze. "Did the Greyhound himself not come to your aid in Denver? In Los Angeles, not just one but two of the Angels? Did the Driver himself not deliver you from danger last month, not once, but twice?"

"How could he possibly know all that?" Seph glanced my way for answers, and when I had none, she looked back at Maddox, her sarcastic gaze a bit more pensive and her display of vehemence deflated. "Mr. Trainor?"

"For a group that occupies every corner of the world, the Ascendant are quite the tight-knit group." Maddox cocked his head to one side. "News travels fast."

"And everyone seems to have their own agendas."

"The smartest thing you've likely said this year." At Seph's raised brow, Maddox added, "No offense, of course." He again met my gaze. "The intricate web keeping the various Ascendant and their many motives and machinations in check was already breaking down when the skiomancers first came for Miss Snow in Albuquerque, and the loss of Danielle Delacroix has done nothing but punch the accelerator."

Hearing my mother's name summoned tears to my eyes. The last thing I wanted was to cry in front of Maddox, but seeing him again after two years, the memory of Mother's smile, and the raw emotion of the moment all conspired against me. It was far from the first time the coyote before us had made me cry. I prayed it would be the last.

"I'm sorry, Rosemary," Maddox said. "I don't mean to be indelicate."

"And yet you showed up here unannounced, nearly got me and my friend mobbed, and danced on my mother's grave anyway. Got it." I wiped away my tears with a crumpled paper napkin. "Please. Continue."

Maddox swallowed back a lump in his own throat, either a sign of his own emotion or an indication of the lengths he would go to in order to convince me he was speaking truth.

"There is one among the Ascendant, one of the newest to the fold as far as we can tell, whose ambitions are beyond that of even the most driven among us. Few have seen this man, and fewer still have lived to tell of the experience, if all the reports are to be trusted."

"A new Ascendant?" My eyes shot to Seph. "Other than my friend here, of course?"

"As far as I know. Though he's only been making waves the last few years, no one knows how long he's been around or even whether he's a known player in a new guise." He looked to Seph. "You may not fully understand all that has changed within you as a result of your Ascension yet, Miss Snow, but trust that far more in you has been augmented than simply your ability to deliver a commanding performance."

"So I've been told." Seph's eyes dropped to the table.

"Ascendant live far longer than their human progenitors, at least so long as no one comes along to cut short their time in this world."

Seph swallowed hard. "And how long exactly is that?"

"Two, sometimes three normal lifetimes." Maddox's eyes shifted to one side. "And occasionally, far longer."

"So, barring badness, I'm supposed to live to see the next century?"

"And maybe the one after that." Maddox's mouth slid into a sarcastic grin. "I would advise investing for the long term. Compounding interest is quite a miracle in and of itself."

"You two can play twenty questions later." I leaned across the table and stared Maddox straight in the eye. "This new Ascendant that has brought you out of the woodwork. Who is he? What does he want?"

Maddox pulled in a breath. "He calls himself the Cardinal, and—"

"Wait," Seph interrupted, "the Cardinal?" She snorted a quiet laugh. "First Ravens and Crows, and now this? What is it with you people and birds?"

Maddox's expression soured a bit at yet again being interrupted. "Ascendant are called such because we have risen above our previous existence. Not all, but many, have taken on appellations of various birds to declare as much."

"But not you and your theriodan friends?" Seph asked.

"I know what I am, Miss Snow." His eyes flicked in my direction. "As Rosemary *never* ceases to remind me, I'm a coyote through and through."

"This Cardinal," I asked, trying to keep the train wreck of a conversation at least partly on the tracks, "what exactly is it he can do?"

Maddox's lips pulled into a thin line. "That, Rosemary, is the million-dollar question."

"You don't know?" I'm not sure which surprised me more, that Maddox was apparently clueless about his opponent's abilities or that he admitted as such. "Then answer me this. Why am I in danger from this person if you can't even tell me what he's capable of?"

"I may not know what his particular talents are, but I understand all too well what he's capable of. The Cardinal is credited with at least three Ascendant deaths, and those only represent the ones I've been able to confirm."

"He's killing his own?" I leaned in closer. "Anyone we know?"

"Likely not. A Redstart out of Morocco who crossed his path two years ago; before that an older skiomancer from Moscow who served as a literal shadow agent for the KGB back in the day and almost certainly the FSB for the last three decades until his death; and most recently, the only one I knew personally: a warthog theriodan I'd had drinks with once in Kenya."

"A warthog?" Seph asked.

"Not all theriodans are dashingly handsome and devastatingly charming, Miss Snow, I assure you."

There it was. The Maddox Trainor swagger. One of my favorite things about him. Right up to the moment he swaggered out of my life.

"A precious few Ascendant have managed to track him down and live to tell the tale."

"And?" I asked. "Who might they be? What happened to them?"

"Well..." Maddox raised his eyebrows and sighed, "you're looking at one of them."

"You?" I asked, hating myself for both the breathless question as well as the pang of fear the single word left in my chest. "When? Where? How?"

He looked away. "I never went into exactly how I earned a living back when we were...involved, but before I'd even graduated high school, a group dedicated to keeping, if not a modicum of peace, at least a certain level of impartiality in Ascendant affairs recruited me into their service."

"You told me you were taking a break from the Peace Corps." The bit of my heart that had perhaps softened toward Maddox in the preceding minutes immediately went the way of week-old concrete. "So, you admit you were a liar even way back then."

"Tell me," Maddox said, "did you ever see the movie *Fight Club*?"

"Of course." I wasn't going to admit it was one of the few movies Mother had ever let me watch growing up and one of fewer still she'd sat and watched with me. She'd thought it would be valuable to see, at least from a training perspective.

Me, I'd never gotten the whole Brad Pitt thing nor even knew exactly who he was until I saw that particular movie.

"Okay, then." Maddox straightened his back. "What's the first rule of Fight Club?"

"Don't talk about Fight Club," Seph and I said in unison, her rendition said with far more verve than I was able to mount.

"Precisely. The group I belong to? I didn't just avoid telling you about it, Rosemary. I didn't tell anyone. Not Linus, not Harold, not Neko, and certainly not a nineteen-year-old girl."

"That nineteen-year-old girl could have kicked your ass." I raised a brow and slid into my most confident smile. "And did, once or twice, as I recall."

"My silence had nothing to do with your capabilities and everything to do with my responsibilities to both the organization as well as to you, your mother, and your father."

"So, you lied to my face for my own good, is that it?"

Maddox nodded, a hint of color rising in his cheeks. "More or less."

"And how do I know what you're telling me now is the truth?"

Maddox let out a low growl. "Why don't you let me finish telling you what I have to say and then decide whether or not you want to believe it?"

"Fair enough." I leaned back in my chair, folded my arms across my chest, and let out a frustrated harumph. "Proceed."

"Okay." Maddox leaned in, his voice a bit weary. "Two years ago, right about the time things between you and me were getting interesting, I was recalled. The organization needed me. A new Ascendant, the one we now know as the Cardinal, had appeared on the scene and was disrupting an already tenuous peace. The group needed me to assume a more forward stance."

"And do what?" I asked.

"I'll get to that." He pulled in a deep breath, as if he were about to make a grand confession. "That night? The dinner, the candles, the flowers, the view? It was all to say goodbye, at least for a while."

"Goodbye?" My cheeks burned anew. "You said a lot of words that night. Goodbye wasn't one of them."

"I know, Rosemary." Maddox shook his head. "I'm sorry."

"You took me to bed with you." I turned to Seph. "Sorry." What was the phrase she always used? "TMI?"

"It's all right." Seph's cheeks were a bit on the rosy side as well. "I'd kind of picked up on that part."

"Right." Back to Maddox. "You had a hundred opportunities to do the right thing, to let me know what was happening. Instead, all I got was a crumpled-up note written in blue magic marker."

"Rosemary..."

"*Hey, R, Heading out early. Didn't want to wake you. Had a great night! See you soon.*" My eyes narrowed to slits. "*Love, M.*"

"Wow," Seph murmured, "you've got that one committed to memory."

I ignored her. "Two years, *coyote*, is not 'soon' by any stretch of the imagination."

"Why do you keep calling me 'coyote' like it's some kind of insult?" Maddox tilted his head to one side. "It's who and what I am, but it's not the cause of any of—"

"I'm not saying it for *you*, Maddox." My entire body shook. "I'm saying it for me. To remind me that at your core is a four-legged beast that acts on instinct, hunts by night, takes what it wants, and leaves when it wants to." I let out a little growl of my own. "I say the word to remind myself that at least part of this isn't your fault in an effort to keep myself from coming across this table and showing you in no uncertain terms exactly how deeply you hurt me."

"Ummm, Rosemary..." Seph stared at me, her hand on my wrist. "I'm, uh, all about the girl power you're manifesting here, but you're kind of scaring people."

I glanced around the space, the intricate chess game that had played in my head before as gone as morning dew at noon. Maddox and his infuriating...everything had completely sent me down a rabbit hole. A very angry, very deep rabbit hole.

But now, I had two tables of women and children staring at me as if they were afraid I was about to throttle the incredibly gorgeous man across the table who "only wanted to talk" and a third table of young men who all pretended they couldn't see or hear any of our conversation, no doubt fearing they might be next.

I'd dreamed of this day for months. How I was going to remain calm and collected. Cool as a cucumber, as Ethan would say. How nothing Maddox said would get the slightest rise out of me. How I'd let his words roll off me like water off a duck's back.

Instead, I'd just hulked out—another Ethanism—in front of the one man who I swore would never get another ounce of emotion out of me.

Damn him. Damn him to hell.

"You know what?" I took three deep breaths, centered myself the way Mother always taught me, and looked again at Maddox, willing away the red from my vision. "Just tell us the rest so we can get this over with. Then we can both move on with our lives."

"Very well." Maddox visibly calmed as well, at least as far as I could tell. The people at the surrounding tables returned to their own business, though I did catch some lingering side-eye from a couple of the young men at the next table. "Where were we?"

"We were at the part where you slept with me and then vanished with nothing but a note so you could get back to your little group—a group Father and I will be very interested in learning more about, I assure you—and get started tracking down the Cardinal."

"Right." He did his best to hide the subtle eye roll at my latest jab. "Let me tell you, for someone whose chosen nom de guerre is a bright red bird, this guy is basically a ghost. Took me six months simply to figure out where to get started and what to call this phantom who was rumored to be slowly working his way through Ascendant after Ascendant with no clear agenda and no link that anyone could determine among his victims. Took me another six to figure out where he was and who was next on his list."

"And that was..."

"The Russian skiomancer I mentioned before." Maddox shook his head. "Didn't get to him in time."

"We recently met a Russian shadow creep ourselves." Seph, the situation finally calm enough for her to eat again, finished off her remaining fish taco and sipped at her Coke. "Right, Rosemary?"

I nodded. "A man named Dmitri Drozdov. Works with Johan Krage who in turn used to work for the Midnight Angel but apparently has taken his little cell of shadow dealers on the road, their services on sale to the highest bidder."

"I'd heard you all ran into Krage, Drozdov, and the others, not to mention Ada and her elementalists." Maddox grinned with surprise. "Not to mention, two Angels, the Greyhound, *and* the Driver. Barely Ascended, Miss Snow, and you've already met a lot of the big guns."

"Enough ego stroking, Maddox. My patience is wearing thin." I waved for him to get on with it. "Can we skip to the part where you tell us why you're here?"

"Of course." Maddox pulled a sharp breath. "So, I hadn't gotten far enough along in my investigation to save the Redstart the Cardinal killed in Morocco and didn't put the data points together quickly enough to figure out he was going for the FSB skiomancer, but I was dead set on catching him before he could kill again." He looked away. "Unfortunately, the closer I got to him, the closer he got to me." An unconscious tremor shook his entire body. "The theriodan I mentioned I knew in Kenya? We'd met up the night before the Cardinal found him. Not twelve hours after we sat together turning up whiskey sours, my friend turned up dead."

A part of me I'd been doing my best to shut down leaped to Maddox's defense, but I shoved the instinct way down and kept any further emotion from my face.

"The Cardinal's way of telling you to back off?" I asked, my words as flat as I could deliver.

"That's my best guess. In any case, I withdrew for a bit, gave the bastard some space, and consolidated what I already knew. And then, once I got wind he'd moved on to bigger and brighter, I started tracking his movements again, trying to determine what he wanted, who his next target might be."

"And?" I asked. "Did you figure it out?"

"Yeah," Seph added, "do you know who his next target is?"

"That's what I've been getting at this entire conversation." He locked gazes with Seph. "Who do you think hired Krage and his team of skiomancers to take you in Albuquerque?" At Seph's wide-eyed stare, he added, "It's you, Miss Snow. You're next on the Cardinal's list."

CHAPTER 4

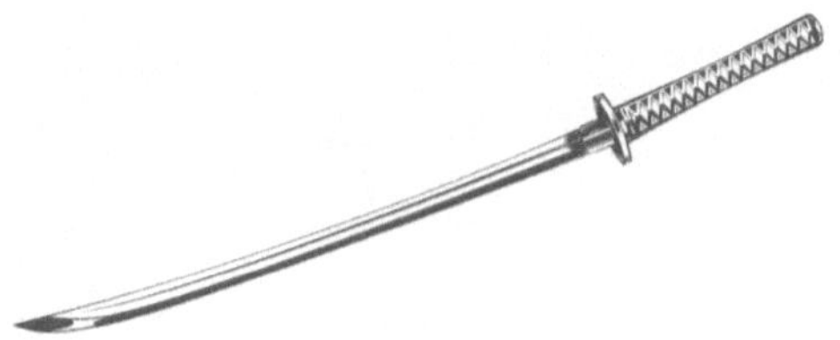

GOODBYE TO YOU

"Absolutely not." Father glared at me with the passion of a lion defending his young from a pack of jackals, whereas Maddox was simply a lone coyote.

"But, Father—"

"You seriously expect me to meet with this animal that treated my only daughter's heart in such a careless manner?"

"He has information." My lips pulled down to a tight circle as I worked to keep any emotion from my face. "Important information."

"What is he doing here?" Father's scowl descended into downright vexation. "And how did he find us, anyway?"

"Like I told you. He said he came to warn us about a new dangerous Ascendant who may or may not be the individual who sent the skiomancers after Seph." As for how he found us or knew all the information about the last month of our lives? I hadn't quite gotten that part out of Maddox yet. "Look, I wasn't thrilled to have him show up in my life again either, but he's right outside, and he says—"

"Wait. He's *here*?" Father glanced at the door of the Commander. "You brought him to our home? We're parked in Miss Snow's driveway, Rosemary. How could you have been so thoughtless to bring that animal to our doorstep, much less hers?"

I let fly an eye-roll even though such obvious expressions usually did little to bring Father over to my side. "He already knew Seph's address and that we were staying here." I let out a frustrated sigh. "In fact, he first approached me in a public place because he knew as well as I did how you'd react if he showed up here unannounced."

"Unannounced, announced, wearing a cowbell, I don't care. He is not welcome in this home or in our lives."

I rubbed at the bridge of my nose. "I'm not asking Maddox back into our lives. I'm asking you to listen to what he has to say, use the information to assess the threat against us, and then send him on his way." I pulled close to Father. "I'm not asking you to do this for me, Father. That's not what this is." I took a deep breath. "I'm only doing this for Seph, to help keep her safe. Will you please back my play?"

Father stood silent and unmoving, other than his enormous barrel chest moving air like a bellows. "This information pertains to the Ascendant who sent the skiomancers after Miss Snow last month?"

"So he says." My stomach turned in knots. "And I'm ashamed to admit that my emotions are too wound up seeing him again to be able to listen objectively." My chin dropped to my chest. "Please, hear Maddox out. Get the information we need. Once he's said his piece, he said he'll go if that's what we want."

"And that *is* what *we* want, right, Rosemary?"

I didn't look up. "Yes, Father."

His eyes narrowed in thought. "Where is Miss Snow, now?"

"I didn't leave her alone, if that's what you're asking." I inclined my head in the direction of the door. "She's with Ethan. I think they were going to take a walk."

"Good." He lowered his voice. "With Maddox showing up out of nowhere with mysterious warnings about nefarious individuals we're not sure even exist, I need her out of the picture while I figure out what to do."

"Why would he lie, though?" I asked myself as much as Father. "Why come here to warn us about a new bad actor among the Ascendant if it weren't true?"

"I don't know, Rosemary, but he's had two full years since we last saw hide or hair of him to find trouble and two full years to come up with a story to get himself out of it."

Two questions fought for supremacy in my mind: why was Father being so obstinate, and why in the world was I defending Maddox?

"Look," Father grumbled, "I'll hear him out…"

"That's all I ask."

"And then, this is over. Maddox climbs back under whatever rock he's been calling home since he vanished on you, and we do with the information what we need to do." He raised his eyebrows in question. "Is it a deal?"

"It's a deal." I nodded. "Thank you, Father."

Without another word, Father rose with a wince, his shoulder still healing from being dislocated by Krage's skiomancers a month before. He forced his lips into something resembling a smile, went to the door, and opened it wide.

"You may enter, Mr. Trainor." His voice cold, Father moved out of the way as Maddox stepped inside our RV home. "Don't make yourself too comfortable, though."

"Father…" I whispered.

"It's okay," Maddox said with a hint of a grin. "Only a fool would expect a warm reception under these circumstances."

Unflappable as ever. Don't know why I'm surprised.

"Have a seat." I motioned to the bench seat next to where I'd positioned myself. "You too, Father." I motioned to the opposite side of the little table where Mother, Father, and I had shared countless meals over the years. "Let's all have a talk."

"Straight to business, if that's all right." Father sat his massive frame down across the table from Maddox, who'd slid in next to me as if a day hadn't passed. "Who or what is this Ascendant you've come to warn us about?"

I was glad Father's arm was finally out of the sling from last month's injuries. As much as he hated showing any sign of weakness—as evidenced by his continued frustrations with his physical therapist—I can only imagine how much he would despise Maddox knowing he sat before him less than one hundred percent.

"First, Mr. Delacroix," Maddox said, "thank you for hearing me out. I—"

"No need for pleasantries. You are here to convey information. Nothing more, nothing less. Now, tell us what you came to tell us."

"Of course." If Maddox was taken aback by Father's brusqueness, he didn't let it show. "The individual in question calls himself the Cardinal. As I told Rosemary, he's responsible for the deaths of at least three known Ascendant, though there are likely many more."

"The Cardinal." Father leaned in on his elbows and rested his chin on his interlaced digits. "And who exactly is this new terror among the Ascendant?"

"No one knows." Maddox cracked his neck. "Though he has a flair for the dramatic, this one. Wears a helmet that covers his entire face: all red, black, and orange, like a stylized cardinal head."

"Of course he does." The muttered comment was out of my mouth before I could stop it. "Not all that dissimilar to Krage and his Ravens with their beaked masks and black hats, I suppose."

"But the Midnight Angel's Conspiracy of Ravens wear variations of the same black avian masks skiomancers have worn for centuries. This person Mr. Trainor is describing may represent a new threat." Father considered for a moment. "You say this man has killed at least three Ascendant? By what means? In what domain does this Cardinal's power reside?"

"That's just it," Maddox answered. "Anyone who has actually seen the Cardinal in action is no longer in any position to pass on what they learned."

"You've seen him, or so you say." Father raised a questioning eyebrow. "Somehow *you* made it out alive."

"I did get a glimpse of him once, though he was over a city block away."

"A block away?" I asked.

"Telephoto lens. Caught him in a rooftop meeting with Johan Krage south of here in Los Angeles not long after the events surrounding Snow's Ascension."

"I'm assuming you brought the photographic evidence?" Father asked.

"Unfortunately, no." Maddox's eyes dropped for the first time since he'd sat by my side. "All I can surmise is that he's either hired one hell of an experienced technomancer to keep him off the world's collective radar, or he is one himself."

"Let me guess," Father raised a brow, "digital camera?"

"I could see him fine through the lens, but when I tried to review the images later, nothing but scrambled color and vague shapes." Maddox patted the shoulder bag resting at his hip. "Went to the camera shop the next day and invested in a top-of-the-line film camera so I'd be ready next time."

"He didn't see you?" Father asked.

"I'm still breathing, aren't I?"

"So it would appear." Father sat silently, his internal wheels working as I'd seen a thousand times before. "In summary, the story you are trying to sell us is that an Ascendant I've never heard of and Danielle never mentioned is stalking others of his kind, taking out his peers one-by-one for reasons you don't know; you're one of the few people who's managed to even see this person without being put in the ground; and you have nothing to prove your assertions beyond your word." He shook his head with a snort. "Am I keeping up so far?"

Maddox exhaled a quiet grunt. "I know I might as well be telling you to check under your beds for the bogeyman, Mr. Delacroix, but real people, Ascendant, are dead, and the only common factor is this man who is a ghost among both them and the world at large."

Father raised a hand. "Second, according to Rosemary, your search for this man is being funded by a mysterious group I've also never heard of, a faction of rich and powerful Ascendant that never once had dealings with my wife in the decades she walked and, frankly, policed some of the most powerful individuals in the world?"

"You are, or were, the consort of the most recent Daughter of Neith—my condolences, of course—but you are not Ascendant and, by this I mean no disrespect, neither was she." Maddox attempted a placating smile. "There are things about our world, Mr. Delacroix, that even you and your late wife were never privy to," he said, "more things than you'd likely care to understand."

Whatever rage had simmered behind Father's eyes quickly escalated to a full boil. "All I'm hearing, Mr. Trainor, is the conspiracy-laden nonsense of someone who didn't have the wherewithal to know to stay away once he'd screwed up." Father crossed his arms, the hue of his face an ever-deepening shade of red. "Masked phantoms and enigmatic cabals of which no one but you has heard so much as a whisper." He glared across the table unblinking at Maddox. "Tell me, boy, how old are you again?"

"Twenty-seven." Any hint of a smile left Maddox's face. "What of it?"

"Danielle and I were helping keep the peace among your kind as well as between Ascendant and the rest of the world when you were still in diapers. Don't come in here telling ghost stories about a war I've been a part of for almost three decades like I'm some kind of wide-eyed novice."

"Father!" I tried to stem the tide of his anger. "He's—"

"Let me talk, Rosemary." He turned his unbridled fury back on Maddox. "I don't know what kind of con you're trying to pull here or why you're attempting to creep back into my daughter's life, but understand one thing. You and your make-believe stories are not welcome here."

"Mr. Delacroix, I only came here to—"

"I couldn't care less why you came here. You were already given wide latitude with this family the first time you darkened our doorway, and you failed miserably." Father rose from the table. "Understand that you will not be given opportunity to hurt my daughter again."

I inhaled to interrupt again, but Father's raised finger held my silence.

"Now, remove yourself from my home, this city, and preferably this time zone at your earliest convenience. Your presence is neither desired nor required."

Maddox shifted his eyes in my direction, speechless for once in his life, and then rose from the table as well. "Sorry, Rosemary. I tried."

"You certainly did." Father strode to the door. "What you tried, I'm not exactly sure, but here we are."

Maddox shouldered his bag and joined Father by the door. "Rosemary," he said, "no matter what your father says, listen to what I told you. Watch your back. No matter what he believes, I came here for one reason and one reason only." He rested his hand on the door handle. "And that was to keep *you* safe."

And with that, he was gone.

"Well, that certainly went easier than expected." Father sat back at the table with me, though no sooner had he settled back in his seat than I was out of my own.

"No matter what he's done in the past," I grumbled, "that was uncalled for."

Father took one of those deep cleansing breaths Mother taught both him and me to regulate our respective tempers. "Someday, Rosemary, when you've had opportunity to scoop your child up from the ground after some unworthy individual leaves them destroyed in the wake of their selfishness and then spend half a year nursing them back to health physically, mentally, and spiritually, remind me again how uncalled for you found my response today."

"But what if all he said was true? What if this Cardinal person is on the loose and after Seph?"

"Oh, we're going to look into it. Me, you, Ethan, and our friends among the Ascendant. But the esteemed Mr. Trainor, even were I interested in his input, apparently has nothing to offer. No name, no description, no photo, only unsubstantiated claims we now need to investigate."

"He tracked down this Cardinal once, though. Perhaps he could find him again." I sat back at the table. "Do you really want to start from scratch?"

"What I want, Rosemary, is to get that coyote as far from you as possible. The last time he entered our lives, you were the collateral damage. Months passed before you were even marginally functional again. If an Ascendant serial killer has entered the scene, I need you at full capacity, not just to help me do what must be done, but for your own safety."

"I'm fine, Father." My face flushed with exasperation and embarrassment. "I'm not the same person I was two years ago."

"No, you're not. You clawed your way back from utter despondence and became stronger than you'd ever been, stronger than I could have imagined, in fact." He came around to my side of the table and pulled me into a tight bear hug. "Your mother was so worried you'd never recover, never be our Rosemary again. Then, one morning, you came to breakfast like a new person. The sheen had returned to your eyes, the spring to your step. Your smile from that morning is forever etched on my soul, the day my daughter returned from darkness."

"You've never shared that with me before." I pulled away and looked up into my father's tear-filled eyes. "Why not?"

"When a wounded and skittish doe emerges from the wood line for help, you don't rush the poor thing. That would only serve to send the animal back into the forest." He brushed away the saline tear trailing down my own cheek. "Instead, you allow the doe to come to you, at its own pace, in its own time, and pray it survives."

"I'm not some helpless deer in the woods, Father."

"Far from it, Rosemary." He smiled. "You are every bit your mother's daughter." A laugh escaped his lips. "And at least a bit your father's."

I sniffed, my nose running. "I miss her, Father."

"I miss her too, Rosemary."

"I don't know if I'll ever measure up to the woman she was."

"Are you kidding?" Father let out a sad chuckle. "Do you have any idea how proud she was to have you as her daughter?" He shook his head. "She didn't tell you nearly as often as she would have liked. Pride is dangerous on the battlefield of life. She wanted to keep you hungry and humble."

"I'd figured as much." I joined him in our quiet laugh. "Mother may not have been the most forthcoming with affection, but I never doubted once that she loved me."

"As much as any mother could, and in many ways few but her could truly comprehend."

Father and I had connected more in the month since Mother's death than at any point in our relationship. By necessity of our line and the responsibilities that went along with who we were, I had grown up closer to Mother, sometimes to the detriment of my relationship with him. To say we'd caught up on lost time in the preceding weeks would have been an overstatement, and I looked forward to continuing our little chat.

But the sound of my phone brought the real world crashing back, and that ringtone in particular: the opening four notes of Beethoven's Fifth.

Ethan.

I snatched the phone from my seat, something telling me before I'd even hit the answer button I wasn't going to like what I heard.

"Hello?" He had yet to speak a word, and I was already breathless with worry. "Ethan?"

"Rosemary!" Seph shouted through the line. "Come quick. That guy Maddox was talking about. He's here!"

Shit. "Where are you?"

"Three blocks down. At the intersection of—" The signal cut out briefly. "—bleeding. My God, he's bleeding! Help us—" And with that, the call dropped.

"That was Seph." I scanned the interior of the Commander for my katana and cursed, remembering it was locked inside Seph's house. "She and Ethan are in trouble."

"Dammit." Father moved like a whirling dervish, grabbing his pistol and a pair of knives he had stashed by the door. "Tell me it's not this Cardinal Mr. Trainor was going on about."

With silence my only answer, he grunted and shot out the door. He had a tracer on Seph's phone and was already tracking her.

"They're only a few blocks away," he shouted. "If Ethan can hold the bastard off until—"

"Seph was calling from Ethan's phone." I leaped from the Commander. "I got the impression Ethan was down."

Funny. Maddox had just warned us about the Cardinal threat and now he was here. Mother's theory about coincidences and how there was no such thing echoed in my mind.

"The Commander is all hooked up to electric and water." Father groaned. "I hate to say it, but we'll be better off on foot."

"Unless Seph left keys in one of her cars." I turned for the door leading to the garage, ready to kick it down if I needed to, but before I could so much as take a step, a squall of tires at the end of the driveway caught our attention. There, behind the wheel of a familiar grey Ford F-150 sat Maddox, sunglasses reflecting the midday sun. After I'd turned down his offer of a ride—"like the good old days," he'd said—he'd followed me and Seph back from the nail salon in Santa Barbara. I'd spent far more time than I'd care to admit staring at the passenger side mirror at the truck where I'd experienced my first kiss and a few other firsts as well.

"Maddox?" I asked, breathless. "How did you—"

"No time for discussion." Maddox thumbed in the direction of his pickup bed. "Let's go."

CHAPTER 5

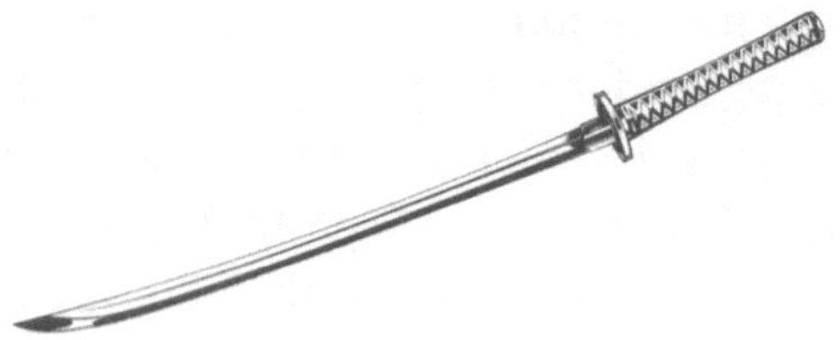

BREAKING THE LAW

Maddox rocketed away from Seph's palatial home at speeds beyond anything the curvy Montecito neighborhood streets were designed to accommodate. Father and I crouched in the back of the truck as my coyote ex-boyfriend took all three of our lives in his hands. A big part of me screamed I had no business trusting this man who magically reappeared in my life the same day as this latest attack.

On the way back to the house, Seph had given me the third degree while I did my best to make sure Maddox couldn't see me watching his every move in the side mirror. I never dreamed that less than an hour later I'd be squatting in the bed of the same truck and holding on for dear life with every turn. I worked to banish the memory of Maddox and me lying side by side, our heads resting on the lowered tailgate, looking up at the stars from the top of Pahute Mesa in Nevada. Had it really just been two years?

"Father, I—"

"Not now," he grunted, mad enough to spit nails. "Hey, Trainor, listen up!" He looked up from his phone and craned his head around to shout at Maddox through the open driver-side window. "Turn right up here, then straight ahead two blocks."

"Got it!" The truck's tires squealed as Maddox yanked the wheel, hung a right straight out of an action movie, and gunned the motor down the street lined with multimillion-dollar homes. Fortunately, the sidewalks and pavement remained empty as we barreled down the asphalt, the usual crowd of children, joggers, and mothers with their babies in strollers notably absent. Only open road and the occasional six-figure car parked at the curb stood between us and our objective.

"Hang a left up here," Father shouted, and then quietly added, "almost there."

I knew that look all too well. Father wasn't happy in the least, and I was going to hear about it later.

Maddox took the left, barely missing a forest green Land Rover. The wide-eyed woman driving slammed on the brakes and pounded her horn with equal gusto as we flew past her. The angry glare, screeching tires, and blaring horn, however, all faded into the background as we arrived at the next intersection, the scene before us straight out of my worst nightmare.

Ethan lay sprawled next to a mansion with a fenced-in yard and five-car garage that made Seph's home, enormous though it was, look like a shoebox. A thin trickle of blood trailed down his cheek and pooled in his ear while his left arm appeared to be bent in the wrong direction.

Seph was nowhere in sight.

I leaped from the truck before Maddox could bring it to a stop and rushed to Ethan's side. "Ethan?" I whispered, my voice quickly becoming a shout. "Ethan?!?"

"Rosemary?" His words came out slurred, as if his mouth were full of marbles.

I'd never in my entire life been so relieved to hear my own name. "Are you all right?" I knelt by his side. "I mean, beyond the obvious."

"Other than feeling like I've been hit by a train, yeah, I'm doing great." He tried to push himself up from the ground and failed. "I'm no doctor," he groaned in pain, "but I'm pretty sure my shoulder is dislocated."

"I'm pretty sure you're correct." That particular injury seemed to be going around. "That has to hurt. Let me—"

"Don't worry about me," Ethan interrupted. "Go after Seph." He swallowed back what I guessed was a mouthful of blood. "He's got her."

"Who, Ethan?" Father appeared at my side with Maddox close behind. "Who's got her?"

"The man in the red armor." Ethan's entire body shook in pain and rage. "I couldn't stop him." He looked up at me, a hint of fear crossing his features. "He's strong and fast, like a theriodan, but different."

Maddox stepped forward. "Which way did he take her?"

"Who's this guy?" Ethan asked, shooting me a confused glance.

"Doesn't matter." I pulled close so Ethan could see me and only me. "Which way did they go?"

"Toward town." Ethan inclined his head toward the road leading west. "Hurry. He took off with Seph on a motorcycle just before you arrived. If there's traffic, you can catch him."

"Come on, Maddox, let's go." I turned to Father. "May I borrow your phone so we can track her?"

"What are you talking about?" Father asked. "You're not going anywhere without me." He glanced at Maddox. "Especially considering..."

"Someone needs to stay here with Ethan." I shot a look Maddox's way as well. "What if this Cardinal person didn't come alone? We can't just leave Ethan lying on the ground injured and defenseless."

"Who's defenseless?" Ethan tried again to push himself up from the ground but only succeeded in falling backward and landing on his bad shoulder. "Dammit," he grunted, "never mind me. Find Seph."

"I hate to say it, but Rosemary's right. We can't leave you here alone." Father shoved his phone into my hand and locked gazes with me, though I recognized he was eyeing Maddox in his peripheral vision. "Go. Find her. Save her."

Maddox and I raced back to his truck. I slid into the front seat where I'd ridden dozens of times, the leather warm against my legs. A river of memories sprang forth, a river I instantly dammed up out of necessity. Seph needed me focused on the here and now, not drowning in the rushing current of what used to be.

Or what could have been, I considered, sneaking a glance at the man behind the wheel, so focused and sure of himself.

Like the good old days, indeed.

Again, I asked myself the question of the hour: if Maddox, as he claimed, wasn't here to rekindle our romance, then why in the world *had* he come back? And why was he helping us?

"Which way?" Maddox asked as we approached another intersection.

"From what I can see, he's made it onto 101 and is heading west."

"Then that's where we're going."

As we raced onto the highway in pursuit of the blue dot on my screen, I took advantage of finally having a moment alone with Maddox since his initial ambush back at the mall.

"I'm curious. Two years. If everything you've told us is true and you've been working with this clandestine organization the whole time, then I guess I can see why you left. Still, why didn't you tell me? That was cruel, and you know it."

"Look, I'm sorry." Maddox changed lanes and rocketed past a VW bug with an out-of-state plate. "The first few weeks, my silence had everything to do with not blowing my cover. That evolved quickly into being crazy busy trying to complete my mission, keep out of trouble, and stay alive. When I finally came up for air, several months had passed." He pulled in a breath. "From that point on, I figured you'd be better off if I stayed away."

"Better off?" My cheeks burned. "That wasn't for you to decide."

"After four months, what the hell was I going to say? 'Hey, Rosemary, sorry about ghosting you the night after we…' well, you know. 'Want to grab coffee when I'm freed up again as long as the psychotic super-powered serial killer I'm after doesn't leave me in a shallow grave?'"

I set my jaw. "Even that would have been preferable to two years of not knowing if you were alive or dead."

Maddox cleared his throat. "Not to rub salt in the wound, Rosemary, but you have to understand, this is hard for me too. Seeing you after all this time." He shot me a sidelong glance. "Honestly, if the Cardinal wasn't after Seph and therefore putting you in his crosshairs, I would have probably continued to keep my distance."

My heart sank, even as my cheeks burned. "Good to know, I suppose."

"To be clear, your dad is right. Even though I'm here for all the right reasons, to keep you safe and to help you find your friend, you should stay away from me. Once this is all done, I'll go and let you get back to your life."

"Hold on a minute." The bile at the back of my throat began to build again. "First, you leave without saying a word, then you show back up without warning, and now you're going to leave again regardless of what I say?"

"I thought that was what you wanted." Maddox weaved around an eighteen-wheeler in the passing lane and continued westward on the busy highway. "That's certainly what your father wants."

"Have you ever once in your life thought to ask someone what they want rather than trying to figure it out, or worse, telling them?" My heart pounded in my chest. "You showing up has opened a lot of old wounds, some of which I thought had healed completely." I stared at him, reserved and completely vulnerable at the same time. "All I'm saying is that when this is all over, you and I are going to have a long talk before you vanish again, understood?"

"Understood." He reached out his hand for mine. "It's a deal."

"Just drive." I crossed my arms before my chest and peered down at the phone in my hand. One second, the little blue dot signifying Seph's mobile continued west on Highway 101, and then, a blink later, the signal was headed north along Highway 154 toward the mountains.

"That's weird." I held the phone across to show Maddox. "Dad's tracking app is as accurate as they come, and yet Seph's signal just jumped a couple of miles in a different direction."

"Maybe the signal is coming from a different cell tower?" He returned his eyes to the road. "Where does it say she is now?"

"It was telling us to keep going straight, but now it says to head north."

His eyes shot in my direction as he passed a stretch Hummer limousine with a trio of teens hanging out the sunroof. "So...we head north?"

The exit for 154 was coming up on our right and fast.

"We take the exit and follow the little dot," Maddox continued, "right?"

Normally, yes, but the dot had jumped.

"You said the pictures you took of the Cardinal came out all garbled?"

"Yeah, What about it?"

"And you also said he likely had a technomancer keeping him off the world's collective radar. What if that same person is now screwing with the tracking on Father's phone?"

"I guess it's possible." Maddox edged off the highway onto the exit leading to Highway 154. "Though we don't even know if he's aware we're following him."

"He's on a motorcycle, so unless he's pulled up inside another vehicle to throw us off, that's all he's got." My brain began to put the pieces together. "But if he had a van or a transfer truck or a..."

Wait a minute. He's not heading to the mountains at all.

"Get back on the highway."

"What?" Maddox said. "What are you—"

With a move I'd never have dared two years earlier, I reached over and grabbed the wheel, jerking us off the exit and back onto the shoulder of the highway. As we were still cruising along at full speed, the move was met with a cacophony of squalling tires and blaring horns, but in seconds we were back on the highway headed west.

"Dammit, Rosemary, if you get us killed, nobody's going to be stepping in to save your friend."

"Keep driving." I shifted the map on Father's phone to look further west. "Follow the signs to the airport."

"The airport?" Maddox asked. "You think a guy dressed in a suit of red armor is going to try to sneak a world-famous superstar through TSA?"

"Not exactly."

"Then where are we going?"

The map showed the airport five miles ahead and the Cardinal likely had at least a mile or two on us. We'd be cutting it close.

"Seph took us on a tour of Santa Barbara the week after we got to Montecito. The main airport terminal is down closer to the ocean, but the north end is where all the private jets are kept. If this guy is as connected and tech savvy as you say, there's no way he flies commercial, and it goes without saying he can't risk staying on the road if he's dressed the way Ethan said."

"You think he's got a private jet?"

"Why wouldn't he? Aren't most Ascendant independently wealthy?"

"Most," Maddox grumbled, "I suppose."

"If they're not at the airport, then we'll—what does Ethan call it? —back up and punt, follow the little dot, and hope for the best. For now, head for the airport and step on it. I'll tell you where to turn. Sound like a plan?"

A quiet growl escaped Maddox's lips, but his only response was, "Sounds like a plan."

Neither of us said much the last three miles other than directions and his dutiful repetition. Either I'd bruised his ego when I both literally and figuratively took the wheel or he simply didn't know what to make of a new and improved Rosemary Delacroix. In any case, though he wasn't quite what I'd consider sullen, something was clearly on his mind. Seeing as how we ran a red light at the end of the exit and were now taking a tight curve at about thirty miles per hour over the posted speed limit, I kept my mouth shut and let Maddox drive.

"All right," he said. "We're back across the highway. Where to now?"

"Hang a right up here on Hollister."

And 'hang a right' he did. The truck went up on two wheels and everything.

"Good," I muttered, trying to keep my fish tacos down. "Now, hit it."

We tore down the four-lane road, past a trio of cabs, a couple Ubers, and a lady in a big grey Volvo who shot us the evil eye as we sped past.

"Up here," I shouted, "on the left."

Miraculously, the light remained yellow as we sailed beneath it. We passed a bar and grill surrounded with tall palm trees on our right and entered the parking lot for Signature Flight Support - Santa Barbara. The two-story grey building boasted a curved roof indicative of the hangar section on the back, the entire edifice blocking any view of the main runway except a peek through the fence to the right that was partially obscured by a large white delivery van. To the left, a long fence stretched down the parking lot and led to a small area of grass, and beyond the fence sat an enormous white hangar with three FedEx planes parked on the tarmac outside.

"Curve around to the right," I ordered. "Let's see what we can see."

"And then what?" Maddox asked. "You want me to bust through the fence and drive onto the runway?"

"I'm not ruling out anything at the moment." I huffed out a breath. "Now, go."

We pulled past the big white van, and I rolled my window down. The sound of a plane engine roaring to life came from somewhere, though it was difficult to pin down a direction. Nothing too out of the ordinary jumped out at me, so I had Maddox pull us back around to the parking lot on the other side of the building.

There, past the fence and at the center of the tarmac, sat a private jet, the source of the low roar I'd heard before. Gleaming white with three parallel stripes running the length of the fuselage, red and black with a thin line of orange between, the plane waited with its door open and boarding stairs down.

"Well," I asked, "what do you think?"

"It's a plane," Maddox replied, "getting ready to take off. At an airport." He shot me a sidelong glance. "Maybe we should call the local news."

"Wait," I said. "Look."

A black SUV with tinted windows that had been parked at the corner of the building pulled away and drove across the tarmac, heading straight for the plane. Behind the spot the SUV had vacated rested a deep purple motorcycle similar to those Krage and his skiomancer friends had used to pursue us a month earlier.

"Again," Maddox said with a subtle shrug, "a motorcycle parked next to a building isn't exactly anything to report to the FBI."

He was right. All I had to support my theory was a basically normal-appearing plane about to take off in the middle of an otherwise ordinary day, a bike that very well might have been sitting there for a month, and a hunch.

That is, until the SUV's driver exited the vehicle and opened the rear door, allowing two strangely clad passengers to step onto the tarmac. The bigger of the two was built like a freight train and wore a full-length duster that fit him like a black circus tent. The other was a woman with a body-obscuring ensemble like a burka on steroids.

A woman about Seph's height.

"You still got those field binoculars?" I asked, judging that the pair stood approximately a football field away. "I've got a feeling we've found our girl."

Maddox reached into his glove box, his hand brushing my knee as it passed, and handed me what I'd asked for without a word.

As I took a closer look, three things struck me. First, the day was a bit hot for the pair to be decked out in such attire. Second, the man was leading the woman to the plane by her upper arm, and she wasn't going quietly. And third, even the minimal struggle between the two allowed me the briefest glimpse of their feet. The man's boot shone a bright metallic crimson while the woman's familiar sandals revealed freshly painted toenails, the turquoise so bright, the color caught my eye despite the distance.

"That's Seph. No question about it." I pulled in a breath. "I'm guessing the other one has to be our guy, red boots and all."

"I'm impressed," Maddox whispered. "You truly are on point

today." He scrunched his nose up. "Still, we're on one side of this fence, and they're on the other. In case you missed it, that plane is about to take off, and while you are a total badass in a fight, Supergirl, last I checked, you can't fly."

"Won't have to," I said with a grim grin. "That plane isn't leaving the ground." I charged the fence and, using a little parkour I'd been practicing with Ethan, danced up the side of a Honda minivan by way of the old school BMW parked in the next spot and was up and over the barbed-wire-topped fence in less time than it took Maddox to start complaining about it.

"Okay, so now we're entering restricted areas," he groaned, his hands on his hips. "I mean, we violated every traffic ordinance in existence getting here. What's one more broken law, right?"

"You think this is bad, I'm guessing a little assault and battery is on the horizon." I inclined my head in the direction of the plane, its door already half closed. "You coming?"

For half a second, a flash of doubt crossed Maddox's gaze, and then, that old devilish smile I'd seen a thousand times materialized across his chiseled features.

"Wouldn't miss it."

CHAPTER 6

UNDER PRESSURE

My little leap over the fence took years of lower body weight training, gymnastics practice, and parkour experience to accomplish. Meanwhile, Maddox cleared the fence with a single running jump and still managed to land with the grace of an Olympic gold medalist. For what had to be the thousandth time, I simultaneously admired and despised the effortlessness of physicality that came to theriodans in general and Maddox in particular.

Must be nice to be a coyote.

"So," I asked, "how are we supposed to stop a plane?"

"You're asking me?" he answered between panting breaths. "This is your plan, remember? I'm just the muscle." No sooner had the words left his lips than the plane's engine cycled up as the jet began to taxi for the runway. "Never mind. We've got to move."

Maddox took off at a dead sprint for the quickly accelerating plane, and I followed close behind, at least for the first few steps.

With nothing but a sword, there wasn't much I'd be able to do to stop a plane on the move, and while a coyote clothed in human flesh might be able to catch a plane, my legs only move so fast. Not to mention it had already been a long morning, and sandals meant for a day at the spa aren't exactly performance footwear.

Fortunately, I had a better idea.

The big black SUV had pulled back into its previous parking place. The driver, a squat Asian man in a dark suit and bowler hat, came around to check on the motorcycle and found the bike had a new occupant.

"All right, little girl." He stalked toward me, hands already out as if he meant to grab me and drag me off the still-warm Suzuki. "Climb down off the boss's bike before you get hurt."

"Okay." I slid off the opposite side of the motorcycle to keep the bike's mass between me and the man in the bowler hat. "Sorry."

"Who the hell are you?" he asked, drawing ever closer. "What are you doing here?"

Here we go. Time to improvise, like Mother taught me.

"I wanted to check out the bike. See how it felt." I shot him a suggestive look Seph and I had practiced for half an hour, much to her amusement, after she and I binged half a season of her favorite show and discussed who was the sexiest of the four. She'd argued Carrie, but my vote was Samantha.

"Want to take me for a ride?" I asked with a Persephone Snow shimmy of hips.

"Get away from there, or someone's going to have a broken arm," the man growled.

Great. This guy's all business. We don't have time for this.

"I don't have all day." I spread my feet apart and distributed my weight in preparation for what was about to happen. "Do you have the keys or not?"

"Look, girlie, step away from the bike or I'm gonna—"

"I'll take that as a maybe." I dropped to all fours and swept out my right leg, catching the man below the knees and sending him to the unforgiving tarmac flat on his back. "Now, hand over those keys."

I rammed my hand into his right front pocket, hoping the small bulge I'd seen was the object of my search and nothing else, and came out with a keychain containing a lone key adorned with the Suzuki emblem.

Jackpot.

No sooner had I turned to hop back on the bike than the man grabbed my ankle.

"You're going...to pay for that...little girl," he grunted between pants, out of breath from his unexpected meeting with terra firma.

Without a word, I spun around, picked up my opposite foot, and brought my heel down on his forearm, the impact producing a sickening crunch. While the sound of fracturing bones, whether my own or someone else's, always turned my stomach, those were the breaks today.

Ethan would be so proud.

As the man howled in pain, I dropped to the ground and brought my elbow down on his breastbone, driving the remaining air from his lungs. I couldn't have him alerting everyone inside the building, at least not until Maddox and I, hopefully with Seph in tow, were long gone.

"Guess you were right about that broken arm," I said as I pushed the motorcycle away from the building and jammed the key into the ignition. I had no idea whether this man deserved such an injury or not, but Seph was in danger and he had what I needed, so all bets were off.

With a deep breath, I tried to recall the last time I'd even sat on a motorcycle, and then remembered it had been with Maddox, my arms wrapped around his broad chest as we rocketed down the coastal highway when my family and I still lived in Oregon, his back so warm against my chest, his scent tripping every switch in my brain to eleven.

Honestly, Rosemary, at every turn an Ethanism.

Dammit girl, no time for getting lost in thought. Mother taught you all you know about motorcycles years before you'd ever even heard of Ethan Harkreader or Maddox Trainor. If you need to focus on a face, focus on the woman who taught you everything you need to know about everything.

Her instructions sounded clearly in my mind as if she'd spoken the words yesterday.

Flip the switch on the right. Squeeze the clutch. Thumb the starter button.

The engine roared to life as I walked the bike around the massive SUV to the wide strip of tarmac leading to the two parallel runways that run north to south.

The plane was making its left turn onto the runway proper, and if my eyes weren't failing me, Maddox crouched atop the right wing. Another minute and it would be too late, and both our cause and Seph would be lost.

Drop the bike into first, came Mother's even tone. *Release the clutch. Pull back on the throttle.*

Like a caged animal released from bondage, the motorcycle rocketed down the tarmac, the high whine of the engine beneath me quickly overpowered by the roar of the private jet's twin engines as I rounded the corner and followed the plane onto the main runway.

Skipping the usual pause before takeoff, the jet engines both cycled up, and the plane began its run down the tarmac. In less than half a minute, they'd all be gone.

I couldn't let that happen.

I pulled back on the throttle with all I had, the front wheel of the motorcycle catching half a second of air as I turned the bike into a two-wheeled torpedo and sent it flying at the plane's left wing.

Funny. I hadn't been feeling particularly suicidal that day.

As the plane and I rocketed down the runway in tandem, I mentally flipped through a dozen plans of how to bring the plane to a halt. Run the bike into the wing at full speed and see what happens? Somehow get ahead of the plane and lay the bike down in front of a wheel, hoping to blow a tire designed to withstand landing nine tons at 150 mph? Send the motorcycle flying into the side of the plane and hope Seph was riding close to the front?

In the end, however, the best plan was the simplest.

The Cardinal apparently needed Seph both alive and well, thus the extra helmet left stashed on the back of the bike.

Last I checked, jet engines don't function as well with three pounds of crash-proof polycarbonate running through the fan and into the turbines.

With a quick glance across the plane at Maddox, who was clinging for dear life to the opposite wing, I hurled the heavy helmet at the jet's left engine, praying as it left my fingers that the bright red hunk of polycarbonate and foam would find its mark. My only valid move spent, I let up on the throttle and crossed to the right side of the runway in time to see bits of the destroyed helmet fly out the back of the left engine along with a ball of fire and an ear-shattering boom. Despite the explosion, the plane continued to accelerate with Maddox still atop the right wing. I brought the motorcycle to a screeching halt and looked on helplessly, certain that the plane would take off, regardless of my actions, with one of my two best friends on board and the only man I'd ever loved clinging to its wing.

Three seconds.

What if my opportunity to finally bury the hatchet with Maddox was about to vanish into the wild blue yonder along with any hope for his survival? Theriodans were tough, but not indestructible.

Two.

What horrible torture awaited Seph at the hands of this man who calls himself the Cardinal because I wasn't good enough to stop him?

One.

The plane reached the far end of the runway before coming to a sudden halt of its own, the nose of the private jet dipping as the front wheel ended up in the grass beyond the tarmac.

Thank you, Mother, yet again, for preparing me for this life. May I continue to benefit from your teachings. God, I wish you were here.

The motorcycle continued to purr beneath me, my metallic steed ready to take me onward. I pulled up my feet and rode to the far end of the runway knowing full well airport security would be upon us in no time. I just hoped they'd listen long enough to get past Maddox and me being in a restricted area to realize they had an international superstar kidnapping on their hands.

Smoke was billowing from the plane's left engine, but I didn't see any flames. Maddox leaped down from his perch on the right wing and jogged over to my side. Relief played out across his features, and I allowed myself to breathe again.

"Are you all right?" I asked.

"Better now that you stopped the plane." He brushed his windblown salt-and-pepper locks from his face and smiled. "Otherwise, it was leap onto the runway at two hundred miles an hour, take a header into the ocean before the plane got too high, or hang on until Big Red and Seph arrived at their destination and hope they didn't fly too high."

"I'm glad you're okay." I felt myself about to reach for him and pulled back. No matter what he'd done in the last hour, he was still the man who ghosted me for two years without so much as a text. "Any sign of Seph or the Cardinal?"

As if in answer, the door to the jet unsealed with an audible clunk and began to descend. From our angle at the rear of the aircraft, however, that's all we could see.

As Maddox and I swept around the wing for the door, my stomach knotted.

And then, yet again, Mother's teachings kicked in.

Breathe in. The memory of her voice calmed me. *Breathe out.*

Focus on the moment at hand. Control your breathing, your heart, your mind. Take command of the situation rather than letting the situation take command of you.

"Moment of truth," Maddox whispered. "You ready to fight?"

"Never more so," I answered, "though I'm feeling naked without my katana."

"A little late to worry about that now." He crossed his hands before his chest and focused, his soulful eyes shifting from thundercloud grey to bright gold and decidedly canine. "Won't be long now."

The door to the plane stood open, a cool wind whipping around us from the shimmering ocean to the south. And then, with a metallic clunk, a boot of crimson appeared at the top step.

"Showtime," Maddox whispered.

Striding down the steps from within the private jet with a fully shrouded Seph in his grasp came a man who had shed one disguise only to reveal another. Dressed head-to-toe in high-tech armor the deep red of his nom de guerre, the Cardinal directed the dark eyes of his avian helmet in our direction. The orange of the stylistic beak faded into the black that covered his face and swept into the crimson that flowed into his headgear's characteristic crest.

"Do you two have any idea the cost of a new jet engine?" His amplified voice struck me as reminiscent of the various armored villains from the *Star Wars* films Father and I watched one weekend when I was a girl and Mother was away. "Leave now, or I shall take it out of your flesh."

"You kidnapped one friend and seriously injured another today" —I directed a finger in his direction—"and you dare speak about matters of money?"

The Cardinal shook his head in faux disappointment. "Even if you had your vaunted weapon of choice, Miss Delacroix, my armor is more than capable of withstanding your steel." He shifted his gaze in Maddox's direction. "And as for the teeth and claws of a lowly animal..."

A low growl sounded from the back of Maddox's throat.

"Silence, theriodan."

No sooner had the Cardinal spoken the venom-filled command than the cry of sirens filled the air from every corner of the airport. A quick spin showed security approaching from three sides, tearing across the tarmac and grass in trucks, cars, and on foot.

"And now, the complications I had sought to circumvent." The Cardinal's augmented sigh proved an unnerving hiss. "My apologies to you all, but it would appear the local TSA wishes to cut short our little meet and greet. Trust that their worthless firearms would prove as ineffective against the technology in my suit as your bare fists. Can you, Miss Delacroix, say the same about yourself or your theriodan friend?" The Cardinal gestured in Seph's direction. "Or Miss Snow here for that matter?"

"Let her go, or I'll show you how effective these fists can be."

"Oh, this encounter has already proven to be an ill-timed catch and release, make no mistake," he answered. "While the various security elements converging on our position pose me no threat whatsoever, I cannot risk even one stray bullet harming the lovely creature on my arm, so for now, I must take my leave." With that, he released Seph's arm, pulled the obscuring hood from her head, and dropped it to the ground, allowing her platinum locks to flow free. A ball-gagged and terrified Seph stared at us wide-eyed and silent as her captor swept her off her feet and lowered her still-covered form to the warm tarmac. "Do stay down, Miss Snow. You being harmed would prove quite unfortunate in ways you do not yet understand." He pulled himself back up to his full height. "In fact, I suggest your hopefully-wiser-than-they-look friends do the same, unless they'd care to roll the dice this early in the day."

I stepped forward. "You can't seriously believe I'm going to let you walk away."

"Don't make a move until airport security establishes your bona fides," the Cardinal said to Seph, ignoring me. "Based on the status your place in the world affords you, I suspect you will be released on your own recognizance." He let out a mirthless laugh, his masked gaze falling again on Maddox and me. "I can't say the same, however, for your friends. Airport security doesn't typically tolerate violent trespassers, as I understand it." The Cardinal stepped away from Seph's supine form. "Fear not, Miss Snow. I will call upon you again, and soon. I sincerely hope our next engagement won't be so rudely interrupted."

The sound of engines cycling up began anew, albeit on a much smaller scale. Before I could process what was about to happen, the Cardinal's armored form lifted into the air, spun in the sky like a pirouette, and with a quiet swoosh of air, flew off in the direction of the Pacific.

In an instant, I was at Seph's side, ripping the ball-gag from her mouth and helping her to sit up.

"Are you all right?" I asked.

"I'm fine, I think," she answered, clearly shaken. She shifted her jaw from side to side. "Boy, that thing sucks."

"Funny. He didn't have you bound in any way other than your mouth." I looked after the Cardinal, his form already nothing but a red dot out over the ocean. "Clearly he knows what you can do." I turned to Maddox. "Meanwhile, you didn't tell me he could fly."

"Hell, you think I knew?" Maddox stared into the distance as the Cardinal's form disappeared into the clear blue sky, his face tight with anger. "I'm the guy that couldn't even snag a photo of the asshole, remember?"

"Right." Already on my knees from helping Seph up, I raised my hands and placed them behind my head as the dozen cars and trucks converging on our position all stopped in a tight circle around us. "In any case, you'd best put your hands behind your head and drop the coyote eyes." Uniformed officers poured out of the various vehicles and shouted at us from every direction, weapons drawn and directed our way. "I'd hate for you to scare one of these guys and end up getting shot."

"Earlier today, you wouldn't have cared," Maddox said with a lone chuckle as he shifted his lupine gaze back to a more normal appearance and joined me on his knees. "I guess that's progress."

"Now we just have to figure out how to explain being caught dead to rights committing several federal offenses." As a dozen airport security descended upon us, I shot Maddox a smile, the faintest hint of forgiveness and warmth bubbling up from somewhere deep within. "Anyway, thanks for the assist."

Maddox returned my grin. "At least you believe me now."

In seconds, all three of us were face down on the tarmac and handcuffed. A particularly rotund officer, at least from what I could see of him, with two days of stubble and breath like a burning cigarette factory, grunted in my ear.

"Stay down, girl."

I tuned out the rest of his canned speech. They were always the same.

And I swear, if one more person called me girl...

No. Both Mother and Father drilled into me that best practice is to respect the local authorities whenever possible and avoid injuring non-Ascendant unless there is no other option, especially when the situation represents something beyond their ken.

"Holy shit," came a voice from a few feet away. "Do you guys know who this is?"

I pulled my head to one side in time to see one of the officers help Seph to her feet.

"You're Persephone Snow," the dumbfounded young man muttered. "*The* Persephone Snow."

"That's right," I got out between clenched teeth. "Now, why don't you and your buddies here take me, my friend, and Miss Snow to your supervisor so we can get this whole mess straightened out?"

CHAPTER 7

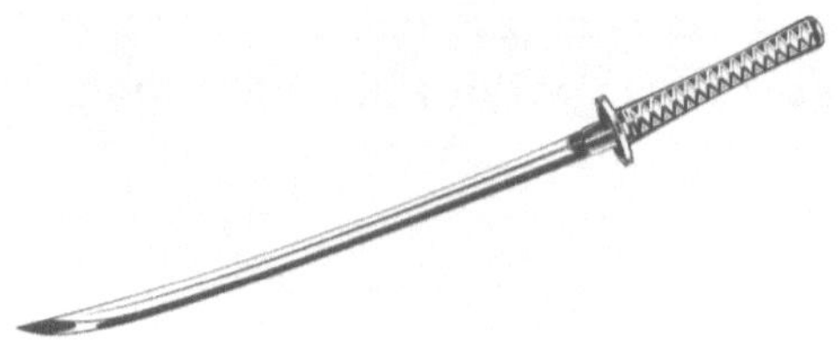

SPY IN THE HOUSE OF LOVE

"So," began the highest-ranking person I'd met yet, a burly man in the standard blue uniform named Mack, "you drove to the airport on a hunch and arrived at precisely the right moment to see Miss Snow's kidnapper drag her onto a plane." He stared across the table at me, the two of us alone in a nondescript room with an obviously two-way mirror to my left. "That's the story you're sticking to?"

"That's right." More or less, at least. I'd already been through the events of the morning several times each with three other TSA officers and could recite my version of what happened in my sleep. "You nailed it."

"And the kidnapper would be this person in the red armor you claim flew—"

"I'm not claiming anything. Two dozen of your officers literally watched the Cardinal fly away." I let out a frustrated groan. "I would appreciate it if you and whoever is coming next stopped with the whole 'pretending that's not a fact' thing. It's insulting."

"Of course." Mack shifted in his chair and glanced subconsciously at the two-way mirror. "So, this 'Cardinal,' as you've called him. He'd kidnapped Miss Snow earlier, gotten her onto a plane without going through security using this black SUV you reported that we can find no trace of whatsoever on camera or otherwise..."

"He's got a technoman...a *computer guy* that engineers things to hide his presence. I've already explained this a gazillion times."

"As I've heard. I'm simply reviewing the report with you."

"Well, review away. The story isn't going to change."

He cleared his throat. "Then, after he attempted to leave with Miss Snow aboard the plane in question, your friend in the next room was able to chase down a plane at taxiing speed and somehow get on the wing—"

"What can I say? He's an ex-track star." That part, funny enough, was actually the truth.

"While you, Miss Delacroix, stole this individual's motorcycle, followed the plane down the runway at breakneck speed, managed to take out the left engine with a thrown helmet, and thwarted the kidnapping seconds before takeoff."

"It sounds even more impressive when you say it, Officer Mack."

"Impressively illegal, in so many ways." He let out an exhausted sigh. "Trespassing. Entering a restricted area. Willful destruction of aircraft." He shook his head. "Not to mention causing an incident that has brought travel to and from this airport as well as every airport across the nation to a screeching halt."

I swallowed hard. Coast-to-coast chaos hadn't been my intent at all. Still, I'd do it again in a second.

"Persephone Snow," I countered, "is an international superstar, beloved by millions, who was in the process of being kidnapped by an individual with technology so advanced that he evaded your airport's every security measure and got her onto a plane your tower wasn't even aware was on the ground. Then, when I stopped him—

you're welcome, by the way—he flew away in a literal super-suit straight out of a comic book movie. Those are the facts."

"Hold on a minute." Mack leaned back in his chair and studied me with an incredulous stare. "Some of what you just said is classified. How could you possibly know all that?"

"Honestly, you just spilled most of it, not to mention, the second guy your people had come talk to me was a real chatterbox." I allowed myself a subtle grin. "Between you and me, you might want to leave him out front with the metal detectors." I crossed my arms before me and banished any hint of mirth from my voice. "Look, cards on the table, I'm not sure why your people have sent in yet another person to interrogate me when you should all simply be thanking me for what I did today." I pulled in a quick breath. "And Maddox as well."

A man in a dark suit who appeared even higher up the food chain than Officer Mack strode into the room. "Fortunately for you, Miss Delacroix, Mr. Trainor's story is miraculously similar to your own, and Miss Snow's version of her morning matches everything you've both reported as well." He sat at the table, excusing Officer Mack to go about his duties. "I still have a few questions, though."

"Of course you do." I stared down at the name badge resting above his heart, either inadvertently or purposefully flipped backward. "And you are?"

He glanced down and adjusted his badge to reveal his name beside a photo with, surprisingly, a rather pleasant smile. "My apologies. Jim Bradley, Chief of Security for Santa Barbara Airport."

"Hello, Mr. Bradley." I continued to work at keeping my temper. "Please know before we get started that you're the fifth person in a row to question me today."

He sighed. "I'm well aware."

"I'm curious, then." I tilted my head to one side in exasperation. "What questions could you possibly have to ask that I haven't already answered?"

"First..." He leaned in, resting on his elbows, his face more interested than interrogatory. "How exactly did you know that Miss Snow was here?"

"For the fifth time, my father is Persephone Snow's personal executive protection agent—"

"Her bodyguard, you mean?" he said with a touch of sarcasm.

I raised a cautious eyebrow. "Don't let him hear you call him that." I cleared my throat. "May I continue?"

"By all means," he said with a hint of a grin.

"She has a tracking device on her phone, and for whatever reason, her kidnapper didn't choose to relieve her of that particular piece of technology."

I opted not to tell him about the false signal leading north, nor the fact that my educated guess was all that prevented the Cardinal from taking Seph to God knows where.

"If you don't mind repeating yourself, how exactly were you able to breach our security and make it onto the tarmac?"

It was my turn to sigh. "For the twenty-seventh time, you allow cars to park right next to your fence on the north end of the airport where we entered. Anyone with the slightest bit of skill can use those vehicles to gain entry." I glanced up at the additional TSA officer standing by the door. "Honestly, I'm surprised it doesn't happen more often."

"Right." Bradley swallowed and somehow managed to maintain his smile. "And how do you think this Cardinal, as you call him, managed to gain access? Not only his plane, but the SUV and the motorcycle? Any thoughts? Maybe even why a man with a suit of armor that lets him fly around like Iron Man needed a private jet in the first place?"

Now, that was a new one.

"I'm afraid I haven't the slightest idea." Especially since using the word technomancer would likely end with me locked up in either a cell or a padded room. "All I knew was that he had my friend and that if I didn't skip standard procedure and do something drastic, she'd be long gone on my watch." I leaned across the table until we were nearly nose-to-nose. "Not to mention, *yours*."

"Well, regardless of the illegal nature of your and Mr. Trainor's actions today, we are quite glad a kidnapping of any kind, much less that of an international figure such as Miss Snow, was prevented. My people will be shoring up security in the areas you were able to breach for certain. However, any help in learning how the man you were tracking and his subordinates seem to be able to come and go at will from our airport would be most helpful."

"Wait, you're asking for my help?"

"A phantom plane no one could see on either radar or camera sat on our tarmac all day today and possibly overnight as well and nearly took off from my airport with a high-profile individual on board." Bradley's mouth quirked to one side. "Consider me...intrigued."

"What are you proposing?" I asked.

He glanced across his shoulder at the remaining TSA officer. "Hey, Gary. Give us a minute?"

"You got it, boss." The officer stepped quietly to the door and pulled it closed behind him, leaving me alone with Bradley.

I wasn't sure if I suddenly felt safer or more exposed, not that I had much say in the matter.

"You know, you're fortunate, Miss Delacroix," Bradley said as soon as the door clicked shut, "that the technomancer employed by the Cardinal took out such a wide swath of our security cameras."

"Wait. What?" It was my turn to be surprised, though I did my best not to appear completely dumbfounded. "Did *you* use the word 'technomancer,' Mr. Bradley?"

"You have more allies than you might believe, Miss Delacroix." Bradley leaned back in his chair. "While most of society remains oblivious to certain aspects of the world around them, there are those of us who, like you and your late mother, work to keep the peace."

"All right." I crossed my arms and adopted my most serious stare. "Cut it with the cryptic bullshit and tell me who you are."

"Very well, Daughter of Neith." He pulled in a deep breath. "What do you know of the Order of Ophanim?"

The Order of Ophanim. Father was not going to like this.

"You're with the Order of Ophanim?"

"Indeed, I am."

"You are aware my father left your Order when his superiors decided that merely observing Ascendant was no longer sufficient?"

"Painfully so."

"And that before it was all over, my mother found herself in the crosshairs of your organization whose charter is simply to watch, catalog, and occasionally assist with Ascendant affairs?"

"Miss Delacroix, I have already violated several oaths simply by telling you of my affiliation with the Order, but I'd hoped my honesty might earn me some measure of trust."

"To be honest, I can think of better ways of gaining confidence than telling someone you're a card-carrying member of a group whose actions nearly led to the death of both their parents years before they were born."

"A calculated risk." He shifted in his seat. "May I continue?"

My heart raced, both my hands curling into fists beneath the table as I struggled to determine if I sat in the presence of ally or enemy. Regardless of his other affiliation, however, he was still chief of security for the airport where Seph, Maddox, and I were being held for questioning. Probably best to "make nice" like Father always says and figure out the rest later. Not to mention I was way more worried about the psychopathic Ascendant serial killer on the loose than I was the bureaucrat in the rumpled suit before me.

"Go on," I whispered. "So, the Order, huh? Yet another secret society with delusions of grandeur." At least I'd heard of this one. I hadn't the first clue about the mysterious group of Ascendant Maddox claimed to be working with, assuming everything the coyote had told me that morning was the truth. "Tell me why I should even consider trusting you."

"First of all, because I can make a lot of this go away with just a few pen strokes." He gestured to the security camera protruding from the corner of the ceiling, its red indicator light from before no longer lit. "Second, it appears that your family and friends, the Order, and the Ascendant population at large currently share a common enemy." He again leaned across the table. "And third, because I thought a lot of your mother and would love the opportunity to help her husband and only daughter in any way I can." He laughed. "Not that your mother was ever too keen on accepting our assistance."

"You knew my mother?" I asked with far more emotion in my voice than intended.

"Only by reputation, though everyone in the Order during my time, top to bottom, held Danielle Delacroix and what she brought to the world in high regard."

My shoulders slumped in disappointment. I'd hoped Bradley might have a story, a memory, a snippet of my mother to fill the void at my core. God, I missed her.

"So, you're offering to let Maddox and me off with a slap to the wrist. What is it you want from us?"

"As sharp as your mother." Bradley pulled in a breath. "In case you haven't put it quite together, Miss Delacroix, the Order needs your help."

"The Illuminati needs my help?" I laughed. "That's disturbing."

"Truth be told," Bradley countered, "while the Illuminati do exist among us, controlling the world and manipulating politics on a global stage toward their own ends, they consist of those your family line polices, not their observers."

"So, your Order is basically a bunch of ineffectual voyeurs basking in the reflected glory of the Ascendant?" My month of hanging with Seph brought one of her least favorite words to the front of my brain. "Like Hollywood paparazzi?"

Bradley cleared his throat, obviously offended. "In a world where gods walk hidden among us, the Order strives to keep a sense of balance and peace in the world and has done so for all of human history. We observe and catalog, guiding relations between Ascendant and the remainder of humankind, and while we may occasionally intervene in a more direct manner, our charge is only to do so when no other option is present."

"Tell that to my father."

Bradley interlaced his fingers and rested his forearms on the table. "This conversation, for instance, is the most direct contact I've ever had with someone from that world. While my knowledge of both the Ascendant and your bloodline is extensive, I've gleaned most of what I know from books, reports, and the like."

"Consider yourself lucky." I gestured around the interrogation room. "Sometimes going into the field leads to places like this."

"My apologies, Miss Delacroix. While my affiliation with the

Order affords me intel beyond that of the remainder of the airport's personnel, the day job does require me to do things by the book. I'm sure you understand."

Funny thing? I got it. The situation was no different than Mother and I sitting back and letting Father fill the role of Chief of Security for Seph for months while we were the ones actually equipped to deal with the threat facing her.

So, if all I'd been told was true, in the space of a day, I'd encountered agents of two different secret societies as well as fought off the superpowered serial assassin both groups were hunting. And it was barely lunchtime.

"If I may, I'd like to offer my personal condolences on the loss of your mother." Bradley lowered his chin in respect and deference. "I've studied her time as Daughter of Neith for years. While the Order of Ophanim has worked with multiple members of your family line, I assure you that none were as brave, skilled, and selfless as her."

"Thank you, Mr. Bradley." I swallowed back the emotion. I'd already let Bradley see more than I desired.

"We were all quite shocked to learn of your mother's untimely death, and saddened further that you were denied both your birthright and your destiny." He raised a questioning eyebrow. "I trust Mr. Harkreader's training is coming along nicely?"

Damn. This Bradley guy did know everything. "Ethan is currently recovering from an encounter with our crimson-clad adversary earlier today, but otherwise, he's doing quite well."

"And that's why you're here with Mr. Trainor instead, I assume?"

"Something like that."

Silence held sway for a long moment.

"Funny thing. Even with all your people did to try to win my mother back to your side after everything that went down, she was never exactly a fan again. I can tell you that with no ambiguity, Mr. Bradley."

"I can't say that I blame her. The element in question has been removed from our organization, but forgiving or forgetting such a betrayal would be not only unwise but next to impossible for most."

"Huh." I studied the man across the table. "I think Mother would have liked you. You strike me as a pretty stand-up guy."

"A high compliment." Bradley sat up a bit straighter in his chair. "I never had the honor of working with your mother and would have loved the opportunity to meet such an individual. I regret that possibility has passed. As I understand it, even before the unfortunate incident that led to your father resigning our ranks, your mother's needs and our organization's goals never quite lined up, and yet, as a student of her career, I assure you the world would be a much different place were it not for Danielle Delacroix." He pulled in a deep breath. "I hope our relationship with you and Mr. Harkreader might be different."

I flushed, my cheeks growing hot, both at the way he spoke of Mother and at the sudden realization that I was being recruited.

"Though she trained me to follow closely in her footsteps, understand I am not my mother. That being said, one thing she taught me is a healthy skepticism of others. Clearly you want something from me. Mind telling me what that is?"

"First," Bradley said, "the video files from the lone camera overlooked by the Cardinal's technomancer that captured evidence of your impressive gymnastic talents as well as your theriodan friend's running eight-foot jump have been deleted and were seen by no one other than me."

"Deleted?" I asked. "But you're the head of security of this airport. Isn't erasing evidence pretty much against your job description?"

"Truth be told, based on your illegal actions today and my public role alone, the decision to turn you and your friend over to the authorities is clear. Between your various offenses, it's unlikely either of you would see the outside of a cell again for many years."

"Mr. Bradley, I—"

"However, I wear at least two hats in this particular scenario. You and I both know that you entered the airport with one goal and one goal only, to save your friend and charge from whatever fate the Cardinal had in mind. Though it is truly unfortunate that the events in question had to occur in such a public manner, had I been in your shoes, I would have done the same." Again, he leaned in, his voice dropping to a conspiratorial whisper. "And I'd like to think I'd have pulled it off with the same level of skill and panache."

"So, we're free to go?" I asked, as baffled as I'd ever been. "Is that possible?"

"Not entirely." Bradley let out a long sigh. "My place within the Order allows me a significantly different view of today's events from the remainder of the TSA agents and officers of this airport, but that doesn't change the rather high-profile situation at hand." He let out a quiet *humph*. "I'm afraid we're going to have to put on a bit of a show to get you and Mr. Trainor away from here with Miss Snow."

"A show, huh?" I crossed my arms, mirroring Bradley. "Funny. You've confided quite a lot in a stranger, and seem to be putting your own neck on the block, and yet I've noticed that you still haven't told me what it is you want from me." I considered for a moment, Maddox's face flashing across my mind's eye. "Or, I suppose, us."

"I have indeed compromised myself in order to gain your trust, Miss Delacroix. Understand that the Order as a whole maintains a decentralized framework of operatives to maintain plausible deniability and the security of our members. Other than knowing of my affiliation, I've offered up very little. Still, you are correct in your assertion that such personal disclosure is anything but par for the course."

"Good lord, did you practice that speech or something?" I let out a frustrated grunt, my mind working overtime to figure out if all I was being told was "legit," as Seph likes to say, or if this was a practiced laundry list of lies. "Quit dancing around the subject, Bradley, and tell me what the hell it is you want."

He bowed his head, though his eyes still met mine. "Things are changing, and quickly. Both the Order and the Ascendant have remained relatively clandestine for centuries." He chuckled. "In the past, word of mouth was dangerous enough for the rare individual who was different. Imagine the Salem Witch Trials in the age of the photograph, the moving picture, the video recording, the camera phone. Ascendant have gone all but completely underground over the last century. The few brazen enough to reveal themselves to the world at large were dealt with either internally or"—he straightened to lock gazes with me—"by the women of your line."

"I know all of this. Mother taught me well." I narrowed my eyes at Bradley. "What's different now?"

"What's different?" He laughed aloud. "In the last month, you and your associates have stopped half a dozen barefaced attempts by various groups of Ascendant to abduct one of the most famous and recognizable people in the world. Skiomancers, elementalists, theriodans, and now, the Cardinal. Regardless of the apparent skill of the technomancer in his employ, the fact that he chose to reveal himself in a public place today, and with a kidnapped international superstar on his arm to boot, shows a blatant disregard for millennia of tradition."

"I still don't see the issue. Mother fought problematic Ascendant her entire life."

"Problematic, yes, though it's the public nature of the recent displays of Ascendant ability that are the concern." He shifted in his seat. "The pair of Angel Sisters you encountered in Los Angeles have each admonished their respective groups and assured both the Order and Ascendant society that any necessary actions will be kept circumspect and quiet, as has been standard operating procedure for decades."

"That's a good thing, right? Your group, the Angels, and the rest working together to keep the peace without freaking out the world at large?"

"Indeed. Still, there remains one bad actor on the stage who needs to be dealt with, as you and yours learned this morning."

"The Cardinal. He's breaking all the rules."

"He's thrown the rulebook out the window. It was his involvement that brought Krage and his people out of the shadows, so to speak, which in turn forced the hand of Alba's elementalists, and now he's taking an even more blatant approach. God knows what he's got planned next." Bradley shook his head. "In any case, the TSA and other federal agencies are trying to contain the repercussions of this morning's events, both to defuse implications on international flight from what would appear to be a terrorist attack on a U.S. airfield as well as, from my perspective, to maintain the status quo between Ascendant, the Order, and the rest of the world."

"Wow." I sucked in air through my teeth. "Though it's not my fault by any stretch of the imagination, I'm sorry about the mess."

"Bygones, Miss Delacroix. As I said before, I would have done the same." His smile faded. "That being said, something must be done. We sit upon a powder keg, one I'm amazed hasn't already exploded. If the world at large learns of the presence of the Ascendant, then all the work done by my Order and your family line will be for nothing."

Finally, down to brass tacks. "What is it exactly that you are asking me to do then, Mr. Bradley?"

"It's more what I can do for you, Miss Delacroix. I've been authorized by the Order to offer you full access to all our information and data on the Cardinal."

"So that I can do what?"

Bradley leaned forward and rested his chin on his interlaced fingers. "We want you and your group to take him down."

CHAPTER 8

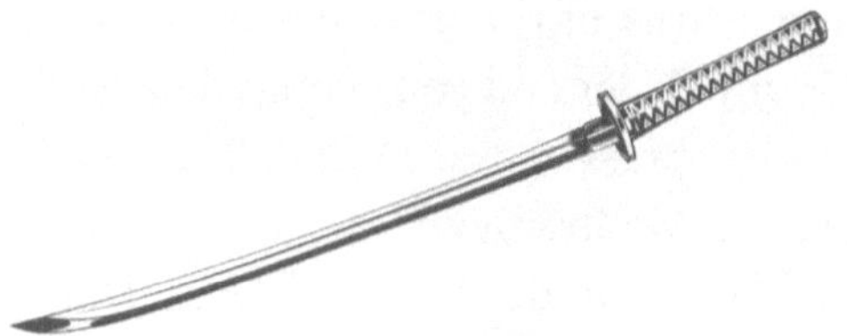

FATHER FIGURE

"And then they just...let you both go?" Father studied Maddox and me, as confused as I'd been at the entire situation. He kept his voice low, as the waiting room of the emergency department at Santa Barbara Cottage Hospital didn't strike any of us as the best place to discuss our involvement in what had quickly become, at least in the eyes of the majority of news networks, an international terrorist incident. "Putting aside this Bradley person's affiliation with the Order of Ophanim, there were likely dozens of witnesses who saw the two of you trespassing in a restricted area and destroying a plane engine mid-takeoff."

"That's not even the strangest thing." I pulled the black leather wallet Bradley had provided me and showed it to Father. "After we were interrogated separately for hours, Bradley had Maddox and me pulled into the same room, gave each of us one of these, reunited us with Seph, and soon after, we were escorted off the property and released."

Father opened the wallet. Inside, as incredible as when I'd looked the first time, rested a five-point star adorned with a bald eagle within a silver circle with letters stamped into the metal proclaiming me a Special Deputy United States Marshal.

As Mother always explained it, Daughters of Neith didn't mix all that well with traditional law enforcement. *"Tread carefully,"* she'd always said.

"Is this legitimate?" Father asked, his puzzlement deepening.

"Legitimate enough to let us walk." Maddox had stayed quiet until that moment, knowing exactly how little my father wanted him there. For better or for worse, though, the events of the morning necessitated my ex sticking around a bit longer.

Father's question raised a two-pronged thought. Suddenly being officially recognized as an agent of sorts for the United States government struck me as surreal and strange. On one hand, I had no idea what responsibilities accompanied this Get Out of Jail Free card I'd been handed. On the other, I couldn't help but wonder if the bona fides Maddox and I had been provided were worth the metal on which they were stamped, and if by carrying them, we were setting ourselves up for a bigger fall down the road. Regardless, Bradley had somehow maneuvered things to avoid felony charges, federal custody, and a lot of pain, freeing Maddox and me to do what needed to be done. Clearly, such intervention was not going to be without cost. Bradley had asked to meet that night, Maddox and Father included, to discuss next steps, and he made it clear that our little group date, as it were, wasn't a request.

"You said Ethan is doing well?" I asked, shifting the subject.

I hated that saying his name in front of Maddox sent my guts into a knot.

"Doctor Charlesworth came out and gave an update earlier. She said Mr. Harkreader is going to be sore for a few days and would benefit from physical therapy for his shoulder injury but otherwise should be fine."

"So his arm wasn't broken?"

"Only a dislocated shoulder, no worse than mine last month." Father answered. "Not the first time, apparently. He said it popped out in high school during a particularly rough tackle on the football field, but hasn't bothered him much since. They gave him some pain meds earlier and were able to reset his arm into the socket." Father shot an annoyed glance in Maddox's direction, and I knew exactly what that look meant. Regardless of his feelings, with Ethan temporarily out of commission, we could certainly use an extra theriodan around. "Fortunately, it's his left arm that will be in a sling."

Father, as always, was thinking tactically. Ethan, as right-handed as they come, had been working with me on some exercises for his left side, as sword work in general and dual blade skills in particular were both new to him. We'd get back to all that soon enough, I supposed. For the next few days to weeks, though, Ethan would have to get back to basics and rebuild strength in his injured shoulder. Fortunately for him, the Light of Neith coursing through his body had likely already kicked in, supercharging his normal healing, not to mention I'd helped Mother rehab enough injured joints over the years that I could probably cruise through PT school if the whole "Enforcer of Ascendant Relations" gig fell through.

In any case, Ethan would be far less miserable with his dominant hand still at a hundred percent as we rehabbed his already weaker side. He wasn't someone who took being relegated to the sidelines well. One of the things I—

I cleared my throat. "I bet Seph was glad to see Ethan."

"Not as glad as he was to see her." Father shook his head. "Even when they were doing the maneuvers to get his shoulder back into its socket, all he could talk about was how he let her down. How he couldn't protect her."

"Harkreader was caught unarmed and unprepared for an armored assailant who likely could defeat him barefisted on his best day," Maddox said. "There is no dishonor in being bested by your better."

"Don't let Ethan hear you say that." Seph reappeared through the door leading to the back of the emergency department. "He's feeling a little defeated at the moment."

"But, he's okay?" My words came out a bit more breathless than I intended. "I mean, if badness is coming for you again, we're going to need all hands on deck."

"He's fine." Seph laughed. "The fentanyl left him a little loopy, but he's coming out of it now." Her eyes took on a wistful cast. "He was like a little puppy. So cute."

The knot in my intestines tightened. "Can I go back and see him now?"

"No need." Seph shrugged. "The nurse back there is giving him his discharge paperwork. They'll be wheeling him out any second now."

"Great." I allowed my body, already halfway out of the seat, to relax back into the waiting room chair. "Then we can go home."

"You're sure you're not hurt, Miss Snow?" Maddox asked, his lips curling into a sly smile. "I'm sure some of the doctors here would be glad to check you out as well."

"I'm fine, thanks." Seph answered his grin, her smile less effortless than usual. "And you can call me Seph." She inclined her head in Father's direction. "He's the only one who calls me Miss Snow."

"And as long as I'm in your employ," Father said stoically with an undercurrent of warmth, "that is how you will be addressed."

Seph snorted. "Don't let him fool you, Maddox. He can be tough as nails when he needs to be, but underneath all the muscles and scowls, he's a big teddy bear."

Father grumbled something under his breath likely not fit for polite company. Maddox wisely kept his silence.

"Hey," came a most welcome voice, "what did I miss?"

A nurse in navy blue scrubs was wheeling Ethan in our direction.

"Nothing important." Seph rose and stole to Ethan's side. "Just catching everybody up." She took over the handles of the wheelchair as the nurse disappeared back through the doorway.

"Then, I'm the one behind the eight ball. What else is new?"

"No worries." Seph leaned in and kissed the crown of Ethan's head. "Plenty of time for the play-by-play when we get back to the house."

"Are you sure returning to your home is the best plan of action,

Miss Snow?" Father stared at her, one eyebrow raised in incredulous question. "After today's events?"

The smile disappeared from Seph's face. "We're not talking about this again, are we, Mr. Delacroix?"

"The Cardinal abducted you mere blocks from your home and managed to incapacitate Mr. Harkreader in the process." At Ethan's cleared throat, Father added, "Despite his best efforts, of course, to defend you."

"He moves fast," Ethan said, a bit defensive, but also likely still under the influence of some of the better pain meds in southern California. "Faster than Neko or any of the theriodans we've run into."

"Present company included, I guess?" Maddox asked.

Ethan shot a cross look in Maddox's direction. "Who is this again?"

"Later," I said. "What were you saying?"

"He's fast, but he's strong too. The armor augments him without a doubt, but I get the feeling both the moves and the muscle are all him." His vexed expression faded into one of bafflement. "How did you two manage to stop him?"

"We didn't," I answered. "Once we disabled the plane—"

"We?" Maddox laughed. "That was all Rosemary. She chucked a motorcycle helmet right through the jet's left engine. Fireball nearly singed my eyebrows off." In what I hoped was a rare moment of forgetful exuberance, he playfully punched me in the deltoid. "Not even Jordan could have made that shot."

There was a time that both the approval and the display of affection, however juvenile, would have made my heart swell with joy. At the moment, they left me cold.

Ethan, on the other hand, stared in Maddox's direction with a glare that could melt steel.

"Once you disabled the plane," Ethan asked, not taking his eyes off Maddox, "then what, Rosemary?"

The smile beaming off Maddox's face diminished, as if a cloud had passed over the sun. Part of me felt for him, but the rest was glad to see him put in his place.

"The Cardinal shut everything down, walked off the plane with Seph, and offered a mix of veiled threats and words of advice before turning and flying away."

"Wait." Ethan scratched his chin. "This guy can fly too?"

I glanced at Seph, then Maddox, before locking gazes with Ethan again. "Right out over the ocean."

"Is he an aeromancer like Falco?"

"Not that I could tell." I again looked Maddox's way, but it was clear no more words were coming from that corner of the room. "No big gusts of wind like in Denver."

"The suit, then?" Ethan looked to Father. "If that's the case, why didn't he just take off with Seph?"

"Limited range maybe?" Father said. "He did go to a lot of trouble to get her on a plane."

"When it was all of us on the tarmac," I added, "the Cardinal said he couldn't risk the TSA agents hitting her." I glanced Seph's way. "For the moment, at least, he needs Seph alive."

"We can only hope." Ethan smiled Seph's way before returning his attention to Father. "You've told me about a lot of Ascendant stuff, Mr. Delacroix. Is 'up, up, and away' something you've seen before?"

"In Danielle's catalog of Ascendant gifts, I don't recall ever learning of someone with simply the ability to fly, though if everything Rosemary learned from her encounter with the head of airport security is true, we may have more resources at our disposal very soon."

"Head of airport security?" Ethan asked as he shot me a puzzled look. "Haven't heard that part yet."

"All in good time, Ethan," I said. "For now, let's get you home."

"Which," Father said, "brings us back to the top of this discussion."

"There is no discussion." Seph crossed her arms, defiant. "I'm not sure what you have in mind, but I'm not going into hiding or witness protection or whatever it is you're recommending."

Father shook his head. "And when he comes for you in the night? What then?"

"Ethan will protect me."

Maddox looked away, sniffing as if his allergies were bothering him, which is funny, because Maddox doesn't have allergies.

"I agree that Mr. Harkreader has done an outstanding job thus far of being your advocate in times of danger, but he's going to be rehabbing that shoulder for a week even with the uptick in healing he'll get from...well, you know." Father shook his head, frustrated. "Are you certain your three-story home with more windows than walls is where you wish to be sleeping when an armored assailant with strength, speed, and flight capability comes calling?"

"And now we're back to last month." Seph's eyes danced with ire. "Where is this magical place you plan to take me that this asshole in red armor along with the rest of the Legion of Doom can't get to me?"

At Father's pause, Seph's lips drew down to a narrow line and her head shook from side to side.

"Staying mobile didn't help last time," she said, "and we already spent a week in your safe house in Nevada." Seph looked to one side. "If I never see ramen again, it will be too soon."

"Miss Snow—"

"Look," Seph interrupted, "I'm not going underground, I'm not going to sit in a jail cell, and I'm not going on the road in your RV, no matter *how* nice it might be." She shot me a quick wink, knowing she was talking about my home for the last several years, a touch point from an earlier tirade. "No matter how long we stayed away, it's not like a bunch of quasi-immortal superhuman demigods have anything but time on their side, right?"

Father considered for a moment. "I suppose you have a point."

"Please note that I'm putting my house, my *very* expensive house, on the line here. If concrete sumo wrestlers or shadow-dealing assassins or armored birdmen show up and blow it to bits, I'll be the one footing the bill, and you know what? That's okay."

"It's not your house I'm worried about," Father interjected. "You know that."

"I do." Seph rested a hand gently on Father's uninjured shoulder and allowed her tender side to come out once more. "This man, the Cardinal. He wants me and is willing to do whatever it takes to get what he wants. He sent mercenaries first, and when they failed, he came for me himself. I'm not certain I buy that he let me go today for my own safety, but regardless, he insinuated that he would be back to try again, and soon. I don't think he's the sort of person you can truly hide from, so isn't the best strategy to simply let him come, defeat him, and then have the Scooby gang unmask him and be done with it?"

Maddox snorted a quiet laugh at that last bit, and even I found the humor in Seph's words, though I didn't dare allow my face to move a millimeter.

"You're offering yourself up as bait?" Ethan asked.

"I'm merely acknowledging that the fox is already in the hen house." Seph shot Father a triumphant glance. "Now, we just need to get this particular fox close enough to poke his little eyes out and break his neck, wouldn't you agree, Mr. Delacroix?"

Father's chin dropped almost imperceptibly, and then he let out a laugh. "From your lips to God's ears, Miss Snow."

"Come on, Ethan. Let's get you home and into some clean clothes." Seph grabbed the plastic bag with all of Ethan's papers and instructions and released the wheelchair brakes. "Then we can have that leftover curry from last night you were looking forward to." And with that, she pushed him out of the emergency department waiting room, which had luckily remained empty throughout our little discussion.

That left me, Father, and Maddox sitting in a tight triangle of uncomfortable silence.

"So," Maddox said, breaking the verbal stalemate, "I know no one here is particularly keen on me sticking around, and though he's barely met me, Harkreader seems to sit at the top of the list. Still, with him down for a few days, you're going to need an extra hand to keep things secure around here. I'd like to offer my services until your boy, Ethan, is back in fighting condition." He swallowed. "That is, if you'll have me."

Before I could answer, Father raised a hand.

"Regardless of the past, you performed honorably today, Mr. Trainor. Your assessment of the situation is on point, and we could use the assistance." Father considered. "Our mutual friend Neko has been a huge help, what with him being mostly nocturnal when he needs to be. He's currently out of town checking on a few things for me, and we could certainly use someone who moves and sees well in the dark to work the night shift." Father's eyes cut my way. "Particularly since Rosemary and I have to go meet with this Mr. Bradley from the Order tonight."

"It's a deal, then." Maddox reached out his hand which Father, after a quiet grunt, reluctantly took and gave a perfunctory shake. "Bradley called the meeting for eleven. Shall I post guard at Seph's an hour or so before?"

"That would be most helpful." Father looked out the doorway where Seph and Ethan had gone. "Just make sure you coordinate with Ethan."

"Of course." Maddox rose from his seat with a sarcastic laugh and headed for the door himself. "That should go over well."

And with that, Father and I were alone for the first time since early that morning. He looked around, taking in the environment, before shifting the conversation.

"Your mother hated hospitals," he said, his tone hushed and contemplative. "Every time I ever brought her to one, it was under duress. Didn't matter if she'd broken bones or had lost a liter of blood. She wasn't having it." He laughed. "Hard to put your foot down when your wife is a Daughter of Neith, right?"

"I'm sorry I let you down today, Father." I hung my head. "If Mother were here, she would have stopped the Cardinal. We'd be done with all this, and Maddox would be on his way."

"First, Rosemary, you don't know that. Had she faced the challenges you did this day, the outcome might have been the same." Father took my chin and pulled my gaze up to his. "And second, Mr. Trainor was right. Michael Jordan himself could not have made that shot."

I chuckled at the compliment, a hint of moisture forming at the corner of both my eyes. "So, you're not disappointed in me?"

Father smiled. "I've never been prouder."

CHAPTER 9

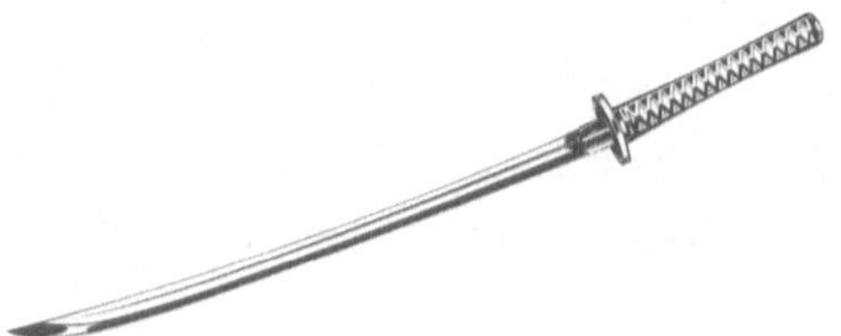

EVERY BREATH YOU TAKE

"Mr. Delacroix."

Bradley took a seat opposite Father and me at the back of Winchell's, a twenty-four-hour donut shop four miles west of Seph's neighborhood and far too close for apple fritters of such quality to exist unless I wanted to add a couple miles to my daily run. The clock had just struck eleven, and the place was deserted except for the three of us, a couple of staff, and two teenagers in the far corner holding hands and staring into each other's eyes across a box of chocolate bear claws. A streetlamp outside the window cast a shadow of their nearness on the tile floor, a literal silhouette of young love.

I'd never experienced a moment so simple and true in my entire life.

"Mr. Bradley, I assume?" Father rumbled.

Bradley nodded. "Thank you both for meeting me so late." He

looked around the all-but-empty shop. "Mr. Trainor isn't joining us this evening?"

"As you are aware," Father answered, "my client, Miss Snow, was nearly abducted earlier today by an armored terrorist." He cracked his neck, the sound like a cue ball scattering its fifteen colorful friends. "While a second attempt in twenty-four hours might seem brazen even for the individual in question, we're not taking any chances, especially after the events of a month ago." Father rested his elbows on the table and leaned in, his hulking presence a stark contrast to Bradley's slight form. "Therefore, Mr. Trainor and others are ensuring her safety while we're engaged in whatever you hope to accomplish with this meeting."

"And by others," Bradley breathed, "I assume you speak of the esteemed Mr. Harkreader." Not kowtowing to Father even a bit, he stared unafraid into the eyes of a man who could easily snap his spine in half. "Do send him my best," he offered with irritating nonchalance.

"We never crossed paths back in the day when I was still a member of your organization, but I trust my reputation precedes me." Father's scowl intensified. "I see that you are as well-informed as I was back in the day, but it will take far more than good intelligence and pretentious smirks to intimidate people who deal with the type of threats I and my family routinely face."

"Just as it will take more than your much vaunted physicality to intimidate me, Mr. Delacroix." He motioned to the arms of Father's suit jacket where his upper arms strained against the fabric. "I understand they actually make clothing in your size if you shop around a bit."

Father's entire body tensed like a sprung trap. "It's been a long day, Bradley. I would advise against tempting me to engage in any, as you call it, physicality."

"Gentlemen." I raised my coffee cup and took a sip of my caramel latte, my taste buds exploding in delight. After years of straight black, Seph's advice to give the rest of the coffee spectrum a chance had been truly life changing. "No need to compare egos in a mostly empty donut shop, wouldn't you agree?"

Each man glared across the table at the other, neither blinking or giving an inch of ground.

"Father?"

"It's fine." He let out a disgruntled sigh and leaned back in his chair, the tiny surrender immediately deescalating the tension at our table. "Everything is fine."

"Right." I turned my attention back on Bradley. "And for you? A maple bar?" I slid the box of various confections across the table so our mysterious hopefully-ally could try some of Winchell's best. "Or you could snag the other apple fritter, I suppose, though you'd be breaking my heart if you did."

"Thank you, Miss Delacroix, but I've already eaten dinner and—"

"Humor the girl, Mr. Bradley." Father smiled. Actually smiled. "Despite your putting her through the wringer at the airport today, my daughter insisted we purchase sufficient pastries for all involved." His eyes flicked in my direction. "Something about providing a warmer reception than the one she received..."

Bradley quirked his mouth this way and that before diving a hand into the box and coming out with an old-fashioned chocolate. "Truth be told, I haven't had a donut in years. When you have a job that involves a lot of sitting, you have to watch the calories." He took out a quarter of the donut with one bite, his eyes sliding shut as he quietly grunted in satisfaction. "Damn. Better than I remembered."

I slid the third cup of coffee we'd purchased across the table to rest at Bradley's elbow. "A little something to wash down your tiny bit of heaven?"

He chuckled despite his mouth being full. "Why, Miss Delacroix, I believe you're buttering me up."

"Just taking care of pleasantries before we get down to business." I offered him a half-smile of my own. "Plus, donuts and coffee are the least I can do for making sure I didn't spend the evening in a cell."

He lifted the cup to his lips and washed down the mouthful of deliciousness with a gulp of Winchell's best. "Regardless of what went down at the airport today, you and I both know that's the last place you deserve to be."

"At least we agree on something." I sucked in a breath. "So, first question." I pulled the wallet containing the Special Deputy badge from my back pocket and dropped it on the table. "Are these for real or simply a forgery to get Maddox and me out of trouble?" I paused thoughtfully. "Or, possibly, into even more trouble?"

"Does it matter?" Bradley asked. "That little tin star allowed you to walk away from a situation that otherwise would have you and your ex-boyfriend sharing a cell tonight God knows where awaiting your fate."

"Of course it matters." Ugh. I never told him who Maddox was to me. Bradley really did know his stuff

"And why, Miss Delacroix? All such indications of privilege are temporary at best. The most decorated soldier or police officer can go from paragon to pariah in a matter of seconds with one bad decision. Did the war criminal not earn their little strips of colored cloth, their shiny little pins and badges? All of it can be taken away at a moment's notice, sometimes deservedly and sometimes less so." His smile returned. "Anyway, isn't it so much better out here among the free this fine evening with your father at your side?" Bradley's eyes dropped to my plate. "They don't serve warm apple fritters in jail, you know."

"Sounds like someone is speaking from experience." Father studied Bradley in that way he does before a fight or argument he knows he has to win. "Am I right?"

"A story for a different day." Bradley, briefly flustered, quickly regained his composure and returned his attention to me. "My point is simply this: whatever badge of honor one chooses to wear on their chest, the bearer will be judged by their actions, not their decorations." He took another bite of his donut and chased it with a second slug of coffee. "In other words, what you do with your freedom now is far more important than the nature of the shell game I played with my higher ups to win you and Mr. Trainor that freedom." He finished his donut and drained the remainder of his coffee. "Though if you must know, Special Deputy Delacroix," he said with a conspiratorial wink, "the badges are as real as they come."

"So," I asked, shooting Father an incredulous glance, "you can make a call and give a twenty-one-year-old woman with no formal law enforcement training carte blanche to run with the big boys?"

"First, your training makes what most of my subordinates go through look like Boy Scout Camp. And second, I can and I did."

"I suppose you think that makes you my boss." I shook my head with a quiet groan. "Am I supposed to jump when you say so now?"

"Actually, I'd prefer if you asked me 'How high?' first." At my less-than-amused glare, Bradley's eyes widened, and he held his hands before his chest, palms out. "A joke, Miss Delacroix." He shifted his gaze to Father. "Neither your daughter nor Mr. Trainor are beholden to me in any way, Mr. Delacroix. Let me make that clear."

Father scowled. "That was already quite clear in my mind, Mr. Bradley."

Bradley cleared his throat. "Still, that doesn't mean I don't want something in return for troubleshooting their potential legal difficulties earlier today."

"Here it comes," I mumbled. "The moment we've all been waiting for."

"Give him a moment, Rosemary." Father, his voice surprisingly calm, rested a hand on my knee. "At least he's finally getting to the point."

Father's pointed glance elicited a quick nod from Bradley.

"The way I see it," Bradley began, "your goals and mine are not that different. You wish for Miss Snow to remain safe—"

"Of course," I answered.

"And for the Cardinal to be stopped so that her life, as well as your own, can return to some semblance of normalcy."

"Two for two."

"My superiors have asked, in return for your freedom, that you and Mr. Trainor continue down the path you've already started, but with Order resources at your disposal."

"Rosemary told me you said as much." Father scrutinized the man before us. "Do you really expect me to believe that the same Order who trained me when I was her age simply wants to help?"

"What *we* want is for this Cardinal threat to be neutralized before he upsets the delicate balance among the Ascendant as well as between Ascendant and humanity at large." The grim line of his lips turned up in a faint smile as he turned to me. "As for what *I* want, please understand that my organization has monitored the activities of the various Ascendant across the globe for centuries as well as those of your family. I've studied your line going back as far as we have records, Miss Delacroix. No other force in history has done more to keep the peace. To be honest, the opportunity to work with a Daughter of Neith has long been a dream of mine."

Heat rose in my cheeks as anger, resentment, and embarrassment warred for supremacy in my mind, all despite the fact that the root of my shame remained as outside of my control as the wind or the sunrise.

"As you are no doubt aware, Mr. Bradley, while I am fully trained in the ways of the family business and well prepared to take on the responsibility of Daughter of Neith, our line stands broken for the first time in recorded history."

"Ah, yes, the regrettable intrusion of Mr. Harkreader on your birthright." Bradley sighed. "I trust that you and your father taking him under your collective wing to bolster his chances at surviving the year is going well?"

No need to keep secrets from this guy. He knew everything.

"Mr. Harkreader is not the topic of discussion today." Father jumped in before I could say a word. "My wife and I trained Rosemary since she was a toddler to take on her preordained role, and I can say without reservation, inheritance or not, that she is as capable as her departed mother on Danielle's best day. That being said, Rosemary is without, at least for the time being, all she would require to allow her to perform her role to its ultimate extent. While I have nothing but the utmost confidence in her abilities and training, I'm not certain she's quite the agent of change you require."

Father couldn't have possibly expressed more confidence in my abilities if he'd tried, but his words still burned like a scorpion's sting.

"To the contrary, Mr. Delacroix," Bradley answered, unperturbed. "While a fully empowered Daughter of Neith would be an even greater boon to our cause, your daughter's knowledge and skills are precisely what I require."

"To take down the Cardinal." My teeth ground together in frustration at the two men talking about me as if I weren't there. "We've already covered this."

"Indeed we have. In return for your shared freedom, Miss Delacroix, the Order wants you and your theriodan friend to track down this man who calls himself the Cardinal and bring him down."

The question I couldn't bring myself to ask in the airport interrogation room sprung to the front of my mind. "You want us to kill him?"

"Dead, alive, it doesn't matter." The wistful half-smile vanished from his face. "As long as he is removed from play and, if left alive, either in a state or a place where he can longer cause mayhem, then order will have been restored."

"With all due respect, how big of a threat are we talking about here?" I asked. "Outside of kidnapping Seph, I understand the Cardinal is responsible for the deaths of three Ascendant for reasons we don't exactly—"

"Three?" Bradley asked, incredulous. "Try eleven, and those are merely the kills my people have confirmed. Truth be told, for all our impressive intelligence on the matter, we have no idea how many Ascendant truly walk the Earth, and therefore, the number could be many more."

Father and I shared a shocked look.

"That many?" I asked. "But Maddox said—"

"It would appear Mr. Trainor has seriously undersold the danger all of you are in." Bradley considered. "Or worse, he is somehow unaware of the extent of this unprecedented crisis." He swallowed, his face momentarily colored with emotion. "While it is true that over the centuries there have been times when Ascendant has killed Ascendant, we've not seen anything like this since before the Common Era."

"So, not totally unprecedented." The words escaped my mouth before I could stop them, drawing a sharp look from both Father and Bradley.

"Much of ancient myth is drawn from Ascendant warring on Ascendant," Bradley continued. "From the labors of Heracles to the tales of Gilgamesh and woven through everything from Homer's epics to Grimms' fairy tales are stories everyone knows, and yet most don't know the real history behind any of them. Ascendant killing Ascendant has at times been a product of war and at others simply a matter of business." He raised a brow. "And more often than any of them would care to admit, sometimes even personal acrimony."

"More than they'd like to admit?" I asked.

"They call themselves Ascendant not only because of their powers and abilities but because they truly believe themselves above the pettiest of human emotions like envy, fear, or hate. For most of history, even when they have to come to blows, or worse, crossed swords with only one walking away, the violence occurred for a reason. Always a method to the madness, if you will." Bradley stared out the window into the halogen-lit darkness. "This is different."

"Different?" Father asked. "How so?"

"These deaths from the last few years seem arbitrary. Of the few Ascendant we know of who escaped the Cardinal's talons, none have the first idea of who he is, what he wants, or why he was stalking them."

"Well, Miss Snow certainly doesn't know." Father rested his chin on his interlaced knuckles. "In any case, despite our history, my wife worked with the Order on more than one occasion, however begrudgingly. Perhaps if they'd involved her when all this started, she'd be sitting here talking with us instead of lying God knows where in an unmarked grave." His voice cracked on that last word.

"Ascendant barely tolerate our existence in our role as observers. Our current ask notwithstanding, calling in the Daughter of Neith, regardless of how respected the position might be in Ascendant circles, would have been tantamount to Switzerland calling a nuclear strike after decades of neutrality."

"And what is different now?" I asked, giving Father a moment to collect his emotions.

"Many among the Ascendant fear for their lives, some for the first time in decades, even centuries, though few would dare admit to such." Bradley's face grew solemn. "Those used to being wolves among humanity's herd have suddenly found themselves sheep, and while most have kept their bleating private, the number who have reached out to us in desperation grows on a daily basis."

"Eleven, huh?" I shuddered. This revelation cast an entirely different shadow on the preceding day. The number suggested the work of a serial killer more than someone with a plan. But if this Cardinal were hunting for sport rather than carrying out some sort of mission, then why in the world did he want Seph? If this Cardinal wanted her dead, why hand her over to us at the first sign of trouble and leave? And why the elaborate plan to escape with her alive in the first place? He could have taken her to any dark alley in Santa Barbara if all he planned to do was make her his next victim.

"Wait a second." I narrowed my eyes at Bradley. "Maddox told us that the Cardinal was the one who hired Krage and his skiomancers last month to come for Seph. Why in the world would any Ascendant, even someone as low as Krage, work with someone like the Cardinal?"

"Did you not hear me say that many among the Ascendant are afraid? Even big bad shadowmancers are going to respect an individual whose kill count is coming up on a dozen and likely approaching their own." Bradley scoffed, clearly not a fan of our skiomancer adversaries. "Not to mention that Johann Krage is an unapologetic mercenary, thus his reported break with his former benefactor."

"How can you possibly know all these things?" Father asked the question that had been on my mind since my prior conversation with Bradley. "I mean, *we* were there that night, with the Midnight Angel and Krage—"

"As were we." Bradley's smug smile returned. "The vast majority of humanity knows nothing of the Ascendant or your family line, Miss Delacroix, but as your father can readily attest, the Order of Ophanim has eyes and ears everywhere."

"And it's gotten so bad," I said, "that both the Order and various Ascendant are reaching out to the Daughter of Neith for help."

Bradley nodded, his expression pensive. "There have been bad actors among the Ascendant before, but over a millennia has passed since anything approaching the existential threat the Cardinal represents. Most Ascendant are happy to keep to themselves and leave the rest of the world to its own devices, enjoying their longevity coupled with the miracle of compounding interest. The current situation, however, has turned the status quo on its ear."

"One lone Ascendant, even a mass murderer such as the Cardinal, can cause that much havoc?" Father asked.

"An unstoppable, anonymous killer with an inscrutable pattern to his killings and motives no one can fathom?" Bradley rested his elbows on the table. "You were one of us once, Mr. Delacroix. You more than anyone should understand the intricate spiderweb of accords and pacts and territorial covenants that exist between the major players in the Ascendant world and the alliances and rivalries that keep everyone in their place, both geographically and otherwise. Sever enough strands in such a carefully woven tapestry..."

"And everything falls apart." A chill ran up my spine. "Chaos."

"Nature abhors a vacuum, and the supernatural entities your line has policed for centuries obey the same law. If world history has taught us anything, it's that peace between superpowers is tenuous and fragile." Bradley leaned back in his chair, a flash of defeat robbing the vigor from his features. "And what are Ascendant if not the very definition of superpowers?"

CHAPTER 10

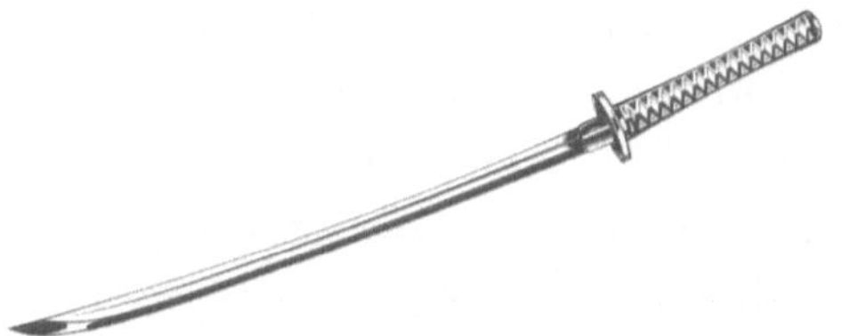

CAN'T FIGHT THIS FEELING

"Hey." Ethan popped his head into the Commander as I was finishing up a breakfast of two boiled eggs, yogurt, and black coffee to make up for the caloric indiscretions of the night before. "Sorry I missed our run this morning. After getting my ass handed to me yesterday trying to defend Seph from that Cardinal freak, she thought I might like breakfast in bed." A wistful look overtook his features. "And you know Seph. One thing led to another and—"

"She brought me breakfast in bed is sufficient information." I noted the color in his cheeks, his relaxed stance, the playful smirk dying to break through his serious gaze. "I take it you managed to get your heart rate up regardless." Before he could parry my stab at innuendo, I changed the subject. "So, how's the shoulder?"

He offered me a quick shrug. "Not bad." He performed a full swing of his arm as if he were a Major League pitcher. "Whatever quick-healing vibes your family has passed down through the ages, I can yet again vouch for the results."

"You think you're back to a hundred percent?"

He motioned for me to join him outside. "Think you can take me?"

I rose from the table with a knowing chuckle. "Let's go."

Seph's fenced-in yard had become my and Ethan's gym, work out area, and dojo over the preceding weeks, just as her driveway had become my and Father's de facto home base as we'd been living out of the Commander. A far cry from the usual campgrounds and backstreets where we'd often parked between gigs, having our run of both the yard and home of a wealthy celebrity represented a huge shift in our standard of living. Father's strict work ethic, not to mention his pride, precluded us from actually sleeping under a client's roof, but the extreme situation meant closeness and rapidity of response were paramount. Crashing each night in the parked Commander with an open invitation to all that awaited inside split the difference, be it movie nights in Seph's home theater, dinners that were basically catered affairs for the few of us in her new inner circle, billiards and beverages—nothing too strong for me—in Seph's basement game room, or half a dozen other enticements.

Not long after we arrived in Montecito, Ethan showed me an episode of *MTV Cribs*, an older program revolving around the lavish lives of the rich and famous in America, in an effort to demonstrate that the opulence of Seph's mansion was simply the standard in these parts. The funny thing was, for all the niceties—six bathrooms each larger than the entire living space of the Commander, a master bedroom suite straight out of *The Great Gatsby*, and an Olympic length pool and hot tub in the back yard—Seph was never a bit pretentious about any of it.

"Something on your mind?" Ethan asked.

"Just how lucky we've been until today. No attacks, no badness. We've had time to breathe, train, and actually enjoy life a bit." I dropped into a low stretch, my inner thigh still a bit angry with me for leaping over a twelve-foot fence the day before. "Couldn't stay that way forever, I guess."

"Nothing gold can stay," Ethan answered. "Isn't that what Robert Frost said?"

"I suppose." I motioned to his recently injured shoulder. "You sure you're up for a couple rounds?"

"A mystery Ascendant in candy-apple-red armor beat my ass and kidnapped my girlfriend in less than half a minute yesterday." His eyebrows and shoulders rose together in a quick shrug. "Call me crazy, but I think we're way past opting to take it easy around here. This Cardinal is coming for Seph. It's not a question of if, but when. On that day, I have to be ready."

"*We* have to be ready." I dropped into a low cat stance and prepared for Ethan's attack. "What shall we work on today? Tae kwon do? Krav Maga?"

"Maybe you can show me some more jiu-jitsu?" Ethan cracked his neck. "For all his armor, the Cardinal had no trouble getting me to ground and tying me up in his legs like an MMA fighter. Stupid armbar popped my shoulder right out of its socket."

"Huh. I was wondering what he did to send you to the hospital."

"He's strong, Rosemary. Not giant-walking-sumo-made-of-asphalt strong, but that armor plus whatever he's got going on under the hood has left him way stronger than you, me, or any of the theriodans we've encountered so far."

"We'd best prepare, then." I shifted into a defensive posture. "All right, Ethan. Come at me. Give it all you've got."

"You sure?" he said with that devilish smile.

"My, someone is getting confident."

"Hey, I've got a great teacher."

And with that, he rushed me, not the uncontrolled young fighter I'd met a month before, but a skilled combatant, his every move filled with the discipline I'd been teaching since we had our first hotel parking lot session what seemed forever ago. His flurry of punches and kicks immediately put me on the defensive even as it brought a smile to my face.

The first thing I'd taught Ethan was the old adage about the best defense being a good offense, and he was applying my teaching in spades. I did my best to demonstrate economy of motion as I deflected his barrage of punches with one arm before shooting out a knee to block his low roundhouse kick.

"Not bad."

With that, I stepped into his space and threw a back fist at his ear to pull his attention to one side before spinning in the opposite direction to attack his other side with an elbow to the head. A quick dodge and a forearm block I taught him saved him from that attack as well, but not from my own sweeping low roundhouse. My kick sent both his feet from beneath him, a move that a month ago would have sent him to the ground like a sack of potatoes, but not anymore. In a blink, he shot out an arm, caught himself before he hit the grass, and rolled away from a trio of stomping kicks, quickly righting himself with a back roll into a low defensive posture.

"Excellent recovery."

He smiled again. "Like I always say, I was taught by the best."

Back on his feet, he wasted no time coming at me again, this time drawing closer and keeping his jabs quick and continuous, doing his best to penetrate my defense.

I didn't have the heart to tell him that Mother and I used to do this blindfolded.

Strike after strike I blocked, keeping my elbows in and fists up to show him how it was done. A couple of his best blows landed, glancing strikes at best, but a far cry from the man who wasn't sure how to make a proper fist. Occasionally, I noticed the Light of Neith informing his actions—his reflexes shifting a little quicker, his punches a bit faster, his blocks more controlled—but when we train, he tries to tamp down everything that isn't intrinsically his own skill, as we both know the centuries of expertise that got downloaded into his head doesn't need much more in the way of practice.

I hoped Mother would approve of my methods. Until now, I'd always been the student. Suddenly being the teacher was a new experience for certain, though it helped to have a student like Ethan. Eager to learn. Humble to a fault. Teachable.

Not to mention, he smelled great first thing in the morning.

Ow. I let Ethan clock me in the chin. That was a first. I'm not sure who was more surprised, me or him. Even as I cursed myself for allowing distraction to let a strike through, a part of me beamed with teacher's pride. That being said, it wasn't going to happen again. Time to follow my own advice.

I went on the offensive, all elbows and knees, driving Ethan back across Seph's immaculately kept yard. Though he met my every punch, kick, and forward thrust with an adequate block or dodge, he was quickly running out of room, and the eight-foot wall that surrounded the yard was coming fast. Disappointment welled within me. I'd tried to hammer home since the beginning not to allow anyone to back you into a corner. Unless...

With a quick grin, Ethan spun around and raced at the wall, employing a bit of parkour himself as he ran straight up the painted concrete and kicked off, landing behind me at the end of a decidedly practiced backflip.

I spun around to face him and found his foot already flying at my midsection. Too late to block, I tightened up my core and took the brunt of the kick.

Suddenly, it was me who was backed into the proverbial corner, and though such positioning tended to limit my options a bit, Mother always told me that fighting with my back to the wall was my specialty.

"Nice move," I grunted, blocking a trio of punches. "Someone's been practicing."

"Gotta keep up." Ethan threw a flying roundhouse, and despite my double forearm block being on point, the force nearly knocked me over.

He *had* been practicing. Time to step up my game even more.

Ethan said he wanted to practice some jiu-jitsu. I decided to oblige. I blocked his next couple of kicks and another barrage of punches as I waited for my moment. And then, as if we'd choreographed the movement, he charged me, giving me the opening I needed.

I dove to his right, palms to the grass at his feet, and whipped my legs around in a scissor strike, my thighs and calves encircling his torso like a pair of pythons. Before he could figure out what I was up to, I combined my momentum and core strength into a twisting motion that forced him to the ground. He landed squarely on his back with me sitting atop his ribcage, the combination of the hard landing and my weight on his chest driving the air from his lungs. His eyes slid closed and for several seconds he didn't breathe.

"Ethan?" I pulled my face closer to his, trying to figure out if I'd yet again accidentally knocked him unconscious. The last time had been weeks before, and we hadn't talked about it since beyond my sincere apology when he'd come to. "Are you okay? Ethan?"

Something was wrong. He hadn't hit his head, so this wasn't a concussion, and I'd seen him get the wind knocked out of him more times than I cared to remember. Less than twenty-four hours had passed since his fight with the Cardinal and his emergency room visit. He'd said he was okay, but what if that wasn't the case? What if the doctors missed something, and I'd just finished what the mysterious assassin in red started? What if—

"Gotcha." A wicked grin filled Ethan's features as he caught my shoulders in his strong hands and kicked off from the ground with both legs, flipping me onto my back. As his firm buttocks took their place across my abdomen, I swatted at him with one fist and then the other, but he caught each flailing punch and forced my arms up and behind my head until my wrists were pressed firmly yet gently into Seph's manicured grass.

"Scissor takedown, huh?" he said. "You said you were going to teach me that one."

"I think I just did." With his full weight atop my torso, it was hard to get out much more than a whisper. "What do you think?"

"I think it's a solid move." His grin shifted to a smirk. "As long as you don't let your opponent fool you into thinking it worked too well."

I struggled against his firm grip at my wrists, my cheeks flushing at his nearness. Not for the first time, my body responded in ways not really appropriate for a simple sparring match, particularly on your sparring partner's girlfriend's front yard.

"Looks like she's got him right where she wants him." Maddox's voice, dripping with sarcasm, hit my ears like a tidal wave. Anger and shame and regret welled up within me, the last flooding my psyche tenfold as I noticed who stood with him, a pitcher of lemonade and a pair of ice-filled glasses in her well-manicured hands.

"Hey there, Ethan," Seph said with a forced smile. "Rosemary." She paused for a moment before continuing in our direction, her steps slow and hesitant. "Thought you two might be thirsty." She stopped a few feet from us. "Is this a...good time?"

"Of course." He shot me a quick wink. "If I let you up, are you going to behave?"

I suspect the question sounded way more innocuous in his head.

"We can take a quick break, I guess." In my mind, I'd worked out at least six different ways to break Ethan's hold and put him on his backside, but the situation was already mortifying enough, and there was no need to prolong it. I had to admit, though, the fact that I'd appeared in any way weak or submissive in front of Maddox burned at my core like a black sun of rage.

Ethan sprung up from my supine form and offered me a hand up. I opted instead to right myself with a quick backward roll, coming to my feet in a low martial stance before offering Ethan a quick formal bow and headed for the covered veranda of Seph's house where we'd shared breakfast a dozen times over the preceding month. Ethan followed with Seph and Maddox close behind.

Funny thing? Of the three, only Ethan seemed confused by the sudden awkward silence. For someone who'd traveled the country and world for years on this or that tour and had seen the seamier side of society on countless occasions, Ethan had somehow managed to hold onto a certain degree of innocence. I envied that about him, and in fact, if I were being honest, that unshakeable streak of naive optimism was one of the things about him I admired the most.

I sat in my usual chair, my back to the wall and facing the open yard and road as Mother taught me. Seph sat to my right and Ethan to my left, which put Maddox directly across the table, right in my line of vision. In the past, I would have treasured every second spent gazing into those cool eyes and admiring the curve of his cheek bones, the hint of stubble at his chin, and the triangle of muscled chest visible at the open collar of his shirt.

That time was long past.

And yet, the maelstrom of revulsion and trepidation and fear and abject anger I'd felt when I first heard his voice back at the mall had also left me. Much like our very first meeting, my entire psyche brimmed with but one emotion: curiosity.

Why was he here? What did he really want? Had he really come back to protect me? Was any of what he told me and Father true?

Did some part of him still love me? Did any part of me still love him?

Of all the questions, I knew only the answer to the last.

Dammit.

Seph poured each of us a glass of lemonade, the heavenly concoction beyond anything you could purchase off the shelf. Nothing but fresh-squeezed perfection for the biggest pop star in the country.

"Training going well?" she asked hesitantly.

"Getting better every session," Ethan answered. "Rosemary taught me a new takedown today."

"I saw." Seph's voice dropped a few decibels. "Looked pretty effective."

The edge in Seph's voice pierced me like a blade to the heart. Though my lifetime dating experience was limited, I knew all too well what the female of the species marking her territory looked and sounded like. And coming from an Ascendant whose power was her voice...

"I think she taught me some similar moves back in the day." Maddox's mischievous half-leer danced between the three of us. "Didn't mind that training one bit."

My cheeks burned. I couldn't imagine a more uncomfortable situation than sitting at a table sipping lemonade with a jealous woman, her clueless beau, and an ex-boyfriend who reveled in wreaking havoc.

And then, the unlikeliest of saviors.

A flash of brown skin and blue hair at the gate of Seph's walled-off front yard caught my attention as a knocking sound brought the awkward conversation to a merciful close.

"Ethan?" Seph whispered. "Who is that?"

"I don't know," he said, rising from the table, "but I'm going to check it out."

I shot out of my seat and motioned for Ethan to stand down. "Don't worry about it, Ethan. I'll take point on this one."

I crept across the yard, my senses attuned to every sight, sound, and smell, but everything appeared to be as it should be.

Was this person lost? A solicitor? Part of a trap or ruse to get Seph out in the open?

I opened the gate on a teenage boy, Ethan close behind on my left and Maddox, uninvited but present nonetheless, on my right. His brown skin marked his descent from the Indian subcontinent, while his hair, a shock of electric blue, revealed a defiant streak I appreciated immediately.

The young man looked at me through wire-rimmed glasses, his expression neither frown nor smile. "Rosemary Delacroix?" he asked with a hint of reverence, his accent and diction marking him as American, specifically midwestern.

"Who's asking?" Though he appeared no older than fifteen, there was no way of knowing if he was Ascendant or, more importantly, friend or foe. "And why are you here?"

"You can call me L.J., ma'am." His chin dropped in a moment of bashful silence. "And though you don't know me, I'm here to help."

CHAPTER 11

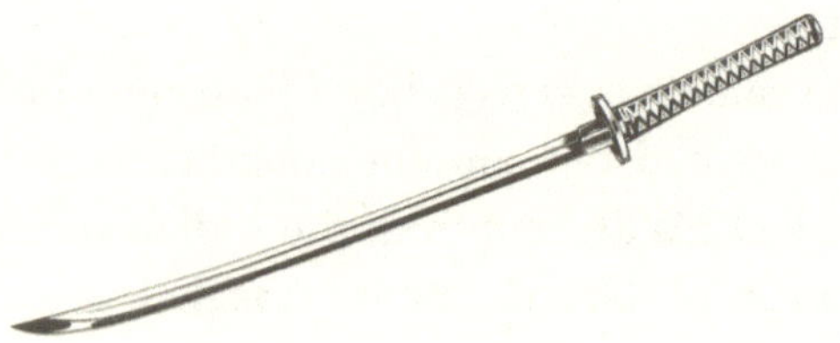

TOGETHER IN ELECTRIC DREAMS

Ma'am? Now, that *was* a first.

Mother never really liked being called the word, though she did her best not to bristle in polite conversation. She assured me that most people meant it as a term of respect rather than contempt and that anyone who meant the latter wasn't worth the time or emotion.

I decided it best to follow suit and assume the best.

As always, however, I prepared for the worst.

"L.J., you say?"

"Yes, ma'am." There it was again. "I'd like to talk to you and Mr. Harkreader, if you will give me five minutes of your time."

He knew both our names and that we were staying at Seph's place. If nothing else, he wasn't leaving until he told us where he got his intel.

"Hello." Seph joined us at the gate. "Do you know who I am?"

"Of course I do. Sorry to show up at your house uninvited, but all pleasantries aside, you need my help." His gaze leaped from face to face: Seph's, mine, Ethan's, and finally, Maddox's. He seemed to linger a bit longer on the features of the coyote in our midst, but I suppose that could have been my imagination.

"Everything all right here, Miss Snow?" Father half-walked, half-jogged across the yard to join us in meeting the neon-blue-coiffed teen at the gate. "Do you know this young man?"

Ethan shot Father a concerned glance. "He knows who all of us are. Says he's here to help."

"Someone who didn't immediately start trying to kill, maim, or kidnap one of us." Father removed his palm from the grip of his pistol, still holstered at his side. "I'd say that's a step in the right direction." Father stepped in front of Seph in a protective stance. "What did you say your name was, young man?"

"Everybody calls me L.J., sir." He stared up at Father through thick eyebrows, his head still tilted forward in a bashful nod. "Sorry to show up unannounced, but as you can see I'm unarmed." He held his arms out to his sides, his Vampire Weekend t-shirt, khaki shorts, and black Chuck Taylor high tops leaving no room to hide any sort of weapon.

"Unarmed and not dangerous are two very different things," Maddox grumbled. "You'd all do well to remember that."

"I'm curious, L.J."—Seph stepped out from behind Father—"what is it you think you can do to help me?"

"A little knowledge and skill," he answered, "not to mention a particular talent."

He focused his attention on the speaker by the gate, a two-way with which Seph could communicate with people without leaving her house. His eyes narrowed at the metal box and music emanated from the speaker, the opening "One, Two, Uh One, Two, Three, Four" of a song I remembered Ethan playing for me once.

"Technomancer," Maddox whispered, his face twisting with concern.

"'A Matter of Trust,' huh?" Ethan smiled, his reaction to a technomancer showing up on our doorstep unannounced the polar opposite of mine and Maddox's. "Hard to be too suspicious of a young person who clearly knows their Billy Joel."

"Being a walking jukebox is the least of what I can do." He glanced up and down the sidewalk. "Look, coming here today wasn't without its own risk. May I please come in off the street? There are dangerous people about."

I'd never heard a truer statement.

A quick scan of faces suggested that Ethan, Father, and Seph were all on the same sheet of music about the young technomancer in our midst, a very different song from the one playing at the back of my mind. Only Maddox's expression echoed the cold certainty at my core that we were being led down a cherry path. Something to discuss if we had a moment alone.

"Come in." Seph entered the gate's key code and allowed entry to the young man with hair the color of the Pacific. "Let's talk."

"First thing," L.J. said as he headed for the veranda, "we're going to need to upgrade your security. My abilities allow me to chat with your little keypad there like we're old friends, but even an everyday hacker with a modicum of skill could break in any time they wanted."

The blood left Seph's face. "Good to know."

L.J. stopped center yard. "Seven security cameras, three keypad locks, window sensors all along the first floor. Pretty standard." He pulled in a breath. "By the way, you'll save a lot of money on water if you have your sprinklers set to go before sunrise instead of the afternoon."

"I'll tell my yard guy." Seph's nervous gaze caught mine. "Anything else?"

"We'll put your private safe on a rotating combination along with the door locks and overall security system. Nothing I can do against a brute force attack on the premises, but I can keep anyone from sneaking about." Arriving at the table, he pulled up one of the extra chairs, sat himself down, and poured himself a glass of lemonade. "Most importantly, once I've put my touch on your electronics, I'll know if anyone else goes mucking about."

I couldn't be sure, but it seemed his eyes flicked in Maddox's direction at that last bit. One thing was certain: either all of us were witnessing a serious case of dislike at first sight, or L.J. and Maddox had history.

Join the club, kid.

Father, who had remained surprisingly quiet during L.J.'s entire discourse, cleared his throat. "Young man," he started, "while I appreciate your rather thorough assessment of our situation and current security measures, I'm still a bit confused as to why you're here." His eyes bored through the turquoise-haired teen. "Are you hoping Miss Snow will hire you on?"

"Oh, I don't want any money, though a flat surface to sleep on and a couple meals a day would be appreciated."

"You don't have a place to stay?" Seph asked, joining him at the table.

"No." For the first time, a hint of emotion played across the young man's face. "Just me."

I took a closer look at the boy's clothes. While in reasonably good shape, they appeared slept in and unlaundered. When married with the scant bit of stubble on his chin, his unkempt hair—stylish blue dye notwithstanding—and the odor of someone who hadn't showered in a few days, one simple fact became clear: he was homeless.

Something in the lines of his young face told me that was just the tip of the iceberg.

"How old are you, L.J.?" I asked.

"Fourteen." The previous confidence in his voice vanished like dandelion seeds in a hurricane.

"Fourteen?" Ethan sat in the chair by Seph and asked the question I'm sure all of us wanted to know. "Where's your family?"

"I don't know." The admission broke him. All but swaggering minutes before, L.J. now choked on his own words.

Seph reached out a hand and squeezed the boy's wrist. "You don't know?"

"I haven't seen them in months. I'm not even sure they're alive."

Father circled the table, his professional side taking a back seat to the paternal, and rested a hand on L.J.'s shoulder. "Young man, why don't you start from the beginning?"

None of us said a word as we waited for L.J. to gather himself enough to speak. Both Father and Ethan maintained respectful silence while Seph continued to squeeze the young man's wrist as if she were comforting an old friend. Maddox alone seemed annoyed by the entire conversation, but even he kept his response to a simple forced exhalation through his nostrils.

There was a story there. I was certain of it. But now was not the time to explore what seemed like clear enmity.

"Before I get started, I have something I need to get off my chest." L.J. looked up from his half-full glass of lemonade. "All the trouble you had communicating last month as you made your way from Albuquerque to Denver and then along your route to L.A.? Most of that was me."

Father and Seph both pulled away momentarily in shock. Ethan remained stock-still while Maddox rolled his eyes as if it were the least surprising news of the day. I did my best to keep any emotion from my face, but it wasn't easy. The various ways each of us had almost died as our little group navigated our first interstate excursion together flashed across my memories like one of the slide shows Mother used to show me of photographs taken by her own mother before the days of digital cameras.

Seph, swept from a rooftop by gale force winds.

Father, held several stories in the air by animated shadows.

Ethan, nearly immolated in a Denver bank vault.

Me, surrounded in a prison of darkness and forced to explode a flash-bang grenade in my own hands to free myself.

And Mother, gutted by a skiomancer's blade for the simple offense of dropping her guard long enough to care for the love of her life in a skirmish that was far from over.

To come here seeking aid from those he'd helped to hurt must have taken a lot of courage, especially for one so young.

Courage, or desperation.

"Krage?" I asked.

L.J. nodded. "He took me from my home in Indianapolis better than six months ago. Right out of my bedroom in the middle of the night. I haven't seen my parents since, though not a day went by I wasn't reminded what would happen to them if I didn't obey."

"He blackmailed you?"

"Among other things. He threatened my family and tortured me with everything from sleep deprivation to starvation." He glanced down at his relatively svelte frame and let out a mirthless chuckle. "First time since I was eleven anyone would describe me as something other than 'chunky.' Guess that's sort of a plus."

"That's horrible." Even as my heart went out to the vulnerable boy, my mind went in the complete opposite direction. "Assuming, of course, what you're telling us is the truth."

"Rosemary!" Seph glared at me from beneath a furrowed brow she usually reserved for Ethan or Father when she wasn't getting her way. "What has L.J. done or said to warrant such a remark?"

"Other than helping us all almost get killed a month ago?" I crossed my arms. "By his own admission, I might add."

"With all due respect, Rosemary, he's barely a teenager." Even Father looked on me with more intensity than his usual stern gaze. "I would hear the rest of his story."

"He's Ascendant, Father. Is it not my role to maintain a healthy suspicion? Is that not one of the basic tenets of Mother's training?"

"A tenet you'd do well to apply more broadly, Rosemary." No one missed the flick of Father's eyes in Maddox's direction. "All I'm saying is that L.J. came here not only waving a white flag but has provided us with intelligence we didn't previously have."

"Very well." I leaned across the table, my elbows resting on the cool metal and my chin atop my interlaced fingers. "Tell us everything. You blocked our phones, kept us from communicating, ensured that any mention of us or our pursuers stayed out of the media and off the internet—"

"I can't take credit for that last one, actually." L.J. squirmed in his chair. "There's an entire network of technomancers across the globe who make serious bank keeping Ascendant matters off CNN and Fox News."

"So, you're the one who made sure we were flying blind?"

"With some significant help, yes."

"And kept us from reaching each other by phone or any other manner?"

"As best as I could at the time, yes."

"And now you want us to trust you?"

"Look," L.J. grumbled, "I'm sorry. I didn't want to do any of that stuff. I came here to offer my help in hopes you all would help me as well. I only just freed myself yesterday and—"

"Wait," Ethan jumped in, "if you just escaped, does that mean Krage is here?"

L.J. rolled his eyes. "Did you all not nearly lose Miss Snow to the Cardinal yesterday? If he is the king of this little game of chess you all are playing, then Krage is his knight and the other skiomancers his pawns." He cleared his throat. "Among others."

"And all trying to take our queen." Father studied L.J., his professional side asserting control, though I recognized the protective father figure who'd raised me from birth lurking within his gaze. "But why?" he asked. "Not to mention, young man, what does that make you in this particular scenario?"

"I suppose I'd like to think of myself as a bishop." A single snorted chuckle fled L.J.'s nostrils. "I travel on the diagonals, can reach all the way across the board, and if you happen to be on my half of the sixty-four squares, you're mine." He took another sip of lemonade, the glass shaking subtly in his hand. "But that's all metaphor. All that matters is that for better or for worse, I am at your service."

"And in exchange?" I asked, drawing frustrated looks from all present except the person to whom I was asking the question. "What is it you want?"

"I'd like you all to help me find my family." He took a deep breath. "Assuming, of course, they're still alive."

"You can't find them?" Maddox asked. "You know what time her sprinklers turn on, but you can't use whatever you've got going on between those big ears of yours to find your own mommy?"

"I may be able to speak to machines..." Any earnestness in the boy's voice evaporated, his words coming out robotic and monotone. "But I'm not God."

"And no one expects you to be." Seph, caught up in the emotion of the moment, brushed a tear from her cheek as she silenced Maddox with a laser glare. "Of course we'll help you."

"Miss Snow?" Father asked.

"Mr. Delacroix?" she answered.

"You should take care making deals with Ascendant," Father grumbled. "You never know what might—"

"In case you've forgotten, Mr. Delacroix, *I* am Ascendant, and L.J. is just a boy. Five years younger than me and possibly all alone in the world." Seph returned her attention to the technomancer in our midst. "I have no idea what discoveries lie ahead, L.J., but until we find some answers, you're safe with us."

A single curt nod was the boy's only response.

"So, you say you're here to help us." Ethan watched him like the proverbial hawk. "How exactly do you propose to do that?"

"Well," L.J. said without missing a beat, "first things first. I locked your comms down a month ago. Now that I'm no longer under Krage's thumb, I can certainly help keep everyone in touch."

"The Angels made all that go away a month ago," Maddox scoffed. "What else you got?"

"Don't delude yourself. You've only had your phones and tech working for the last month because Krage told me to back off other than keeping tabs on you and reporting what I learned."

"Wait. You've been spying on us?" Ethan asked.

"I've been protecting you, if you want the truth." L.J.'s cheeks went a darker shade of red. "Only reporting the bare minimum. Leaving out important details. Making sure no one else screwed with your tech. Once they realize I'm out of pocket, they'll probably just bring in another technomancer, and I can guarantee the next guy won't be so benevolent."

"Benevolent?" Ethan said. "If it wasn't for you, half the shit that went down last month wouldn't have happened."

L.J. shook his head. "Truth time? I may have caused your phones to stop talking to the sky, but I didn't have your GPS take you over a cliff, did I? Your engines, brakes, headlights? They all kept working, didn't they?" He let out a quiet sigh. "And the occasional self-driving car you encountered along your many hours on the highway? Did any of them torpedo your tour bus or RV?" His eyes shifted left and right. "I never told my captors, but I was keeping you all out of danger even while I was gumming up your communication."

"But you didn't know us then." Seph studied L.J. with compassionate eyes. "Why did you risk everything for people you had never met?"

"Wouldn't you have done the same?" L.J. asked.

Okay, the kid was beginning to win me over as well.

"In the end, Ascendant and the rest of the world? We're not that different." L.J. looked off into the distance. "The only trouble comes when those who Ascend forget the time before they discovered who and what they were." He met Seph's tender gaze. "I may be only fourteen, but I've been making everything from microchips to combustion engines dance to my tune since before I could walk. Some advice? Always remember when you believed you were like everyone else."

"So," I asked, "you managed to tiptoe through the minefield of captivity and keep us all alive, and now you're with us. What do we do now?"

"Like I was saying before, I've got some work to do locking anyone else with my particular skill set out of your phones, homes, and vehicles. It's going to take some time and energy, but I can likely be done in a few hours."

"A few hours?" Seph asked. "Wow."

"Like I said, I've been doing this longer than I've been walking."

She laughed. "If you're joining the team, L.J., you can call me Seph."

He raised an eyebrow and smiled. "I'll take that under consideration." He stretched out his hand. "I guess I'll start with you. May I see your phone?"

"How does she know you're not going to put a whammy on it?" Maddox asked.

"I already put a 'whammy' on it a month ago, Mr. Trainor," L.J. answered, his tone slightly irritated. "Now I'm simply fixing it to make sure no one else can do the same."

He turned his attention back to Seph who hesitated in handing over the pinnacle of her most prized possessions. As much as she'd accepted L.J into the fold, her phone was basically her third hand.

"What are you going to do to it?" she asked.

L.J.'s mouth quirked to one side. "Just think of it as an upgrade to your operating system." He tilted his head to one side. "I won't even make you sign a EULA."

She held back another second and then handed L.J. her phone. He, in turn, studied its dark screen for a moment as if reading words only he could see, then closed his eyes. At first, nothing changed, and then the world went briefly still. The hair on my arms and neck stood on end as if lightning were about to strike. Then, a brief shimmer of blue surrounded Seph's phone and L.J.'s hands. Lasting but a second, the flash of energy was so subtle, I almost wondered if I'd imagined it.

"Done." Opening his eyes with a slightly fatigued grin, L.J. placed the phone on the table and held out his hand to me. "Next."

CHAPTER 12

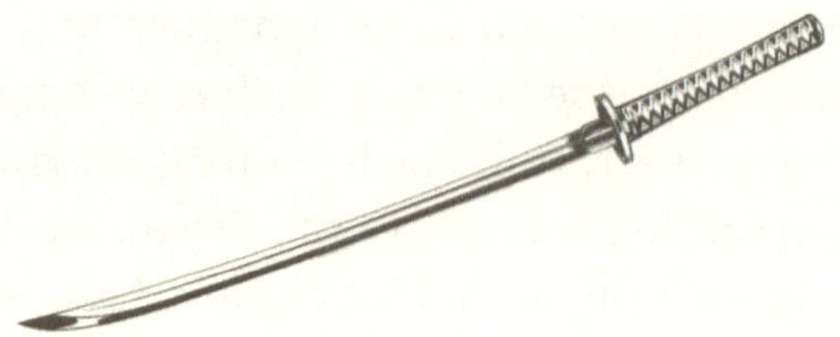

WANNA BE STARTIN' SOMETHIN'

"Round Two?" Ethan beckoned from the bottom step leading back into the yard. "My collection of bumps and bruises from this morning feels a little lopsided. Maybe a few more to even them out?"

"You got it."

I rose from my chair, unsure of what to say to Maddox, the only other person still sitting around the table. Father had taken Seph and L.J. inside to get to work putting up what the kid called a "technomancer firewall" around all of Seph's tech from television to toaster and everything in-between. The tiny exodus had left me, Ethan, and Maddox alone on the veranda, the last three people on Earth I would have ever put together.

To call the conversation awkward would have been an optimistic take, as none of us had the first idea of what to say to the other. Ethan's idea to return to training seemed a flash of brilliance until Maddox chimed in, "Mind if I tag along?"

The energy as we squared or, I guess, triangled off on the cut grass felt completely different. When it was just me and Ethan, the whole thing felt very much like a dance. One of us would lead, then the other, the entire process rewarding even if one or the other of us took a stray kick to the head.

This was ugly. Whatever trust I'd built with Ethan over the preceding month seemed on the chopping block now that Maddox was involved, and any faith I'd ever granted the coyote had gone the way of the dodo two years ago. Now, we were all going to fight, a lupine predator in human form, a man possessed by two millennia of inherited power and skill, and me. Though trained in every fighting technique from aikido to zui quan, I remained at my core a normal human being. As I dropped into my fighting stance, the sun slipped behind a massive cloud sending the world into a premature twilight. An omen if I ever saw one.

I hoped all of us survived the next five minutes.

"So," Maddox tilted his head to one side, "you're the latest 'Daughter' of Neith?"

"I'm going with *Agent* of Neith, if it matters." Ethan dropped into a low fighting stance. "And you used to hang with the theriodans we met in Vegas? The dog of the group, as I understand it?"

Maddox's puffed out chest deflated, his face twisting into a feral snarl. "Coyote."

"They're all related anyway. You know, wolves, coyotes, dogs." Ethan slid into a practiced smile, far from the usual carefree grin I've always enjoyed when he's learning a new skill or when we're hanging out after training. "The wonders of evolution, right?"

Maddox pulled in a deep breath through his nostrils. "I spoke with Linus recently, Harkreader. He said you were pretty good in a fight, though Rosemary here had to bail you out when the shit hit the fan. No judgment, of course. I used to run with a tough crew."

"Of course not." Ethan's smile resembled more a baring of teeth. "You know, your little pack jumped me and Seph in Vegas while we were having dinner. Three on one seemed chickenshit at the time, especially for a trio of big bad theriodans, but predators are gonna predator, right? Not to mention we got Neko out of the deal, and he's been a cool addition to the bunch, so there's that."

"Thanks, Ethan," came a voice from the gate. "That means a lot."

Striding across the yard, our resident 'Crouching Tiger, Hidden Fabulous,' as Seph liked to call him, fought to keep his usually infectious smile from turning into a frown as he digested the identity of the third in our impromptu sparring match.

"Maddox." Neko posted up as if unsure whether he was about to fight for his life. "What are you doing...you know what? Never mind." He shifted his attention to me. "What the hell is *he* doing here, Rosemary?"

I immediately stepped into the space separating the two theriodans. The last time I'd stood between the coyote and the tiger, the three of us were on the dance floor at a club in Miami after an ill-advised night of jello shots I'd prayed Mother would never learn about.

Maddox's idea, of course.

Neko was relatively secretive about his sexual identity back then, having maintained a facade that kept even his best friends at arm's length.

I guess I should have picked up on the fact that he kept pointing out all the good-looking guys before I could even notice them. And that takes into account that Mother trained me to notice everything. To be fair, I only had eyes for Maddox back then, and boy did Maddox know it. Still, even though I'd known him for years, I only felt like I got to meet the real Neko a month ago. And though one of the two predators in human flesh before me was one I used to call lover, the other was the only one I trusted at the moment.

"Hello, Neko." Maddox stepped out of our triangle as if greeting a long-lost friend. "Been a while."

"Not long enough." Neko stepped past him and fist bumped Ethan. "How's it going, Ethan?"

Ethan's eyes flicked in Maddox's direction. "Interesting day."

"Hold on a sec." Maddox stepped back, hands before his chest, palms out. "In case everyone here is suffering from short term memory loss, I'm the one who broke cover to warn you all about the

Cardinal, went with Rosemary to track him down to the airport, and risked my skin to help you get Seph back."

"*Seph*?" Neko said. "Already on a first name basis, I see." He shot me an incredulous gaze. "I've only been gone a week."

I raised a finger in Neko's direction to quiet him and took a half-step toward the man who used to be my every day's first thought. "You've got a point, Maddox. I've never actually thanked you for all you've done since yesterday morning."

Maddox relaxed, if only a bit, at the closest thing to gratitude or apology he was likely to receive. "I appreciate that."

"You have to understand, however, that dropping off the face of the Earth after—well, you know—and leaving not only me but your entire pack of friends high and dry without a word was unacceptable. Expecting an open-armed welcome back from people you unceremoniously dumped, no matter the reason, is a bit unrealistic."

Maddox inhaled, his eyes narrowing the way they did when he was about to go full coyote in a discussion. In the end, however, he stepped back and answered with a simple, "I guess that's fair."

"And your acceptance of that, I'd argue, is a step in the right direction." I beckoned Neko to enter our circle. "All right, Neko. Let's catch you up. As Maddox alluded to earlier, he's been on the trail of the Ascendant behind all our problems for many months and has come out of hiding to offer us his help." I shot Maddox a quick nod. "At no small risk to his own safety, I might add."

Neko studied his former friend for a long moment, sniffing the air for scents Ethan and I would neither perceive nor understand if we could. "You're back, then."

"For now." Maddox shot a questioning grimace my way. "I was worried about Rosemary. Wanted to make sure she was okay."

Neko shook his head in disgust. "You weren't too worried about her two years ago when you shrugged her off like yesterday's trash."

The tension in the air went electric. Neko refused to back down, and Maddox responded the way Maddox responded to such things. The two animals in human form circled like predators in the wild. Ethan wisely stayed out of the whole thing, but against my better judgment, I tried once more to intervene.

"Look, Maddox is here to help." I raised a hand to each of them. "The rest of it, at least for now, has to remain in the past." I glanced in Ethan's direction. "What's that saying you like? We have bigger fish to fry?"

At Ethan's subtle nod, Neko's entire body relaxed.

"Of course." Neko studied Maddox for a moment longer, then strode over and extended a hand in welcome. "Just say goodbye before you head out this time." His eyes dropped to the ground. "Some of us might have missed you after you left."

Maddox, a look of surprised emotion blossoming across his features, accepted the tiger's olive branch with a firm handshake and smiled. "Just because I didn't call doesn't mean I didn't miss all of you as well, you know."

"Let's just put a pin in it." A mix of hurt and doubt flickered in Neko's tiger eyes, but he did his best to hide it all behind a dashing feline smile. "For the moment, we're good, but step out of line and all bets are off, understand?"

"So, Neko," Ethan said as Maddox nodded his agreement, "how was your trip?"

"Overall, it went well." His raised hackles continuing to smooth with each passing moment, Neko stretched his back like a cat in a sunbeam. "Caught up with Mom and Jess. Saw some friends from back in the day. Even dropped by to see Dad." His shoulders slumped an inch. "That went about as well as could be expected."

"Still no traction?" Ethan asked.

Neko shook his head. "Like I told you before I left, he never accepted who I was, Ascendant or otherwise, not that I ever told anyone in my family about my inner tiger. After he and Mom split up, dear old Dad decided his queer son was to blame rather than his own stuff, and not much has changed over the years."

"Sorry to hear that." Ethan let out a solitary laugh. "It's funny. I'd give anything to be able to talk to my dad one more time. I can't imagine what it would be like if he were still here and we weren't on speaking terms."

"It's pretty much the definition of suck." Neko pulled in a breath. "But that's nothing new." He shifted his eyes left and right, his gaze landing on each of us briefly. "So, what's this? Did I interrupt a sparring session?"

"Rosemary was showing me a couple of moves since I got my ass kicked yesterday."

"Wait." Neko stiffened. "That thing at the airport. That was you guys?"

"Maddox and me." I gestured in the coyote's direction. "An Ascendant I'd never heard of before yesterday—he calls himself the Cardinal—jumped Ethan and took Seph while they were out on a walk. Father took Ethan to the emergency room while Maddox and I went after them."

"It took breaking a few federal laws," Maddox jumped in, "but Rosemary managed to stop the Cardinal's plane mid-takeoff, and though the Cardinal got away, we did rescue Seph." He shot Neko a sharp look. "I mean, Miss Snow."

"If you run into this guy, be careful." Ethan rubbed absently at his upper arm. "You may be strong and fast, Neko, but this Cardinal guy? He's stronger and faster, not to mention he walks around in a suit of armor out of a sci-fi movie." He gestured to the hint of purple at his cheekbone. "He took me down without even breaking a sweat, I'm ashamed to say."

"You have nothing to be ashamed of, Ethan." I walked to his side and rested a hand on his still-healing shoulder. "He ambushed you in the middle of a residential neighborhood wearing high-tech armor when you were on a stroll with your...girlfriend." I hated that a part of me didn't want to utter that last word. "None of us would have been ready for such an assault."

"You would have been." Ethan scowled, more sullen than he'd been minutes before. "If it had been you, this Cardinal guy never would have taken Seph in the first place."

"Hey." I hated seeing Ethan beat himself up that way. "Maddox and I had him outnumbered two-to-one, and he escaped without us laying so much as a finger on him. He's a professional, and you're still learning this game. Give yourself a break."

"Don't need to." He rubbed again at his injured shoulder. "A guy dressed like he was waiting for a spot at the bird feeder already did that for me yesterday."

Neko and Maddox caught each other's gaze.

"If this guy is as fast as you say," Neko said, "then none of us would have had much of a chance at taking him one-on-one."

"And as armored as he is," Maddox added, "even on your best day, you probably couldn't have hurt him."

I flicked Maddox a withering look that communicated as clearly as possible he wasn't helping.

"Look, Ethan. I know you want to be the one to keep Seph safe and secure, but from what Maddox has told us and what we've seen, this Cardinal is as dangerous as they come." I locked gazes with him and offered a grim smile. "You weren't ready for him this time—that much is simple fact—but next time, you will be." I dropped back into a fighting stance. "And on that note, now that we have enough for two-on-two, what say we see how you handle a full-on brawl?"

"I'm game, I guess." Ethan raised a brow. "Teams?"

I hadn't thought that far ahead.

Me with Ethan would've put us up against two theriodans who, for all their current friction, had fought together more times than either could likely remember. I was as well-trained as they came and Ethan carried the Light, but at the end of the day, he was still relatively green, and neither of us shared our soul with the spirit of a feral predator. Such a sparring arrangement would be lopsided at best.

Me with Neko would've stuck Ethan with Maddox. Talk about a recipe for disaster.

That left me with Maddox as the only viable option. This day kept getting better.

Still, this was for Ethan, both for his training as well as to help break him out of his funk. Taking a few hits, physical or otherwise, was part of the deal.

"Neko, why don't you and Ethan work together against me and Maddox? We'll see what happens."

Neko raised an eyebrow. "You sure?

"You've trained with Ethan nearly as much as I have. He's good to go."

"That wasn't my concern." Neko dropped into his usual cat stance without another word and motioned Ethan to his side. "Come on, Ethan."

Our resident tiger had trained with Ethan before, but usually either as a sparring partner or in an advisory role as he worked on his strength, reflexes, and balance. Not since the final night of Seph's tour had they fought side-by-side, and that entire evening was one big blur for all of us.

Maddox chuckled. "Boy Wonder there may carry the Light," he proclaimed as he adopted a low fighting posture, "but I'm glad to know that Rosemary still calls the shots around here like the old days." He cracked his neck and directed his full attention in Neko's direction. "Defend yourself, tiger."

Neko bared his teeth, the expression almost a smile. "Defend yourself, coyote."

The two theriodans circled, leaving me to face Ethan alone, at least for the moment.

"Can't tell if those two are best friends or mortal enemies," he murmured as he dropped into a fighting position I taught him the first day we trained together.

"You know what they say," I shot out with a palm strike which Ethan easily blocked, "love and hate are simply flip sides of the same coin."

Ethan countered with a low sweeping kick I dodged only to catch a quick back fist across the chin.

"Nice." I rubbed at my jaw. "You continue to get faster." I whipped out my hand, grasped his wrist, and pulled him to me. Dropping into a roll with Ethan still in tow, I used our combined momentum to flip him onto his back behind me. Another quick shoulder roll, and I was again atop his chest, my knees and shins pinning his arms to the ground.

And though he wasn't playing possum this time, I was still careful. He'd become quite the cagey opponent over the preceding month, and I wasn't going to be fooled twice the same day.

"Surrender, Harkreader," I hissed, doing my best movie supervillain—Seph, Ethan, and I had binged at least half the Marvel movies over the last month—with a purposeful wicked grin plastered across my face. "Give in, or face the—"

A compact ball of muscle, bone, and sinew rammed into me from behind, knocking me from my perch. Neko, his eyes feline and his grin like the cat that ate the canary, stood over me, hands on his hips.

"Looks like someone forgot this is a partners match."

Maddox dove at Neko, his movements as graceful as I remembered. Neko evaded him with ease, but I quickly realized the tiger wasn't Maddox's target. Spinning out of his near miss with the other theriodan, Maddox flew into a roundhouse kick that caught Ethan mid-abdomen before he'd recovered from my takedown. Ethan shot both forearms up in an effective block, but the sheer force of the kick still knocked him back to the ground.

"All right." Ethan performed a quick backward shoulder roll and shot back to his feet. "So that's how we're going to play today." He took a step in Maddox's direction, fists raised and face red.

"What was it your mom always used to say, Rosemary?" Maddox's lips curled into a grin as he motioned for Ethan to come at him. "Your enemy won't pull punches, and neither will I."

Hearing Maddox spout one of Mother's aphorisms filled me simultaneously with nostalgia, sadness, and rage, but before anyone could say another word, Father exited the house with L.J. and Seph in tow.

"Get your things, everyone." Father's eyes burned with intensity. "We've got a lead."

"A lead?" Ethan asked.

He motioned to L.J. "Our newest addition discovered something as he was setting up his array of defenses across all of Miss Snow's tech."

"Most everything had been left alone," L.J. added, "but the closed-circuit security camera system was anything but 'closed circuit' before I cleaned house." He shook his head. "A technomancer and whoever it is they work for has almost certainly been spying on Seph."

"And do you know who this technomancer is?" Ethan pulled

Seph to him and wrapped the clearly shaken pop star into a comforting embrace.

"No, but I know where to look." He mimed running his fingers across an invisible keyboard, a subtle shimmer surrounding his hands as he focused his concentration. "Denver."

"Denver?" I asked. "Like the whole city?"

L.J. cracked his knuckles. "You might not think it, but technomancy is very personal. Each of us approaches technology in a subtly different way. In doing so, every technomancer leaves behind a specific fingerprint."

"What does that have to do with Colorado?" Ethan asked.

"Once I purged this place's technology of the other technomancer's manipulations and set in place my own set of bells and whistles, I stretched out through the internet and phone lines to see if I could isolate the origin of the manipulation."

"And?" I understood about half of what L.J. was saying. "What did you find?"

"Whoever infiltrated the house's security camera system is currently expending a lot of time and energy doing the same to cameras across the entire Denver downtown area."

"They're looking for something," Ethan murmured.

"Or someone," I added.

"While it's possible they're doing all of this remotely, I've usually had better results with larger scale tech systems when I was on site." L.J. crossed his arms. "Unless I miss my guess, this technomancer, and possibly whoever they're working for, is there."

"Denver is sixteen hours away." Maddox crossed his arms. "Even if you left now, you'd be lucky to get there by tomorrow morning."

"If we went by ground." A flash of inspiration hit me, courtesy of a piece of advice Mother hammered into my head years ago: always start with the resources you have at hand. "I think I have an idea."

CHAPTER 13

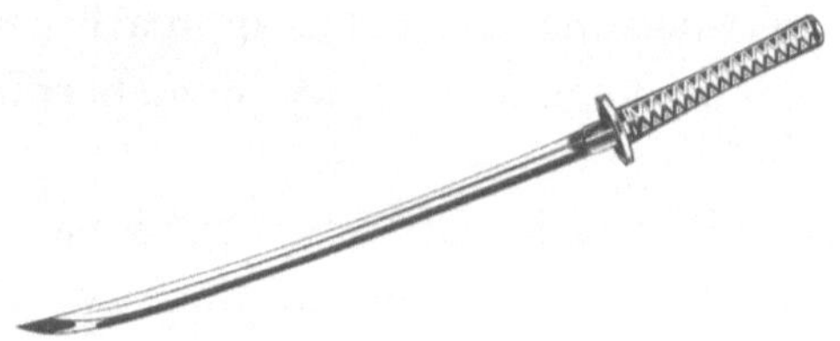

MYSTERY LADY

"Fifteen minutes out." Bradley smiled like a kid at the theater about to see the sequel to his favorite superhero movie. "I've arranged for us to have clearance to land, and there will be a car waiting for us."

Impressive, I had to admit. We went from stuck in Montecito with a day's drive ahead to Denver airspace in less than three hours. It helps to have friends in high places, I guess.

If only I knew whether or not we could count Bradley as a friend. But I suppose I could say the same about L.J. and Maddox. Honestly, I'd only just moved Neko back into the angel column on my internal ledger, and we'd left him alone with Seph while we went on what I hoped wouldn't be a wild goose chase to Denver.

Some might say I have trust issues, though I'd argue I inherited Mother's intuition even if Ethan was the one who carried the Light.

"So, Mr. Bradley. You've acquired us a private jet, a relatively sequestered arrival location, and a vehicle." Father cast a concerned look in L.J.'s direction. "Now, to see if we can keep up our end of things."

L.J., silent for half an hour, looked up from his laptop. His screen sat filled with code that might as well have been the arcane scribblings of a wizard's grimoire, the protective measures he put in place back at Seph's home in Montecito more spell than cypher to me.

We were talking about a "technomancer," I suppose.

"L.J.," I asked, "anything?"

"Just that whoever this other technomancer is, they're good. They've blocked me out of the major metro area. Can't access cameras, security systems, phone lines, nothing." He shook his head. "Not many cities where I can't see whatever I want whenever I want, I'll tell you that."

Father's face deepened a few shades of crimson. "With all due respect, son, we've moved heaven and earth to get you and the rest of us to Denver before sunset. I certainly hope you have more to offer than flying as blind as the rest of us once we get on the ground."

L.J.'s face turned up in a mischievous grin. "Just because I can't see the city all that well doesn't mean I can't lead us to whatever the technomancer is trying to hide."

"What is that supposed to mean?" Ethan asked. "You can't access the tech but you can see the person manipulating it?"

L.J.'s smile doubled in intensity. "Precisely." He stroked his chin like a wizened professor rather than a gangly teenager with blue hair. "Think of the city like, I don't know, a redacted document. I may not be able to read the blacked-out words—"

"But you can absolutely see where the black marks are." Ethan's epiphany became all the more evident as a wave of L.J.'s hand flipped on a light above his head. "That's cool."

"The thing is," L.J. continued, "from the way this technomancer is setting up their combination of surveillance and blackout, it's clear they're looking for someone." He stiffened as he had an epiphany of his own. "Not to mention setting up whoever it is for an ambush."

"But who are they after?" I asked. "And why?"

"There's no way of knowing that, but what I can tell you is that our unseen enemy wasn't anticipating another technomancer showing up. To the untrained eye, all the tech across the city likely appears to be working as designed, but for people like me, they might as well have painted everything they've touched neon orange." L.J.'s eyes focused on a point in space across the room. "They're not even bothering to cover their tracks."

"Maybe this other technomancer simply doesn't see you as much of a threat," Maddox grumbled.

"Not helping," I whispered loud enough for all present to hear.

Maddox tilted his head back to study the lone teen in our midst. "Anyway, I don't get it, kid. You say you can see this technowizard's handiwork from a mile away. What's keeping them from noticing you the same way?"

L.J. considered for a moment, though I suspected from the look on his face that he wasn't having difficulty coming up with an explanation as much as he was trying to find a way to express it that didn't make Maddox look like an idiot.

"Think about it this way," he said eventually. "Imagine you suddenly appear in a darkened wood. You haven't moved or done anything to give away your position or even your presence. You can listen and observe all you want, but as long as you don't make a move yourself, you don't make a sound."

Maddox shook his head. "In this little scenario you've concocted, you're still breathing, right?" He crossed his arms and raised a questioning brow. "And even if the various jungle predators hidden in the darkness can't see or hear you, I suspect their noses are working just fine." His lips parted in a snarl as a quiet growl sounded in the tiny cabin. "Don't forget who you're talking to, kid."

"L.J.'s metaphor may not be perfect," I jumped in quickly to keep what had remained a relatively conflict-free two hours from going off the rails ten minutes before we landed, "but I get what he's saying."

"As long as he stays in observer mode," Ethan spoke slowly, as if processing the information himself, "we should have the upper hand in figuring out where they are."

"*Should...*" Maddox grumbled.

"But what if we need L.J. to, you know, do his thing?" Ethan asked, ignoring Maddox's quiet gripe.

"That will be a good problem to have," I answered, "because that will mean we have found them."

"Any idea where to start?" Father asked, pointing to L.J.'s laptop. "I know you can interpret all those numbers and symbols, but it all looks like screen gibberish from those *Matrix* movies to me."

"Of course." L.J. typed a few keystrokes and waved a hand across the keyboard and the screen shifted into a map of what I guessed was Downtown Denver. "Whoever we're dealing with has spent considerable effort taking out the various surveillance systems of the city." He pointed to the center of the screen. "But nowhere as concentrated as right here. Basically, he's created a null. No signal in or out. A perfect hiding place."

"But what's there?" Father asked.

L.J. looked up from his laptop at the large flatscreen mounted at the front of the private plane's cabin. With another wave of his hand, he cast the image onto the larger screen and then manipulated the image with a series of finger motions until we were looking at a satellite image of a large open area in Denver's western Downtown area filled with shops and restaurants.

"This is Larimer Square." L.J.'s voice dropped into a monotone as if he were reading from a script rather than simply speaking. "*Come shop and dine in Denver's most distinctive district amid our Victorian buildings and our unique chef-driven restaurants and specialty boutiques.*" He shook his head and both his eyes and voice resumed normalcy. "Not sure why, but this other technomancer's blockade has basically turned the Square into an electronic black hole. The rest of the city is locked down, but this place? I'd be surprised if the cash registers are still working."

"Sorry if I'm being dense," Ethan's face twisted with confusion, "but what exactly does all that mean?"

L.J. maintained an air of calm detachment, which was pretty impressive coming from the youngest person in the room. Even at my own tender age of twenty-one, I'd been told more than once I came across as world weary, and in L.J. it appeared I'd found a kindred spirit. He'd clearly seen some things, and one day when all our lives weren't on the line, I planned to sit down with him and hear the rest of his story.

Today, however, wasn't the day.

"What it means is that whatever is going down is either about to happen or is happening right now at this Larimer Square place"—L.J. let out a quiet sigh—"and we're still in the air."

"I couldn't have gotten you here any sooner," Bradley whispered. "I've got connections, but jets only fly so fast." His eyes dropped to the plane's carpeted floor. "In any case, we'll be down in five minutes."

"No one's blaming you, Mr. Bradley." I waited for him to look up so I could speak to him eye-to-eye. "If it weren't for you, we'd all either still be at the airport awaiting a commercial flight or half a day away on the interstate." I glanced out the windows at the lights of Denver. "We're all doing the best we can here. Either we'll get there in time or we won't."

"But if we don't," Ethan said, "another Ascendant is going to pay the price."

"I know, Ethan." I met Father's grim gaze. "I know."

~

Bradley's Denver connections got us off the plane and out of the airport in record time. Though the gleam in his gaze let me know he wanted nothing more than to tag along, Bradley agreed to stay behind with the plane in case another quick takeoff was required. In the final minutes before landing, L.J. forged what he hoped would be an inseverable connection between all our phones, Bradley's included, to make sure this other technomancer couldn't block our communications once the feces hit the fan.

One of Mother's favorite aphorisms.

It's funny. Though I'm not sure if Mother let swear words fly when she and Father were alone, I didn't recall her ever saying one in my presence. She would have said such words were beneath a Daughter of Neith, but between hanging out with Seph and training with Ethan, I'd learned exactly how emotionally satisfying such utterances could be.

In any case, the five of us were stuck on the sidewalk at the Denver Airport, Larimer Square was twenty-seven miles west of our position, and the little flashing dot on the Uber app hadn't moved in five minutes. I wasn't sure which of Seph's favorite four-letter words best represented the moment, but a couple flirted with the tip of my tongue.

I pulled to Ethan's side, leaving Father standing a few feet away with L.J. and Maddox, the latter watching me with those coyote eyes of his full of suspicion.

"So, the way I see it, we've cashed in every favor we might have had with a mysterious organization that Mother never liked in the first place, all to get to Denver to stop an event that we know nothing about based on information we gleaned from a fourteen-year-old technomancer who last month did everything in his power to help our enemies thwart us at every turn." I pulled in a deep cleansing breath. "And now? The badness we've flown cross-country to stop is going to happen anyway because our transportation is stuck in traffic due to a stupid ball game."

"We'll get there, Rosemary. Whatever it takes."

Ethan rested his hand on my arm, his strong fingers warm against my skin. Maddox responded to the touch, his reaction likely imperceptible to the rest of our crew, but I knew the coyote well enough to pick up on it with ease. He didn't like Ethan much to begin with, and he certainly didn't like him anywhere near me. Though to be honest, I'm not sure he was doing all that much to hide it from anyone.

"Careful, boy." A middle-aged-appearing woman with skin like polished ebony and long curly tresses that flowed like a pitch-black waterfall down her back stepped from the shadows. Her outfit, consisting of a glowing ivory tunic, matching pants, and a pair of spotless white designer sneakers, would have elicited a well-earned nod of approval from Seph. "The first rule of bargaining is knowing what you are and aren't willing to sacrifice to achieve your ends."

I dropped into a fighting stance, my blade half out of its scabbard and resting in my light grip as I studied the gaze of this newcomer for even a hint of malice. Ethan and Maddox both followed suit, their shift into defensive posture oddly mirror-like. Father pushed L.J. behind him and rested his hand on the pistol at his side.

"And who might you be?" I asked, working to inject equal parts civility and gravitas into my tone.

The woman held her hands before her, palms out in mock surrender, and smiled. "No one deserving such a martial response to a well-timed piece of simple advice."

I hesitated for half a second and then slid the katana back into its scabbard, working all the while to answer the woman's confident smile with one of my own.

"My apologies." I tilted my head to one side. "Though today may not be the best day to drop in unannounced on this particular crowd." I motioned for Ethan and Maddox to hold their position and let me take point. Offering the woman the subtlest of bows, I stared deeply into the woman's dark brown eyes. "In any case, you seem to have all of us at a disadvantage." When she didn't say anything, I added, "I am Rosemary Delacroix."

She crossed her arms. "And here I thought my dramatic entrance and immaculate ensemble would be all the introduction I would need." She clucked her cheek in disapproval. "Ah well, yet another of a long life's little disappointments." She drew herself up straight, her arms dropping to her sides in a disarming gesture. "You are quite correct, Miss Delacroix. We haven't met, though I understand you and some of those who stand with you met my Sisters a month ago."

A breathless moment passed as I made the connection half a second before Maddox let out an astounded gasp.

"You're one of the Angels," he said, his eyes narrowing, "and, as I understand it, quite far from your home."

Her smile faded into a faraway gaze. "While it is true, coyote, that I rarely venture far from my little slice of paradise these days, I still go where and when I am needed." She studied the five of us in turn. "Today, I am needed here." Her eyes shifted to the west. "Or, more precisely, the lot of you are needed elsewhere."

"This is all very cryptic. Your Sisters would approve." My lips pulled down to a pensive moue as I channeled what I always used to call Mother's "business face" during private chats with Father. "Now, you've clearly come a long way, and I assume you're here to help us. What do you bring to the table?"

"Very direct, girl." The Angel looked on me with both kindness and curiosity. "You remind me so of your mother."

I fought to keep the emotion from my face. "You knew my mother?"

"Better than either of my Sisters. Alba always imagined herself above dealing with such as the Daughters of Neith, and I'm quite certain that Danielle Delacroix felt the same about the darkest of the Three Angels."

"Midnight." The word fell from Ethan's lips like an oath. "While I admit that meeting her didn't inspire me to invite her over to hang out by the pool, in the end, she wasn't our enemy in L.A." Ethan's eyes cut in Maddox's direction. "Her underlings perhaps, but she actually seemed appalled at what they'd done."

"She has her own sense of honor, my dark Sister, which serves a person well if their goals align with hers. Cross her or interfere with her plans, however, at your peril." Her eyes went up and to the right, as if reminiscing. "I can't believe it's been so long."

If there's one thing I can say about Ascendant, it's that I have yet to meet one that didn't love the sound of their own voice.

"If you knew my mother as well as you as you say, then you know she wasn't much for chit chat when the mission was at stake. So, please, Ms.—"

"The last few years, I've been going by Lady Day," the Angel said with a dazzling smile. "And trust me, I'm keeping tabs on the situation." She cast her sparkling eyes around our little clutch. "Anyway, it's not quite time for you all to make your grand appearance"—she bit her lip as if witnessing something unpleasant none of the rest of us could see—"though it won't be long now."

"So, Ms. Day—" Father began.

"Lady," the Angel interrupted, "Lady Day."

"Very well." Father cleared his throat. "Lady Day, if you've come to provide us with transportation, perhaps we should move out smartly? Larimer Square is a good forty minutes from here, and every minute we waste could mean someone's life."

"Ah, leave it to Dani to marry one so linear in his thinking." She twirled her finger in the air. "Leave now and trust that you'll arrive later than if you wait here with me, and far too late to accomplish what you've come to do."

"Great," I muttered, "more riddles."

"The Cardinal." L.J., quiet the entire time, stepped from behind Father's broad form. "He's here."

"Indeed, young man." Lady Day beckoned the boy closer. "My, aren't you something to behold?"

Color rose in L.J.'s brown cheeks. "I'm just the team technomancer, ma'am."

"And Van Gogh was just another man who liked to—" Her motherly smile twisted into a grimace of pain, her entire body stiffening as if an electric current ran through her. "No, no, it's too soon. How could that monster have already—" Her sentence cut short by clamped teeth, a shriek flew from her parted lips that sent ice down my spine. "You were right, Daughter of Neith. I tarried, and now the one I came to save may be lost. Gather close, all of you, quickly, while there's still time."

"What are we doing?" Ethan whispered even as he followed my lead and drew close to Lady Day. "I mean, I'm totally in, but—"

"I can't believe I'm saying this," Maddox added, "but I'm with Boy Wonder. What the hell is happening?"

I looked to the one man whose cool head had seen me through two decades. "Father?"

"We'll figure it all out later." He rested a hand on L.J.'s shoulder and pulled the last of our quintet into the tight circle around the third Angel I'd met in a month after a lifetime of knowing them only by reputation. "For now, we do as the Lady says."

"I get that," Ethan countered, as bold as I'd ever seen him speak to Father, "but that still doesn't explain what it is we're doing."

"What you're doing young man," Lady Day invoked, her voice at once full of wonder and fear and magic and morbidity, "is following instructions so I can get the five of you exactly where you need to be." Her eyes shimmered with the golden glow of the midday sun. "I just pray that we're not too late."

CHAPTER 14

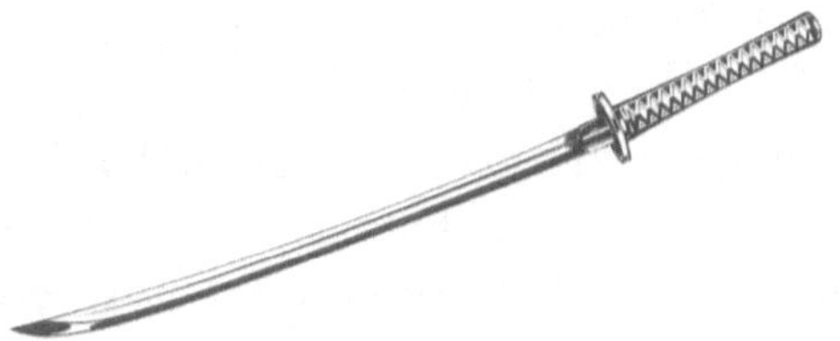

NIGHT MOVES

"Aplace, a person, a time." Lady Day's harsh whisper hit my ears in stark contrast to the almost melodic quality of her voice from before. "Tell me, Daughter of Neith."

"Larimer Square," I looked to Ethan, "right?"

"As for the time," Father caught my gaze, the cast of his eyes as incredulous as Ethan's, "as soon as humanly possible."

If what I thought was about to happen was in fact the case, the fact that we had to name a time sent my thoughts spiraling.

"And the person?" Lady Day peered around the circle. "To whom shall I send you five?" The air crackled with electricity. "Be quick with your answer."

I had no idea what to say. We'd come to save some faceless Ascendant from our shared enemy, but outside of the media blackout put in place by this other technomancer, we had no idea whatsoever of the situation we were about to encounter.

"The Cardinal." Maddox spoke for us all. "Send us to the Cardinal."

"Thank you." Lady Day visibly relaxed. "That closes the circle." She spun a finger in the air, and the smell of ozone filled the space as crackling static pops echoed like tiny thunderclaps from her fingertip. "Now, all of you, get ready. The first time can be quite wrenching for some."

"The first time?" Ethan asked.

"For what?" L.J. finished the thought.

A couple other questions ricocheted around inside my own skull. The Angel with glowing eyes before us had said "the one I came to save may be lost." Whom did she mean? And why wasn't she just sending us to that person?

"Go, all of you." Lady Day's eyes continued to burn like the noontime sun. "Save him, if you can."

"Save who?" I asked as gravity seemed to shift ninety degrees, nearly sending me flying from my feet.

"Save him." The light from the woman's eyes grew blinding in intensity as her twirling finger curled down, her hand balling into a fist. "Go."

The golden radiance emanating from the Angel's eyes flared, the blinding burst of light like the flash of an old-timey camera. Dazzled by the shimmer of gold, I blinked a few times to clear my vision.

The first thing I noticed was the difference in the ambient noise; the honking of horns and purr of engines and overhead roar of planes landing and taking off were replaced in an instant by the rush of scrambling feet and raspy breaths, all punctuated by a shrill scream in the distance. The combined smells of car exhaust and travelers far too many hours from their last shower transitioned to an odd mix of the delectable aroma of grilled meat and the acrid odor of gunpowder. And then, as my vision finally recovered from the blazing light that shone from the third Angel's eyes, everything became crystal clear.

The five of us stood in a circle on one side of a two-lane city street that clearly hadn't allowed cars in years. An intricate spiderweb of hanging lights drooped overhead from the shops and restaurants on both sides of the street. Tables, chairs, and potted plants stretched from the sidewalks onto the worn asphalt. Most of the tables sat empty with half-eaten plates of food and full glasses of drink left behind. A few people remained, most cowering behind light posts or under tables while an unfortunate few lay sprawled and unmoving, apparently trampled by a rushing mob minutes before.

And then, the cause of the terrified exodus.

Half a block away, two combatants stood on either side of the street. On one side, his crimson armor on full display and avian helmet sinister in the dim light, the Cardinal waited, his body position relaxed as if he were simply biding his time. On the other, his face turned down in frustrated exhaustion, stood the Greyhound.

"Wait." Maddox gasped. "Is that—"

"Yeah, that's him," Ethan answered. "The Greyhound."

"Or," I added at a whisper, "what's left of him."

After hearing all the legends and then finally seeing him in action for the first time a month ago in this very city, I never would have imagined even a flicker of defeat in those slate-grey eyes.

The times, it seemed, were a-changin'. And not for the better.

The Cardinal noticed us first, the overhanging lights reflecting off his smoked glass lenses as he looked our way. Though his helmet completely obscured his features, I imagined the man's lips turning up in a wicked smile behind the metallic-orange beak.

The Greyhound followed his opponent's gaze, the momentary relief in his features shifting immediately to terror. "Why are you here?" he bellowed, his voice holding none of its usual vigor. "Don't you know what he intends for all of us? Flee, Daughter of Neith, before it's too late."

"We're not going anywhere." Ethan drew his paired swords and filled them with Mother's Light, directing the longer blade at our foe. "Ready for round two, bird man?"

The Cardinal turned to acknowledge Ethan's taunt. "You have no idea," came his electronically augmented voice. "A shame that you didn't take time to digest the lessons from our last encounter, boy."

"You're not ambushing me from the shadows this time," Ethan answered.

"And this time, he's not alone." Father locked and loaded a round and pulled his weapon to his shoulder. "Do you really think you can take all of us at once?"

The Cardinal swept his arms wide and offered a bow. "The real question, Mr. Delacroix, is whether the five of you truly believe you have what it takes to stop me from taking what I've come for."

"We'll see how tough you are when we cut you out of that tin can." Maddox dropped into a three-point stance, his eyes shifting from human to lupine. "Now, step away from the Greyhound and face us."

"Gladly, coyote," the Cardinal said with a passing glance at his exhausted adversary. "The old man isn't going anywhere, and, unlike earlier at the airport, I don't have to concern myself with a pack of hot-tempered fools with guns who might inadvertently injure my quarry." He beckoned us to come closer. "So, are we going to talk all night, or shall we dance?"

Father kept both eyes firmly on the Cardinal, but subtly waved in L.J.'s direction. "Find a place to hide, kid," he whispered. "You're good at what you do, but this is not your fight."

As L.J. scurried away, I directed the remaining four of us into a combat wedge with Ethan on my right, Maddox on my left, and Father off Ethan's flank. I drew my katana, checked that Ethan and Maddox were good to go and that Father had his Glock at the ready, and then signaled for the group to advance as a unit.

"All at once, eh?" The Cardinal swept his arms out to either side as if welcoming us to a party. "Excellent. A far more efficient use of my time." He glanced over at the Greyhound, who was slowly limping away from his attacker. "Fear not, Grandpa; I haven't forgotten about you. When I'm done with these four, I plan to circle back around and finish what I started."

I paused mid-step. The thought of fighting an Ascendant who could stand against the Greyhound, much less leave him in such a state, sent ice running through my veins. I worried for Father, for Ethan, and even for Maddox.

This, however, is what we came to do. What *I* was *born* to do. Mother faced worse than the Cardinal for years and survived time after time, not to mention had a family, raised a daughter, and more than lived up to the expectations of our line. Could I do any less?

"All right, Ethan," I whispered, "you know the drill."

"I go high, you go low?" he answered, a grim smile etched across his features.

"You got it."

"Not sure how effective bullets will be against that armor of his," Father added, "but I'll do what I can."

"And what about me?" Maddox growled. "Other than Boy Wonder here—"

"Keep him off us," I interrupted, already tired of his preferred nickname for Ethan.

"And try not to get killed," Ethan added. "You wouldn't be the first theriodan this asshole has taken out."

"Duly noted." Maddox's features darkened, but he didn't speak another word as we went into action.

Ethan leaped into the air, Mother's blades held crossed before him, as I raced forward, my katana a long diagonal before my body. I slashed across the Cardinal's midsection as Ethan sent the longer of his two blades hurtling at our enemy's neck. My blow struck true, though my steel glanced off the Cardinal's body armor without so much as a scratch. Our crimson adversary deigned to block Ethan's strike with his armored forearm, the angular ridge that went from wrist to elbow like a metallic wing an effective counter. Sparks flew from the blow, but the Cardinal moved not an inch and instead caught Ethan midair by his recently injured arm and hurled him to one side.

As soon as his line of sight was clear, Father took two shots at our opponent. Each hit center mass—Father doesn't miss—but both ricocheted off his armor like hail off a tin roof. Maddox, his eyes fully coyote, came up on my left and dove at the Cardinal, his teeth bared like the animal that lived at his core. The ferocity of the attack, surprisingly, took me aback. The two years since he left, it seemed, had blunted my memory of the coyote's capability for violence.

"Leave this place," Maddox growled, his clawed fingers flying at the Cardinal's neck, "or I swear I'll rip out your throat myself." He nearly made good on his threat, climbing the Cardinal's armored form in an instant and nearly dislodging his avian helmet. A whirling spin, however, transformed our enemy into a red tornado that dislodged Maddox's grip and sent the coyote flailing to the ground.

The better part of me lamented watching my first love hurled to the unforgiving asphalt. But the tiny part that remembered the pain and hurt and destruction he'd left in his wake? That part cheered, if only a little. Nevertheless, I couldn't leave him there defenseless.

I shot to my left and stepped across Maddox, my feet straddling his broad shoulders in a martial stance and my sword held high above my head.

The crack of gunfire as Father unloaded another three bullets at our enemy left the air sulfurous and thick. The third bullet caught the Cardinal in his right shoulder, and though his crimson armor deflected the round, the momentum actually knocked him back a foot, the first indication that our foe wasn't invincible.

Ethan, back on his feet, moved on the Cardinal with caution. "What do you want with the Greyhound anyway? What do you want with Seph?" Step after step, he continued, making sure to keep his weight above his feet and distributed evenly like I taught him. "What do you hope to gain by killing your own kind?"

"What do I hope to gain?" the Cardinal asked with a laugh. "Do you truly not know?" He pointed in the direction of his retreating quarry. "Ask the old man, why don't you? The fear in his eyes shows that he understands."

My eyes flicked in the direction of the Greyhound as I completed my flanking movement on the Cardinal, freeing Maddox to return to his feet, albeit with a little less spring in his step.

"What is he talking about?" I shouted to the Greyhound, a man who up until a month ago had only been a legend to me and now had been brought low by our shared enemy. "What does he want?"

"Your mother never told you?" The Greyhound's dark eyes shot to Father. "Nor even you, Mr. Delacroix?"

"Ah," the Cardinal chuckled, "the pain of family secrets never shared." He gestured to the Greyhound. "Tell them, old man. Tell them of your fate, should the lot of you fail to stop me." His head shifted to one side inside his armor, cracking his neck in preparation for the next round. "And fail, you will."

"You understand, Daughter of Neith, that your power flows from your mother, and hers from her own mother, and so on and so on as far back as history has been written on the matter." The Greyhound's shoulders slumped as his eyes shifted in Ethan's direction. "Your current situation notwithstanding."

"Of course I understand." Keeping one eye on the Greyhound and the other on the Cardinal, all the while trying to keep even a hint of disappointment from either in case Ethan looked my way, I asked, "What does that have to do with anything?"

"Your line may not be Ascendant, but just as your power may be passed on at the time of your death, so may ours." His eyes narrowed, in paired exhaustion and frustration. "Have you never been present at the passing of one of my kind?"

I hadn't, and if the words that were about to come out of his mouth were what I suspected, the entire world had just become a whole lot scarier.

"Ascendant are born with whatever ability sets them apart from the rest of humanity," the Cardinal spoke, his voice reverberating through the amplifiers of his helmet. "Though some are quite showy and others more subtle, all require a certain spark that comes from within, a wellspring of power that remains with them until the moment they leave this world."

"Should an Ascendant pass on alone, that power simply returns to the universe from whence it came, completing the grand circle of life." The Greyhound pointed a shaking finger at the Cardinal. "But should another be present at the time of their death, or worse, commit the forbidden offense this piece of offal has committed time and again..."

"No," Ethan whispered in disgust.

"Yes, Harkreader." The Cardinal swept his arms wide in a quick bow. "The moment they cross the veil, their power is mine."

Ethan drew back, the revulsion I felt at my core mirrored on his face as well as Father's. Even Maddox, who had always remained unfazed even in the face of insurmountable odds, stood agape at the revelation.

"You're nothing but a vampire feeding off others." Maddox spat on the ground. "Despicable."

"That's rich," the Cardinal countered, "coming from the closest thing this world has to an honest-to-god werewolf, you pathetic coyote."

Maddox's hair stood on end, his eyes squinting in anger. "I am theriodan, you monster. Call me 'were' again at your peril."

Wow. While I'd noted the similarities between theriodans and various creatures of urban legend when we'd first met, I'd never spoken of it and suddenly found myself glad I'd kept my own counsel on the subject.

"So," Father asked, "you're not just killing Ascendant, but stealing their powers and abilities as you go?"

"And with each kill, the next becomes easier." A twirl of his finger sent the shadows around our feet swimming. "That pathetic skiomancer was the first, though adding his essence to my own barely moved the needle. The Redstart out of Morocco, however, ironically proved to be the real beginning to this little campaign." In a blink, he leaped backward, the move a gymnast's fever dream. "I thought I moved fast until the day I crossed paths with her. Even in the moment I took her essence, however, I learned that speed and reflexes only carry you so far." He tapped his helmet with a steel-covered finger. "Against such as us, resilience is where it's at."

"Is that why you killed Omari?" Maddox blurted out, his chest working like a bellows.

"Omari?" The Cardinal considered for a moment. "Wait. The warthog?" An amplified laugh echoed in the urban canyon. "Yes, coyote, at least in part." His gauntleted hand balled into a fist before the dark avian eyes of his helmet. "I indeed took his strength, his fortitude, his power, but most of all I sought to put the poor creature out of his misery." The mocking tsk-tsk hit twice as hard as it echoed off the brick walls on either side of the Square. "I mean, can you imagine being born a warthog?"

"You bastard!" Maddox raced at the Cardinal in a loping run that used hands and feet alike. I'd only ever seen him that angry and out of control once, and it didn't end well for the person on the other end of the exchange.

That individual, however, hadn't been an Ascendant augmented by the essences of the three victims he'd just admitted to and God knows how many others as well as sufficient armor to defend against every weapon brought to bear so far.

However much of me hated the coyote who broke my heart, no part of me wanted to watch him die.

"Maddox," I shrieked, "don't!"

Too late. Maddox hit our armored adversary with a flying tackle, taking the both of them to ground in a heap of flesh and claw and steel. For a brief moment, it seemed that Maddox might have a sliver of hope as he straddled the Cardinal, his muscular arms working to free the angular helmet from our adversary's head. The armor's designer, however, apparently had done their job quite well.

A blindingly fast armored gauntlet to the head sent Maddox's body limp.

"No!" I screamed.

The Cardinal pulled himself up from the ground, holding Maddox before him by his naked throat, his still form as vulnerable as a newborn babe's. "Funny, I came here today to feast upon the energies of one Ascendant." The beady dark eyes of his helmet focused on Maddox's drooped head. "Didn't know there'd be an appetizer."

CHAPTER 15

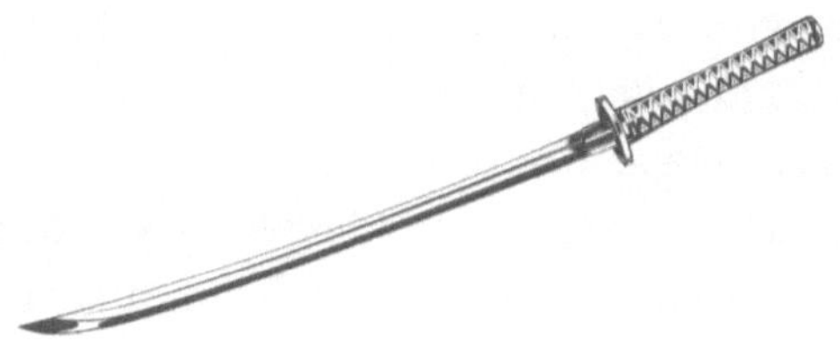

LET'S DANCE

"Let him go." I advanced on the Cardinal, katana at the ready. "Or my face and this blade will be the last two things you ever see."

"And without that blade of yours, what exactly do you bring to this fight, little girl?" He chuckled, the amplified sound dark and ominous. "You may be trained as a Daughter of Neith, but without your mother's essence, you're nothing but a finely tuned sports car with no gas in the tank." He shifted his attention in Ethan's direction, making a point to ignore me.

My core went simultaneously ice cold and white hot. "Try me, Cardinal, and you'll see that I possess all I need to put you in your place."

"Not to mention," Ethan added as he moved to flank our enemy, "she's got me."

"Ah," the Cardinal said, "the two of you together is quite the sight: the most lethal girl in the world, denied the power that was her literal birthright, fighting alongside a boy brimming with that very power who barely knows one end of his sword from the other." His helmeted head shook sadly from side to side. "I'm not certain which is more pathetic." He glanced across his shoulder at the Greyhound who continued his slow hobble away and then allowed Maddox to fall into a puddle of flesh at his feet before actually deigning to adopt a fighting stance. "But it seems the two of you are hell bent on an exercise in futility and pain. Let's get this over with so I can resume the day's business."

Okay. I had his attention. Now, to keep us all alive.

I quickly ran through our assets.

Though the Greyhound's timely arrival may have turned the tide the last time we were in Denver, we couldn't count on any help from that corner.

Father remained in position, his Glock at the ready, though he dared not waste any of his remaining twelve rounds, as the first five bullets had indeed found their target and accomplished nothing beyond proving the defensive capability of the Cardinal's armor.

Ethan's swords, with the Light of Neith pouring from their shining steel, might have a chance at penetrating our enemy's defenses. Still, for all his virtues, the current vessel of my line's power had less than five weeks of training under his belt.

And then there was me.

The Cardinal's taunt echoed in my mind, and a part of me answered. The part that believed, despite two decades of training, that I was nothing but a girl with a sword. That I didn't have what it took to fight big scary Ascendant serial killers in mechanized battle armor the color of fresh blood. That this day, despite all our effort and bravado, we were going to lose.

"Well?" the Cardinal asked. "You and your brood have come all the way from Montecito—and in record time, I must say—to face me. Are you going to stand there, or are we going to fight?"

Shocked out of my reverie, I glanced in Ethan's direction. The question in his wide-eyed gaze broke my heart.

"Different tactic," I whispered, hoping to win back both his trust and at least an ounce of confidence. "No high, no low, just together."

He shot me a crooked smile and a wink. "I can do that."

My heart may have skipped a beat, and it had little do with the fact that we were about to charge into the lion's maw.

No time to think about that now.

About Ethan.

About Seph.

About Maddox.

"Let's do this."

As one, Ethan and I rushed the Cardinal in as coordinated an assault as we could manage after only a month of working together. Mother and I had such intricate martial interplay down to a science, but with me and Ethan, it was at best a work in progress. I prayed to whoever might be listening that my limited training and the voices of generations of Delacroix women whispering in his mind would keep us from skewering each other in our mad attack.

The Cardinal's armor left our choice of target areas limited. The main plates guarding his torso had deflected five rounds from Father's gun and nothing short of Ethan's blades empowered with Neith's Light was likely to penetrate the crimson metal. That left the joints: his neck, shoulders, elbows, hips, and knees. I was more than capable of such precision, but I had a new partner, and that was going to require some modifications to my technique.

Ethan barreled straight ahead, his already-glowing blades flashing beneath the countless lights of the Square. His hold on the blades connoted that he meant to strike from above, so I focused on our enemy's lower half, hoping to land a well-placed blow to the bend in his leg and bring him to ground.

In a move we practiced for hours last week, Ethan slashed with both blades in a scissor strike aiming for our enemy's neck. The Cardinal deflected the longer blade with his armored forearm while the shorter blade glanced off the lower edge of his helmet. My own blade similarly clanged off the crimson-armored thigh of our opponent twice, my third strike kicked away by his steel-soled boot.

And then, it was his turn.

His movements a blur of metallic scarlet, the Cardinal shot both his fists at me like twin cobra strikes half a second apart. I deflected one blow with a quick forearm block that hurt like hell. The other punch, however, hit me center chest, driving me back several feet and forcing the air from my lungs. Winded as if I'd been hit with a sledgehammer, I stepped back into a balanced stance to catch my breath, leaving Ethan alone in the breach.

Not surprisingly, he did me proud.

Without a word, he launched into a barrage of coordinated strikes, at times bringing both blades to bear and at others feinting or probing with the first only to attack from the opposite side. His movements were fluid and lightning fast and all with the full power of the Light of Neith at his beck and call. I watched with awe and, admittedly, a tinge of envy as he executed what should have been my destined role: a valiant battle against a rogue Ascendant. How much of the prowess on display represented Ethan's inherent athleticism, how much my limited training efforts, and how much the influence of centuries of hard-won experience passed down via the women of the Delacroix line, I'd likely never know.

The Cardinal remained on the defensive for what seemed a long segment of the fight, blocking Ethan's various attacks with gauntlets and greaves, all while holding back from any form of counterattack. At first, it seemed that Ethan was actually driving back our crimson foe, but in the end, the Cardinal had only been biding his time and taking Ethan's measure.

"Not bad for your first month on the job, kid," the Cardinal mocked, "but I don't have all night to give you fighting lessons, so we're going to have to end this now."

A low whirring sound buzzed from the Cardinal's helmet followed a moment later by a piercing repeated chirp, the first of which shattered a nearby wine glass. More deafening than a jet engine taking off—my ears still rang from my little race down the runway with the Cardinal's private jet—and maddening in its echoing rhythm, the bursts of sound emanating from the Cardinal's armor sent Ethan's hands to his ears. His paired blades fell to the ground, dropped like a pair of hot potatoes forgotten in the midst of the sonic onslaught. The clatter of the two steel swords hitting the ground didn't even register as the Cardinal's latest attack drove away all other sound. Despite the agony, I managed to hold on to my katana with one hand even as I pressed one ear against my shoulder and held the heel of my free hand to the other.

For all the good it did. At this range, the blasts of sound hit with physical force.

"Stop," Ethan mouthed, the words shouted at the top of his lungs and yet unheard in the face of the deafening attack. "Please, stop."

A glance in Father's direction revealed he fared no better. Down on one knee, his weapon rested on the ground by his foot while he protected his own ears with the palms of his hands.

Maddox, on the other hand, lay unmoving despite the ear-splitting torture. I envied his unconscious state even as I lamented the vain hope that maybe he was playing possum and planning a counter attack against our shared foe who now stood over his crumpled form.

Though hard to admit, I had to face facts.

The Cardinal had the four of us at his mercy, and we weren't even his actual target.

The Greyhound, already compromised before we arrived, now crouched half a block away, his hands over his ears the same as the rest of us. Rumor had it that among his far-more-obvious talents, he could hear at least as well as his nom de guerre should suggest. Regardless of how much the Cardinal's sonic assault devastated the rest of us, I could only imagine the poor man's suffering in that moment.

With a dismissive salute, the Cardinal stepped over Maddox's still unmoving form and casually strolled past both Ethan and me, giving Father a sidelong perfunctory glance as he moved on the injured Greyhound. With no more haste than the masked madmen in the slasher movies that both Seph and Ethan love to watch, he stalked his prey. Without so much as a look back, he took position before the downed Greyhound and retrieved a short sword from a compartment of the miniature faux wing formed by his armored shoulder. The blade as red as the Cardinal's armor, I wondered briefly how much of the crimson of the metal was design and how much the blood of his prey.

Time slowed to a crawl as he raised the short blade above his head and prepared to strike. The Greyhound couldn't so much as raise an arm to defend himself as the pulsing high-pitched blasts continued to echo in the brick and glass canyon, the sonic barrage drowning out every other sound.

And then, a miracle.

The multitude of stringed lights over our heads went from pleasantly dim to outright blinding half a second before they began to burst three and five at a time as if they were popcorn in a microwave. Shattered glass flew in every direction, and I averted my eyes as the remaining strands exploded all at once. The air filled with static and ozone as a loud crackle like a lightning strike silenced the Cardinal's sonic blasters, leaving the Square simultaneously dark and eerily silent.

Lit now by only the half-moon overhead, the Cardinal looked about, his newly-stilted body language conveying anger and frustration. Whatever tech his armor used to facilitate his movements had clearly been disrupted by whatever caused the burst of electricity. His voice no longer amplified by his helmet's electronics but rather muffled by the steel, plastic, and rubber surrounding his head, his curses fell on deaf ears that still rang from his sonic attack.

With one last burst of defiance, the Greyhound leaped up from the ground and tackled the surprised Cardinal, sending his armored form to the asphalt before awkwardly loping away and disappearing around the corner of the Square. I briefly wondered if the Greyhound had been feigning his injuries, but the obvious truth was far more poignant. Despite being on his last legs, the legend had hung back and risked his very life to remain by our side in case things went south. No other explanation made any sense, and I swore as my Mother's daughter one thing: such bravery in the face of death would not be forgotten.

A part of me hoped that the Greyhound's tackle along with the Cardinal's compromised armor would keep him down long enough for us to gather for a counter-offensive, but as fortuitous as the electrical surge had been, it seemed the designer of our foe's tech had built in some fail-safes. Back on his feet in less time than it took to say it, the Cardinal glared at us through the smoked glass lenses of his helmet before stalking off after his prey.

Though I prayed for the Greyhound's safety, I found myself relieved that the Cardinal didn't make good on his threat to "feast" upon Maddox. As our enemy disappeared into the shadows at the far end of the Square, relief washed over me knowing that the coyote who used to hold the key to my heart was, at least for the moment, safe.

The fact that I still cared would be something I'd have to think about when everyone's life wasn't on the line.

I went to Ethan and helped him up from the ground. Dazed from the sonic onslaught, he did his best to offer me a smile, though his features remained filled with a mix of shame, anger, and pain. I retrieved the paired swords from the ground and returned them to his hands. Guessing neither of us would hear a word I said, I touched his cheek and smiled in an effort to show that despite our momentary defeat, he had earned my Mother's blades beyond any shadow of a doubt. He shook his head slowly in answer, and yet his gaze showed understanding that though we'd been bested, we'd also survived to fight another day. If there's one thing I respected about Ethan, it was that he never lost hope, even in the darkest moments.

Father stumbled over, the blasting sonic assault having left him drunk and off-balance. "Are you two okay?" he shouted, the words registering as muffled grunts.

"Other than the fact my brains have been turned to mush," Ethan bellowed with an ironic smile, "I think I'm fine."

I opted to save my voice and simply shot Father a quick nod. In turn, his eyes dropped to the ground where Maddox lay unmoving. Blood leaked from his visible ear, as he'd been closer to the Cardinal's sonic blasters than any of us. I sheathed my katana, knelt at his side, and placed my fingers at the angle of his jaw. Though faster than I liked, his pulse was strong and steady. At my touch, his chest rose and fell. His entire body shifted as if he were sleeping and in the midst of an unpleasant dream. Relief again washed away the inescapable dread that had built within me since the moment the Cardinal took Maddox by the throat.

It was one thing to wish someone dead in the heat of a break up and another altogether to nearly watch their life be snuffed out right before your eyes.

I rose from the ground, the steady ringing in my ears taking on a new quality. A flash of blue light at the far end of the street revealed the truth: an actual police siren was competing with the ringing in my ears I guessed would be keeping me company as I tried to sleep that night.

"We'd better go," Father shouted. "We're in no shape to face the police." He stooped by Maddox's supine form. "Ethan, give me a hand."

Ethan joined Father, and together they lifted Maddox from the ground and headed for the opposite end of the Square from where I'd seen the flashing blue lights. Though we were following in the Cardinal's footsteps, he was almost certainly long gone. I again prayed that the Greyhound had gotten enough of a head start to escape our shared foe.

Before we could take a dozen steps, however, a forgotten face emerged from one of the boutique shops across the way.

L.J., his ears covered with noise-canceling headphones, rushed toward us. "This way," he shouted, his words barely loud enough for me to appreciate their meaning over the combined tinnitus and police siren. "Hurry!"

Father and Ethan followed L.J. with Maddox slumped between them and me bringing up the rear as we passed beneath an arch marked with a fleur-de-lis and a French welcome under a large sign that read "KETTLE ARCADE." Straight ahead, a set of stairs led down to a place advertised as "GREEN RUSSELL," the sign barely visible in the muted darkness. A large arrow at the bottom of the stairs, all but spectral in the dim, pointed to the left, leading us to the door of an establishment that was most likely quite exclusive, at least on days when the lights were working.

When darkness falls, however, particularly unexpected darkness, I've found that many of society's rules tend to fall by the wayside.

We stole inside the establishment, the complementary aromas of beef and bourbon filling my nostrils as I took the lead. With the pitch black of the room interrupted only by the tiny candles that adorned each table, I felt my way through the darkness, leading our group to the closest thing to safety we were likely to find. A nearly invisible horseshoe-shaped booth sat empty at the back corner, likely vacated when everything went to hell. I directed Father and Ethan to help Maddox in from one side, and then L.J. and I slid in from the other.

I suspected our newest friend was one of the youngest patrons such an establishment had ever seen.

"All right." My voice dropped a few decibels, the ringing in my ears quieting at least a bit. "Looks like we're safe, at least for the moment."

Ethan helped Father get Maddox situated. The coyote who'd both won and broken my heart sat propped up, his head lolling to one side but his airway clear as we waited for him to come to.

"I don't know what caused that electrical surge," Ethan grunted, his words still barely audible despite the comparative silence of the bar, "but we're all lucky to be alive."

"Luck had nothing to do with it." L.J. took a sip from an ice water that had been left at the table. "I may not be much use with a sword, but if you need a well-placed EMP, I'm your man."

CHAPTER 16

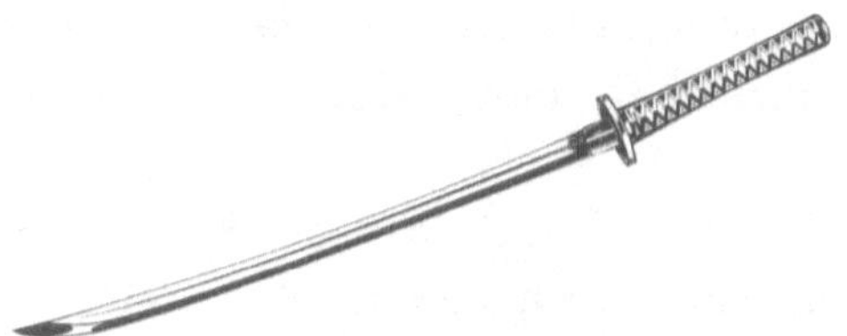

ELECTRIC AVENUE

Several long minutes passed before Maddox opened his eyes. The claxon going off between my ears had regressed to a low roar, and I could almost hear normally again. The lights had just come back up, revealing the trendy interior design of the pub we'd invaded and the staff trying to get everything moving again. Though the server in charge of our section kept shooting us the stink eye, as Seph called it, he accurately surmised that we were not in the mood for talk and wisely left us alone other than bringing a fresh round of ice water to the table.

"Maddox," I asked, "can you hear me?"

"Rosemary..." My name came out more grunt than actual speech. "You're alive." He ran a hand up his chest, his fingers resting at the bruises at his neck, no doubt tender to the touch after the Cardinal's assault. "Am I?"

"Alive and kicking," I answered, "or at least you will be soon, if I know you."

"Did anybody get the license tag of the Mack truck that hit me?" His hand continued up to his face, then his temple, and then his ear, the last of which had finally stopped dripping blood a few minutes before. "Someone should really get him off the road."

"Maybe you'll get that chance." I smiled at Maddox, unabashed. Nothing had changed between us, but there would be time to work out all the hurt and pain later. At the moment, what he needed was support and care, things I would have gladly given two years before and could still manage to convey regardless of my feelings. "But for now, rest."

Without asking, he pulled close to me like the wounded coyote he was and rested his head on my shoulder. My cheeks flushed with heat as I glanced in Ethan's direction. Ethan pretended not to notice, but his eyes avoided Maddox as his face blossomed with color as well. Father, in a show of measured restraint, merely crossed his arms and snorted through his nostrils without a word.

"What now?" L.J. asked. "We gonna sit here all day, or are we gonna do something?"

"What would you have us do, L.J.?" Father, who had been studying the door since we first sat around our impromptu table, narrowed his eyes at our young technomancer friend. "We were just trounced by the man we came to stop, though we outnumbered him four to one. Maddox can barely move, my best shots are ineffective against his armor, and even Ethan and Rosemary together were unable to slow him down. We lived to fight another day, fortunately, but going after the Cardinal again right now is suicide."

L.J. studied us all from his end of the table. "Maybe I'm missing something, but who was it that jumped in to save all your asses right here in Denver a month back when the Morning Angel's elementalists were trying to take Seph and kill all of you in the process?"

I lowered my head in shame. "The Greyhound."

We didn't even have to ask for his help. He appeared out of nowhere and rushed in to save our collective skins, at great risk to not only his personal safety but possibly his stature among the Ascendant.

I let out a plaintive sigh. "He did risk a lot for us."

"He risked everything, going up against a foursome of Ascendant who could have ended him to defend a bunch of people he'd never met. He could have let you all go down in flames, and he didn't. Now he's wounded and limping through a darkened city with an armored assassin hot on his tail." L.J.'s head tilted to one side. "Not to mention, I heard everything the Cardinal said. Are you all going to sit back and let an already unstoppable foe take on the power and prowess of an Ascendant legend?"

"Of course not." I pulled in a deep breath through my nose. "What would you have us do, L.J.?"

"I want you to get out there and fight this Cardinal asshole. Find the Greyhound and save him from a fate worse than death. Be the Daughter of Neith that I've been hearing about since I first figured out who and what I was."

Damn. The kid's a natural orator. And deep in his heart, a warrior.

But more important than any of that, he's right.

"Father, can you stay here with Maddox?"

He nodded, as if he'd decided his answer hours before. "We'll stay right here."

"What?" Maddox scowled. "I'm not staying here. I'm coming with you."

"No offense," Ethan jumped in, "but you were unconscious like five minutes ago." He looked on Maddox with something bordering on admiration. "No one wants to stay on the bench, but you'd better sit this one out."

Against my better judgment, I rested a hand atop Maddox's trembling fingers. "Look, we've all had a bit of time to lick our wounds. Stay here with Father for now. Gather your strength. We need you alive, understand?"

"We?" he asked.

"Father." I dodged the leading question completely. "Now that Maddox is awake, get him some food while Ethan and I go after the Cardinal."

"I said I'm not staying here." Maddox sat up straight and tried to push his way past Father's massive form, the futile effort bringing a groan of pain. "Please. I can fight."

"Another day, Maddox." I squeezed his hand, still beneath mine. "Stay here with Father and gather your strength. Regardless of the outcome of the next hour, I have a feeling we're going to need it soon."

"Fine." Maddox's eyes narrowed in frustration. "Just be careful out there." He shifted his attention to Ethan. "And you watch her back, Harkreader. Understand?"

"With my last breath, Maddox." Ethan gave him a quick nod. "We'll be back soon."

Ethan slid out his side of the horseshoe-shaped booth as I raised an eyebrow at L.J.

"You want me to go kick some ass, kid, you're going to have to let me out."

"Let's go, then." L.J. scooted to his left and stood next to Ethan. "I'm ready."

"What?" I came to my feet as well. "You can't go out there with us. He'll kill you."

"If it weren't for me, the Cardinal would have already killed all of you." He puffed up his chest. "Like I told you before Maddox woke up, I may not be able to put a direct whammy on the Cardinal's armor —it's been locked down much like what I did for Seph's house by a technomancer that's at least as good as me—but there's a lot I can do, and you're going out there down a couple of warm bodies." L.J. looked to Father for support. "Please, Mr. Delacroix. Tell them. Tell them I can help."

I locked gazes with Father, though his steady gaze revealed his answer before I could even ask the question.

"I'm sorry, Rosemary, but L.J. is right. You need him out there. Maddox is in no shape to fight, and I'm not sure if my bullets even scratched the paint on the Cardinal's armor." He shook his head. "So far, he's the only one of us who has so much as slowed this murderer down. Honestly, I wouldn't go out there without him."

"Glad that's settled." L.J. crossed his arms, having won the argument, though trepidation shone in his young eyes. "Shall we?"

"Let's go. We'll come up with a plan on the way." I turned for the door with Ethan on one side and L.J. on the other. Mother would have chided me for moving forward without a clear path, and yet, L.J. was right. Regardless of the odds or even the outcome, we owed it to the Greyhound to at least try.

"Oy," our server said with a British accent I wasn't sure was authentic or mere affectation, "you lot have been occupying that booth for the better part of an hour and now you're going to take off without even ordering?"

Father pulled his wallet from inside his jacket, whipped out his fanciest credit card, and rested it on the center of the table. "Unfortunately, my daughter and her friends have to go, but the lad and I will take a slab of ribs each with all the trimmings." He shot Maddox a sidelong glance. "I suspect my young friend here is quite ravenous." Father's eyes narrowed. "Please be sure to add a generous tip of your choosing to the tab, if you will."

The server's demeanor shifted immediately. "Excellent, sir." He turned on one heel and walked away.

Alone again, Father met my gaze one last time before we headed out. "Take care, Rosemary." His gaze shifted to Ethan. "And like Maddox said, you watch after my daughter, Mr. Harkreader."

"Fear not, Mr. Delacroix. I've got this."

"We've got this," L.J. said with a nervous smile. "But one last request?"

"Of course." I studied his mercurial features, at once brave and terrified. "And that would be?"

"Can the both of you watch my back as well?"

Ethan, L.J., and I emerged from our makeshift underground bunker and stepped out onto Larimer Square. Though no longer plunged into darkness, the absence of the multiple strings of overhanging lights left the area in a strange twilight state. Vacated and as silent as a city at night can be, one thing was clear: both the Greyhound and the Cardinal were long gone.

"How the hell are we supposed to find either of them?" Ethan asked before I could vocalize the same. "Any thoughts?"

"We follow the way they went?" I racked my brain for ideas. "Try to guess which way a wounded man would go to evade his pursuer?"

"Too many variables." L.J. stepped forward. "Fortunately, though I have no way to track the Greyhound, I think I may know how to find the Cardinal."

"You're telling us this now?" Ethan asked.

"I wasn't sure before we arrived in Denver, and until we were ready to pursue, it was kind of a moot point."

"It's okay, L.J." I shot Ethan a silencing glance. "What have you got?"

"Before, when all of you were under attack, I was doing everything I could to infiltrate the Cardinal armor's computer systems to shut it down, but like I was saying back in the restaurant, that tech has been locked down tight by his technomancer. I can't even get a toe hold to climb that particular mountain."

"All right," Ethan said, calmer than before. "How does this help us?"

"In a way, it's like how I found Larimer Square. Tons of tech in this town is blocked by various security measures, firewalls, etc., both human and otherwise, but only one is locked down as tight as the Cardinal's red suit." A hint of smile L.J.'s face. "His tech may be impenetrable."

"But that doesn't make it invisible?" I asked.

"I can sense every piece of technology in the vicinity out to a mile or so, kind of like a bloodhound can detect scents." His smile faded into a thoughtful grimace even as his eyes narrowed in concentration. "And what I can detect, for the most part, I can manipulate."

"Except for one, I'm guessing." Ethan's features blossomed with understanding.

"An enormous room full of doors, and I can open most of them. Find the one I can't—"

"And then we go there and knock it down." I patted L.J.'s shoulder. "Good job, kid."

"*Kid...*" Ethan said. "That's what the Cardinal called me when we faced off. Like he knows me or something."

"Forget it, Ethan." I shook my head. "He was just trying to get under your skin."

"It was more than simply a taunt, though. It was the way he said it. So familiar."

"The only thing his voice reminds me of is James Earl Jones screaming at all the stormtroopers to 'Tear this ship apart until you've found those plans.'" A tremble overtook L.J.'s body. "At least Vader wanted the passengers alive."

"I know you're scared, L.J., but like you said, the Greyhound needs us. Reach out with whatever you have and see if you can get a hint as to where we should start."

Without another word, L.J.'s eyes slid shut. An audible hum I wasn't exactly sure was coming from his vocal cords filled the air. His arms rose slowly out to either side, as if he were a satellite dish feeling for a signal from the sky. Slowly he spun counterclockwise until he faced the direction both Greyhound and Cardinal had fled and pointed due north.

"That way." He waved into the distance. "There are multiple nodes of technology all over the city against which my powers have been blocked, but only one of them is currently on the move." He took off at a run. "Let's go."

"What's that song say?" Ethan raised an eyebrow. "Teach them well and let them lead the way?"

"I have no idea, Ethan. You're the walking music encyclopedia." I took off after L.J. with Ethan close at my side. "Stay sharp, understand?"

"Of course," he got out between breaths as he jogged beside me. "You know, one thing we haven't discussed?"

"The fact that we have no plan and don't have the first idea about how to change the outcome of a fight we just fought and lost an hour ago?"

"Precisely."

"Yeah." I let fly a frustrated grunt. "I was thinking the same thing."

"I mean, it's not exactly a suicide run." Ethan took the lead with those long strides of his. "With L.J. with us, maybe we have a chance?"

"You two need to work on your pep talk skills." L.J., already huffing and puffing as we caught up to him, looked left and right at each of us. "This is the part where the coach pulls everyone in at halftime and gives the big speech about how they're going to turn it around and win, not how they're going to get their asses beat in the second half."

"Life isn't a football movie, L.J." Ethan grunted as he took point in our trio of runners. "Just keeping it real."

At the teen's slumped shoulders, I slowed to run alongside him. "It's like you said back in the restaurant. We fight today because it's the right thing to do, and believe me, we will fight, as long and as hard as we can." My mother's words, leaving my mouth as if they were my own, sent chills down my spine. "And then, as with every day of our lives, what will be will be."

"But it's not every day that you go up against a psycho in impenetrable battle armor with a penchant for slaying other Ascendant and stealing their souls, right?"

"There is that, kiddo." A pang hit my chest, whether from the run or the comment, I wasn't sure. "Wish I knew what else I could say."

Over the next block, L.J.'s pace continued to slow. Though younger than Ethan and me, it was clear that most of the running he did involved a video game controller and a screen. With neither the endurance of eighteen years of daily training nor the benefit of Ethan's long legs, natural athleticism, and a month of rigorous conditioning courtesy of yours truly, he was doing his best. I prayed that would be enough.

"You all right?"

"I'll be fine," he huffed. "Half a block to go."

I sucked in a breath. "Till we catch up to the Cardinal?"

"No," L.J. answered, "till I get us some wheels."

Half a block later, we all stopped by a short white car with a long orange stripe down its side and numerous sophisticated looking cameras atop its roof.

"One car," L.J. said between puffs, "no waiting."

"This is one of those self-driving cars," Ethan said, crinkling his nose. "You sure this is the safest thing you can find?"

"Safer than you driving," L.J. answered, "statistically speaking of course." He let out a quick laugh. "Not to mention, it's a little late to be throwing safety concerns into the mix, don't you think?"

"Fair point." I stepped to the car and unsuccessfully tried the door. "Can you get us in?"

"Of course I can." L.J. rapped three times at the window and with a simple, "Open Sesame," pulled the same handle and opened the door with a deep bow. "Your chariot awaits, milady."

Huh. A bit of a charmer in there, it would seem.

Ethan climbed into the back, I slid into the passenger seat, and L.J. sat himself in the driver's seat where a standard steering wheel and pedals awaited.

"So, you can drive this thing the way you would any other car?" Ethan asked.

"You could"—L.J.'s eyes slid closed—"but I picked this car for a reason."

All at once, the car locks engaged, the engine roared to life, and the tires squalled as we hit the road with the literal pedal to the metal and L.J.'s eyes screwed shut.

"What the hell are you doing?" Ethan shouted as we weaved in and out of traffic like a professional quarterback facing a team of sixth graders. "You're going to get us killed!"

"Are you kidding?" L.J. laughed, clearly having the time of his life. "I can see in literally every direction and know to the centimeter the distance between us and every car around us." A wide grin stretched across his face. "No blind spots in this car."

"Okay." Ethan actually looked a little green, but I suspected he would be fine as soon as we stopped. "Where the hell are you taking us, anyway?"

"Let's see." L.J. went silent as he focused not only discerning our destination but also on keeping the three of us alive at breakneck speed. "Ah. Assuming the Cardinal is as good a tracker as he is a fighter, it looks like the Greyhound fled to a place where he could at least count on being able to see his enemy coming."

"And that would be...?" I asked

"You'll see soon enough," he answered, his tone as no-nonsense as Father's. "We're almost there."

Half a dozen more lefts and rights and, as promised, we arrived. Before us rose a three-story brick structure, the facade for an intricate metallic structure that rose just beyond the wall. A pair of large gates led inside, and though the ground before us was dark, the entire area was backlit by halogen lights that erased the stars from the sky with a yellow haze. A bronze statue of a baseball player with a bat thrown across his shoulder stood at the midpoint between the two doors as if acting as a silent guardian. Above him, on either side of an enormous round analog clock face marked with Roman numerals, the words "COORS FIELD" shone down.

"A baseball field," I murmured.

"Yep," L.J. whispered as he and I exited the car, "the home of the Colorado Rockies."

"Now, all we have to do is track down a wounded legend in a deserted ballpark that covers several city blocks and get to him before an unstoppable assassin finds and kills him, becoming even more unstoppable in the process." Ethan clambered from the back seat and closed the passenger door behind him. "Better hope we knock this one out of the park."

CHAPTER 17

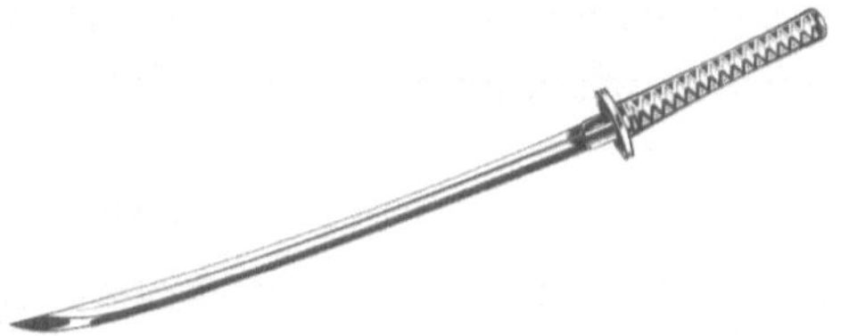

CENTERFIELD

"You're sure they're inside?" I asked, directing a glance through the fence at the darkened ballpark. "Don't want to get involved in breaking and entering unless we know for sure."

"I'm not sure about our injured friend," L.J. answered, "but the big black blob of tech I can't interact with is somewhere straight ahead." His face, only half-visible beneath the light of the nearest streetlamp, clouded over. "And something else. Like a thunderstorm along the technosphere."

"The technosphere?" Ethan asked.

"Much like the planetary ecosphere made up of all life on Earth, the technosphere is composed of every piece of tech on the globe. From the simplest pocket calculator to the biggest data center in the world, and everything in between, the technosphere is how I see the world. I can't perceive it all at once—that would drive anyone insane —but like you see brick, concrete, and the wrought iron fence surrounding this place? I see wires, transistors, microchips, the electrical pulse of everything around me." He returned his attention to me. "Oh, and as for *breaking* and entering, we can simply do the latter."

At a simple snap of his fingers, the nearest gate opened as if a ghost were beckoning us to enter. The silent blackness on the other side with all its new dangers and horror gave me momentary pause. And then, Ethan stepped forward and summoned what he's brought to every situation we've encountered since our first meeting.

Light.

Mother's paired blades glowed like twin rods of lit magnesium, filling the area with sufficient luminescence for us to see a block or so in every direction before Ethan brought the brilliance down to a less blinding level.

"Sorry," he muttered, "I was going for torch, not beacon."

"It's all right," I answered quietly, blinking in an effort to get my eyes readjusted to the darkness. "At least we know our immediate surroundings seem to be safe."

A part of me bristled. Such an artless show of power announced our presence without any hint of subtlety. Both Mother and Father had hammered home a hundred times the incalculable advantage of the element of surprise, and any possibility of that had just evaporated.

On the other hand, two encounters was all it had taken for me to understand that the Cardinal, regardless of any underlying weaknesses we hoped he might possess, was unlikely to ever find himself on the receiving end of a surprise attack.

With a deep cleansing breath, I called upon every bit of training, insight, and perception Mother had instilled in me over my twenty-one years in an effort to ensure it was not we who were caught unawares and stepped through the open gate.

"Any ideas?" I asked.

L.J. considered for a moment. "Let me see if I can break into the closed circuit tv cameras and take a look around."

"The field may be lit," Ethan said, "but everything out here is dark. You think you'll be able to see anything?"

"Let him try, Ethan," I whispered. "He got us here, didn't he? Let L.J. see what he can do, and we'll take it from there."

"All right." Ethan crossed the pair of glowing blades before his chest, and their light combined with the streetlamps outside and the regularly spaced LEDs along the stadium walls provided sufficient illumination to keep the area from being pitch black. Still, I had no idea what the cameras were going to pick up besides three people breaking and entering through the main gate armed with a pair of glowing Middle Eastern blades, a samurai sword, and a backpack full of whatever a technomancer brings on a field trip.

"Got anything, L.J.?" I asked after a pause. "Any sign of—"

"Quiet," he grunted, and then immediately backpedaled. "Sorry, navigating a system this big requires a bit of concentration."

"Sorry." I stepped back, palms out. "Do what you've got to do."

L.J. stretched his arms out to either side again. His eyes slid closed, and a low hum escaped his lips as if he were brimming with electricity. But that wasn't it at all. He was simply humming a song we'd heard on the radio on the way here, one of his "faves," I believe.

Recognizing he was completely vulnerable standing in the darkness with his eyes shut to any world but that of wires and electricity, I stepped quietly to one side of our resident technomancer, katana raised, and motioned for Ethan to guard his opposite flank. And that's where we remained for the better part of three minutes during which L.J. changed up his subvocal humming, opting for a song from a generation or two earlier. One of the more popular songs from Father's favorite station on the satellite radio, I knew the tune by heart, if not the words. A song of teenage rock and roll dreams and young love lost, I'd always liked the singer's voice: just the right mix of clarity and grittiness to give the story within the song the raspy edge it needed.

Apparently the tune was one of Ethan's favorites too, a fact made evident by his tapping foot as L.J. continued the quiet melody.

The two of them, my boys of summer.

"I've got something," L.J. said, interrupting my brief reverie, "though neither of you are going to like it."

"What is it?" Ethan asked.

L.J. scanned the area, his gaze stopping on a beverage station with several darkened big screen monitors used to display prices for various drinks and snacks. He stretched out a hand like a wizard from a storybook and after a couple pops of static electricity, the screen came to life with a horrific scene.

At the center of the outfield wall, the Greyhound stood hunched over beneath the bright lights of Coors Field.

And striding toward him, strangely nonchalant and focused at the same time, came the Cardinal, the mechanics of his armor clearly back at a hundred percent.

Viewed from the Greyhound's left, the images L.J. was intercepting must have come from one of the dozens of security cameras that kept tabs on the stadium's comings and goings every night. I guessed that he'd sought a place to hide where he could watch his own back and couldn't be caught unawares, but looking at him now, eyes wide and nostrils flaring, he appeared very much the proverbial cornered dog.

"Come on," Ethan shouted as he raced deeper into the darkness, "he needs us."

The last thing I saw before I took off after him was the silent image of paired two-foot-long crimson blades sliding out from within the Cardinal's gauntlets, completing the avian appearance of his crimson armor with razor sharp wing tips that had almost certainly tasted blood in many a fight.

We raced up the stadium concourse and through the nearest gate leading to the seats and the field itself. Within seconds, we emerged beneath the thousands of lights illuminating the grassy diamond as if it were midday. The entire facility abandoned but for the two figures at the far end of the field, the eeriness of the space hit me full force.

Mother once told me the word for the emotion: kenopsia, the strange feeling of entering a usually bustling space when no one was there. Mother always knew the best words.

The preternatural sensation was only compounded by the fact that we'd soon be witnessing a murder if things didn't go significantly better than the last time we faced this exact situation. Which was, by my count, three hours ago.

"So, what are we going to do different this time?" Ethan asked between breaths as we sprinted down the concrete stairs between the rows of seats—the boy's a mind reader sometimes. "Only difference is that Captain Redbird out there gets to see us coming from farther away."

"And we're down both Father and Maddox this time." I glanced back to find an exhausted L.J. trailing us and getting farther behind with every step. If he stuck around long term, we were going to have to work on his cardiovascular endurance, but that was a problem for another day. "Hopefully, our resident technomancer will think of something."

"The Cardinal seems to be back in full swing, and if he's had a chance to connect with his technomancer since we saw him last, I'm betting L.J.'s EMP trick isn't going to work twice."

As much as I hated to admit it, Ethan was right. We couldn't count on any particular strategy being effective more than once. The Cardinal, if nothing else, seemed both prepared and adaptable, perhaps even more so than me, with state-of-the-art tech to back it up.

Mother would have known what to do. Meanwhile, I was making it up as we went along.

Maybe if I possessed the wisdom of centuries currently floating around inside Ethan's head, I'd have felt more confident and assured in my actions, but after our near defeat before, I'd never felt more like a fake, a pale reflection of my Mother, undeserving of my stolen inheritance.

Perhaps the Light of Neith chose the better vessel after all.

"No time for any of that talk, Rosemary," I grumbled. "Time to fight."

As we hit the bottom of the steps, Ethan and I vaulted the wall overlooking first base and took off across the closely mown grass of right field, heading straight for the miniature forest of pines the stadium designers had built at the apex of the outfield beyond the back wall. The Greyhound stood his ground as the Cardinal bore down on him, ready to stand and fight for better or for worse.

With a good two hundred feet left in our race to defend the man who'd saved us all a month before, I prayed it wasn't the last decision he'd ever make.

"Think L.J. can pull another miracle out of his hat?" Ethan asked between huffing breaths. "Otherwise, it's you and me against that psycho."

"Save your wind," I grunted. "We're going to need it."

As we covered the last fifty yards between us and the one-sided melee, my heart sunk with each not-nearly-fast-enough step. Despite the Greyhound's considerable strength, superhuman reflexes, and unparalleled prowess, the Cardinal dominated the battle, his stolen power and technological edge against the Greyhound's bare fists leaving little doubt as to the outcome. We were close enough to see the beads of sweat coursing down the Greyhound's face when the deciding blow was dealt, a vicious slash of the Cardinal's wing-blade across his broad chest that tore both cloth and flesh, leaving a line of bright scarlet in its wake.

The Greyhound dropped to one knee, grunting in pain and panting with exhaustion, but as the Cardinal drove his bladed gauntlet straight at his quarry's face, the Greyhound yet again proved his mettle in battle. Both of his massive hands shot out and caught the Cardinal's gauntlet on either side, stopping the tip of the blade an inch from his neck.

Unfortunately, the Cardinal understood all too well a lesson Mother taught me at a very young age: the reason why she always carried two blades.

The Cardinal swung his other arm in a downward arc and opened the Greyhound's shoulder with a gout of blood, sending the mountain of muscle to the grassy ground.

"No!" I screamed, as I crossed the last few feet between me and our shared enemy. "Don't!"

"Scream all you want, girl." The Cardinal pulled back his fist from the Greyhound's chest and then drove the tip of his wing-blade into the man's chest with a sickening *shunk*. "Despite your best efforts, the night is mine, and now, I shall be taking my reward."

The Greyhound turned his head and looked at me, sadness and

anger and a touch of fear in his eyes as a trail of crimson tracked its way from the corner of his mouth to drip onto the manicured grass.

"It's over for me," he gurgled, his lips wet with blood. "Save yourselves before..." The last word came out as a wet hiss as the Greyhound finally succumbed.

"No!" I cried out again. "No..."

"You bastard!" Ethan launched himself at the Cardinal. "Get away from him."

"I'd be careful with name-calling, Harkreader." The Cardinal withdrew his blade from the Greyhound's ribcage and parried a trio of blows from Ethan's glowing paired swords before landing a kick center-chest and sending him winded and sprawling to the ground. "You never know when your words might circle back to haunt you." And with that he directed a sweeping gesture at Ethan, the arc of his blade ending with its tip pointed directly at me. "And now, I highly recommend you both stand back. What comes next is often dramatic, and with the passing of an Ascendant of such status, all bets are off."

"What are you talking about?" I asked.

"Oh, how little you know for someone who has spent their entire life training to police my kind." The Cardinal positioned himself above the Greyhound's crumpled form, arms held wide. "Regardless of what their specific nature allows them to do, each and every Ascendant carries within them the spark that sets them apart from the rest of humanity. In some, the spark remains just that, and then there are others who learn to fan what they've been given into an *inferno* of near godlike power."

At the word, the white light surrounding Ethan's blades took on the appearance of blinding white flame, if only for the briefest of moments. The Cardinal, his attention focused on me, didn't seem to notice, and even I wondered if I had imagined the entire thing.

"At the moment of their death, the flame of their Ascendance is not extinguished but instead returns to the universe from which it came." I could almost imagine the wicked grin spreading behind the red and black helmet facade. "And here I am, ready to warm my hands by the fire."

"You're a murderer," Ethan seethed. "That's all you are."

"Omelets and eggs, boy. Omelets and eggs."

The Greyhound's body shimmered with a golden glow, and in response, the Cardinal threw his head back in victory. The warm radiance emanating from the sprawled body of the man who leaped into the breach to save us all in Denver grew in brightness until it outshone even the countless lights illuminating the stadium. With a burst of brilliance and a rush of air like a localized hurricane, the golden shimmer leaped from the Greyhound's body like a swarm of tiny insects and circled the Cardinal's armored form as if intending to devour him whole. The miniature cyclone of golden light lasted but a few seconds before flowing into the Cardinal with a crackle of electricity followed by a deafening thunderclap. And then, without warning, both the golden glow and every light in the stadium extinguished at once, leaving Ethan and me blind in the darkness, as vulnerable as babes.

The pitch black lasted but a few seconds as the lights above returned to life, dim at first but back up to their full brightness in no time at all.

At our feet lay the Greyhound's body, still and lifeless.

And the Cardinal? He was gone, the faint imprint of his armored boots in the grass the only evidence he'd been there at all.

Aside from the body of his victim, of course.

"Is he..." Ethan stared at the Greyhounds twisted frame. "You know..."

"I believe so." I stepped forward. "Unless I'm wrong about what we just saw."

Like a man possessed, Ethan rushed to the Greyhound's side and knelt by his lifeless form. Bringing both of Mother's blades to bear, he crossed them over the Greyhound's unmoving chest, and with a deep breath, allowed his eyes to slide closed. The dim silver glow of each blade grew in intensity with each passing second, the intersection of shining steel brighter than burning phosphorus, all leading to undeniable confirmation of what I'd seen before.

There, where the two swords that until a month ago had been fated for my hands met, a flame of silver-white sprung to life, blinding in its intensity, and yet I found it impossible to look away from the tiny inferno's indescribable beauty.

The silver flame grew and grew until each of the two blades were engulfed in white fire. Brighter and brighter, the crossed conflagration of silver-white blazed, and then, just when it appeared that Ethan himself might burst into flame, the silver fire poured down onto the Greyhound's body like liquid light.

I had no idea what was happening, but the entire spectacle was unlike anything I'd ever seen, even after all my years of training under Mother's watchful eye. I had never dreamed that Mother had kept secrets from me, at least not when it came to my destined role. What else didn't I know? And why had details of such importance been left out of my nearly two decades of preparation?

My mind filled with more questions than ever, one on top of the next, and though I had no idea where to start, I swore in that moment that I would discover the truth to each and every one.

For me.

For Ethan.

For us all.

CHAPTER 18

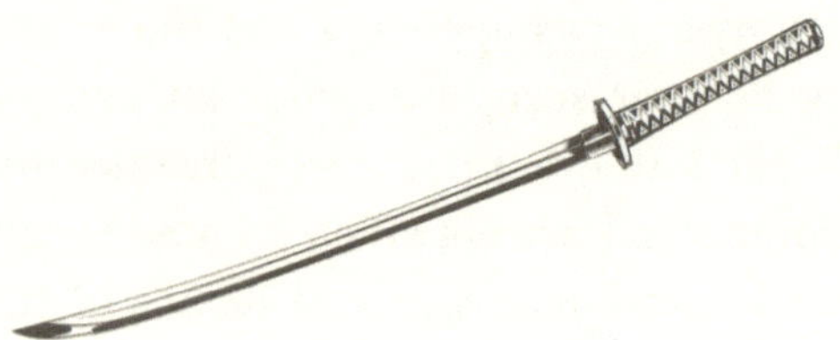

THE UNFORGETTABLE FIRE

Ethan's entire body convulsed as if he held a live wire rather than a pair of ancient swords, though to be fair, those same ancient swords were currently channeling mystic white fire from God knew where. A torrential flood of silver-white power like something straight out of the Old Testament, the fire fell upon the Greyhound's crumpled form, but rather than immolating his corpse, the mysterious flame seemed to flow into him—his eyes, his ears, his mouth—animating his limbs as if the fallen giant were suddenly a puppet on strings.

For a moment, I wondered if the fire pouring from Mother's— Ethan's blades might somehow revive the legend that lay on the manicured grass of the baseball stadium's outfield, but in the end, the flame extinguished, the Greyhound's form again went limp and lifeless, and Ethan dropped to his knees, spent.

"It's no use." Ethan slumped forward. "He's gone."

Casting my eyes left, right, up, and down to make sure the

Cardinal wasn't circling back around for Round Three, I stole to Ethan's side and knelt by him.

"You were trying to save him?" I asked.

"I don't know what I was doing." He stared up at me from the corner of his vision. "Something told me to hold the swords crossed, to stand there, to maintain the flame or whatever that was. I did exactly what the little voice inside my head told me to do…" His voice trailed off as his gaze returned to the ground. "Until I couldn't."

I placed two fingers beneath the angle of the Greyhound's bloodied jaw and checked for a pulse. For half a minute, I didn't move a muscle other than my eyes as I worked to maintain situational awareness even as I prayed to whomever would listen that my fingertips might register even the feeblest sign of life.

But no. Ethan was right. The Greyhound, already old the day my grandmother was born, was lost to us forever.

And God only knew how many more had gone before him at the hands of this madman.

"That fucking vampire," Ethan spat. "He killed him."

"I'm sorry." I rested a hand at his shoulder. "We both did everything we could to prevent that outcome."

"And we failed." Ethan drove his fist into the grass. "Now we're down a powerful ally and friend, and unless I'm missing something, our enemy just added the Greyhound's power, strength, and speed to his own." He glared up at me again. "Like the bastard wasn't already hell on wheels."

I leaned back and sat on the grass by Ethan and draped my arm across his shoulders. Our closeness felt a bit strange, but in that moment, Ethan needed a friend.

Yeah, that's it. A friend.

"I've got to know," Ethan asked. "Is that what it looked like? You know…when me and your mother…"

"Mother?" I asked. "What are you talking about?"

"The Greyhound's life force, or whatever that was we saw, left him the moment he died and went into that creep." Ethan shook his head slowly. "I want to be angry about what he did, but I can't help but think that's exactly what I did by mistake when your mom died." He met my gaze again, his rage fading into sadness. "I stole what wasn't meant for me and made a bad situation far worse."

My heart ached at his words. "What happened with you and Mother is nothing like what the Cardinal just did."

"Isn't it?"

"You didn't kill anyone, Ethan. You were trying to save her." I pulled him closer to me, his arm warm against my side. "And for that, I am forever grateful." I sucked in a breath of air. The scent of Ethan's hair mixed with the smell of freshly mown grass left my head spinning. "And as for making the situation worse? You have to know there's no one I'd rather be stuck with in all of this than you."

He ground his teeth. "If you had the power or Light or whatever instead of me, you'd have known what to do. Whatever that white fire was, you would have made it work. Hell, if you were the Daughter of Neith instead of whatever the hell I'm supposed to be, the Cardinal might never have put down the Greyhound in the first place." He rose from the ground, brushing off my arm as if my attentions were undeserved. "I'm trying and trying and trying with everything I've got, and yet all I've managed to do since the latest big bad hit town is let him get away with Seph, watch helplessly as he beat the snot out of Maddox, and now, with all the chips down, I've screwed up saving the Greyhound not once, but twice."

"Twice?" I asked.

"I couldn't stop the Cardinal from killing him, and then I couldn't bring him back despite the fact my every instinct screamed I was supposed to do just that."

"If it makes you feel any better, I didn't even know what you did with the fire was a possibility."

Ethan furrowed his brow. "Your mother never did that?"

"Not to my knowledge. She never told me about any sort of abilities beyond what we've been working on in training, and I certainly never saw her summon magical fire from crossed steel." I put on a subtle smile. "That was a cool trick, even if it didn't end up being enough to bring back our friend."

"That's just it, Rosemary." Ethan stalked off. "I'm not sure if you noticed, but we only survived everything a month ago because no less than three major players among the Ascendant showed up to call off the bad guys. Without their help that night..." He hung his head. "And today? One screw up after another. I'm not sure if I'll ever be ready at this rate."

"And with every death, the Cardinal only grows stronger." L.J. approached from the direction of second base, mere feet away from where we stood. I'd been so focused on Ethan's pain and watching the sky for any sign of the Cardinal that he'd effectively gotten the drop on me. Mother would have assigned an additional hundred pushups for such a mistake.

Something to add to tomorrow morning's workout, I suppose.

Ethan ran a sleeve across his eyes, unwilling to let L.J. see the emotion welling at their corners, and slid into his practiced smile.

"You doing all right, kid?"

"Better than you two," L.J. answered. "I watched the whole thing on the closed circuit."

"And?" Ethan asked.

"To be honest, I don't know what else you were supposed to do. This Cardinal is serious bad news, and that's before you put him in an Iron Man suit and equip him with sonic blasters that can scramble your brain like an egg."

"That little black out," I asked, "I'm guessing that wasn't you?"

L.J. shook his head. "Call me crazy, but it seems you two aren't the only ones who brought their technomancer to this party." His dark eyes scanned the lights around the periphery of the stadium. "I got the lights back up and running as fast as the electrical lines and bulbs would allow, but in all the hubbub, both Big Red and his tech support seem to have flown the coop." L.J. sniffed at the air, his eyes tracing a path in the sky that only he seemed able to see. "Literally, it would appear."

"As far as we know, it's the suit that lets him fly, right?" I asked. "Now that you've seen him up close and personal, is that still what you think?"

"As best as I can tell," L.J. answered. "Definitely a shift in the sounds of his armor at takeoff, though I can't rule out some sort of Ascendant ability playing a part." He shivered. "Especially if he's taken as many Ascendant lives as we suspect. I've never heard of simple flight, mass control, or gravity manipulation being an Ascendant thing, but there are way more of us than anyone really knows."

"He's certainly full of surprises," Ethan whispered.

L.J.'s dark eyebrow rose to meet his turquoise bangs. "Says the man who just summoned white fire out of two hunks of sharpened steel simply by thinking about it."

Ethan actually chuckled at that. "So, he's super strong, super fast, can fly, can control shadows, and can take the abilities of anyone he can defeat, not to mention has a technomancer who is likely already creating counter measures against everything we've got."

"At least we share that advantage." I patted L.J.'s shoulder. "Great job tonight, L.J."

"I'm doing all I can." L.J. shook his head. "I suspect the Cardinal's technomancer has racked up a few more merit badges than me."

"Maybe," Ethan said. "If their person can make someone fly though, can you?"

"Theoretically, it's possible, but my talent has always been more manipulating existing tech than creating stuff from scratch." He paused, his eyes shifting left and right in silent calculation. "There's electromagnetic manipulation, gravimetric pulses, and various forms of propulsion, some quieter than others. Then there's how you power the thing. Big screen superheroes may be able to build an infinite energy source in a cave in the Middle East with nothing but scrap parts, but out here in the real world, it's not so easy." L.J. shoved his hands in his pockets. "Unfortunately, I'm like a fifth level wizard, which is nothing to sneeze at, but this guy working for the Cardinal? He's truly next level."

"So," I tried to interject a joke, "sixth?"

Both L.J. and Ethan shot me the same withering stare.

Note to self: leave the one-liners to Ethan.

"Basically," L.J. continued as if I hadn't spoken, "besides the capability almost certainly being a part of the suit, I don't have any idea how the technomancer has rigged Big Red to be able to fly around like he's on wires." His wry smile returned. "Except for one thing."

"And that would be?" Ethan tilted his head to one side, his expression a mix of curiosity and annoyance.

"Whatever technology they're using, it leaves a trail." L.J. rubbed at the wispy hairs at his chin. "Or, at least like with everything else so far, an absence of one."

"Like before?" I asked, my tone so bright, it surprised even me. "When you were able to track him here?"

"So far, our one ace in the hole seems to be that our friend the Cardinal thinks he's the only one with a technomancer wide receiver on the team." At Ethan's incredulous raised eyebrow, L.J. added, "So I know D&D *and* football. Nothing wrong with being multifaceted."

"Nothing at all." My gaze went skyward. "So, which way did he go?"

L.J.'s eyes traced an invisible path in the sky. "East," his eyelids fluttered, as if his brain were downloading a few gigabytes of data, "toward the airport."

"He needs another plane," Ethan said. "If that's correct, that would suggest the armor's flight range is limited."

"And may only be able to support so much weight," I added. "I mean, he didn't take Seph with him when he flew off yesterday. He had her in his grasp and then left her behind."

"Which begs a question I've been trying to figure out since we hit Denver." Ethan's eyes filled with concern. "If this guy is killing Ascendant and stealing their life force and power—" Ethan started.

"Then why is Seph still breathing?" I finished.

A distant siren filled the air, soon followed by another.

"Shit," Ethan grumbled. "*Now* the police show up."

"Another problem no one has taken the time to figure out," L.J. said. "What are we supposed to do with a three-hundred-pound corpse in the middle of a professional baseball field?" He hung his head, ashamed at the brusqueness of his words. "With all due respect to the recently departed, of course."

"Of course." I looked to Ethan. "L.J.'s got a point. We're both in tip-top shape, but there's no way even with all three of us working together that we could move the Greyhound's body before this place is crawling with police."

"So," Ethan's face screwed into a disgusted grimace, "we leave him here to rot?"

"The authorities will get him to the coroner. We can check on what happened later. For now, though, we don't do anyone any good if we get caught out here beneath ten-thousand lights standing over a dead body."

"Agreed." Ethan shot a sidelong glance at L.J. "Any thoughts on how to evade the police while we get the hell out of here?"

"Actually, I'm two steps ahead of you on that one." L.J. spun in a slow circle, eyes closed. "I redirected all the various closed-circuit signals to pipe straight into me rather than the central video repository soon after we arrived, so there shouldn't be any visual evidence we were ever here."

"That's convenient," Ethan said.

"And with the feed of all those cameras in my head," L.J. continued, "I should be able to lead us out of here without any run-ins with the police."

"Should?" I asked.

"Hey," L.J. grumbled, "unless there's some master plan you two failed to tell me about, I got the impression that all of us were just making this up as we went along."

"Forgive me." I raised my hands before me and offered an apologetic smile. "I don't think I can handle another surprise tonight."

"Not all surprises are necessarily bad." Lady Day appeared atop the wall that separated the well-tended grass from the even-better-tended park that lay beyond centerfield. Her waist-length locks of black tied up in a makeshift ponytail, she had changed outfits and now sported a far more urban appearance of torn jeans, graphic tee, and dark shades, though the spotless white designer sneakers remained on her feet. "I'm somewhat responsible for this predicament in which you find yourselves embroiled. Please allow me to aid you all before you end up either in a jail cell, or worse, on the run from the law." She looked left and right. "Wait. Where are the other two of your party?" She fixed me with a concerned gaze. "Your father and the coyote?"

"They're both back at Larimer Square." I looked to one side. "The Cardinal very nearly took Maddox before his time."

"And then two friends would be dead." She stole to the Greyhound's crumpled body and knelt by his massive chest, stroking his pale cheek with the back of her dark fingers. "All these years, and now, I don't even have a chance to say a proper farewell."

"He went down fighting," Ethan offered, "but nothing any of us could do worked against this...this..."

"This monster." I motioned for L.J. to come closer. "So, Lady Day, can you get us out of here?"

"Would I be here if I couldn't?" She held out her hand. "Come."

Each of us took her hand in turn: L.J., Ethan, and lastly, me.

"And now, Daughter of Neith," she said as before, "a place, a person, a time."

"She always asks for a time," L.J. whispered. "Can she..."

"Shush," Lady Day let out between closed teeth, her dark eyes regaining the golden glow we'd all seen at our first meeting. "Time for questions later." She returned her attention to me. "A place, Miss Delacroix."

"Back to Larimer Square."

"A person."

"M-my father," I stammered, though my mind's eye saw only Maddox's face and attempted to make my lips and tongue follow suit.

"Good." Lady Day pulled in a breath. "A time."

"How about right now?" L.J. frantically pointed to the stands where half a dozen police scrambled down the concrete steps with weapons trained in our direction. "Like before it starts raining bullets?"

"Now it is."

As it had back at the Denver Airport, the air crackled with static pops as if lightning were about to strike. Lady Day spun her finger in the air, and I half-expected a tiny bolt of electricity to strike her digit like lightning to rod. Ozone filled the air, the light surrounding us dimmed, Lady Day's eyes pulsed with dazzling light, and for the second time that day, everything changed.

A blink, and the baseball field, bright as day, shifted to darkness, the low hum of thousands of lights overhead to the sound of roaring car engines and honking horns. In seconds, my eyes adjusted back to the dim left in Larimer Square by L.J.'s miraculous EMP to find Father and Maddox seated on a park bench as if the two were actually on friendly terms. Maddox looked up at me, a question haunting his exhausted gaze, a question Father verbalized a moment later with similar weariness.

"The Greyhound?"

"Gone," Ethan, to my right, muttered, "despite our best efforts."

"Leaving the Cardinal stronger than ever," L.J. added, appearing on my left. "How in the hell are we supposed to fight this guy? Every time we cross him, he's tougher than the time before."

"We'll find a way." I rested a hand on L.J.'s shoulder. "He hasn't killed us yet."

"Yet being the operative word." The first words to pass Maddox's lips since we reappeared, they dropped like a stone into the ever-deepening well of fear that had gripped my heart since our first encounter with the Cardinal, which already seemed like ancient history. "Face the facts, Rosemary."

"What facts?" I asked as Father turned to glare at Maddox.

"That maybe the Cardinal isn't your enemy to fight." Maddox's eyes filled with passion. "No matter what has gone before, Rosemary, I don't want to watch you die."

"The Cardinal is a rogue Ascendant, and I am the Daughter of Neith. He is precisely my enemy to fight."

"No offense, but last I checked, Harkreader here was the 'Agent of Neith' in our group." Maddox studied Ethan with a gaze just shy of derision. "The only question now is which combination is more likely to get one of you killed: immense power without the skill to wield it"—his gaze drifted back to me—"or a lifetime of training without the raw power to back it up?"

CHAPTER 19

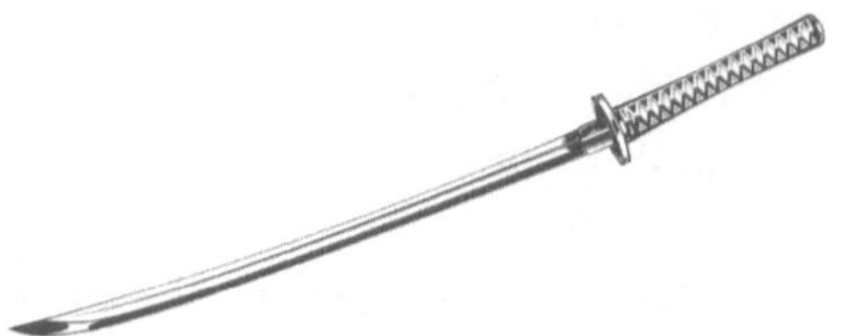

FLIRTIN' WITH DISASTER

My cheeks burned in anger and embarrassment at Maddox's words. Ethan grew very quiet while L.J. looked away, unwilling to meet either of our gazes. Worst of all was the sentiment I found in Father's eyes: the acceptance of Maddox's statement as not only correct but at the forefront of his mind as well.

"Does no one here think we can stop this guy?" In turn, I met the gaze of each of the four men in my presence. "None of you?"

"You've touched the red-hot burner three times now, Rosemary," Maddox answered, his voice a bit louder than I suspect he intended, "and each time it's left you blistered." He shook his head. "How many times do you want to get burned?"

"And yet you're going to keep pursuing him?" I asked. "He almost killed you."

"Don't you think I know that?" Maddox bared his teeth, his not-so-inner coyote making an appearance. "The world needs you."

"Yeah, to do the very thing we're—"

"Please, let me finish."

I kept my silence, doing my best to keep the anger from my eyes.

"The world needs you and everything your line brings with it despite its current—I suppose you'd call it—interrupted nature?" His eyes shot to Ethan. "No offense."

Ethan rolled his eyes but also stayed quiet.

"I couldn't bear it if I knew that anything I'd done, or worse, didn't do led to the end of the line of Neith."

"That's all you care about?" I asked. "My lineage and what it brings to the world?"

"Of course not." Maddox peered around the circle, at Father, L.J., and Ethan, his gaze eventually landing back on me. "You have to know how I feel."

The statement struck me as atypical for Maddox. Though admittedly among friends—or at least a group who at the moment didn't want to kill him—offering up his jugular in such mixed company was still a bold move. Especially for a coyote.

"Can we do this when an Ascendant murderer in impregnable body armor who gets stronger with every slaying isn't on the loose?"

"But can't you see? That's the whole point. Two years ago I loved you so much that not being with you was physically painful, then I loved you enough to leave and stay away because the situation I was dealing with was far too dangerous to be involved with anyone." A lone tear slowly made its way down his cheek. "Now I'm telling you I still love you, and I'm asking you to stand down and let me handle this."

Damn. That took serious guts.

L.J. stared at Maddox, eyes wide like car headlights.

Dad studied Maddox as well, a rare bit of admiration in his gaze.

And Ethan stood there gobsmacked, a hint of sadness invading those blue eyes of his.

"I don't know what you want me to say to that." My voice, somewhere between whisper and grunt, left my lips as if spoken by someone else. "You say you love me after disappearing for two solid years, and I believe that you believe that." Fire entered this other

Rosemary's voice, a fire built on the fuel of two years of sadness and anger, regret and loneliness, disappointment and loss. "I haven't the first idea how I feel about you in return." I finally locked gazes with Maddox, drawing close and resting one rigid finger against his sternum. "But if you think for a second that I'm leaving you to die at the hands of this monster after all we've meant to each other, regardless of where our relationship might be at the moment, then you never knew me at all."

Father moved to my side. "What my daughter is trying to say…"

He paused mid-sentence as I inhaled to tell him exactly how much I needed him to mansplain what I'd just said in plainest English and looked at me with that look I'd known since I was a baby that meant simply, "Trust me."

"Rosemary no more wishes to see you die than you her, and from my perspective, it's going to take all of us if we plan to bring down this miscreant."

"Wow." L.J. murmured under his breath. "Great word."

Father continued as if no one had spoken. "While I do appreciate the sentiment of you wanting to keep Rosemary out of danger, she has been training for this her entire life, and our chances of defeating the Cardinal will be magnified by her efforts, empowered or otherwise. The mission is what is important here. It was important enough for you to break my little girl's heart two years ago, and the stakes now are only higher."

"So, no matter what," Ethan added, "we're all in." He looked in my direction. "For better or for worse."

When I was old enough to appreciate the words, Mother had shared with me the vows from her wedding, handwritten in her elegant script on a folded sheet of parchment paper she kept with her most prized possessions. As unique as the woman herself, one phrase that she'd incorporated from the traditional vows used countless times across the world for centuries was "for better or for worse." Marrying into the Line of Neith was no small proposition, and they'd both known it.

Hearing those same words from Ethan's lips sent a shiver up my spine I only half-understood, but I filed the sentiment away along with the countless other emotions and questions and quandaries warring for my attention under "Things to worry about when we've defeated the psychopath Ascendant serial killer and are back in Montecito with our feet kicked up watching Netflix."

Maddox glared at all of us like a cornered animal before finally muttering, "Fine, but if everyone here dies—"

Father stepped forward and extended his hand to Maddox. "Then we will have gone down fighting."

I stepped to Maddox's other side. "Together."

Ethan strode over. "I've got your back."

This left L.J. alone in the shadows of Larimer Square, squinting at all of us through the dim. "You know, I'm really vibing on the whole 'All for one and one for all' thing you have going, but now that we've decided we're going to stick this out regardless of the danger, what's our next move?"

"I was thinking about that," Father lowered his chin in deep thought. "The Cardinal came to Denver to lay claim to the Greyhound's power and ultimately killed him despite our best efforts. Per the reports of the other Ascendant deaths that we know about, this seems to be his standard M.O."

"When he came for Seph, though," Ethan added, "he wasn't out for blood, but rather was doing whatever he could to keep her in one piece, right, Rosemary?"

"Sure seemed that way." I studied Father's features in the dim. "What are you getting at?"

Father pulled in a breath. "While we're still not sure why the Cardinal attempted to abduct Miss Snow, one thing is clear: he needs her alive." He drove a fist into his opposite palm. "I say we give him another shot at her."

"At Seph?" Ethan asked, dubious. "We couldn't protect the Greyhound, a man who eats Ascendant for breakfast, from this monster. How are we going to protect her?"

"By calling in a few favors," Father said with a grim smile.

"Favors?"

"Don't worry, Mr. Harkreader. We'll be ready this time." The shine in Father's visage dimmed as he added. "Though I suspect you won't be thrilled to learn what I have in mind."

~

"You want me to fly you where?" Bradley, in a departure from his usual unflappable smugness, stared at Ethan and me incredulously from across the airplane cabin.

"From the top, then." I kept my voice calm and even. "First, we need you to drop Father and L.J. off in Montecito so they can check on Seph."

"And after seeing what the Cardinal is really capable of," Ethan added, "to get her the hell out of that house." Father's nod backed Ethan's assessment of the situation. "She's not safe there...or anywhere, I suppose."

"After that," I jumped back in, brushing Ethan's leg with the back of my hand in an effort to keep him from alarming Bradley further, "we need you to get us to Los Angeles."

"The City of Angels." Bradley studied us, flabbergasted. "The homeplace of two quasi-immortal entities who a month ago, along with every foot soldier in their respective ranks, fought tooth and nail with all they had to lay claim to the very woman you're trying to protect."

"And who both stood down once Miss Snow Ascended, according to their custom." Father spoke quietly, maintaining my attempt at calming the situation. "Neither have made a peep since."

Bradley crossed his arms and snorted. "You, of all people, Mr. Delacroix, should understand the difference between someone who has given up and someone who is merely biding their time."

"Times are desperate, and the Cardinal isn't simply biding his time." Father looked to me. "Continue your plea, Rosemary."

"Mr. Bradley, I don't think we've made ourselves clear." I leaned across the aisle, resting my elbows on my knees and my chin on my interlaced fingers. "We can't stop the Cardinal by ourselves. Ethan and I, Maddox and Father? We gave this monster everything we had back in Denver, but in the end, only L.J.'s EMP even slowed him down."

"I still feel that delivering you to the Angels is tantamount to rescuing you from the frying pan only to hurl you into the fire." Bradley raised a questioning brow. "What makes you think they'll help you?"

"They let Seph walk last time, and I can't imagine either of them is too keen on letting an Ascendant serial killer continue to get stronger with every line of red in his ledger." I raised my shoulders in a quick shrug. "What's the worst they can do? Say no?"

"I've studied the two individuals in question for most of my life, Miss Delacroix." Bradley shook his head. "You really don't want to know the answer to that question."

"Can't you just call them?" L.J. asked. "Or text?" His brow furrowed. "Why do you all have to go all the way to Los Angeles?"

"Like I have the Angels of the Ascendant on speed dial." Father laughed. "Alba did give Miss Snow her card, but I'm hoping an in-person plea might carry more weight."

"And you're sure you don't want me to come along with you three to L.A.?" L.J. asked. "As you've seen, urban tracking is kind of my specialty."

"We appreciate the offer," Ethan interrupted, "but what we really need is for you to help keep Seph out of harm's way while we're gone. Mr. Delacroix, Neko, and Mr. Bradley are going to get her someplace safe. I need you to do whatever you can to keep the Cardinal and his own technomancer from tracking her down until we can execute the next step of our plan."

"Plan?" Bradley laughed coldly. "Begging for assistance from the very people who were doing their level best to kill you at every turn a month back isn't a plan. It's insanity. We've talked about what happens if they say no. What if either or both say yes? Have you even thought about the repercussions?" His voice grew very quiet. "Do you understand what it means to owe a favor to such as the Angels of Midnight or the Morn?"

"Do you have a better plan, Mr. Bradley?" Father asked. "Can you keep Miss Snow safe? Mr. Harkreader? My daughter?"

"We'd certainly do everything in our power to protect you all until the Cardinal can be brought low."

"And what exactly is it you and your people bring to the fight?" Maddox finally spoke up after growing visibly more agitated with every word from Bradley's smug lips. "Your bullets can't hurt this guy. Unless you have an Ascendant or two of your own on retainer, I'm not sure who or what you're planning to bring to bear."

None of us said another word as Bradley turned without a word to look out the window at the lights below. Somewhere down there, Colorado would soon give way to Utah, then briefly to Nevada before all of us reentered California airspace. We had no idea how the Cardinal and his people were getting around, what with Maddox and I trashing his plane—an event that already felt like it happened a month ago—but he'd somehow beaten us to Denver by a significant margin. I prayed for both Seph and Neko's sake that he didn't somehow beat us back to Montecito as well.

"So," Bradley grumbled after a long sixty seconds or so of deep thought, "this grand plan you all are dead set on me helping you implement involves splitting your forces, moving three of your most powerful agents several hours from your enemy's known target, leaving her vulnerable while delivering yourselves into the hands of known mercenaries who have already attacked you unprovoked on multiple occasions. Did I miss anything?"

L.J. raised his hand like a kid in a tenth-grade classroom, which I had to remind myself had likely been his daily reality until he was taken by the Cardinal's forces. "Maybe an armored convoy waiting on the runway for you, me, and Mr. Delacroix when we land so we can minimize exposure to...like...death?"

Bradley inhaled as if to laugh again, but instead rested his chin on his fist with a quiet, "You know, that's actually not a bad idea." He whipped out a smartphone more the size of a tablet computer and began tapping out a message, I guessed to someone on the ground in Montecito. Ethan and I both attempted to restart the conversation, but a raised finger each time from Bradley let us know he expected quiet while he worked.

I wasn't used to being hushed. Not surprisingly, I didn't like it.

On a different day, I planned to remind Mr. Secret Agent Man that we don't actually work for him. For the time being, however, we needed his cooperation, so I held my tongue, the sharpest blade in my arsenal, as Mother never failed to remind me.

A smile spread across Bradley's face a few seconds later as he looked up from his phone. "It's settled. A detail will be waiting when we land to pick up Mr. Delacroix and our resident technomancer and get them to Miss Snow, and then, as soon as we are adequately fueled, we're off to Los Angeles."

"Wait," Ethan said. "What do you mean we?"

"You didn't think I planned to send the last descendent of the Line of Neith and the current repository of her power—no offense, Mr. Harkreader—into the maw of the lion without coming along to supervise, did you?"

I ground my teeth. "We can manage our own business, Mr. Bradley."

Bradley cocked his head to one side. "Then you can arrange your own transportation, Miss Delacroix."

I gave the idea more than a passing thought, but the clock was ticking. "Fine, but let's keep one thing very clear. You may be in the know about all things Ascendant, but as you said, I am Danielle Delacroix's daughter, so please, leave the heavy lifting to me."

"I wouldn't have it any other way." He crossed his arms. "Though you might be surprised if you actually give me a chance. I'm more than just some guy who thinks and knows things."

Ethan snorted at that last comment for reasons I didn't quite understand. He'd fill me in later. Pop culture recap was basically our standard operating procedure.

"So," Father interjected, "this detail waiting for us at the airport. What can we expect?"

As if in answer, Bradley's phone buzzed in his hand. "Looks like..." He studied the lit screen. "All right, three armored SUVs with bulletproof glass, standard issue for POTUS detail so they're top of the line, and a dozen armed guards."

"And the plan?" Father grumbled.

"Straight from the airport to Miss Snow's house where you two will pick up both her and her theriodan friend. From there, we'll be taking her to an undisclosed location where we'll keep her under wraps until I return with Miss Delacroix and Mr. Harkreader, hopefully both in one piece and with the assistance they're hoping to enlist."

"Just like that?" I asked.

"Just like that." Bradley raised a shoulder in a half shrug. "I'm not an unreasonable guy." A furtive smile broke across his features. "And if you had any idea how long I've been waiting for something like this..." In that moment, the man's inner fanboy made a reappearance.

"In your zeal to be a part of the bigger picture," I warned, "don't forget to keep your head down, Mr. Bradley. This is dangerous business."

"You don't have to tell me, Miss Delacroix. I'm not the most experienced in the field, particularly with direct Ascendant contact, but this isn't exactly my first rodeo either."

"Well, we have the whole flight to L.A. for you to fill me and Ethan in on your experiences."

"Why wait? We're still an hour out from Montecito." He opened his arms in a welcoming gesture. "What would you like to know?"

As Bradley launched into story mode, detailing his long history with the Order of Ophanim, I found myself impressed with his unabashed candidness, though another of Mother's favorite aphorisms ricocheted through my head time and again with every twist in his tale.

Even an open book can be filled with lies.

CHAPTER 20

PASSENGERS

As we exited the Los Angeles International Airport beneath a sign welcoming us to "The City of Angels," Ethan and I drew up short at a sight both reassuring and ominous: a black Mercedes stretch limousine parked at the curb directly outside. Leaning against the rear passenger door, the Driver waited, his dark skin setting off wise eyes that fastened on mine as if there were a physical connection. Dressed immaculately in his black tuxedo, white shirt, black silk tie, and black leather shoes that reflected the fluorescent lights of the airport entryway like mirrors, he waited patiently, unsmiling, his muscled arms crossed before his chest. The engine of his well-maintained machine purred like a metallic black panther waiting for the order to run.

A strange relief filled my heart even though I knew deep down the Driver's presence meant that the situation was likely worse than we already understood.

"Good evening, Miss Delacroix, Mr. Harkreader." His nose

crinkled, though he kept any emotion from his gaze as he added, "Mr. Trainor." His dark eyes shifted past me to the fourth in our party. "And who might this be?"

"Jim Bradley, Chief of Security for Santa Barbara Airport, among other titles." Bradley stepped forward and offered his hand. "I'm guessing you must be the Driver." The man trembled like a kid meeting his favorite celebrity. "It's an honor to make your acquaintance—"

The Driver didn't so much as shift his arm a millimeter. Completely ignoring Bradley, he continued his conversation with me, albeit slightly more annoyed.

"What is he doing here, Miss Delacroix?" The deep bass threatened to shake the concrete beneath our feet. "And where is your Father?" His eyes went briefly up and to the right as he answered his own question. "I suppose he is with Miss Snow. Finally going to ground, I see." His head shook subtly from side to side. "Unfortunate, but good. I would not see her harmed."

I offered a conciliatory smile. "Mr. Bradley here was instrumental in keeping Maddox and me from incarceration after everything that went down in Santa Barbara yesterday morning."

"The newscasts were quite vague," the Driver said, "but between the limited footage from the runway and what both was and wasn't said, I detected the handiwork of a well-prepared Daughter of Neith."

"Actually, it was a team effort." Maddox puffed up his chest. "Me and Rosemary against an Ascendant who has so far, unfortunately, proven unstoppable. It was something to see."

"I am quite certain you performed admirably, Mr. Trainor." The Driver's lips shifted into a smug half-smile. "The tricks of a well-trained dog can be impressive."

A low growl sounded from deep within Maddox's chest. His hands curled into fists at his sides, but he held both his position and his tongue.

Good. For all of Maddox's natural ability and martial skill, I had zero doubt that the Driver would mop the floor with him. In our relatively infrequent encounters with the man, neither Mother nor I had ever seen him so much as lift a finger against another individual, primarily because no one to our knowledge was foolish enough to challenge him to a fight.

"As for Mr. Bradley, his connections were all that kept us free, not to mention allowed us quick passage to Denver to confront this new enemy."

"You faced the Cardinal." The Driver's chin dropped, almost imperceptibly. "Is it true? The Greyhound, is he…?"

"We fought with everything we had," Ethan said, "all of us and the Greyhound together, but in the end, everything we had simply wasn't enough."

The Driver stroked his closely trimmed beard and then ran his fingers along his tightly buzzed scalp, a wince of mixed pain, anger, sadness, and acceptance flashing across his features. "That is unfortunate. He was a friend, and one of the few who walked this planet whose motives I never questioned."

"And now his power, strength, and abilities belong to a madman who will use what he has gained to kill again." Maddox tensed, like an animal in a cage. "Look, I've spent the better part of two years tracking this asshole and studying his every move. Though I've always ended up a step behind him despite my best efforts, I've seen enough to develop serious respect for his abilities, if not his motives." His eyes shifted left and right. "Now that we've actually come face to face, I've gotta say, he terrifies me."

The sobering admission hit me like a ton of cinderblocks. The Maddox I knew two years ago would never have admitted something so personal even to me, much less in the company of one he considered a competitor, a legend he'd always hoped to meet, and a complete stranger.

"As dramatic as I was led to believe," the Driver said, studying Maddox with a modicum of compassion, "though your assessment of both your enemy and the situation, Mr. Trainor, couldn't be more on point." He drew himself up to his full height and turned to open the door he'd leaned against. "Get in, all of you. We can continue our discussion en route."

"En route?" Ethan asked. "Where is it you think we're going?"

"It is well past midnight, and simple math coupled with my

understanding of the various flight routes on this end of the United States would suggest that you are all exhausted and almost certainly famished." The Driver allowed the last of us into the rear of his limo, shut the door behind us, and circled around to perform the service embodied in his chosen appellation. "Our first stop, the Midnight Diner, and then a bed and breakfast for some much needed and well-deserved rest?"

"With all due respect," I said, "we're on a bit of a timetable. Can you take us to—"

"Miss Delacroix, I know why you're here in Los Angeles." The Driver glanced at me through the rearview mirror. "I already had the car prepared when my sources confirmed you were indeed headed my way."

His "sources." Fantastic. And here I thought private jets run by ancient secret orders would buy us at least a few hours when the whole world didn't seem to know our every move.

"You will eat, you will sleep, and I will ensure you are all awake for your meeting with Alba and her entourage."

"How did you know we were hoping to meet with her?"

He held up his mobile. "She called me. You're scheduled to meet at ten tomorrow morning. She thought you might want to sleep in after the couple of days you've had."

"She knew we were coming?"

"She likely knew before you did." He hit the button to raise the partition window. "Now, all of you rest your eyes for a moment. I'll let you know when we've arrived at the Diner, and we can continue our conversation over some hot food."

"But—"

As the tinted glass slid into place, I bristled momentarily at being cut off so succinctly. But then the heated leather seats, the cool air from the vents, my utter exhaustion, and even the hint of momentary safe haven all conspired to send me off to dreamland, if only for a moment.

～

The Driver rapped at the glass three times, shocking me awake. A quick check of my watch showed no more than half an hour had passed, and yet if anyone had said I'd missed one or two major holidays, I'd have believed them.

Except for the sore muscles. They were still there. And they'd made friends.

I peered out the side and rear windows and discovered we were parked at the far end of a deserted lot with a dumpster to our rear and a fence separating us from the next parking lot a couple feet past the window glass.

The rear driver's side door opened. "Midnight Diner, as promised, though the clock sits way past that particular witching hour." The Driver peered inside at the lot of us, a hint of a grin playing across his features. "I called ahead. They have our table waiting."

"He called ahead to a diner?" Ethan asked under his breath as we exited the limo. "At two o'clock in the morning?"

"Again," I answered, my voice low, "the aspects of the Ascendant world that surprise you the most never cease to amaze me."

"It's the little things." Ethan smiled that thousand-megawatt smile of his. "By the way, you snore when you sleep."

"I don't typically sleep curled into a ball in the back of a limousine." I held him back for a second, letting the other three go on ahead. "Anyway, I'm surprised you didn't drop off for a quick cat nap like I did. Aren't you exhausted?"

"I'm totally beat." A bitter chuckle parted his lips. "But I kept my eyes open in case there were any more surprises." He inclined his head in Bradley's direction. "Secret Agent Man stayed up as well. Cool as a cucumber, at least on the outside."

"Huh." I dropped my voice to the barest of whispers. "And what about Maddox?"

Ethan followed my cue, pulling close to keep our conversation private as the five of us approached the diner's main entrance with him and me bringing up the rear. "He barely took his eyes off you the entire trip." He cleared his throat. "Not trying to be mean, but watching him reminded me of a hunting dog pointing at a rabbit. He barely even blinked."

"Funny thing," Maddox growled. "Coyotes have not only superb night vision, but exceptional hearing as well." He shot a look back across his shoulder before entering the diner behind Bradley and the Driver. "Careful with reporting your little observations, Harkreader. You're not the only one taking notes."

"Just calling things like I see them," Ethan answered. "Wasn't trying to offend." He took the door from Maddox and held it for me, closing the door behind us after a quick scan of the parking lot.

Good. He was learning.

The Driver motioned to a svelte waitress in black with her hair up in dark pigtails and her arms tattooed with the various slashers from the last four decades of horror movies. Funny thing? I'd never seen a horror movie other than *Rosemary's Baby* before a month ago, but between Ethan and Seph, I'd been introduced to several of the more popular franchises and was suddenly quite familiar with the likes of Michael Myers, Jason Voorhees, Freddy Krueger, Pinhead, and Ghostface.

Mom would be horrified, no pun intended, but not as horrified as Ethan and Seph would be if I told them I picked up a tip or two from a couple of their favorite flicks, and not from the hapless screaming teens running around in the dark trying not to end up the latest statistic in their little town.

We all have our pet interests, I suppose.

The five of us huddled around a table at the back of the diner. The Driver sat with his back to the wall, and though he appeared calm, I had little doubt he'd already assessed every soul in the room and had a plan to disable or kill anyone between him and the door if the need arose.

Just like Mother taught me to do.

Maddox and Ethan sat on either side of me, each trying to outdo the other on vigilance and preparedness, though the fatigue wafting off both of them was obvious.

Bradley, on the other hand, nonchalantly perused the menu as if he didn't have a care in the world. "I'm feeling like hash browns." He placed the laminated list of every greasy food under the sun back on the table. "Definitely hash browns."

"Opting for an early breakfast rather than a late dinner, Mr. Bradley?" The Driver motioned for the waitress with the slasher tattoos to come over.

"Yes sir, tall, dark, and handsome," she purred. "What will it be?"

The Driver motioned to Bradley, who in turn smiled at our well-inked server. "I'll have an omelet with everything, hash browns, and black coffee, please."

"I'll have the same." The Driver peered around at the rest of us. "Anyone else?"

"Steak," Maddox grunted, "rare. With a Coke." His usual.

Ethan inhaled to speak, but instead of ordering, he glanced down at the menu I held in my lap. "You first, Rosemary."

The tiny bit of chivalry brought a slight smile to my face. "I'll do egg whites, three, scrambled with provolone, a Greek yogurt, and another black coffee."

The waitress turned to Ethan, bringing the red-headed killer doll tattooed at her elbow—Chucky, as I recall—around to stare at me as Ethan ordered his usual western omelet and bacon, though he did throw on a side of sliced avocado, something he'd never really tried until Seph and I made him give it a shot at breakfast last week.

Again, he was learning.

As our server vanished into the kitchen to turn in our order, Bradley and the Driver simultaneously rested their elbows on the table as if both were indicating they were ready to get down to business.

The Driver quirked his mouth to one side, amused. "Yes, Mr. Bradley?"

Bradley pulled himself upright in his seat. "First, again, I'd like to tell you what an honor it is to meet one of the most respected—"

"You may dispense with the pleasantries." The Driver raised a hand. "While appreciated, I've heard it all more times than you can possibly imagine."

"Of course." Bradley cleared his throat as he searched for a conversational course correction. "May I at least thank you for your timely transportation and for delivering us all to a place of..." He peered around the diner, the keenness in his eyes matching that of the coyote sitting next to him. "Relative safety?"

"Even if your armored adversary were to walk in the door at this very moment, let me assure you all that you are as safe as you can be in this place."

"Big talk," Maddox said. "That guy tore the Greyhound apart. Call me crazy, but for all your reputation, all I get from you is 'buff dude with a nice ride' and a frankly suspicious tendency to show up exactly where and when you're needed." Maddox looked away and muttered. "Speaking of the Greyhound, I'm sure he would have accepted a ride earlier tonight."

"I was three states away when the Greyhound fell." Any hint of mirth vacated the Driver's features. "And preparedness often looks like luck to the unprepared, young man." He cracked the knuckles of his massive hands, his skin like well-brushed mahogany. "You of all people should understand that individuals are often more than they appear." His raised eyebrow made clear that his insinuation included far more than the coyote who lurked behind Maddox's human features.

"Don't be fooled by his simple moniker, Mr. Trainor," Bradley interrupted before I could clarify exactly what the Driver was getting at. "There's a reason this man travels the world unassailed, a reason beyond either his mere physicality or his excellent taste in transportation."

"Yeah," Ethan added, "seriously, dude. I may be new to this, but even I know that the Driver is basically a legend, not to mention this is the third time he's helped pull my can out of the fire since we met, and—"

"Thank you both, Mr. Bradley and Mr. Harkreader." The Driver crinkled his nose, as if unsure how to respond to Bradley's barely veiled awe and admiration. "Though I am quite capable of fighting my own battles."

"Again," Bradley said, his voice growing quieter with each word, "of course."

Our server reappeared with our drinks, four coffees and Maddox's Coke, and distributed them among our table, her black-painted lips turned up in a pleasant smile. "Food should be out in a couple minutes. You all need anything else?"

"We're doing fine." I answered her smile with one of my own, though I was certain the expression didn't make it all the way to my eyes. "Thank you."

Our server, her name tag flipped backward at the top of her apron, shot me a quick nod and again disappeared into the kitchen.

"Now." I needed to say my piece before the four heaping helpings of testosterone all started going after each other again. "I'm guessing there's a reason you brought us all here besides simply making sure we all got fed and watered. You know why we're here. Can we discuss how we're going to track down Alba in the morning, or are you four going to continue your little manhood measuring contest?"

All present but me, the Driver included, squirmed at the remark. Good. Like Mother always taught me, it's always a good idea to keep the men on their toes.

Before anyone could speak again, the lights in the establishment flickered as if they might go out. Maddox, Ethan, and I were out of our seats in an instant, though both the Driver and Bradley sat sipping at their coffee as if the brief interruption of electricity were not only inconsequential but expected.

"And here we go," Bradley muttered. "I've been waiting for this."

"Waiting for what?" Ethan asked.

In answer, the door to the diner swung open as if by unseen hands, and into the diner swept a woman dressed head to toe in black, her torn jeans and long sleeve top hugging her every curve. Her leather boots from a different decade were well worn yet they shone in the fluorescent light. From under the dark bangs of her pixie cut, her deep brown eyebrows rose as her fervent gaze met mine.

"The Midnight Angel?" I whispered. "Here?"

"It's 2:30 in the morning in the City of Angels, and you're all sitting inside a place called the Midnight Diner." Bradley chuckled even as he gazed upon the Angel in awe. "What did you think was going to happen?"

CHAPTER 21

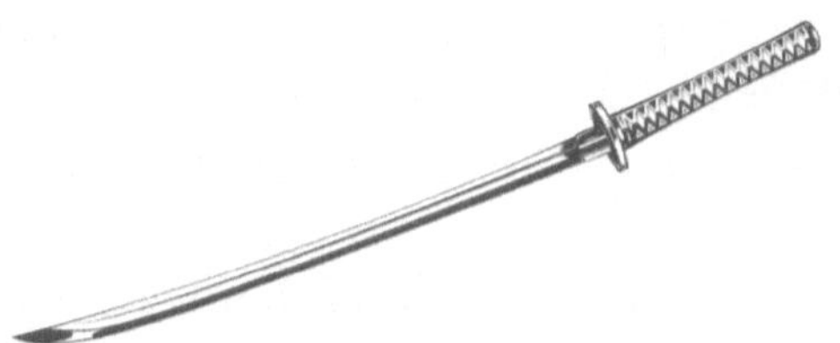

MIDNIGHT AT THE LOST AND FOUND

"No offense," I whispered to the Driver, "but a little advanced notice would have been nice."

"You came all this way to speak with the Angels, Miss Delacroix." He motioned to the short-haired brunette who strode in our direction and smiled. "What is the saying? No time like the present?"

Madame Midnight slipped into the lone empty chair of our table I noticed was actually set for six and snapped her fingers. In an instant, our server reemerged from the back and hurried to the Angel's side.

"Yes, Mistress."

"A light repast, Katrina, so that I might partake with our guests."

"Your usual?" Katrina asked.

"Surprise me." As Katrina scampered off, Midnight turned her attention back to us. "Is it true?" she asked. "The Greyhound?"

"Gone." I lowered my head. "We did all that we could, but—"

"We will speak more of this later." The Angel's gaze swept the table. "I see you've added to your ranks since last we met, Daughter of Neith." She studied Maddox for a moment. "Let's see...I detect some canine undertones with this one." Her appraising eye turned to Bradley. "This one, on the other hand, reeks of abject normalcy and unfortunate bureaucratic entanglements."

"Been a while since anyone called me normal, Madame Midnight," Bradley responded, "though your assessment is on point, I must admit." He bowed his head in a show of respect bordering on reverence. "As I said to the Driver earlier, I am honored to be in your presence."

"Hmm. A bit unctuous for my taste, but not sickeningly so." She gave him a full once over and then turned to me. "You vouch for this man, Daughter of Neith?"

"Inasmuch as I can vouch for anyone other than myself. Mr. Bradley, though a recent adjunct to our group, has already proven both dependable and resourceful."

"And he knows of us, I see. How came he by that information, Miss Delacroix?"

I shot Bradley a questioning glance, not sure why I was deigning to ask permission from a man I'd known for less than two days. He'd proven trustworthy to that point, however, at least as far as I could tell, and not "throwing him under the bus," as Ethan would say, seemed the least I could do. Fortunately, after a few seconds of consideration, he shot me a quick nod letting me know I could speak of what we'd discussed.

"He belongs to a group called—"

"The Order of Ophanim." The Midnight Angel crossed her arms and grunted in exasperation. "I feared that you had brought one of *them* into my establishment."

"You're familiar with our Order?" Bradley asked.

"Mostly by reputation."

Bradley puffed up his chest with momentary pride, the figurative balloon popping a moment later with a derisive grunt from the Angel in his presence.

"I didn't say the reputation was good," she clarified with a withering stare. "I've hoped over the many years I've walked this planet that your archaic organization would eventually wither and die like a garden weed, outcompeted and made obsolete by the various intelligence agencies of the modern world's nation states. Unfortunately, your roots appear far deeper than even I dreamed."

Bradley's cheeks pinkened. "With all due respect, Madame Midnight, my Order seeks only to observe, record, and occasionally facilitate matters between Ascendant and the rest of the world."

"Facilitate?" the Angel scoffed. "Tell that to the Ascendant hunted down and slain throughout history simply for being born different."

"The rules and regulations of the organization as it stands today precludes any direct action against your kind."

"And yet, here you are, helping the Daughter of Neith and her friends hunt an Ascendant. Do you plan on 'observing and recording' him into ending his killing spree?"

"The circumstances of the last few months have necessitated an unusual exception to policy." Bradley's face went from pink to crimson, even as his eyes narrowed into steely points. "Unless you're saying you don't want our help."

"Humans. The most enlightened among you study that which you do not understand, but the rest seek either to worship or destroy things beyond your ken."

Bradley's shoulders fell, deflated. "I swear to you, Madame Midnight, the Order's only goal is to bring down the Cardinal and protect your brothers and sisters."

"Keep telling yourself that, Mr. Bradley. I've spent many lifetimes on this planet and have seen what happens when studying and cataloging becomes a bit more pointed. Pardon me if I don't wish to have my name, likeness, and location recorded in your ledger when your leadership inevitably decides that simply understanding Ascendant no longer makes them feel 'safe.' As one who has narrowly escaped being burned at the stake in more than one century, not to mention my fair share of bullets over the years, I'd prefer to keep my anonymity, thank you very much."

Bradley leaned back in his chair and considered for a moment. "In that case, it is truly unfortunate that our trip to Los Angeles ended up so noncontributory. I'd truly hoped that Miss Delacroix, Mr. Harkreader, and Mr. Trainor might find the help they needed here, but it seems I will have to report that all the Ascendant within city limits apparently went to ground before we arrived."

The Angel studied Bradley, her lips eventually shifting into a faint smile. "You will bear watching, Mr. Bradley, but you may stay."

"Thank you." And Bradley left it at that.

Apparently, he was learning too.

"So," the Angel shifted in her seat, "I assume you have come to talk to me about this individual calling himself the Cardinal who is causing such distress among my community."

"How do you know about him?" I asked. "Mother never mentioned him once, and I only just learned of him myself."

"The monster has been killing Ascendant for at least a year." The vigor in Midnight's dark gaze faded for a second. "It is my business to be aware of such things."

"And you haven't tried to stop him?" Maddox blurted out. "I mean..." His eyes went wide as the realization of exactly who he was questioning dawned on him.

The Angel furrowed her brow in annoyance. "Actually, I've had emissaries searching for this murderer of our kind for months, Mr...?"

"Trainor. Maddox Trainor."

"Ah, I've heard of you. You run with that pack that has taken up residence east of here in Las Vegas, do you not?"

"Not at the moment," Maddox answered, "but Linus and I go back a ways."

"And what have you and your theriodan pack done to staunch the bleeding from our community?" The Angel leaned in. "Please, I'm all ears."

Maddox hesitated.

"Tell her." I might not have thrown Bradley under the bus, but a tiny part of me enjoyed calling Maddox out in front of someone of the Angel's stature, almost as if I were pleading my case before a judge. "Bradley's not the only one here affiliated with an organization that operates off the books."

"Oh really?" The Angel asked, her eyes narrowing at Maddox like a soaring hawk's tracking a mouse in a fallow field. "Do tell."

Maddox glared at me, his eyes twin lasers burning through my soul. A part of me immediately regretted the betrayal of his trust, but in the end, the truth is the truth, and if we were laying all our cards on the table, as the Driver had said, there was no time like the present.

At least, that was what I was going to keep telling myself.

With a quiet sigh, Maddox began. "Two years ago, I went underground at the behest of an organization of Ascendant whose interests align with all present. My mission was to gather intelligence so that we might put an end to the threat posed by our mutual enemy, the Cardinal."

"An organization of Ascendant of which I'm neither a member nor even aware..." The Midnight Angel leaned back in her chair. "Go on, Mr. Trainor. You have my attention."

Maddox's angry glower continued to smolder in my direction. "It's been said that I have a nose for such things, though despite my best efforts, it's taken me two years of failure after failure before I finally got to one of the Cardinal's victims before the fact." He looked to one side, color rising in his cheeks. "Not that the outcome was any different."

Despite all that had transpired over the last two years and the preceding two days in particular, my heart went out to the coyote who had first stolen and then broken it.

"Come on." I leaned across the table and rested my hand atop his. "You know we did all we could."

"And it wasn't good enough." Maddox shook his head.

"This mysterious group of Ascendant of which you speak," the Midnight Angel asked, "what resources did they put at your disposal to bring down such a formidable opponent? I sense that you perform well in a fight, but I can't believe anyone expecting results would send out a lone theriodan to bring down such a high-level threat."

"I wasn't always alone, but I am the only one left." His already flushed cheeks went positively crimson.

Everyone at the table, myself included, took a moment to process this bit of news. First I'd heard of it. I wasn't sure exactly how this new revelation made me feel—or even how it was supposed to make me feel. All I knew was that despite all we'd shared over the last two days, Maddox still hadn't told me everything.

"Who else was lost?" the Angel asked. "What other names must we add to the list for which this monster must be held responsible?"

"Three other Ascendant, young and insignificant like me. You've likely never heard of any of them."

"You might be surprised, Mr. Trainor." The Angel motioned for him to speak. "Their names, if you please."

"Actually, with one exception, we never learned each other's names. The powers that be thought it would be best if we maintained, as you said before, a certain degree of anonymity."

"And the one you did know?"

"Her name was Jia Li, a Chinese empath." Emotion twisted Maddox's features into a mask of pain. "We called her Jade. I...we lost her three months ago."

"What happened to her?" Ethan, content with listening until that moment, jumped back into the conversation. His sudden interest struck me as strangely intense, even personal. "Was it...him?"

"I believe so, at least indirectly. The organization that contracted the four of us has extensive resources at its disposal, but so, as we found out, does the Cardinal." Maddox hung his head, his gaze not rising from the checkered tablecloth. "The first two of our group were killed a month before in an ambush in New Zealand."

"And Jade?" I asked, not quite understanding why saying the name hurt my heart so much.

"A hit outside Buenos Aires. Nothing I could do in either case. To be honest, I'm lucky to be alive."

"How did you get back?" Ethan asked.

"As best I could. Between buses, hitching, and the occasional hike, it took me the better part of two months to make my way safely back to the States."

"Right around the time that I met Seph and Ethan." Considering our current company, I left off the second half that went something like, "the night the skiomancers first attacked."

"I'm curious." The Angel continued her low-key interrogation. "Did not this group you speak of offer their aid in your return home, or did they simply leave you to fend for yourself?"

"I suppose they might have," Maddox whispered as he continued to avoid all our eyes, "if they didn't believe me already dead."

Wow. Maddox was chock full of surprises tonight.

"Anything else you haven't told me?" I murmured under my breath, despite the fact that the only thing I truly cared about was already painfully obvious.

"I loved her," Maddox answered, as if reading my thoughts. "Jia Li." He finally dared look up and met my gaze. "And I'm not going to insult either her memory or your intelligence trying to deny it."

The sliver of ice that had slipped between my ribs moments before shattered into a thousand razor shards.

"And with her gone, you came crawling back to me." I let out a growl that would have made any theriodan proud. "Is that it?"

Maddox's eyes lowered yet again. "I had nowhere else to go."

Question after question I'd been asking myself for two years were suddenly answered, the revelations going off in my head like popcorn over an open fire.

"You said you came to me for my benefit and to help keep Seph from harm, but in the end, all you were really doing was saving your own skin."

"Truth be told, if you must know, it was a bit of both."

"And there it is." My teeth ground audibly. "I can't even look at you."

"Things happened, Rosemary. A lot of things, and—"

"And you chose this moment, in front of all these people, to come clean?" My hand went instinctively to my hip where my katana usually rested, the razor-sharp sword the only friend I could truly count on. Finding only empty air, my fingers balled into a fist.

Maddox was lucky we'd all left our weapons back with the plane.

"Miss Delacroix," Bradley spoke, his tone confident yet tenuous, "if I may?"

"Yes, Mr. Bradley?" I did my best to keep my voice even, but the venom in both my words and stare came through regardless. "What could you possibly have to add to this conversation?"

Bradley cleared his throat and straightened his tie as he searched for the right words. "All personal matters aside, you strike me as someone whose focus is on the end result rather than the means."

"Careful. You don't know me as well as you think you do."

He quirked his mouth to one side. "A trashed aircraft back at my place of employment would speak otherwise." He pulled in a deep breath through his nose. "While it is clear that you and Mr. Trainor here have some unfinished business of a romantic nature that you need to explore, no one would argue that each and every person at this table has a vested interest in bringing down our shared enemy."

"Your point?" I asked.

"I believe what Mr. Bradley is trying to say, Miss Delacroix, is that regardless of what history exists between the two of you, the Ascendant community and Miss Snow in particular need everyone working together if we are to have any hope of defeating this threat to our way of life." The Angel turned her attention back on Maddox. "I do, however, wish to address a certain matter with Mr. Trainor."

"Yes, Madame Midnight." Despite the emotion of the moment, Maddox swallowed back his pride and gave the Angel the respect she was due. "What is it you'd like to know?"

"This organization you speak of that contracted you and the others in an effort to stop this latest scourge of Ascendant. Who are they? What do they want?" She held her hands before her palms up, a sly grin creeping subtly across her face. "It is rare for me to hear of an Ascendant matter of which I am not already patently aware."

"I can imagine," Maddox muttered, dodging the implied question.

Managing to keep the vexation from her voice, the Angel continued her interrogation. "Who was your contact among this group?" she asked. "I would know their name."

"I wish I knew," Maddox answered without batting an eye. "All instructions and reports between me and the group were conveyed via email or scrambled phone transmission, and all funds were sent via online transfer. And before you ask, they clearly employed an expert-level technomancer for all their communications, as our own

—who was no slouch, mind you—couldn't place the origin of the various messages to even a continent, much less a specific location." His hands, one atop the other on the table, trembled. "That was the way it was until—"

"Until Buenos Aires?" Ethan asked.

"Yeah. After that, not another peep." Maddox returned his attention to me. "You have to understand. When they first reached out to me, they said I'd be responsible for bringing down a murderer of our kind. That's what your Mother was all about, Rosemary. What you spent your entire upbringing learning to do. I thought you'd be proud of me." He looked away. "At least in the beginning."

"You fell in love with somebody else." I hated the words that were coming out of my mouth. "It happens."

"Day in, day out, training and fighting alongside another? Putting your life in their hands and taking theirs in yours? Doing everything you can to make sure you're both still alive at the end of the day? That kind of closeness changes things."

"I understand." The heat of Ethan's eyes burned into my neck, and I utilized every last iota of willpower to keep my gaze firmly on Maddox rather than give in to his palpable stare. "That doesn't mean I don't need a little time to process all of this."

"Of course," he whispered. "Take all the time you need."

"So," Bradley said with faux ebullience, "we're all one big happy dysfunctional family again. Excellent." He rested his elbows on the table and steepled his fingers at the bridge of his nose. "Might I suggest we proceed from here with more of a plan than simply 'Stop the Cardinal'? Blind luck and last-minute saves are only going to get us so far before somebody else ends up dead." He glanced around the table, his roving gaze resting the longest on Maddox. "No disrespect, of course, to the recently deceased."

Maddox's solemn nod was the only answer Bradley was going to get.

At that moment, Katrina returned with everyone's food. Bradley's plate mirrored the Driver's right down to the slice of grapefruit that occupied the third of the plate not covered in carbohydrates and cholesterol-laden deliciousness. Maddox's steak was so red, I swore it was going to rise to defend itself when he raised his fork and knife. My egg whites were done the way I like them, with just the right amount of cheese, and the yogurt even had fresh raspberries mixed into its top layer.

When all of us were served, Katrina set her mistress's plate before her. At its center rested a halved avocado stuffed with a chopped hard-boiled egg, peppers, cucumber, olives, and a dash of Parmesan and balsamic dressing.

Didn't see that one on the menu.

Everyone took advantage of our meal's arrival to put a pin in the conversation, not the least of which, me. We were all exhausted—physically, mentally, and emotionally—as well as famished, and we made short work of the diner fare.

Then it was time to get down to brass tacks.

"So, Madame Midnight, as you probably suspect, we have come tonight with a question."

"Of course you have." She smiled, her eyes dancing with something like perverse glee. "You still have to ask it, though."

"We need your help. Despite our best efforts, I fear we will never prevail against the Cardinal alone. Would you join your power with ours, come with us, and help us bring his rampage to an end?"

She considered for seconds that seemed like years. "I'm afraid I can't go with you, Daughter of Neith. As much as your goals and mine align at the moment, I have responsibilities here in Los Angeles, and my absence at this particular juncture would be ill-advised."

Ethan's shoulders slumped with the same disappointment that filled me from head to toe. "You mean, you're not going to help us?"

"I didn't say that." The Angel motioned for Katrina to refill her glass of sparkling water. "Katrina dear, that little business trip you and I were discussing? How quickly can you be packed and ready to go?"

"Everything is in readiness, Mistress." She scanned the table. "I thought these might be the ones of which you spoke."

"Wait." Maddox grumbled. "We came all this way to get the help of an Angel and all she's sending with us is the waitress?"

"Oh, Mr. Trainor, for one with the senses of a feral canine, how little you appreciate that all is not always as it appears." She cast an appraising eye up and down Katrina's lithe form. "Rest assured that Katrina's skills extend far beyond that of humble server, however excellently she might perform that role."

Katrina looked down at me with a friendly smile bordering on amusement, and then, so quickly I almost swore I imagined it, the psychopathic doll tattooed on her arm shot me a knowing wink.

CHAPTER 22

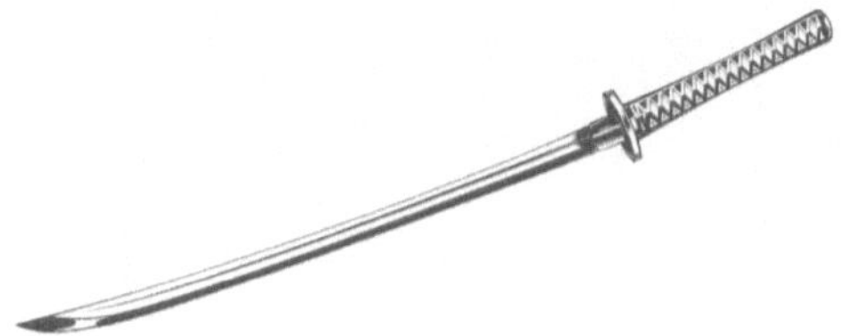

DEVIL INSIDE

We'd all crashed for a few hours at a small hotel off the beaten path whose owner owed the Driver a favor or two. Ethan and I took a two-bedroom suite with Maddox offering to take the couch in the central area to keep watch over us. And by "us" he meant me. Bradley and the Driver opted to stay with the vehicle, Bradley in the back and the Driver up front. I had no idea if the Driver required sleep but understood it would be rude to ask.

Our succession of alarms coupled with the Driver's rap at our door had us all up and ready to go bright and early at eight the next morning. My body craved another twelve hours of unconsciousness, but the three to four we'd been able to get would have to suffice.

Katrina had been waiting for us in the parking lot with a collection of coffees from a local shop, her selections spot on for a woman we'd met the night before. More than simply a server, as Madame Midnight had said, but a superb one nonetheless.

Most interesting of all, when the Driver told us where we were going, she was the only one who didn't raise an eyebrow.

"As crazy as last night was," Ethan said as he peered out the limousine window at the block of modern-appearing townhomes at our destination, "I can't believe we're here of all places, asking for help from...them..."

"We're sure this is the place?" Maddox asked. "I mean, as nice as they look, townhouses? Really?"

"I don't know." I rolled down the window and stuck my head out, craning my neck to look up and down the block. "You two see townhomes." I pulled back inside and dropped into my seat. "I see a compound."

"As perceptive as your mother, Miss Delacroix." The Driver watched me over his right shoulder, a hint of a smile playing across his dark features. "And this is definitely the address."

"Oh, don't worry." Katrina giggled under her breath. "This is definitely the place. The Mistress has us skirt this entire end of the city unless we're on official business."

"Funny." Bradley cleared his throat. "I was under the impression the Angels all got along." He twirled his finger in the air. "I mean they both live in the same city, right?"

Katrina laughed even harder. "As if either would allow the other to lay sole claim to the City of Angels."

"What of the third Angel we met?" Maddox asked. "The one called Lady Day. Does she call Los Angeles home as well?"

"Not a chance." Katrina's expression transitioned into one of utter reverence. "Lady Day is a New York City girl. Always has been. She owns several properties in the heart of Harlem as I understand it and rarely sets foot outside the city." She met each of our gazes in turn. "I must ask, did she really expend the energy necessary to convey herself to Denver as you said? Things must be dire indeed."

"Dire enough for us to come begging for help from people who were trying to kill us a month ago." Ethan pulled in a breath. "By the way, what do you mean energy?"

"First law of thermodynamics, boyo: energy can neither be created nor destroyed. Do you think Ascendant are like appliances plugged into the wall, sucking electricity from the universe all day long without repercussions?" She patted Ethan's leg, and I fought the urge to answer with a pat of my own. "We all have our limits. None of us are bottomless wells, not even the Angels." She lowered her head, as if in shame. "Don't tell the Mistress I said so, though. She likes the world to think her invulnerable."

"So, everyone's battery, no matter how big, can run out of juice?"

"Even yours, Ethan." Her hand returned to his knee, but this time she gave it a quick squeeze. "Even yours."

Hands off the merchandise, girl. No matter what you bring to the table, Seph won't be having any of that.

"One last time," Ethan said, trying to change the subject and distract us all from the faint pink rising in his cheeks. "Are we sure this is the way to go? We've already got Katrina, and we're not sure if—"

"Whoa, whoa, whoa," the tattooed woman said, the eyes of the ghost-faced murderer on her right deltoid growing as wide in shock as her own, "I agreed to be part of the solution, not to take a dive headfirst into a blender. You pull away from this curb without at least a couple more folks in the back to go up against this Cardinal asshole, and you can drop me off at the next bus stop."

"I guess that's that, then," Ethan said. "Let's do this." He grasped the door handle and gave it a yank only to find it locked. "Driver?"

The Driver opened his own door and stepped onto the sidewalk. "Perhaps we'd all be better off if I handled initial contact this time." His gaze meandered along the side of his vehicle. "Last time, a stray piece of flying rubble put a ding in the car." He poked his head back into the vehicle. "You can all imagine how much I like dings."

The man my mother trusted like a brother strode to the center door of the complex of townhomes and rapped at the door. Moments later, he disappeared inside, leaving the five of us alone in the back. Though I recognized we had more than enough power among our group to leave whenever we wanted, I conceded that it was in our best interest to do exactly as the owner of the vehicle recommended.

"So," Ethan asked Katrina, "I'm guessing there are shadowmancers across the globe. How did you end up one of the Midnight Angel's Crows?"

My heart sank. If there was one thing you didn't call one of Midnight's Ravens…

"We. Are. Not. Crows." Katrina pulled in a deep breath, any hint of her previous flirty smile evaporating like rain on a lava flow. "We are her Conspiracy of Ravens, and don't you forget it, Mr. Harkreader."

Ethan raised his hands before him and backpedaled as well as he could while stuck in the back of a limo. "Sorry. Didn't pick up on the distinction."

Katrina stared into her own lap, her voice becoming as ephemeral as the shadows that acted at her whim. "As you said, Ethan, many skiomancers walk this world of ours, but only a few ever attain an audience with the Mistress, much less receive an invitation to train under her. Those few are Ravens, or at least the ones who meet her exacting standards."

"And the rest are relegated to Crow status?" Bradley interjected. "Not exactly a term of high praise, I'm guessing."

"My apologies," Ethan whispered, mortified, "I meant no disrespect."

"Of course you didn't." Katrina shook it off, her smile returning in spades. "You're new to all this, Ethan, and therefore, all is forgiven."

Of course it is. I've got news for you, shadow-girlie. Ethan is spoken for, and not by just anyone, but one of the biggest pop stars in the world. Those big blue eyes? Those muscular arms? That great big heart of his? All property of Persephone Snow, Queen of the World.

Deal with it, like the rest of us.

"Ravens, then." Ethan worked to dig himself out of the hole. "How many of you are there?"

"Here in L.A? A handful. Across the world? A few dozen. The Mistress keeps us all under her dark wing until we're ready to fly and then sets us loose upon the world to find our own path."

"A few dozen?" Bradley asked. "And those who have been banished from her side? How many of those?"

"As I said, most with talent for shadow never achieve the favor of an audience with the Mistress, much less her protection, training, and succor. Those of us who comport ourselves with honor and remain in her good graces may remain a Raven for life."

"And those who don't?" Bradley asked.

"Crows are few and far between. The fact that Krage and his three associates continue to breathe speaks volumes of the Mistress's near boundless grace and represents more mercy, frankly, than any of them deserve." She crossed her arms, her gaze shooting to one side. "Most of the rest, those who have brought the Mistress embarrassment or shame, or worse, attempted to supplant her, have all shared a similar fate. Now, their shadows live on in her."

"Hold on a second." I could almost hear my brain making the connection. "We're hunting a man who kills other Ascendant to steal the power that is their birthright and you're telling us the Midnight Angel is guilty of the same?"

"Like I said, sweetheart, First Law of Thermodynamics. When an Ascendant dies, that power has to go somewhere. Sometimes, if they're alone at the moment of their passing, the energies of their existence return to the ether, but like goes to like in our world." The tattoos of Ghostface on one arm and Pinhead on the other turned to face each other, the former closing its dark eyes and dissolving as if in death and the latter sucking the remaining "ink" into its mouth as if inhaling the other's essence. This transference of darkness left the blackened image of the Cenobite Hell Priest—I couldn't believe I knew those words—larger than the remaining monstrous portraits that decorated her slender arms. "If a skiomancer proves fool enough to challenge the Queen of Shadows to a duel to the death, their fate is their own doing."

"That's cold," Maddox said.

"So are shadows," Katrina answered.

Her eyes slid closed and her arm art returned to its previous state, though the Pinhead tattoo bore even more of a scowl while Ghostface's demeanor showed a touch more relief in its new manifestation.

"How do you do that?" Ethan asked the question that was likely on all our minds. "Are those..."

"Something the Mistress taught me. So many skiomancers seek only to control the shadows around them." She ran a hand down her body, a bit too sensuously for my taste. "I have learned to embrace the shadows within."

"That's awesome." To his credit, Ethan kept his eyes on hers. "And your personal shadows come out as the faces of late twentieth century horror movies?"

"I started with My Little Pony, but a jet-black Twilight Sparkle jumping over a shadowy rainbow didn't have quite the same badass effect as Captain Spaulding and his amazing friends." She pointed to a demented clown face on her forearm who I swore was staring at me through the entire conversation. "Besides, these movies are my jam, and I believe in truth in advertising."

Ethan chuckled at her joke. With his love of all the same movies, I couldn't help but think that, in Katrina, he'd found a kindred spirit. I'm not sure why that bothered me. I mean, Seph and Ethan were as committed as a couple can be after a single month, and Ethan wasn't the kind of man who'd have a wandering eye. Still, this Katrina chick needed to back off. Ethan Harkreader already had two women in his life, thank you very much.

"What is your favorite of these films, Katrina?" I asked in a half-hearted effort to stay part of the conversation.

She looked at me askance, as if I'd walked up on a coffee shop date that was going well. "Um, I suppose the original *Halloween* from 1978. Some of the sequels stand up, and I totally dig the Rob Zombie remake, though I'm a little done with all the retcons in the recent movies." She offered as genuine a smile as she could manage. "The original, however, will always be the standard for me."

Wonderful. Ethan had said almost the same thing to me and Seph a couple weeks back. And now, I was practically serving as her wingman—wingwoman, whatever...

"And you, Rosemary," she asked, launching my volley right back at me, "what's your favorite horror movie?"

Suddenly, I was the one taking a pop quiz, though this time I actually cared about the grade. "I'm not sure if it counts," I said after a moment of self-conscious panic, "but it's a black-and-white film I watched with Mother a few years back. A movie called *The Bad Seed*. To me, that little girl with those evil eyes and pigtails is scarier than any hulking shadow with a machete will ever be."

"Old school." Katrina shot a fist out, and before I had a chance to consider whether or not answering in kind was giving her my full endorsement, I'd already given her a bump. "A classic. I like it." She focused for a moment and on her upper arm, Leatherface's horrific mask twisted into Rhoda Penmark's piercing grin. "I'll keep this one right here, in honor of my new friend."

Friend? Not so fast, girlie. Not so fast.

"If I may interrupt this stunning display of one-upwomanship," Maddox grumbled, "can we talk about what the hell we're going to do when the Driver comes back?"

"As fascinating as this review of twentieth century horror cinema has been," Bradley, who had been uncharacteristically quiet, added, "I couldn't agree more."

"I guess we wing it," Ethan muttered, his gaze focused just beyond the window, "because here he comes."

Pulling at the bottom of his tuxedo jacket as he exited the townhome's extremely secure-appearing door, the Driver strode toward the limo with urgency in his every step. With a click of his key fob, the doors unlocked, and he opened the rear driver side door, letting us all out onto the sidewalk. Bradley went first, followed by Maddox and Ethan, then Katrina, and I brought up the rear.

"She's agreed to see you," the Driver said, "but no weapons." He glanced in Katrina's direction. "You, unfortunately, are not invited."

Katrina crinkled her nose and crossed her arms. "I'm not surprised," she grunted with a quiet huff. "I'll wait out here."

"I shall wait with you," the Driver said, "just in case."

"I can take care of myself."

The Driver shook his head. "Though we stand upon one of the safest places on the planet, it would be best if none of you were alone until all of this is over."

"And when will that be?" Bradley asked.

"When the Cardinal is in the fucking ground." Maddox stalked off toward the door from which the Driver had emerged moments before. "Come on, all of you. Let's get this over with."

I took off after Maddox and then shot a look back at the rest. "You heard the man."

Ethan shot Katrina and the Driver a polite salute, Bradley straightened his tie as if he were about to meet the Queen, and then the three of us followed Maddox up the concrete.

"Is there some kind of secret knock or something?" Bradley shouted across his shoulder.

As if in answer, the door opened when we weren't even halfway up the walk, revealing a man I never thought I'd be even remotely glad to see.

Dressed exactly as the last time I'd seen him, Dietrich Falco waited in the open doorway in his tailored ivory suit of linen, a narrow silk tie, silver cufflinks finishing off the just-visible sleeves of his shirt, and white Chuck Taylors that looked as if he'd taken them out of the box that morning. His straight silver hair, pulled into a tight ponytail that hung down his back, had wisps that waved to and fro, all subject to a gentle breeze not appreciable to the rest of us. As we approached, he studied us from behind his mirrored sunglasses.

"Why, Rosemary Delacroix," he uttered with a distinctly German inflection, "I never dreamed a Daughter of Neith would darken our doorway." He shifted his gaze to Ethan. "Greetings, Harkreader."

"Falco." Ethan crinkled his nose in disgust. "Suffocated anybody lately?"

If Ethan's comment ruffled Falco's feathers at all, the aeromancer didn't let it show.

"Nice to see you as well." He returned his attention to me. "The Driver has secured you all safe passage while here at our humble abode so long as everyone behaves." His gaze flicked back at Ethan. "Understood?"

"Understood." Ethan stepped past Falco and into the foyer of the massive townhome. "See you inside."

"Trainor I recognize," Falco continued, "but who is this individual?" He inclined his head in Bradley's direction.

"Mr. Bradley is with us." I offered my most conciliatory smile. "He arranged for our transportation to and from Los Angeles so that we could attend this meeting." I switched my face to "All Business" like Mother taught me. "He's not Ascendant, in case you were wondering, but for the time being, he's with us."

"Outstanding." Falco motioned for the three of us to join Ethan in the large foyer. "Come inside, all of you." He grumbled something under his breath about not remembering the last time they'd had a "normal" inside their walls.

Ascendant snobbery was nothing new. Such elitism came as natural to many of them as breathing. Mother always taught me that for those who walked among the rest of the world with the power of gods, to not feel implicitly superior would be the anomaly. Still, the comment rubbed me the wrong way, a fact I worked to keep from my features.

People are people, after all, as that song Ethan loves incessantly repeats.

After closing the door and turning a series of locks as if we'd entered a maximum-security prison, Falco stepped between the four of us and headed down the hall, his arms folded behind his back. "Come this way. Our mistress is waiting, and her time is valuable."

Though the outside facade resembled a series of townhomes, the interior was more like an enormous mansion: well designed, equipped, and furnished with state-of-the-art everything. Falco led us through a maze of immaculately kept hallways filled with various hung art and statuary to a double door at the end of a long wide passage, the dark wood of the door detailed with intricately carved Mayan iconography from top to bottom.

"No need to genuflect or anything, but I'd highly recommend you all mind your Ps and Qs once you cross that threshold." Falco chuckled. "Hope may spring eternal, but never forget that every sunrise is someone's last."

CHAPTER 23

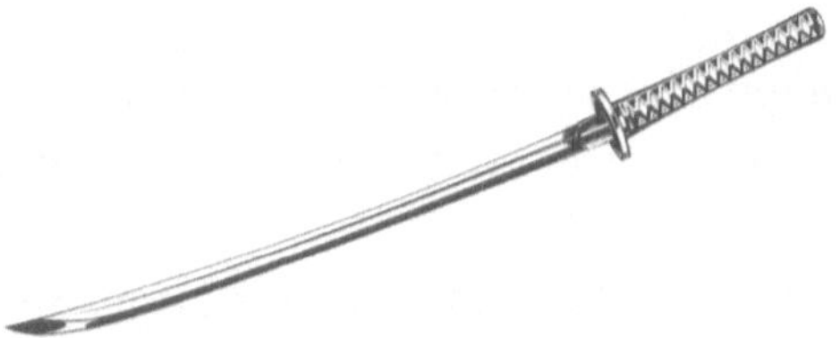

NITE AND DAY

"Greetings, El Ángel del Alba," I voiced as we entered the room, and regardless of Falco's sage advice, I did offer the resplendent woman before us a deep bow. "My eternal gratitude for granting us this audience."

Reclining barefoot atop a chaise of deep brown wood and white cloth, she sat and studied us each in turn. In her tawny features and keen emerald eyes, I found both youthful energy and the wisdom of more years than seemed possible given her flawless visage. Her full head of hair that had hung to her calves at our last meeting now rested coiled in an intricate braid atop her head. Despite the early morning hour, she was dressed to the nines in a form-fitting gown with stripes of sky blue, faint pink, and rich gold indicative of her station as Angel of the Morning.

"Come, child." She stretched out one bare arm and beckoned us closer. "Let us speak." Her twenty nails all shone with opalescent light reflecting from the crystal chandelier that hung at the circular room's center. Though such pampering was more Seph's thing than mine, I'd enjoyed my nail date with her, and even my untrained eye recognized the quality work at Alba's fingertips.

"Not jealous at all," I grumbled to myself as I peeked down at my own nails, all chewed up from the last forty-eight hours, not to mention two decades of wear and tear. The nice lady at the salon had finished my toes, but Maddox's arrival had nixed her getting to my fingertips.

Ah well, if Seph and I both somehow made it through this with ten fingers and toes apiece, I'd spring for the mani-pedi this time. After all, fair is fair.

We all gathered at the center of the room, the metallic tiles beneath our feet laid in an intricate pattern that formed an enormous compass rose. The four cardinal directions and their corresponding intermediates each bisected into silver and gold; the overall effect was that of a giant sun. And unless my usually inerrant internal compass was off, the Angel's dais rested at true east, right where it belonged.

"I, of course, know why you have come," Alba breathed through a strangely benevolent smile, "and I am happy to provide aid to both the Daughter and Agent of Neith, especially since this concerns Persephone Snow. I'm not certain, however, why you chose to visit my Sister before you came to me. Did you think my assistance would prove insufficient for your needs?"

I shook my head. "It seems that all of Los Angeles knew we were coming before even we did." I glanced back at the closed doorway through which we'd entered. "As he likely told you already, the Driver awaited our arrival at the airport. He took us straight to see your Sister at her place of business before we'd barely gotten boots on the ground. We were famished, and the diner's staff rose to the occasion." I chanced a slight smile. "We meant no disrespect, but as the saying goes, darkness usually comes before the dawn."

"Clever girl," Alba answered. "And no disrespect taken." She crinkled her nose. "I understand Midnight has already offered to bolster your forces."

"She has."

"Some would argue that you come to me then from a position of power."

"A position of power?" Ethan muttered under his breath.

"Simple, Mr. Harkreader." Alba spoke as if Ethan had actually addressed her. "If my dark Sister has already assigned one of her lieutenants to accompany you, how can I refuse?" She sat upright on her chaise, allowing her bare feet to descend to the golden carpet below. "The day Midnight proves more magnanimous than Morning is the day I relinquish my role to one more worthy." Her eyes narrowed at me. "So, if we may cut straight to the chase, Daughter of Neith, tell me, what is it I can do for you?"

"You know our situation?"

"I do."

"And you know of the Greyhound's fate?"

She grimaced. "Unfortunately, yes."

"Then you understand that we must stop this menace who threatens us all." I motioned to Ethan and Maddox. "The three of us and my father fought this monster with all we had, and yet, if it weren't for a young but extremely competent technomancer with whom we've recently allied, none of us would have survived."

"The Cardinal." She savored the word on her lips like a sommelier picking out the hints of a fine wine. "Such an innocuous little bird in the grand scheme of avians. I'd be interested in what led this...man to choose such a nom de guerre."

"He's anything but innocuous, Lady Alba." Ethan looked left and right as if making sure he hadn't totally screwed up addressing Ascendant royalty. "Beyond an electromagnetic pulse that took out an entire city block, nothing we've done so far has even slowed him down."

"And what say you, theriodan?" She directed her attention to Maddox. "Whispers suggest you've spent the last two years hunting this man. I would hear your thoughts on the matter."

Maddox's eyes darted left and right, very much a wild coyote backed into yet another corner. "To be honest, Lady Alba, it's difficult to fully assess the threat level outside what we've directly experienced in the last two days. That being said, the situation is grave. The Cardinal has not only dispatched an unknown number of Ascendant over the last many months, but taken their powers, their abilities, their very essence to augment his own. He's strong, fast, and durable, likely from killing one of my theriodan brethren, and we've seen him manifest skiomancer ability, but God knows what other abilities he holds in reserve." He shook his head sadly. "And that doesn't even take into account the armored suit he wears that allows him the power of flight, a sonic defense system that can incapacitate anyone with eardrums, and protection from bullets as well as Harkreader's steel." He let fly a mirthless laugh. "Even empowered with the Light of Neith, Danielle Delacroix's ancient blades scarcely scratched the paint."

The Angel let out a quiet sigh. "Quite a thorough assessment, Mr...?"

"Trainor."

"Oh." Surprise flashed across Alba's gaze for the first time since we entered the room, followed by an instant understanding as her eyes flicked briefly in my direction. "Thank you, Mr. Trainor."

"He can fly, eh?" Falco asked, the first words he'd spoken since we entered the room. "Are you all sure he hasn't simply taken an aeromancer's power as well? The sky, after all, is our purview."

"We considered that," I answered, "but other than flight itself, the Cardinal hasn't manifested any other wind-related abilities."

"As best we can tell," Ethan answered, keeping the hostility from his tone, if not his face, "his flight is a function of the suit. After our technomancer hit him with the EMP in Denver, he appeared grounded, at least temporarily."

"Not that it helped the Greyhound," Maddox grumbled.

"So," the Angel breathed, a hint of exasperation in her tone, "at least we have that as a last resort, when and if he attacks again."

"I wouldn't count on it." Maddox ground his teeth. "We have our technomancer, but the Cardinal has his as well. His suit is already cutting edge—pardon the pun—and likely being updated as we speak to prevent an EMP attack from working a second time. Between his likely continuing assumption of Ascendant power as well as an ever-improving arsenal of offensive and defensive technology, I fear the Cardinal will only become more difficult to defeat with each encounter."

The Angel considered all our words for a long moment. "It would appear then, Daughter of Neith, that you are in need of some significant reinforcements." Alba looked to Falco. "Dietrich, it appears this murderer of our kind despoils your element with his very presence. What say you accompany Miss Delacroix and Mr. Harkreader and lend them your expertise?"

"Somehow, I knew when I awoke this morning that I wouldn't be returning to my bed tonight." Falco raised a questioning brow. "Should I gather the others, Mistress Alba?"

"Yes, Lady Alba," I asked, "as you said, the more firepower, the better. Anyone you can spare would be greatly appreciated."

"Would that I could help more." The Angel dipped her head forward in the slightest of bows. "Violeta is currently out of the country while Daichi just returned from a rather strenuous errand and would not be at his best, especially against such a threat as you all have described." She lowered her head. "As for Ada, she is... indisposed for the time being."

I knew better than to ask for Alba's personal involvement, especially after Midnight's earlier pass on our request.

"Understood. We are happy with the involvement of your aeromancer and appreciate both his help and your leave to allow him to join us." I tried to penetrate the mirrored lenses of Falco's shades in an effort to get a read on his true feelings regarding coming with us, but failed to pick up on anything other than his usual smug smile. "Know that we'll do everything in our collective power to return him to you unharmed."

"Dietrich can take care of himself, as I regret to admit you all had to learn the hard way." She looked to her aeromancer. "I look forward to your full report."

"At my earliest convenience, Mistress." Falco opened the doorway leading back to the main passage. "Shall we, Miss Delacroix?"

As the four of us plus Falco returned to the hallway, it occurred to me that Bradley hadn't said a word the entire time we'd been in the Angel's presence.

"You were unusually quiet in there, Mr. Bradley." I patted his shoulder. "Everything okay?"

"Are you kidding?" He shook his head and chuckled before letting loose a satisfied sigh. "I have spent the better part of my life studying everything known about the Ascendant, pored over the Order's archives into the wee hours of the night more times than I can count, and now? I've encountered two of the three Angels and nearly met the third, all in the space of a day." He looked at me as moisture welled at the corners of his eyes. "You might as well ask a priest or rabbi how they feel five minutes after their first time seeing the face of God."

~

Though substantially more packed than before, the back of the Driver's limousine was notably quieter on the return trip to the Los Angeles Airport. Maddox alternated between glaring at Ethan and pretending not to stare at me. Katrina and Falco shot daggers at each other with their eyes, the latter quite impressive as his ever-present mirrored sunglasses remained in place. Bradley sat in the middle of it all, alternating between nervous glances left and right and giddy smiles as if he were a child on Christmas morning. Then there were the tense stares between Ethan and me, as we communicated silently as to our next steps and what we'd do if the bomb we'd assembled over the preceding hours blew up in our face.

Surprisingly, Falco was the one who finally broke the ice. "I'm curious," he addressed Katrina, "I've been with Alba since I was a gangly teen, so long that I don't remember what it was like before I came to be in her employ."

Katrina cocked her head to the side. "Is there a question in there somewhere?"

Falco's lips curled into a sideways question mark. "I guess I was wondering, as you appear rather young, how long have you worked for Madame Midnight?"

"Long enough." At the uncomfortable silence, she went on. "So, I didn't really have much of a home life before my abilities manifested.

218

But after?" A morbid chuckle escaped her lips. "You think parents look sideways at goth kids? Wait until they start making shadows dance, then see how fast Mommy and Daddy kick them to the curb. I was thirteen and homeless when Midnight took me in, gave me a roof and three squares a day, taught me how to do my thing, and gave me a place where I belonged."

"Homeless?" Being raised by a mother who made the tiger moms you read about in magazines look like absentee parents, I couldn't imagine. "How terrible."

"And you have already achieved the rank of Raven in her eyes?" Falco continued. "Impressive for one with so few years under her belt."

"To be honest," Katrina's eyes dropped, "I'm more like a Raven in training at this point."

"Raven in training?" Maddox scowled around at all of us. "We fly all the way to L.A. to get help from two of the most powerful individuals on the planet, and all we get is a junior shadowmancer and a guy whose most useful skill is making a sailboat move?" He shook his head in frustration. "We're all going to die."

"Hey," Ethan said before Falco could stir the pot even more, "the only reason anyone in Dietrich's presence continues to breathe is because he wants them to." He shot Falco a knowing glance. "Trust me, I've experienced the pain he can bring firsthand."

As Falco settled back into his seat, his ruffled feathers stroked by Ethan's almost-compliment, Katrina leaned forward to defend her own honor.

"As for my status among Madame Midnight's entourage," she whispered, "just because I'm the youngest of her skiomancers and have yet to claim the title of Raven doesn't mean I don't know what I'm doing."

The ink-black image on her upper arm of the killer from the Halloween movies swirled down over her biceps like a wave coming to shore. The two-dimensional cyclone of shadow trailed down her arm, picking up all the other slashers that stared from her porcelain flesh. A moment later, darkness poured from her clawed fingertips like ink from a quintet of fountain pens, the five swirls of shadow coalescing into a pair of jet-black forms with curved horns and wings of night. One monstrous silhouette leaped at Falco's face while the other lunged for Maddox's throat, simultaneously eliciting a jump from the aeromancer and a quiet yip from the coyote's lips before each dissipated into the darkness within the limo.

"Do not tempt me, girl," Falco whispered. "I've ended individuals for lesser offenses."

"I'm certain you have, Mr. Falco," Katrina said, her tone respectful even as her face twisted into a wicked grin. "To misquote my yoga teacher's favorite saying, the darkness in me recognizes the...hot air in you?"

"How glib." Falco looked out the limo window. "I certainly hope you fight as well as you snark, skiomancer."

"Going for the jugular, eh?" Maddox growled. "At least we agree on basic tactics."

"I may not be as in touch with my inner animal as you, Mr. Trainor, but you'll find I'm full of surprises nonetheless."

"Well," Bradley cut in, "now that everyone is on friendly terms, what say we start working out how we're going to win this thing?" He paused for a moment, giving everyone a moment to reframe. "The way I see it, our problem is three-fold."

"How to find the asshole," Maddox offered.

"How to defeat him," I added.

"And how to keep Seph out of danger while we're doing it," Ethan finished.

"Wow," Katrina laughed, "did you guys practice that or something?"

"You missed a key element." Falco considered for a moment. "Two, in fact."

"Go ahead, then." I motioned for him to continue. "We're all ears."

"First, what does this Cardinal want? If you can answer that, you'll be well on your way to answering the other three questions."

"What he wants, Mr. Falco, is to kill, to take that which isn't his birthright and make it his own, to become more and more powerful until none can stand against him." Maddox's fists clenched and unclenched at his sides. "That is what this monster wants."

"But why?" Falco asked. "I've killed normals and Ascendant... never unprovoked, mind you. But doing what this maniac does, the seemingly arbitrary murders of others of our kind, has never so much as crossed my mind."

"When you have taken another Ascendant life," Ethan asked, "did you do what the Cardinal does? Did you take their power, their abilities, their...essence?"

I had little doubt that Ethan was again beating himself up over taking Mother's Light at the moment of her death. We'd talked about it dozens of times, but the guilt he carried over simply being in the wrong place at the wrong time was like a wound that continued to bleed no matter how many times repaired.

"First," Falco said, "no, I personally have never feasted on the essence of another Ascendant. Second, even if I chose to do so, most of us simply cannot do what the Cardinal does. At the time of an Ascendant's death, another in close proximity can indeed absorb their essence."

"As I understand it," Katrina added, "my mistress has ushered many a skiomancer to the other side of the veil, sometimes in combat when one of our kind has attempted to supplant her and other times simply at the end of another skiomancer's time in this world. Nevertheless, each time, she takes on their shadows, their darkness, their very souls so that some small part of them might live on."

Ethan shuddered at the revelation. "And that's...okay?"

"It's not all that different from my family line, Ethan. With the death of each Daughter of Neith, the power, skills, and memories of all that have gone before pass on to the next in line. For the moment, that very Light lives on in you."

"The difference," Falco said, "is that the Cardinal seems capable of taking on not only the raw power but also the specific abilities of virtually any Ascendant."

"Has there ever been another Ascendant with such an ability?" Ethan asked.

"One that I'm aware of," Falco answered. "We do not speak of him."

Ethan raised an eyebrow. "Any chance the Cardinal could be this guy?"

"Almost certainly no. Not only was the Ascendant in question put down centuries ago, but were it the individual in question, not one of you would still be standing after your encounter in Denver." Falco paused and looked left and right, as if he feared the Devil himself might appear before us. "Fortunately for us, to appropriate a little Shakespeare, there appears to be method in the Cardinal's madness. These killings are not the random violence of some rabid animal—no offense to the theriodan in our midst—but clearly the acts of a man with an agenda. Figure out what that agenda is, and you can stop him."

"Agreed." Bradley raised an eyebrow. "What else, Mr. Falco? Anything else we're missing here?"

"A corollary to the first. A question that I'm certain has plagued you all the last two days. The marked break in his pattern of killing."

"It's all I've been thinking about," Ethan said. "What does he want with Seph?"

"For a man who has stalked and slain who knows how many fellow Ascendant, to set up such an elaborate kidnapping of a recently Ascended public figure, and then, in the heat of the moment, to release her rather than jeopardize her life?" Falco turned his head in Ethan's direction "In this aberrancy exists a multitude of questions, though the answers, Mr. Harkreader, may be ones you don't like."

"Whatever the truth is," Ethan said, "I can handle it."

"I certainly hope so," Falco said, "for all our sakes."

The smoky barrier that separated the Driver's area of his vehicle from the rest of us lowered, revealing his broad shoulders and his close-cropped scalp. He peered back at the lot of us through the rearview mirror. "We're a few minutes out from the airport, Mr. Bradley. I trust you have notified your people to be ready."

He checked his phone and watch. "Everything is proceeding as planned, Mr. Driver."

"Simply 'Driver,' if you please."

"Of course," Bradley answered. "My people tell me the plane will be fully fueled and ready upon our arrival. Security is already notified to allow us all safe passage." He looked to Ethan and me. "And then you two will be happily reunited with your favorite respective lengths of steel."

"Excellent," I said as Ethan nodded with vigor.

I wasn't sure who took more convincing to leave our weapons behind, Ethan or me, but Bradley's instincts to not tempt fate in a major U.S. airport nor to show up asking for the Angels' help armed to the teeth had been the right call.

Still, his assessment was on point. I was distinctly more comfortable with a sword at my side, and unless I misread his body language, Ethan was quickly coming around to my way of thinking on the subject.

"We've gathered our army, such as it is," I whispered to no one in particular. "Now, we go to war."

CHAPTER 24

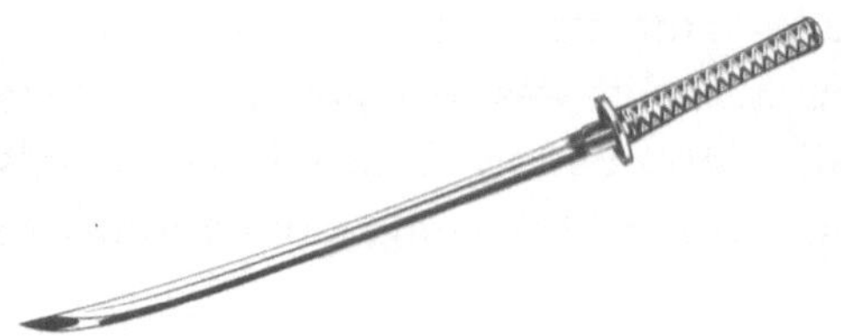

WE'RE READY

"Ethan!" Seph sprinted barefoot across her front yard in a tank top and sweatpants, threw her arms around Ethan's neck, and covered his face with kisses. "Thank God."

"Nice to see you too," Ethan barely got out as he contended with what to the untrained eye might have resembled a piranha attack. "Everything okay here?"

"It is now."

Simultaneously sweet and awkward, the passion of their reunion was undeniable. Guilty heat rose in my cheeks for reasons I only half understood, and yet I found myself captivated by the moment. Only at the height of our relationship had my feelings for Maddox poured out of me with such vehemence. That all-too-brief time, however, had left an indelible mark and a big part of me desperately wanted to feel such passion again.

An embarrassed glance my way from Ethan finally convinced me to turn away and give them their moment. I chuckled to myself.

Despite working for weeks to prepare Ethan for any possible attack, an onslaught of kisses from his girlfriend hadn't made the syllabus.

Girlfriend. What a weird word. I mean, she's not exactly a girl, and what they're likely doing behind closed doors goes way beyond friendship.

All right, Rosemary. Enough fun with etymology. Let the moment pass and move on.

Funny. In private, I could only imagine that Ethan and Seph had the whole intimacy thing down to a science. Still, Ethan was like me in a lot of ways, including our general discomfort with public displays of affection, and it showed.

A solid thirty seconds later, Seph finally came up for air.

"In case you couldn't tell," she said with rosy cheeks and furtive eyes, "I missed you."

"I missed you too, Seph." In a moment I'd been dreading since we first touched down back in Santa Barbara, Ethan asked the question that had been on all our minds for the last half hour. "But what are you still doing here? I thought Mr. Delacroix was going to—"

"For the thousandth time, Mr. Delacroix works for *me*." Where only unfettered adoration had been moments before, exasperation stole across Seph's features. "But, if you must know, he and I agreed once we made it back to the house that it might be safer to wait until you all returned before taking me to whatever godforsaken place he has in mind." She glanced back at her palatial home. "Not to mention, with all the work L.J. did to proof my home against others with his particular skill set, it's actually one of the more secure places in town." She motioned to the pair of black SUVs along her street. "And Mr. Bradley really delivered on the security—" Finally noticing the rest of us, Seph stopped mid-sentence, her eyes fixing like lasers on something across my shoulder. Or someone. "Wait. What is *he* doing here?"

Ethan followed her gaze, briefly meeting my own, and then turned back to Seph, palms out before his chest. "Hold on, Seph. Let me explain."

"You brought that Falco creep to my home?" Though Seph's eyes filled with a mix of terror and disbelief, her body language made a very clear decision between fight and flight as she dropped into the low cat stance I taught her weeks ago. Not that her self-confidence needed much of a boost, but Ethan wasn't the only one who'd been training with me the last few weeks. Her weight on her back foot and her hands before her in fists, I couldn't help but feel a bit proud of the current reigning pop princess of the world.

From the periphery of my vision, I witnessed Father poke his head out the door. Upon seeing Falco, he rushed to Seph's side, his hand resting atop the pistol at his hip.

"Everything all right, Miss Snow?"

"I don't know." Her glare shifted back and forth between Ethan and Falco. "*Is* everything all right?"

"Persephone Snow." Falco stepped forward and extended his hand "I humbly beg your forgiveness regarding our various encounters last month. I hope you will accept my deepest apologies as well as my assurance that I am only here with your best interests at heart."

After several seconds of staring at the offered handshake as if it were a viper poised to strike, Seph rested her fingers atop his with a decided wrinkle of her nose. Falco, in turn, raised her hand gently and tickled her knuckles with a proper European brush of the lips.

"Please understand that when we last met, I merely performed my duty as an emissary of the Angel of the Morning and at the moment, ironically, continue to do the same, albeit in a quite different context." He bent forward at the waist in a deep bow. "Regardless, until all this is over, I remain in your service."

Seph shot a puzzled look at Ethan. "You actually trust this guy?"

"Like he said, Alba herself sent him," Ethan answered. "He was a model citizen the whole way back to Montecito and has been extremely helpful as we've been trying to figure out our next steps."

"Give him a chance, Seph," I added. "The list of Ascendant who wish you ill may be long, but Dietrich here isn't among them."

Seph let out a mirthless chuckle. "Wow, this Ascendant stuff really turns on a dime." She turned her attention on Katrina. "Let's see. Alba sent Falco, so I'm guessing you must be Midnight's offering?"

"I'd prefer envoy." She held out her hand. "My name is Katrina Wellen." With a smile, she added, "It's German."

"Welcome." Seph took her hand and gave it a firm shake. "I'm curious. How old are you, Katrina Wellen?"

"Nineteen." Color rose in Katrina's pale cheeks. "Just like you, Miss Snow."

"Nineteen." Seph considered for a moment. "And how long have you been doing...whatever it is you do?"

"Since before you were cast on *Teen Spies*." The shadowy figures of horror up and down her arms blurred momentarily before returning to their previous sharpness. "I must admit, if I'm being totally honest, I've seen every episode multiple times."

"A fan, then." Seph's perturbed facade cracked a millimeter or two. "She can stay." She shot a look at Falco and, with a purposeful eye roll, added, "Him too, if he loses the stupid shades."

"Stupid?" Falco bristled. "I'll have you know these frames cost four figures."

"You want me to trust you, yet you won't let me look you in the eyes?"

"Look." Falco cheeks flushed a bright pink. "My condition leaves my eyes very sensitive to light. I wear the sunglasses so I don't walk around squinting." He looked to one side, and his voice dropped to a low mumble. "And the lenses are prescription, if you must know."

Seph's jaw dropped at the sudden vulnerability of a man that had a month before held her life in his hands—or a mentally controlled mini-cyclone, to be more specific. She considered for a moment, and then, in a move that was one hundred percent Persephone Snow, reached out and rested a hand atop Falco's shoulder. "Please excuse my insensitivity, Mr. Falco. I had no idea."

Falco studied Seph for a moment, and then his face broke into a legitimate smile. "Thank you, Miss Snow."

"No. Thank you, Mr. Falco, for coming to help keep me safe from harm." She flashed the skiomancer in our presence her most winning grin. "You as well, Katrina."

"My pleasure." Katrina squirmed with joy.

Huh. I hadn't seen the whole fangirl thing coming, but Katrina was the correct demographic. And unlike me, she likely had a television in her house growing up.

Seph turned to the remaining two of our returning clan. "Welcome back, Maddox. Glad you appear none the worse for wear." Her eyes narrowed as her attention shifted to the last of our group. "And you must be this Mr. Bradley I've heard so much about."

Bradley stepped forward, his bearing rigid as if he were addressing royalty. "Yes, ma'am. I'm here to offer my services and whatever resources my organization can bring to bear to help you make it safely through this ordeal."

"No need for such formality." She smiled. "Thank you for all you've done already and your willingness to stick around despite all the insanity."

"To be honest, Miss Snow," Bradley smiled like a kid in a candy store, "I wouldn't miss it for the world."

Seph laughed again, an amused twinkle in her gaze. "Then you and I have very different tastes in spare time activity, Mr. Bradley."

"Which we can discuss in detail at your leisure, but might I suggest we get under roof." He glanced left and right. "Considering the Cardinal's initial attempt two days ago was mere blocks away, it would seem we're rather exposed at the moment."

"I couldn't agree more." Father rested his fingers at Seph's shoulder, the touch gentle but firm. I still remember those same hands keeping me from stepping in front of a bus when I was three, and the sentiment here was no different. "Shall we reconvene inside your lovely home?"

"Of course." Seph turned and headed for the door. "There's plenty of space in the dining room, and L.J. and Neko have ordered more pizza than even this crowd can eat in a night."

"Indeed," Father grunted. "You'd think the two of them had never seen a credit card before."

Seph headed to the front door of her house and allowed us all inside what had over the last month become almost as much home as our RV. The twenty-foot ceiling sported a crystal chandelier straight out of the fanciest hotel I'd ever set foot in, and the walls all gleamed white as if every square inch bore fresh paint.

Original paintings, not prints, decorated the white stucco. Seph had told me all the painters' names half a dozen times, but the French and Russian and Spanish names all evaporated the moment they hit my temporal lobe. While a few of the pieces were to my taste, a lot of the paintings looked like a three-year-old had been let loose in an art store and allowed to go to town on a blank canvas. Personal tastes aside, however, I had to admit Seph had a keen eye for what looked good where.

After spending my entire life in a trio of progressively nicer recreational vehicles and a countless succession of hotel rooms all over the world, I'd have been lucky to remember to even put something on the wall of a home, much less pick out something that was, as Seph would say, "aesthetically pleasing."

We passed the long hall that doubled as museum art gallery and entered her cavernous great room with the sunken oval couch where I'd curled up watching dozens of movies with Seph, Ethan, and even Father occasionally over the preceding month: laughing at comedies I'd never seen that Ethan knew by heart, holding back tears with dramas I'd heard of but never experienced, and fighting off goosebumps to a bevy of horror flicks that left me wondering about the sanity of the movies' creators. At the moment, however, the center of the couch was occupied by L.J. and Neko armed with video game controllers playing one of those three-dimensional military games, what Ethan called a "first person shooter."

What this game has to do with the golden circles that hover over the angels' heads in Christian iconography, I had no idea.

"Ethan!" Neko paused the game with a quick push of a button. "You're back!" He hopped up off the velvety cushion, leaped from the recessed oval to the main floor, and went straight for the hug.

Quite the affectionate tiger, that one. Good in a fight, but at home, a big pussycat.

"Everything go okay?" Neko asked, pulling back from Ethan and perusing the rest of the crowd with the dubious feline eye. "Funny, I was expecting a bigger army."

"Mind your manners, kitty cat," Falco said, his gruff German running roughshod over my eardrums. "I may be here at Alba's request, but it was my choice to come."

"Same for me and Madame Midnight." Katrina pulled up at Falco's side. "It would be nice if at least one of you had an initial response besides eye rolls around here." She looked genuinely upset, more than what I would have expected from such a relatively benign complaint, but before I could ask what was wrong, another voice filled with jubilant enthusiasm from the opposite end of the emotional spectrum hit all our ears.

"Wow!" L.J. approached from the far end of the room, having taken the long way out of the sunken mini-amphitheater. "Your tattoos are so cool." He headed straight for Katrina, his eyes wide with admiration. "Is that the skull from *The Evil Dead II* poster?"

"Now, that's more like it." Katrina shot me a wicked grin, and then turned back to L.J. who appeared to be mid-internal debate as to whether or not to touch the skiomancer's "inked" skin. "Great hair, by the way!" She mussed his turquoise locks with her black-nailed hand, and L.J. jumped like he'd been hit with a cattle prod.

"Thanks..." he said, as if his every word had abandoned him. "I'm L.J."

"Nice to meet you, L.J." She laughed. "I'm Katrina." She pulled her lips to one side in consideration. "If you think that's cool"—she pointed to the skull-face occupying her deltoid—"watch this." The eyebrows of the gruesome face wriggled, eliciting another jump from our young technomancer friend. "What do you think, kid?"

"Coooool..." His pupils dilated, even as he balked almost imperceptibly at being called kid by a woman only five years his senior. I'd both seen and experienced such moments many times already in my few years. L.J. was either in love or well on his way.

As if this group needed more emotional entanglements.

"Shall we set up in your dining room, Miss Snow?" Indifferent to introductions—polite, sarcastic, or otherwise—Bradley headed for Seph's dining room table, the expanse of dark wood backlit by the enormous window looking out on Seph's gigantic backyard pool where I'd been swimming laps every morning for weeks. "We have no idea how long this current respite will last, and we need to get everyone on the same sheet of music if we're going to survive the next few days, defeat the Cardinal, and return your life to some semblance of sanity."

"Agreed again." Father strode over to his typical chair at one end of the rectangular table and took a seat. "Everyone?"

Bradley went to the opposite end and occupied his space with similar conviction.

I smirked, wondering who would win the argument between the two men as to who sat at the head of the table and who sat at the... other end.

"So..." both Father and Bradley began as if they'd rehearsed it, each clearly trying to keep up a semblance of cool though the tension in the room had spiked.

Seph took charge immediately. "All right, alpha males. I'm going to head this one off at the pass." She nodded in Father's direction. "In matters of my security, Mr. Delacroix, you're in charge as always." She then turned to Bradley's end of the table. "And you, Mr. Bradley, are our highly appreciated consultant who I fully expect to keep any plans we make on the straight and narrow." She rested both fists on the rich wood tabletop before her. "We're all on the same team here, and both of you are essential. Just making sure we're all on the same page."

Both Father and Bradley stared silently in Seph's direction, each avoiding the other's gaze.

"Gentlemen?" Seph asked.

"Yes, ma'am," Bradley whispered, his entire body relaxing into his chair. "Agreed."

"Of course, Miss Snow." Father leaned back, arms crossed but his features resigned to Seph's terms.

"Great." Seph motioned for everyone to join her around the massive slab of wood. "All right, babe," she nodded in Ethan's direction after everyone had taken a seat, "now that we're peopled up and all in one place again, what's the next step?"

My entire body puckered at the question.

First, I'd never been a fan of cutesy pet names, never allowing Maddox to call me anything other than my given name and having vetoed the various diminutive versions of my name Seph had tried to institute over the preceding weeks, but I had no control over how she and the man with whom she shared a bed addressed each other.

And second, while I appreciated Ethan's skills and tactics in a fight, he wasn't the most experienced strategist in the room by a long shot.

Still, Seph's feelings for Ethan notwithstanding, having him serve as a relatively impartial arbiter of all the room's opinions wasn't the worst idea.

"We were all talking on the way back from L.A," Ethan began. "The way I and the others see it, waiting for the Cardinal to strike again and hoping our defense is adequate leaves him with every advantage: surprise, time to plan—"

"We take the fight to him," Falco interrupted. "Tear him from that armor of cowardice."

"We make him pay for what he's done," Katrina added, "for the lives he's taken, and the wisdom that can never be passed on."

"Wow," Seph said. "Glad you two are on our side." She turned to me. "What do you think, Rosemary?"

It was the first time she'd directly addressed me since our return. For someone who'd spent the whole morning two days ago proclaiming us BFFs, the silence had hit me hard. Truth be told, even I had to admit being in the woman's spotlight felt good and that the world seemed a little darker when you weren't.

"Though our last attempt at tracking him down and stopping him once and for all proved unsuccessful, I have to agree." I took a step toward my usual spot at the big table, next to Father. "The adage about the best defense being a good offense seems apropos."

Bradley, who'd remained silent along with Father since their dress down moments before, cleared his throat. "We are far better prepared this time, Miss Snow, with far greater numbers and power to bring to bear."

"Not to mention, L.J. and I have been working on a couple things to at least try to level the playing field from a technological standpoint." Father cast a glance in our resident technomancer's direction. "When he hasn't been blowing up imaginary bad guys on a screen with Neko, that is."

"Some people listen to music to concentrate." L.J. retreated into a self-conscious shrug. "I descend into the nearest video game."

"Sorry, L.J." Father laughed. "I'm just ribbing you. Whatever your process, keep those good ideas flowing."

"Thanks, Mr. Delacroix." Genuinely touched, L.J.'s voice warbled with emotion. "That means a lot."

Though we'd barely gotten to know each other, I got the distinct impression that L.J. didn't have much of a father figure in his life, and as far as fathers go, mine had gravitas to spare.

"So," Father continued, "it appears we're all in agreement that going on the offensive is the way to go. Let's discuss logistics." He looked to the young technomancer. "I suspect that even if you can't pinpoint him as well as you did last time, L.J., you can at least get us in the right ballpark, so to speak."

As L.J. let out a rapid, "Yes, sir," Ethan shook his head at Father's unintentional joke.

"We have a coyote and a tiger to help sniff him out once we're on the ground," Ethan added, "assuming you're both in, of course."

"Oh, I'm in," Maddox growled, shooting me a perturbed glance. "Payback is going to be a serious bitch."

"You can count on me as well." Neko made a point to not look Maddox's way.

"We have air support, tech support, and our very own shadow agent," Bradley offered, "not to mention Mr. Harkreader's special abilities and Miss Delacroix's incomparable skills."

I tilted my head forward at the compliment. "As well as both your and Father's tactical acumen and firepower."

"Don't forget about me," Seph said. "I haven't exactly figured out all my capabilities quite yet, but I don't want to be treated like I'm just the damsel in distress here." Her eyes flicked in Ethan's direction. "I want to help too."

"Of course." Ethan nodded Seph's way. "It's going to take all of us if we're to win this fight. The Cardinal kicked our collective ass *before* he absorbed the Greyhound's essence. I can only assume he'll be even tougher this time."

"I suggest, then, that we allow our esteemed technomancer to get started triangulating our quarry's current location while those on the front line discuss tactics to bring this madman down." Bradley cast his gaze up one side of the table and down the other. "No time like the present."

"I couldn't agree more."

Amplified to near-deafening volume, the words shook the enormous window to my rear. I spun in my chair to look out the back of Seph's home, already knowing what I would see.

With crimson wings of steel emanating from each arm, the Cardinal hung effortlessly in the sky above Seph's Olympic-size pool, the water showing only the tiniest of disturbance at his presence.

"I thought I'd save you all the trouble of hunting me down." He offered a mid-air bow, the enormous rectangle of glass separating us from him shuddering as if about to shatter. "Here I am."

Seph rose from her chair and moved behind Ethan, who had already sprung out of his own seat, his gaze filled with surprise, anger, and disbelief. Father and Bradley both came to their feet, drew their respective firearms, and trained them on the Cardinal. Maddox and Neko were out of their chairs an instant before Katrina and Falco, the latter churning the still air of the room until my ears popped with the pressure change. Only L.J. remained in his seat, frozen to the spot, though whether in fear or concentration, I couldn't be sure.

I leaped onto the dining room table, wishing my sword rested in my hand rather than against the wall twenty feet away.

"You have our attention," I shouted, doing my best to keep the fear from my voice, "and obviously, you can hear us." I narrowed my eyes at our armored foe. "What do you want?"

"Believe it or not, Rosemary Delacroix," the Cardinal swept his arms wide, "I've joined you at Miss Snow's lovely home in hopes that we could make a deal."

CHAPTER 25

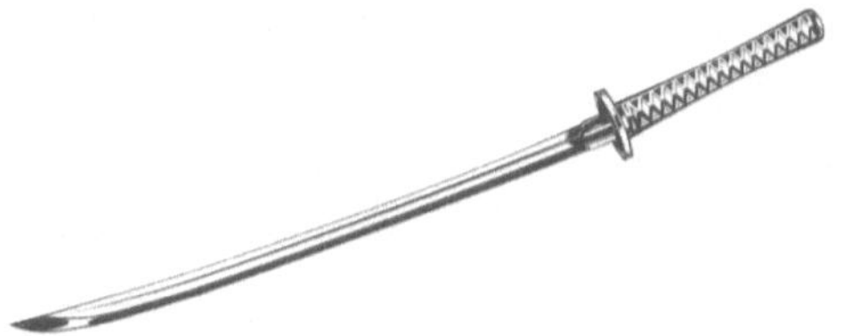

COME GO WITH ME

"First," came the Cardinal's augmented voice, "I would feel terrible if the lot of you felt you had to shout to be heard during our negotiations." A single blast from his sonic cannons sent a spiderweb of cracks through the gigantic window from one end to the other, even as it sent an unprepared Neko howling to his knees.

The sensitive ears of a theriodan, both blessing and curse.

Maddox stood fast as the massive sheet of glass for which Seph had undoubtedly paid through the nose fell to the ground in a million pieces. He'd confided in me on the way back from Los Angeles that even then his ears still rang and that he suspected the attack in Denver had ruptured one of his eardrums. The rest of us, on the other hand, collectively winced at the thankfully brief sonic onslaught, and then awaited the Cardinal's next words.

With only the whisper of whatever his armor used for propulsion, our crimson enemy passed through the destroyed window and lit before us with a decisive thud of metallic boot on expensive hardwood.

"I knew I sensed something amiss," Katrina muttered, the horrific faces up and down her arms expressing varying reactions of fear, shock, and outrage. "Dammit. Violated Midnight's first rule."

"To always trust your gut?" the Cardinal asked. "Good advice if I've ever heard it." He held up a fist surrounded in a sphere of swirling darkness. "If you must know, the shadow in me sensed the shadow in you as well."

L.J. looked on in disbelief, clearly scared out of his mind as he truly came face to face with the Cardinal for the first time, but wisely kept his own counsel regarding his place on our team. Ethan, meanwhile, inched backward toward the far wall where Mother's swords leaned in the corner.

The Cardinal raised a gauntlet in Ethan's direction. "Take one more step toward Danielle Delacroix's blades, Mr. Harkreader, and our negotiations end."

Ethan froze in place, though he maintained his balance over both his feet, ready to move in any direction should the need arise.

Just like I taught him.

"And don't try to sing me a lullaby, Snow," the Cardinal continued. "You may not be gagged this time around, but the same tech in my helmet that filters out the sound of my sonic cannon does the same for your pretty little voice. I may hear your words, but I'm afraid the melody would be lost on me." He stepped forward, confident and without an ounce of trepidation. "You must all feel quite foolish, preparing your little battle plans in earnest only to learn the enemy you plot against heard everything." He cracked his neck, as if preparing to step into the proverbial ring. "I considered listening to the entire diatribe before making my entrance, but then again, I wouldn't appreciate it if someone wasted my time in such a manner." A quiet laugh echoed from his armor's loudspeaker. "I will say I'm quite honored that you've taken such drastic measures in an effort to win this fight. Makes me feel like I'm finally getting somewhere with my current course of action." All mirth left his voice as his words grew quiet, the quiet vibrato of his armor's speakers lending a strange gravitas to his words. "Don't delude yourselves, however, into thinking you can defeat what you barely comprehend."

"I was reared and trained by Danielle Delacroix, Daughter of Neith." I somersaulted off the table to land before the Cardinal in a show of fearlessness, though at my heart, I wondered if the demonstration of gymnastic ability might be my last act. "By the way, as far as villainous speeches go, that one was almost worthy, though I'd go heavier on the menace and a little lighter on the sarcasm if I were you."

"Trust me, child. You all stand to benefit from me maintaining a sense of humor." He swept an arm, his hidden eyes taking the measure of each and every foe gathered against him. "The way I see it, I'm showing a significant amount of restraint, all things considered. The guards outside, for instance: to the man, I left them alive, if not exactly conscious." The Cardinal's sigh echoed in the space. "The lot of you, without a whit of understanding as to who I am and why I've set myself on this path, now sit in judgment of me and have gathered every force possible to your side to bring about my demise. Anything I do now could easily be construed as self-defense. Truth be told, I'd be justified in ending you all where you stand, and please, spare no thought as to whether or not I could make good on such a threat."

"Then why are we all still breathing?" Maddox's hand went involuntarily to his throat. "Why not finish us all here and now?"

"Simple, coyote." The Cardinal stepped forward, the tiny servos of his armor working almost silently as he joined our circle. "Contrary to what you and those gathered here have been led to believe, I'm not simply the latest Bogeyman of the Ascendant, though there have been many of those over the centuries. I have a purpose, a plan, a mission of my own."

"Said every megalomaniac in the history of the world." Ethan scoffed. "Any thoughts of sharing this grand scheme with the rest of us?"

"I will keep my own counsel in these matters, Mr. Harkreader." Yet again, the Cardinal cast his armored gaze over us all. "Suffice it to say that most of you have nothing to fear from me." He gestured in Falco's direction. "I have no need of his command of the wind." He raised his other gauntlet at Katrina. "And I have already tasted of one skiomancer and have gained all I need from that well." He directed his attention to Maddox and Neko, who appeared to be having a conversation only the two of them could hear. "The same for your tiger and coyote. While the wild boar that races through my veins and invigorates my soul longs to learn how its hooves and tusks would fare against their teeth and claws, such a conflict is superfluous to my mission."

"The warthog you murdered and whose essence you stole had a name, you know." Maddox seethed, barely able to hold himself back despite knowing all too well how his last fight with our armored intruder went. "Omari was a person. He had a life, a family who loved him, a purpose of his own. You ended all that."

"And you, coyote? You've never killed in the service of a higher cause?" His head tilted to one side, taunting the man I once swore I'd love forever. "Or maybe just for the hell of it?"

"I have never killed," Maddox proclaimed loudly, and then softer, barely audible, "without reason."

"Then you and I have far more in common than you would care to admit or even realize." The Cardinal's snarl, invisible behind the crimson and black helmet, came through loud and clear, amplified by his suit's speakers. "Does a coyote in the wild not kill to stay alive? If it goes against its baser nature, does it not simply starve?"

"Enough," Father interjected before Maddox could come back with an answer. "You've made it imminently clear that you've come to talk." He studied our armored foe. "Say what you've come to say and then get out."

"If only it were that simple, Mr. Delacroix." The Cardinal shifted his stance, clearly working to keep us all in his field of vision. "I've come not to chat, but to negotiate."

Father's expression drew down to a focused glare. "Understand that any negotiation that involves you leaving with Miss Snow is unacceptable."

"Yeah," Ethan said, continuing to inch his way toward Mother's blades, "not happening."

"The both of you as well as Miss Snow herself may wish to hear me out before making such grand declarations." He turned his avian gaze on Seph. "In the end, however, no matter how much the men in the room wish to beat their chests and howl at the moon, she will be the one who decides not only her own but all of your fates."

"You can talk all you want." With a quick spin, Ethan retrieved the paired blades that by every definition were his but a part of me wished were mine. "We're still going to kick your ass six ways from Tuesday." He set the razor steel in each hand glowing with the Light of Neith. "Say the word, Seph."

"Hold on, Ethan." Seph stepped forward and motioned for Ethan to hold his position. "As much as I hate to admit it, the Cardinal could have just flown in and taken me had he chosen to, possibly hurting you or the others in the process."

"What are you saying?" Ethan asked. "You can't seriously be considering doing what this guy says, can you? Look what he did to your window. If he truly wanted to negotiate, why didn't he just knock?"

"Admittedly, I'd have preferred he hadn't broken my *very expensive* window, but I know a show of power when I see it. All of you have gone above and beyond to keep me from this outcome, but despite all our efforts, the Cardinal now stands among us, ready to fight." She bit her lip, a move I've seen dozens of times when she's trying to hold back emotion. "He didn't kill me before when he had the chance, nor did he come in today guns blazing. If it will avoid violence, shouldn't we at least hear him out? Find out what he has to say?"

"Listening to the Devil's words is a slippery slope." Falco inserted breathily. "One second you're acting in good faith, and the next you've agreed to the unthinkable."

"You think *I'm* the Devil." The Cardinal's helmet tilted forward in an almost imperceptible nod. "Regardless of how much or little the lot of you think you understand the bigger picture, at least you finally comprehend the futility of going against one who is your better in every way."

"Better, you say?" Maddox stepped forward, his coyote blood hot in anger and defiance. "Only due to spilled blood and stolen power."

"A truth, coyote?" The Cardinal pulled himself up straight and directed a gauntleted finger at Maddox. "If you had the first inkling as to what it is I'm trying to accomplish, you'd heel at my side in an instant."

"And what is that?" I asked, taking Seph's lead. "What is it you're after with all this mayhem and death?" I allowed my hands to drop to my sides, though I kept my guard up and my senses sharp. "Surely there must have been another way than the path you have chosen."

"Would that such optimism could be true." He paused, as if in introspection. "In a former life, I learned that some problems require knowledge and skill while others benefit from more of a brute force approach." He studied all of us with a sweeping gaze. "Ingenuity and finesse have never been deficiencies of mine." His roving eyes landed on Seph. "And as for raw power, I simply take what I need."

"But you didn't kill me like you did the others." Seph worked to keep the tremor from her voice, though I'd heard her on the edge of tears more than once over the preceding days and understood well how close she was to losing it. "What is it you want from me?"

"Not your death, if that gives you any solace." The Cardinal took a step in Seph's direction, a move that brought Ethan and Father to her side in an instant. "My needs and plans require you to remain very much alive."

Seph shuddered at the electronically modulated words.

"She's not going anywhere with you." Ethan directed the longer of the two glowing blades at the Cardinal's heart, keeping the other low at his side. "I think we've all heard quite enough. I suggest you leave while you still can."

"How very brave, Harkreader. You do your family proud, though never forget the line between courage and stupidity is narrow indeed."

"Good lord, do all you assholes take a class in these stupid speeches?" Maddox shot a look in Ethan's direction. "Like Harkreader said, we've heard enough."

"More than enough." Father aimed his pistol at the Cardinal's center of mass. "I've got you covered, Mr. Harkreader."

I'm not sure which hit me harder: that Maddox deferred to Ethan instead of me, or that Father went along with the boys without so much as a glance in my direction.

"Do what you must." The Cardinal raised both arms before his chest and assumed a martial stance. "Just know that in the end, I will be taking Miss Snow and she will be well cared for. How many of her self-appointed guardians are injured or killed in the process, however, is completely up to you."

"Let's see you put your money where your mouth—"

Without waiting for Ethan to finish his sentence, the Cardinal let fly with another sonic barrage. The shattering glass of every window, drinking glass, and framed picture in the room filled the air like a rain of razor blades. The deafening chirps from the Cardinal's sonic cannon hit like shotgun blasts, dropping everyone to their knees— everyone, that is, but L.J., who slid into the headphones hanging at his neck as fluidly as I might draw my katana from its scabbard. Even with my thumbs in my ears, it took all I had to maintain a visual lock on our technomancer.

Pulling a blue shock of hair from his eyes with one hand, L.J. freed what appeared to be a car remote from his pocket with the other, held it in the air above his head, and pressed the button. From Seph's kitchen appeared a trio of tiny metallic balls, their weight held aloft by something between electromagnetism and magic, that flew at the Cardinal like a tiny swarm of angry hornets. In an instant it was over, two of the balls hitting either side of the Cardinal's waist while the third struck him center chest. All three burst upon impact into what appeared a gallon of pink foam that immediately returned the room to silence save the continued ringing in my ears.

"Clever boy," the Cardinal said, the speaker that amplified his voice clearly unaffected. "The only one who actually prepared for my return." The Cardinal rushed L.J. "How unfortunate for you."

Wing-like blades along the long gauntlets of the Cardinal's armor popped into place, and with one downward slash, he sent L.J. bleeding to the floor, a diagonal cut stretching from one shoulder to the opposite armpit.

"L.J.!" Seph screamed. "No!"

"Anyone else?" The Cardinal motioned for us to get up. "The 150 decibels may hurt, but my razor wings leave far more scars—if you survive the experience, that is."

Maddox rose from his crouch, the coyote behind his eyes clearly both enraged and terrified as he prepared for the Cardinal's next move.

Both Father and Bradley got off a couple of rounds, for all the good it did. The Cardinal's armor proved as effective against small arms fire as it had previously, and our shared enemy barely gave either of the men a second glance.

Katrina sent a quartet of shadows from around the room flying at the Cardinal, only for the Cardinal to assume control and send them hurtling at Ethan and Falco. Ethan, in turn, went to work on the quartet of ephemeral attackers, Mother's blades aglow with power, defending both himself and Falco from the shadowy onslaught.

That left Neko, Seph, and me.

"Stay back, Neko." I dropped into a reverse combat roll and snagged my katana from its position along the wall. "I don't think your reflexes and fists will do much against that armor." I shot a look at Seph as well. "Same goes for you and that magic voice of yours."

She didn't say a thing, the terror in her quick nod relaying her emotion far more effectively than words ever could.

That meant it was up to me.

I leaped at the Cardinal, katana held high, and remembered the strategy that Ethan and I had employed before. The only hope of breaching our enemy's armor with steel lay in striking at the joints. I had little doubt the suit's designer had done everything in their power to make the armor's wearer invincible, but if a teenage technomancer with next to no hand-to-hand combat experience could lay their life on the line to shut down this monster, then the daughter of Danielle Delacroix needed to represent.

I led with the decapitation strike Mother taught me to reserve only for life-or-death situations. The Cardinal blocked my diagonal downward slash an inch from the interval between his avian helmet and breastplate.

"Going straight for the neck, I see." He stabbed at me with the opposite razor wing, its point headed straight for my eye as I batted his arm away with my katana. "Noted."

The Cardinal whirled around and sent his right arm and its crimson wing-blade flying at my own neck. I barely got my katana up in time to block the attack, a strike that was only the beginning. Wasting no time, he launched a series of short jabs aimed at my face, neck, chest, and abdomen. Mother and I had spent countless hours training in defense against just such a rapid-fire attack. Still, it was only by the grace of God that I wasn't skewered on the spot. Between his various attacks, I struck at his neck, shoulders, elbows, hips, knees, anywhere I thought I could actually land a blow that might do some good.

Two things, however, became crystal clear very quickly: the Cardinal knew the weak points in his armor far better than I did, and he was well versed at the use of his paired wing-blades in combat against a single sword.

Fortunately, I and my lone katana were not left without reinforcements for long.

Having made short work of the squad of shadows sent against him and Falco, Ethan appeared at my side, both of Mother's blades in his hands gleaming with white light.

"Two on one, eh?" the Cardinal mocked. "Bring it, then, Harkreader. Show me what you've got."

Without wasting a word, Ethan launched into the Cardinal from our enemy's right, leaving his left flank to me. As we'd practiced dozens of times, he slashed first with the shorter of the swords before lashing out with the longer blade, exercising the one-two combination again and again in an effort to keep our opponent's attention fully on him. Meanwhile, as the Cardinal parried Ethan's attacks, I probed his defenses with my katana's razor tip. Though most of my blows struck metal on metal, a few struck true.

A blow to the right hip. A slash across his left knee. A blow to the neck that seemed to nearly send him tumbling.

"You two fight well for a pair who only just met." The Cardinal leaped backward, his armor deflecting another barrage of bullets from Father and Bradley. He shook out his left arm where I'd landed a quick jab at the shoulder and then raised his arms before him again. "But I can already sense you slowing, your limbs growing tired, your reflexes diminishing. Do you really want me to end one of you before you finally give up?"

"They are not alone in this fight." Maddox flew growling at the Cardinal from one side while Neko attacked from the other. The coyote went high, leaping for the jugular, while the tiger went for their shared enemy's knees, attempting a low tackle. Falco and Katrina both waited in the wings, anticipating their moment to strike. Father and Bradley held their fire to avoid hitting Neko or Maddox as Seph tended to L.J., who lay wounded and bleeding nearby.

I too awaited the moment to attack, as Mother had taught me, when a chink in the Cardinal's armor, both literal and figurative, might open and allow me to make the strike that would win the fight.

Ethan, however, didn't have the years of discipline under his belt that I did and rushed forward, his blades held low at either side. "Hang on," he shouted. "You guys hold his arms and I'll finish—"

It was over in an instant, though my trained combat eye saw the sequence of events as if in slow motion.

The Cardinal kicked Neko to one side, the servo motors of his leg armor amplifying his strength enough that the tiger's flailing form fractured the drywall upon impact. He then spun and hurled Maddox directly at Father, sending the two sprawling to the hardwood floor in a tangle of arms and legs. The Cardinal's tight whirl brought his razor wing flying at Ethan's blades, knocking both from his hands and sending them flying end over end at Katrina and Falco. An instinctive burst of wind from our resident aeromancer sent the paired swords flying into wall and ceiling respectively, saving the two Ascendant from being shishkabobed. The blast of air and flash of Mother's Light-filled blades clashing midair, however, left Ethan momentarily blinded.

As Mother drilled into me from a very early age, a moment is all it takes for a fight to turn from triumph to tragedy.

CHAPTER 26

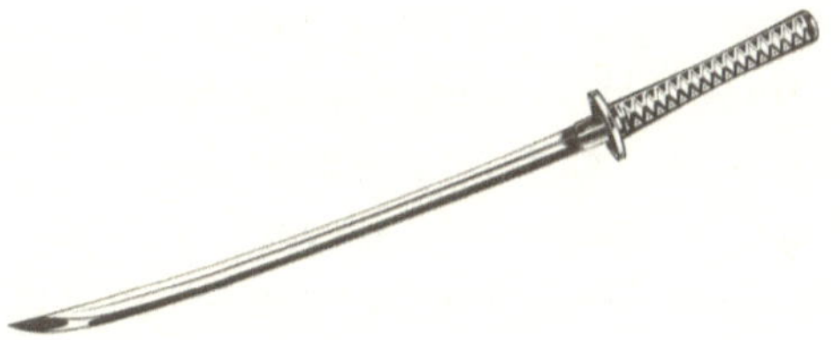

IT'S A MIRACLE

"Ethan!" Seph and I screamed in unison. "No!"

Ethan and the Cardinal stood there like two dancers frozen in a moment. The razor wing of our armored enemy rested a foot deep in Ethan's belly, its gore-covered tip protruding from his back an inch below where his kidney lay. A trickle of blood ran from the corner of Ethan's mouth as he turned his head in my direction and mouthed a silent apology.

"This could have all been so easy." The Cardinal raised his free arm, an accusatory finger pointed directly at me. "As I said, in the end, Miss Snow will be leaving with me. Do you want anyone else's blood on your hands before that inevitable outcome, so-called Daughter of Neith, or shall I continue?"

"Don't...let him...take..." Ethan got out between gurgling coughs, his sentence cut short as the Cardinal ripped the wing-blade from his abdomen.

As Ethan dropped to the floor, I rushed to his side, tore my shirt from my body, and wadded it around my hand to apply pressure to his wound. Seph raced over and dropped to her knees, desperate to help Ethan as well, but seeing that there was nothing for her to do but watch him bleed, she looked up into the Cardinal's hidden eyes and whispered two tiny words.

"I'll go." Rising from the ground, her head bowed forward in resignation, she shot me a doom-filled glance. "Please, save Ethan."

"No, Miss Snow." Father leaped up from being tackled by Maddox's flailing form. "I can't let you go with—"

"I can and will do exactly as I please." She stared trembling at Ethan's writhing form. "Help him, please, all of you. Get him to a hospital. Save him. Whatever it takes, no matter what it costs."

"Money is the least of our concerns at the moment, Miss Snow." Father positioned himself between his charge and her would-be abductor. "Please, don't—"

"I'm not talking about money, Mr. Delacroix." She strode purposefully over to our armored enemy and glared directly into the triangular white markings that served as the Cardinal's eyes. "You want me? I'm yours." She directed a willowy arm toward the door, her fingers trembling with fear and anger and adrenalin. "Shall we?"

"See?" The Cardinal crossed his arms before his chest, his head tipping back in a show of victory. "Was that so hard?"

"No time for gloating." Seph jabbed her finger into the Cardinal's armored chest. "The man I love is bleeding out before my eyes, and you have precisely who and what you came for today. Don't make me stand here and watch him die."

The Cardinal let out a surprised chuckle. "I don't think you understand who is in charge here, Miss Snow."

"Look." Seph narrowed her eyes at the monster in crimson armor, her eyes as steely as a sky before a thunderstorm. "You'd best take me now before I change my mind. I'm only surrendering myself to you to save a life. If Ethan dies, I swear I'll spend every moment of every day of the rest of my life ensuring you're next in line. Do I make myself clear?"

"Such spirit." The Cardinal turned for the door. "The coming weeks are going to be so invigorating."

Seph met my gaze one last time. "Save him, Rosemary. Save Ethan." And with that, she strode from the room and out the front door before Father or I could say another word.

"Do not attempt to come after us," the Cardinal warned before following Seph. "You've already forced my hand enough this day. It would be unfortunate were we to meet again."

The sound of the door closing behind them possessed a strange finality.

"Ethan!" I pressed my already drenched shirt further into his open wound, hoping to staunch the rhythmic pump of scarlet between my fingers. "Don't move, okay?"

Father dropped to his knees next to me and wrapped his jacket around my all but naked torso. "Rosemary..."

"Don't say it." I silenced Father with the harsh whisper and returned my attention to Ethan. "You're going to be okay, you hear me? We've got this."

"Move." Falco pushed Father to one side, knelt between the two of us, and placed a hand on Ethan's belly. "Maybe I can buy us some time."

"What are you doing?" I asked as Ethan's wound began with a wet sucking noise and his abdomen began to swell beneath my hands.

"Same as you, trying to apply pressure to the wound." He met my gaze through those mirrored shades, his features filled with worry. "Long term, this would do more damage than good, but in the short term..."

"The more blood that stays in the body, the better." Father nodded grimly. "Thank you, Mr. Falco."

"Maybe this is the way it's supposed to be, Rosemary," Ethan gurgled between wet coughs. "I failed today, and now I'm paying the price." His entire body trembled as his skin continued to pale. "At least you're here." A pained grunt escaped his lips. "Get ready for your birthright, Daughter of Neith."

"No one is dying today, Ethan." I pressed even harder into his swollen belly. "Not on my watch."

I shot a quick glance in L.J.'s direction. He sat under his own power as Katrina tended to what appeared to be a relatively superficial slash across his chest. He was going to be left with a monster scar for the rest of his life, but that life, at least for the moment, wasn't on the line.

Neko and Maddox pulled up on Ethan's other side along with Bradley, who barked orders into his phone. Maddox sniffed the air and looked down at me, shaking his head.

"We're going to have to move him if we're going to save him," he said.

"If you try to move him," Neko countered, "it might make him worse."

"Look," I whispered, "I don't know when everybody here suddenly became a combat medic, but we're doing the best we can." I looked up at Bradley. "In between checking in with your stupid Order, did you bother to call 911?"

His dead stare spoke volumes. "I'm getting someone here as fast as I can."

"Get them here faster," I said, as a bloody bubble parted Ethan's pale lips with another gurgled breath. "We're running out of time.

Bradley's brow furrowed as he was clearly not used to taking orders from a girl, but he nodded and scooted back a few feet to give us room as he returned his attention to his phone.

"Rosemary," Ethan whispered, "it's okay." He swallowed back the blood in his mouth and sucked in a quick breath. "I did my best, and it wasn't enough. Please, take what's rightly yours and go save Seph." He let out a series of wet coughs. "The Light was never supposed to be mine in the first place."

Wait.

The Light.

How could I have been so stupid?

"Maddox, Neko," I whispered, "bring me Mother's swords."

"What?" Maddox's eyes went wide in surprise. "You going to put him out of his misery? That *is* cold."

"Get me the swords." The time for niceties was over, and my words came out little better than shouts of frustration. "Now."

Maddox shot across the room to where one of Mother's blades protruded from the wall while Neko leaped up onto the table and retrieved the longer blade from Seph's dining room ceiling. In seconds they returned, each holding a blade intended for me since before my birth.

"Here." Maddox extended the shorter sword to me. "Seems a little premature reclaiming your mother's weapons while he's still breathing, but—"

I took the blade and turned to the tiger in our midst. "The other one, Neko. Quickly."

Neko placed the longer blade's hilt in my opposite hand as Father took up the job of keeping pressure on the gaping gash in Ethan's belly. In turn, I crossed the two blades and rested the razor-sharp intersection of steel on Ethan's chest below his chin.

"Ethan," I whispered, "I'm so sorry."

"No," he gurgled, "I'm the one who's sorry." His eyes flicked downward as he took in the position of the two blades an inch from his throat. "Just do it."

"To the contrary." I narrowed my eyes and stared directly into his. "This is your task. Now, take your blades."

"I can barely lift my arms." A blood-tinged wheeze parted his lips. "Just let me go."

"Listen to me, Ethan Harkreader." I pulled close to his ear so he couldn't miss a word. "I didn't spend the last month training you so that you could give up after one setback."

"But—"

"No buts." I took one of his hands and wrapped the fingers around the hilt of the longer sword. "Now. Take. Your. Blades."

His grip on the one sword grew strong at my command, and then, with no further prompting, he brought the trembling fingers of his other hand to the shorter blade's hilt. For a moment, his hold on the crossed swords left him looking somewhat like a pharaoh's sarcophagus.

But Ethan wasn't dead yet.

"Now, summon the Light."

He focused for a moment, but nothing happened. "Can't. Too weak."

"I didn't ask for excuses. Right or wrong, the Light of Neith lives within you. I need you to bring it."

"But why?"

"No questions, Ethan. Summon the Light."

His eyes slid closed, and for a moment I feared he'd lost consciousness, but after another gurgling breath, the crossed steel began to shine with an inner glow that grew stronger with every passing second.

"There." He coughed, the sound weak and phlegmatic. "The Light."

"Perfect." I drew even closer so that my lips brushed his earlobe. "Now, the Fire."

Realization finally overcame the oblivion in Ethan's stare. "Wait," he said, his voice fading. "You mean?"

"Bring it, Ethan. Like you did back in Denver."

"But...that didn't work."

"The Greyhound was beyond help. You are not. Now bring the damn Fire, Ethan, before it's too late."

"Do it, Ethan." L.J. crawled over, reluctantly leaving Katrina's side, and propped himself up next to us. "We need you."

Katrina joined us next, and then Father and Bradley, making our circle complete. Frozen in place, we prayed, or at least I did...harder than I had in years, possibly in my entire life.

I'd already watched one person I loved bleed out before my eyes. I'd be damned if I'd allow another.

"The Fire, Ethan." I gripped his thigh, as if trying to push my own life force into his failing body. "Now. You can do this."

His eyes squinted closed in effort, his weakening hands clutching the blades with a tremor that grew worse by the second.

"The Fire," he whispered. "It won't come."

"The hell it won't." I pulled my hand from his leg, straddled him, and grasped both of his wrists. "Listen, Neith," I screamed to the sky, "whoever or whatever you are, bring your Fire and save this man who does you honor with his every action, or I swear this line of yours will end with me."

Father and Bradley both gasped at my declaration, though Katrina and Neko both nodded in understanding. L.J. looked on, his eyes awash with tears. Maddox alone looked away, unable to watch.

"It's now or never, Ethan. Do it."

He focused a few seconds longer, and then his eyes rolled back in his head as if he were losing consciousness.

"Ethan!"

Without warning, his entire body shook as if he were having a seizure, and then an electric charge ran from his body into my inner thighs, up my torso, and out my scalp and fingers still wrapped around his wrists as if the two of us had been hit with a cattle prod.

The sensation was...not unpleasant.

My knuckles burned as, for the second time in their existence as I understood it, Mother's blades burst into glowing white flame. As before, the metal neither melted nor diminished, but rather exuded the flames as if they'd become a gateway to a dimension filled with nothing but blinding white conflagration.

Ethan opened his mouth to take a breath, and the fire answered. A spiral of dazzling brilliance flew from the crossed blades and raced for his mouth, his nostrils, his eyes, his entire form.

And, as I remained atop him, the tiny inferno engulfed me as well.

The white flames burned, yet did not damage. Scorched, yet did not wound. The Fire swept away all that was bad or imperfect, replacing every pain, sadness, and suffering with comfort, joy, peace.

It lasted but a second.

It lasted an eternity.

And then, it was over. He lay beneath me, unmoving, eyes closed, chest still.

"Ethan?"

Nothing.

"Ethan!"

His eyes flew open as he sucked in a lungful of air.

"Rosemary?"

A rush of conflicting emotions filled me, and it took all I had not to show Ethan in that moment how glad I was to hear him say my name, not to mention with a voice that was again strong and sure.

I released his arms, rose quickly from his body, and offered him a hand up from the floor. Before he could so much as reach for my outstretched hand, however, Katrina slumped to the floor with only L.J.'s quick reflexes keeping her head from impacting the ground. Ethan rolled to one side, apparently restored, even as Katrina's already pale skin grew whiter still.

"What's wrong with her?" he asked.

"You didn't see?" L.J. asked, staring up at us through quickly reddening eyes. "The Fire..." He ran his hands down her suddenly bare arms. "Whatever that power represents may have fixed Ethan but the Light from the Flame burned the shadows right off her flesh." L.J.'s lip trembled, as did his voice. "She didn't even have time to scream."

"And yet..." Father pointed to L.J.'s chest. His shirt, still shredded by the Cardinal's razor wing, did little to hide a torso completely healed and devoid of even a scar. A scan of Ethan's recently impaled midsection as well revealed the absence of even a hint of injury. "You and L.J. are as good as new, and for the first time in a month, my shoulder isn't reminding me that a pair of shadowdealers tried to rip my arm out of its socket a month back."

All good news, miraculous even, and yet, poor Katrina still lay there unconscious, her breathing shallow and skin damp with perspiration.

The Fire giveth and the Fire taketh away, it would appear.

"Neko, help L.J. with Katrina," I asked, breathless. "Get her to the couch."

Neko knelt by her side and grasped her upper arm. "Damn. She's like ice."

After being burned by otherworldly flame. Great.

"Warm her, however you can, both of you." I returned my attention to Ethan. "Are you okay?"

He rose from the ground, almost as if he were rousing from a nap. "Never better." He strode over to the couch where Neko and

L.J. piled blankets atop Katrina's shivering form. "Did I do that to her?"

"I don't know."

"What about when your mother used the Fire? Did it—"

"Mother told me all about the Light, taught me about its power, its majesty, its peace." I lowered my head. "She never once mentioned the Fire. I'm not sure she even knew it existed."

"And yet, I've been able to summon the White Flame twice."

"And in both instances, only when the need was greatest." I stepped forward and touched Ethan's belly where moments before gaped an open wound. "The Fire may have healed you and L.J.," my gaze shifted across the room where our resident technomancer monitored Katrina beneath her mountain of knitted yarn and pile while Father and Neko worked to get the gas logs working, "but it certainly didn't do Katrina any good."

"The Fire and the Shadow fall at opposite ends of a spectrum." Ethan's voice grew distant and mysterious, his eyes glazing over as if another spoke with his voice. "Never forget."

"Ethan?" I asked, almost afraid to speak. "What are you saying?"

"What?" he asked.

Before I could inquire further, Katrina let out a scream that sent chills from my teeth to my toes.

"The lights," she screeched. "Turn off the lights!"

"She needs the darkness," L.J. stared around at all of us, a half-crazed look in his eyes. "Don't tell me how I know that, but—"

"Do it," I shouted to no one in particular. "Now."

Falco, who had stood by dumbfounded at Ethan's miraculous recovery, rushed to the main set of light switches for the room and flipped them all off as Father and Bradley ran to opposite ends of Seph's gargantuan home and commenced with closing off every door, shade, and curtain that allowed in light. The sound of rushing footsteps and slamming doors filled the space as Neko and Maddox together hefted the enormous dining room table and, as well as they could, blocked the light coming through the gigantic shattered window. In less time than I thought possible, the four of them rendered the room as dark as they could for midday California and, other than the occasional breath or sniffle, as quiet as a freshly closed tomb. None of us dared speak, which was fortunate, for even the slightest distraction might have caused me to miss the subtle but undeniable phenomenon that followed.

Shadows, simultaneously ephemeral and tangible, swirled through the room as if alive. Silent in their motion, only the contrast between them and the remaining light allowed me to track the progress of the vortex of darkness. Countless vague contours of gloom all spun around and through the blackened space, and at their epicenter, the lone skiomancer in the room floated in the air as if held in her mother's arms.

As with Ethan's moment with the Fire before, the maelstrom of shadow seemed to last forever and yet was over before my five senses could truly make sense of what had occurred.

And then, in the darkness, two quiet words let us know that everything was okay.

"Thank you." A flick of Katrina's finger, and a tiny shadow resembling her slender arm flipped on the overhead lights. What color the pale girl normally possessed had returned to her, and she no longer appeared drenched in sweat, though she did appear weaker than when we'd first met.

"What happened?" I asked, going to her side. "Are you going to be all right?"

"Light and Shadow," Katrina whispered, her voice low and feeble, "as the Angel explains, are not so much polar opposites as they are reflections of the other. Without light, there is nothing to cast a shadow. Without darkness, there is no need for light." She looked at Ethan. "To be so close, however, to a light so intense, a flame so pure..." Her entire body shook. "It was more than the darkness in me could withstand."

"But you're going to be okay?" L.J. asked, coming up on one side with his arm stretched out behind Katrina as if he feared she might fall. "Right?"

Along her right upper arm, a haunting figure she'd not worn before appeared. I'd not seen the movie, as even a month wasn't enough for Ethan and Seph to introduce me to every horror movie of the last half-century. Still, the image of the girl with the long stringy black hair climbing from the television set had been left indelibly imprinted on my mind ever since seeing a snippet from one of Ethan's "modern classics" called *The Ring*.

That being said, I certainly never imagined such a figure would stare at me from another woman's flesh, smile, and shoot me a gruesome wink.

CHAPTER 27

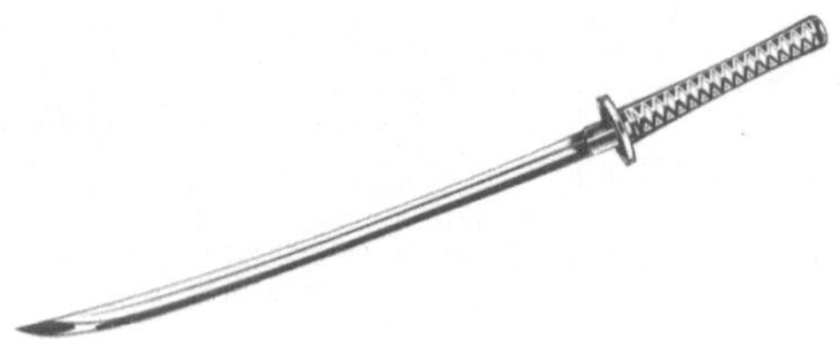

I WON'T BACK DOWN

"All is not lost." Father peered around at each of us from the head of Seph's dining room table, returned to its previous position none the worse for wear. "Thanks to Mr. Harkreader and his mysterious healing flame, we at least have our entire team back to a hundred percent."

"Except for the one we were all here to protect." Ethan sulked at the far corner of the table, as despondent as I'd seen him. "We just let that bastard waltz in here and take her and—"

"*And*, therefore, we proceed with the plan," Bradley said from his position at Father's shoulder, the only one of us not sitting. "Right?"

"Except for the fact that our plan was to launch a surprise attack and stop the Cardinal from taking Seph in the first place," Ethan grumbled, "not a half-baked rescue mission when he knows we're coming."

"Every good plan incorporates a certain level of...flexibility, wouldn't you agree, Mr. Harkreader?"

Ethan looked up from the table and glared in Bradley's direction. "In case you haven't noticed, the so-far-undefeated Ascendant serial killer we've been chasing just broke into our main base of operations without breaking a sweat and walked out of here with my girlfriend while I lay on the ground half dead and bleeding."

"Mr. Harkreader," Father began, and then, softer, "Ethan, take solace. The Cardinal himself said that he needed Seph alive."

"Alive and well are two very different things." He pounded a trembling fist on the table. "And call me crazy, but are we really taking the word of a man who just rammed a foot of steel through my stomach?"

"We'll save her, Ethan." I worked to keep any doubt from my face. "I promise."

"We couldn't even stop him on our own turf. Now we're going to go confront him wherever he's holed up and expect a different outcome?" Ethan shot a look at L.J. "Hell, if it weren't for our resident technowizard's little science project, none of us would have even gotten in a hit." He let out a heavy sigh. "Look. Everyone here knows I'll go down swinging if that's what it takes to help Seph. I just wish it didn't feel like we were fighting a lost cause."

"No such thing, Harkreader." Falco rested both elbows on the table and placed his chin atop his interlaced fingers. "There are causes never taken up and causes abandoned, but lost?"

Ethan raised a curious brow. "Didn't think you'd be the one giving me a pep talk today."

"I'm not done." Falco rose from his seat. "When we attempted to take Snow back in Denver a month ago, do you have any idea how close we were to success?"

"You had her. Helpless."

"Indeed." Falco's lips spread in a grim smile. "And you, with no more than a day of experience with your newly inherited power and skills, leaped into battle and fought against those with the powers of gods." He let out a lone chuckle. "And, as I recall, won."

"I got lucky." Ethan cast his gaze around the room, catching first Father's eyes, then mine. "Not to mention I had a lot of help."

"And now, Harkreader, you have even more help. Living shadow, the wind at my command, technology limited only by a young imagination, a pair of beasts in human form." Falco caught my gaze. "And a true friend whose sword's edge is matched only by the razor sharpness of her mind." He reclaimed his seat. "How can you possibly fail?"

Ethan's voice grew quiet. "That very group just failed, in case no one noticed."

"And yet, do we not all sit here awaiting your direction, each of us ready to dive once more unto the breach?"

Ethan's jaw dropped in disbelief, and I had to fight to keep mine from following suit. Falco's words hung in the room, strangely heavy and yet uplifting at the same time.

"Alba knew what she was doing when she sent you." I spoke to break the awkward silence. "Thank you."

Katrina gazed at the aeromancer with newfound admiration. "And here I'd always been told that you were nothing but a big bag of hot air."

"My reputation precedes me, it would seem." His features went a bit pensive. "If there's one thing I'm quickly learning about this group, it's that everyone is full of surprises."

"Glad to know everyone is the president of everyone else's fan club now." Maddox's scowl brought everyone right back to earth. "So, if the rousing speech segment of the afternoon is over, will someone please tell me how we're supposed to track down the Cardinal and what we're supposed to do if and when we find him?" He shot Ethan a cold look. "You're not the only one he's almost killed in the last couple of days, you know?"

"If I may," L.J. interjected with a quiet clearing of his throat. "Now that the Cardinal and his technomancer know that I'm on the team, I suspect my previous method of tracking their whereabouts will be significantly hampered."

"Another dead end, then," Maddox grumbled.

"Think of it more as a reframe," L.J. countered. "Now it's chess, and I'm a pretty good chess player." He looked to me. "I may not be able to track him like before, but I've figured out another way to determine where he's gone. As for what we do when we find him, though, I think I'll leave that to you guys."

"I don't know, L.J.," Ethan said, "those bubblegum balls of yours saved the day earlier." He raised a brow at our resident technomancer. "What have you got?"

"Well," L.J.'s eyes narrowed, "as I understand it, the Cardinal arrived in town aboard a certain private jet that two members of our group left scrapped a few miles away, right?"

The plane. Why hadn't I thought of that?

"The Cardinal's private jet is cordoned off for a full FAA investigation," Bradley said. "That's some major league stuff you're talking about there."

"Last I checked, one of us is head of security of a nearby major metropolitan airport." I rose and strode over to Bradley's side to give his deltoid a light punch. "Unless you're thinking you don't have enough pull."

"Oh, I have the pull." Bradley puffed up his chest. "Just making sure that you all understand the ramifications if we're caught messing with evidence in a federal investigation."

"You'll have to make sure we don't get caught, then." Maddox came up on his other side.

"You're in, then?" I asked.

"I said we were up against long odds." Maddox shot a hint of a smile in Ethan's direction. "If you think I'm letting Harkreader hog all the glory when we beat that armored asshole, though, then you never knew me at all."

And just like that, for all his posturing, that little part of me that simply got what Maddox was all about awoke as if from a long sleep. "Good to hear, I guess." I looked to Ethan. "Looks like Maddox is up for the fight, Ethan." I allowed a slight smile. "And in case you had any doubt, you have my sword."

Katrina tilted her head forward, a grin blossoming across her face. "And you have my bow."

Falco's shades did little to hide his eye roll. "And my axe, I suppose."

L.J. rose from his chair and stole over to Bradley's side. "Well, if the Fellowship is ready to rock, I guess we get right to Step One." The eager technomancer tented his fingers below his bottom lip. "How are you going to get me up close and personal with that plane?"

~

"Just the three of us, then?" L.J. looked extremely uncomfortable in the ill-fitting suit. "What if there are booby traps?"

"Any traps would likely have already been set off by the inspectors," Bradley said from behind the wheel of the black SUV as we slowly made our way across the tarmac. "Guess I should have thought of that before now."

"Water under the bridge." I pulled at the collar of my own hastily put together outfit: a button-down blouse, skirt, and blazer I'd borrowed from Seph's closet, far from my usual t-shirt and jeans. "You sure they're going to buy this, Mr. Bradley?" Between our shared youth and L.J.'s. blue hair, the two of us couldn't have looked less like a pair of aviation forensics experts if we tried. "I mean, look at us."

"If L.J. can't dazzle them all with technobabble, then I'll befuddle them with bullshit." Bradley pulled the SUV to a stop at the end of a line of similarly imposing looking vehicles and dropped it into park. "It's what I do."

"And if they call us on it?" L.J. asked. "Tell us one more time."

"You stop talking and do exactly as I say. Don't forget, this is my airport. You two may be subject matter experts on kicking ass and all things technological respectively, but aeronautic bureaucracy?" He stopped the engine and cracked his door. "This is my turf."

We exited the vehicle and stepped out into the muggy evening. The sun had dropped below the horizon, and the tarmac was lit by yellow halogen lights. L.J. and I followed Bradley in a tight triangle, the three of us reminding me very much of the three raccoons in a trench coat postcard that adorned Seph's refrigerator. As we approached the hangar where the remains of the Cardinal's private jet was being stored, I reviewed the plan for the hundredth time in my head.

As my attack only took out one of the engines, the rest of the plane remained for the most part intact. Still, the national and international groups responsible for safety in the air required a full investigation due to the "terrorist" nature of the event.

I'm not sure if Mother would be ashamed or proud.

The flight recorder, which I'd learned was an "international orange" box rather than a black one, rested inside along with various navigation systems, all of which were awaiting full diagnostic evaluation. Fortunately for us, the focus of the investigation remained on the destroyed engine.

Truth be told, I found myself strangely pleased with the pile of wreckage left in my wake, though I wouldn't be sharing that observation with Father or Ethan.

Our part of the plan revolved around getting L.J. close enough to read the data off the flight recorder and any other systems from the plane and then stalling as long as it took for him to do his thing. What we could expect remained uncertain, but his theories regarding what we could do with the information was sound. He hoped that analyzing the plane's traffic patterns, assuming this was an aircraft the Cardinal had been using for a while, would reveal a consistent location: a place to start our needle-in-a-haystack search for the biggest pop star in the world and her thus-far-unstoppable kidnapper. Once we knew where to start looking, that would be when the other part of the plan that was being hatched back at Seph's house would come in. Our assets included L.J.'s technomancer eyes on the world around us, the enhanced senses and fighting skills of two theriodans, Bradley's government connections, Father's extensive experience in all matters Ascendant, Falco's command of the wind along with his bird's eye view of the battlefield, Katrina's stealth and shadow abilities, and Ethan's absolute commitment to bringing Seph home.

Still, unless we could come up with something better than overpowering the Cardinal with sheer force of numbers, I feared we would simply end up repeating history. He'd bested Ethan in one-on-one combat, taken us in Denver, defeated and killed the Greyhound right in front of us, and trounced our gathered forces just hours before.

If only I could have talked with Mother for five minutes, sought her advice or at least her encouragement, I'd have felt better, but the woman who taught me everything I knew about everything was gone. All that remained of her resided in a man who, despite the power at his fingertips, nearly died earlier defending his love because I hadn't prepared him well enough. Another burden on my soul.

Not to mention, a tiny part of me was curious if a quarter as much effort would be expended to get me back if it were me in the Cardinal's clutches.

In any case, the truth was that no plan could truly prepare us for what we might face if and when we caught up to the Cardinal again, and the alternative of simply leaving Seph to her fate was unthinkable. Therefore, the only plan that mattered was to do what the Daughters of Neith have always done: our best.

"Good evening, officers." Bradley approached the two TSA personnel, their blue uniforms and badges bright in the otherwise drab evening. A mid-thirties Black man with close-cropped hair and a well-groomed mustache rose from his chair to greet Bradley, while his partner, a Latina woman a few years older than me, remained seated and drank from a steel thermos. "Everyone doing okay this evening?"

"Yes, sir, Mr. Bradley." The officer who'd stood eyed the other agent. "Hey, Garcia, on your feet."

Officer Garcia shot out of her chair and deposited her thermos atop her chair. "Pardon, sir. Literally just sat down to take a break. Been a long day."

"Relax, you two. I just came out to check on everything with the wreckage before heading home for the evening."

"Wow." Garcia checked her watch. "Long day all around, then."

Bradley let fly a sarcastic chuckle. "You have no idea."

"Officer Buckner and I have duty here until two am."

"Only a few more hours," Buckner added, "then right back at it bright and early tomorrow."

"Thank you both. You're doing an excellent job." Bradley eyed the door to the hangar. "Mind if I take a look around before I head out?"

"Of course not, sir." Buckner brought up his clipboard. "Just log in yourself and your two associates here."

"Wait." Garcia studied my face, her expression somewhere between a curious grin and outright concern. "Don't I know you?"

"Don't think so." I offered an innocent shrug. "Though I do get that a lot."

I suspected that every TSA officer in California had reviewed the footage of my and Maddox's attack on the plane in question. Katrina had expertly utilized Seph's extensive makeup arsenal on me to the point I barely recognized the face that looked back from the mirror, but in the end, I'm still the same woman who single-handedly kept a jet from taking off with a flung motorcycle helmet not forty-eight hours earlier.

I reminded myself that Officer Garcia was simply doing her job and prayed her competence would not necessitate me doing mine even more competently.

"If you must know, everyone says I'm a dead ringer for the 'best friend' actress from one of last year's big rom-coms. Maybe that's it.

A month ago, I'm not sure I knew the word rom-com. Seph would be so proud.

"Are you sure?" Garcia squinted at me in the dim light. "I swear I've seen your face before, and recently."

Buckner stopped his continued conversation with Bradley and peered at me as well. "Yeah, Garcia, I see what you mean."

"Look," Bradley stepped in, "Agent Cohen and Agent Patel may not look the part, but they've just arrived from out of state and their respective areas of expertise are needed to expedite this investigation."

"I'm certain, sir," Garcia said, "but with all due respect, it's pretty late."

"And no one mentioned any additional investigators," Buckner added. "Our orders are to keep this hangar secure until morning."

"I'm the head of security for this entire airport." The friendliness in Bradley's tone dropped a few notches. "Who do you think gave that order?"

"Apologies, sir." Buckner went to the hangar entrance and unlocked the door. "Let us know if you need anything."

"Thank you." Bradley showed us through the door as Garcia reported in over her field radio and closed the door behind us.

"She just called in that we're here," I said. "That means we're either good to go…"

"Or we're on the clock," Bradley finished. "Get to it, L.J. You're on."

As Bradley flipped on the hangar lights, I was astonished at the progress the investigators had already made. The engine I'd trashed had been partially dismantled, the various parts labeled and laid out on the floor in a grid. The fuselage itself appeared to have been gone over with a fine-tooth comb. And there, in one corner, a bright orange box rested open like the Ark of the Covenant, waiting to reveal its secrets.

L.J. meandered slowly between the various pieces of destroyed engine, his hands stretched out to either side as if he were listening to their cries and doing his best to assuage their pain. His twisting path through the debris led inexorably to the flight recorder, the *pièce de résistance* as Father would likely have called it. As he knelt before the vermilion box of steel, he took on the manners of a young man of manners joining a woman for dinner.

Even with all I'd seen, the world of the Ascendant never ceased to amaze.

From the moment he planted himself before the flight recorder, a silent conversation began, with L.J. passing his hands through the air above and around the orange box, the lights of the hangar dimming in time with the arcane gestures. With eyes closed and breathing regulated, L.J. sat unmoving other than the bizarre gesticulations for the better part of ten minutes while Bradley and I stood by the door and let him do his thing. I barely breathed while he worked, afraid that even a cough or sniffle might break his concentration.

And then, when he'd apparently gleaned all he could from the cold metal box, L.J. rose from the chair by the flight recorder and rested a hand atop the orange-painted steel as if saying goodbye to an old friend.

"Were you able to get what we needed?" Bradley asked as L.J. rejoined us. "Do you know where the Cardinal is?"

L.J.'s eyes darted left and right, up and down, as if he were a machine himself in the middle of an immense calculation.

"L.J.?" Bradley asked. "Everything okay?"

Another few seconds, and then his eyes focused on me. "That was...informative."

"What did you discover?" I asked. "Anything we can use?"

"First," L.J. answered, with a half-embarrassed smirk, "the plane forgives you for what you did and understands you were doing what you had to do to save a friend."

"The plane...forgives me?" I raised an inquisitive brow. "Like I hurt the jet's feelings or something?"

"Everything under the sun feels in one way or another, Rosemary." L.J. looked away. "The trees don't exactly notice when we cry, now do they?"

What do you know? Not only can he talk to machines, but the kid's a poet as well.

"We understand, and we thank the plane for its help," Bradley said, a little louder than he needed to. "All of us." He returned his attention to L.J. "Now, did this crazy plan of yours work? Do you know where the Cardinal is?"

"I'm on the right track." He let out a yawn and rubbed at his eyes. "But if you want me to get coordinates we can actually use, I'm going to need a map of the United States, a computer with some serious RAM and bandwidth, and the biggest cup of coffee this town can brew."

CHAPTER 28

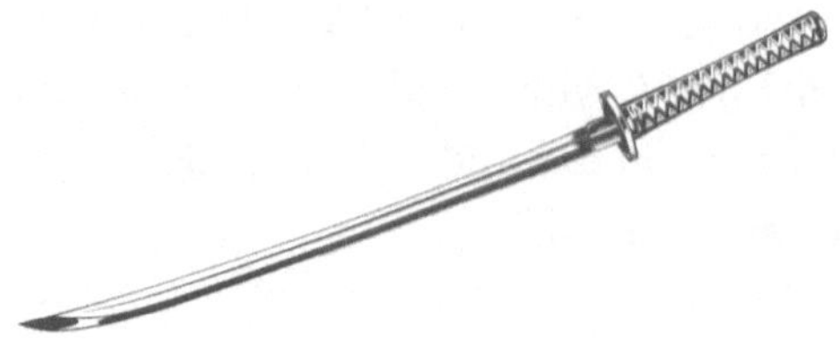

PATIENCE

"There?" I stared across L.J.'s shoulder at the double computer screen full of U.S. geography and the large paper map stretched across Bradley's desk, both dedicated to Middle of Nowhere, Pacific Northwest. "What the hell is in Idaho?"

"I don't know," L.J. said, "but for all the dozens of trips the Cardinal's jet has taken in the last couple of years, visits to central Idaho sure take up more than what would seem their fair share. A couple to Boise, but mostly to this tiny airport in Challis almost two hundred miles to the east."

"But why?" I asked. "There's nothing there."

"Exactly," Bradley reinserted himself into the conversation, having stepped aside to make a mysterious phone call a few moments before. "You want to get lost in the woods, there aren't many better places in the lower forty-eight than Idaho."

"Check out this area." L.J. jabbed his finger down on the map over what appeared to be a mountainous region devoid of cities or even roads, the words inscribed across that section of map ominous in their own right.

"River of No Return Wilderness, huh?" I asked. "Sounds about right."

"3,700 square miles of untouchable wilderness." Bradley chuckled. "About half the size of New Jersey."

"Well," I snorted an ironic laugh, "aren't you the font of information?"

"What can I say?" Bradley shook his head, half-amused. "Geography is kind of my thing."

"If it's so untouchable, though, what would the Cardinal be doing there?"

L.J. looked up from the map to meet my questioning gaze. "Does our murderous friend in the crimson armor with bladed wings strike you as someone who gives a lot of credence to pesky things like trespassing laws?"

"I suppose not." I looked to Bradley. "You think this could be his base of operations?"

"Potentially," he answered. "Could be one of many." He paused. "Or not at all."

"No guarantees we're even heading in the right direction."

"We won't know until we check it out," L.J. said. "The area has low to no tech for hundreds of square miles. I'd need to be a bit closer than Southern California to be able to tell much of anything."

"Same needle, slightly smaller haystack." I shook my head in frustration.

"I don't imagine someone with equipment as high-tech as his is living in a tent." L.J. focused on the screen. "Not to mention, he's got a technomancer of his own helping him out. If I get within a few miles of his location, no matter their precautions, I'll be able to pick up on something."

"But in Denver, the only thing you could find was a blank area, a black spot in a city full of gadgets and gizmos." I pointed to the area on the map we were considering. "How do you do that in the middle of a wilderness? And, like you said, won't the Cardinal's technomancer be expecting you this time?"

"I'm sorry, Rosemary. I don't have all the answers." L.J.'s shoulders slumped. "What I got from the flight recorder is just a bunch of data points. The best thing to do with that information, though, is anybody's guess. Please know I'm doing my best here." He shook his head in dismay. "But no guarantees."

I inhaled to reply, and then remembered that for all his maturity and skill with technomancy, I was still talking to a high school freshman who had been kidnapped, had his parents taken to God knows where to guarantee his compliance, and then forced for months to do horrible things with his technomancer abilities. The fact that he was holding it together at all was a miracle.

Taking a different tack, I rested a hand on his shoulder and leaned in with a quiet whisper. "Thanks for all you're doing. Seriously, I don't know what we'd do without you."

He pulled in a deep breath through his nose and leaned back in his chair.

"What now, Mr. Bradley? Everything I've been able to put together says we should start searching here." He stared down at the map of Idaho. "Another flight on your private jet?"

"Unfortunately, I've been informed it's down for a minor repair." Bradley's lips turned up in a grim smile. "I think I've got a solution, though." He motioned to my phone resting on the desk. "Call the others, Rosemary. Tell them to meet us at the spot where you and Mr. Trainor breached the airport grounds." He raised a brow. "This time, of course, they should stay *outside* the fence."

"Of course." I pulled up Ethan's number on my phone. "Anything else?"

"The gear that L.J. said he'd need? Make sure they bring it with them along with everything else we discussed. Hard to know how long it'll be before we make it back this way." Bradley pulled out his own mobile and studied the screen, his eyes lighting up as the chime of a text filled his office. "And above all, remind them time is of the essence."

~

Just shy of an hour later, our reassembled group convened in the sultry Santa Barbara evening on either side of the chain-link fence I'd nimbly conquered with Maddox two mornings prior. Not surprisingly, the airport had installed concertina wire along the length of the fence where before they'd only had triple strand barbed. L.J. and I stood inside the fence and did our best to keep the others, all stuck waiting in the parking lot outside, as calm as possible despite the heat, humidity, and stress. A part of me wanted to scale the chain link and vault the razor wire to prove I could—to Maddox, Father, Ethan, or just myself, I wasn't sure—but Bradley had assured me he'd be along with the keys shortly.

He and I clearly had very different ideas about wait times. Half an hour after we'd each made our respective phone calls, he'd sent me out to the fence with instructions to keep everyone in one place no matter what happened. The directive had seemed strange to me at the time, and now, with all of us separated by chain-link and concertina wire, I couldn't help but feel like we were stuck in some sort of trap.

That being said, fifteen minutes had passed since everyone had gathered and, for once, not a single untoward thing had occurred. Other than the waiting, of course. That had to be some kind of record.

Mother had done everything in her power to teach me patience, and whatever tenacity she'd instilled in me had done nothing but grow after spending a month as the teacher to two relative novices rather than as her student. Still, all the training and meditation and mindfulness in the world seemed to have no bearing whatsoever on my intense loathing of wasted time.

Though Neko came across as perfectly happy with the whole situation, his social nature coming through as it always seemed wont to do, I could sense that Maddox felt the same as me. His inner coyote, sensing its foot in a trap, seemed to be giving serious consideration to gnawing off its own leg. He kept up appearances, however, and I suspected I was the only person present who knew him well enough to see through his cool front.

L.J. did his teenage best to flirt with Katrina through the fence, though the whole scene was awkward to watch, much like the 80s rom-coms Seph had force-fed me when she and Ethan weren't introducing me to yet another piece of pop music from the last forty years that I'd never seen or heard.

Still, it's not like I hadn't paid attention.

The cute boy that nobody notices because he's too much of a brain or not confident enough yet or a thousand other reasons? That's L.J. through and through. A heart of gold, that one. A lot like Ethan, actually.

Maddox was more the good-looking jerk the heroine falls for in the first half of the movie before she figures out what she really wants. Back in the day, I'd thought I was dealing with the hard-shelled bastard with the ooey-gooey center, and maybe that was true as well.

It just wasn't me he went ooey-gooey for.

Now he was back, surly as ever, and sniffing around with his "one true love" gone forever. What was I supposed to do with that?

"Rosemary?" Ethan's voice from beyond the chain-link fence snapped me back from my 80s-pop-culture-fueled reverie. "Everything okay? You seem distracted."

"Everything's fine." I mentally backpedaled, looking for anything to discuss other than my actual train of thought as he squinted at me through the fence. "Just wondering what's holding up Mr. Bradley."

"I'm here." Bradley appeared out of the evening haze in an out-of-season black trench coat straight out of a spy novel. "Had to make final arrangements."

"Final arrangements?" I asked. "For what?"

"For our transportation," Bradley answered. "They should be here soon."

"So," Falco joked through the fence before I could inquire further, "based on your attire, Mr. Bradley, you've identified yourself as the secret agent of the bunch, but don't you think you're going to get a little hot in that?"

"I suspect I'll be fine." Bradley walked to one end of the fence and brought out a key to the padlock keeping everyone out. "Come in, all of you." He motioned the others through the gate. "I need to get everything secured, and we only have a short while before our ride arrives."

As they passed through the fence, Bradley gave each member of our group a cursory inspection.

"Going a little light there, Mr. Trainor," he said to Maddox who carried no more than the clothes on his back. "We may not be seeing anything resembling civilization for a while."

Maddox stopped and shot Bradley a withering stare. "I've spent the last two years on the hunt or on the run. I've slept in back alleys, on rooftops, up trees." He shook his head. "I think I'll be all right."

"Your call." He turned to Ethan whose pack sat filled to the brim with supplies and foodstuffs. "Meanwhile, look who turned out to be the Boy Scout."

"That was a long time ago," Ethan answered with a sigh, "but yeah. 'Be prepared' and all that, right?"

"Excellent." Bradley stepped around Ethan to study the military style backpack. "Were you able to obtain all the items L.J. needs to... you know?"

"Whatever I could find at the electronics store before they closed." Ethan let out a quiet chuckle. "Next credit card bill is going to be something else, I'll tell you that."

"A problem for another day," Bradley countered.

As the last of our group entered the airport proper, Bradley relocked the gate and turned to face us all. "And now, we wait." In the distance, as if in answer, the distinct wop-wop-wop of helicopter blades split the otherwise silent night. "Huh. They're here. Must've topped off their tanks earlier in the day."

"A helicopter?" Maddox asked. "For all of us?"

Bradley's face shifted into a pacifying smile. "The amenities may not be the most luxurious, Mr. Trainor, but I suspect you'll find the transportation I've arranged more than meets our needs." He pulled a plastic bag filled with orange earplugs from his pocket. "The helmets will have headphones to allow us to talk, but you'll need to wear these to protect your hearing."

"I don't need any stupid earplugs." Maddox rolled his eyes as if he were a toddler getting a lecture from his mother about wearing his seatbelt. "I'll be fine without—"

"As I understand it, a coyote's hearing is rather exceptional. You've already taken significant damage from the Cardinal's sonic assault. Please don't let obstinance or pride leave you worse off than you already are, young man." Bradley placed the pair of earplugs in Maddox's palm and moved on to Katrina. "Miss Delacroix, help him."

"Come on, Maddox," I whispered, "just do the thing."

"But—"

"I know you hate it, but they're for your own good." I took the earplugs. "Here, I'll help you." I slid one triple flanged cone into one ear canal, then the other. "See? Not so bad, right?"

"What did you say?" he shouted, a wicked gleam in his mischievous coyote eyes as he pointed to his ears. "Can't hear a damn thing."

"Funny," I shouted as I pushed my own earplugs into place. The staccato whopping drone of the approaching helicopter dropped in volume immediately, though remained audible. "Now, get your stuff."

"All of you," Bradley shouted at the top of his lungs once everyone had their earplugs in, "keep your heads down, and do whatever the crew chief tells you to do."

The nine of us gathered our things and waited by the hangar for barely a minute before our dark chariot came into view.

Descending out of the hazy night sky, the whine of its engine and roar of its rotors all but silenced by Bradley's timely intervention, the helicopter landed before us like an enormous drab green dragonfly. As I studied the military grade UH-60 Black Hawk just like the ones I'd seen on television over the years, I couldn't help but wonder what strings Bradley had pulled to get us such an aircraft and crew.

The side door facing us slid open, and a man in a green jumpsuit and flight helmet climbed out and onto the tarmac. He motioned us over, and Bradley led the way, his body bent forward at the waist as he rushed to the man's side. The crew chief handed Bradley a flight helmet of his own and helped him aboard before motioning for the rest of us to approach.

Ethan went next, following Bradley's example of keeping his head down as he walked. Once he had his helmet on and had flung his overpacked bag into the belly of the aircraft, he and the crew chief together helped the remaining seven of us inside the helicopter. The passenger section of the Black Hawk had five seats in the front where Bradley and the crew chief were set up, but the rest of us all piled into the eight spots in the back.

The seats reminded me a bit of the metal cots we'd slept on during family camping trips when I was a kid, with little cushion and less comfort. Ethan sat to my left and Katrina and L.J. to my right, much to our technomancer's delight. Facing backward and knee-to-knee with me, Father did his best to maintain his composure, though I could tell that all of this was happening a bit fast for him. Rounding out our group in the other three reverse seats, Maddox and Neko sat to Father's left and Falco took the reverse window seat to Father's right.

No sooner was I in my seat with my helmet on than the crew chief came around to fasten everyone's seatbelts and plug us all in so we could communicate. I fought the urge to break his nose when his hand slid up the side of my thigh as he felt around for the buckle, but I kept my calm and told myself the man was just doing his job. Not like he'd feel much of anything through those thick aviator gloves of his anyway. Still, it was the principle of the thing.

Once we were all strapped in and ready, the crew chief pulled both side doors closed, moved up front with Bradley, and plugged himself into the communication system.

"We're good to go for takeoff, Chief," came a deep Southern voice. "All nine passengers are strapped in, and comms are up."

"Roger." This accent came from farther north, maybe Chicago. "Good evening, everyone. I'm CW4 Anthony. CW3 Roth and I will be spending the next six hours with all of you as we head up to Idaho."

"Six hours?" came Maddox's plaintive voice. "Seriously?"

Father shut Maddox down with a quick elbow to the ribs, allowing the pilot to continue.

"Chief Roth and I will be focusing on the flying this evening, so direct any questions to Specialist Shaw who helped you all aboard." Past Father's shoulder, the crew chief, adjusting his seat and preparing for takeoff, offered Bradley a quick thumbs up as his name was mentioned. "Please stay buckled up throughout the flight for your safety." Anthony chuckled across the comms. "Hope everybody had a chance to visit the latrine before takeoff."

Shaw took over, his Southern accent a stark contrast to Anthony's inland inflection. "Like Mike said, please stay strapped in until we arrive at our destination. We're estimating at least six hours total flight time. Challis is seven hundred and fifty miles as the crow flies, give or take, and though we could make it there in one hop, we're probably going to stop and top off in northern Nevada in case we need to bring everyone back south in a hurry."

"Contingencies," Bradley spoke across the comms. "Best to be prepared for anything."

"Roger," Shaw agreed. "Make yourselves as comfortable as possible for the duration and do try to get some rest. If anyone has an emergency along the way, we'll do our best to accommodate, but our orders are to get you there as fast as possible. Any questions?" He gave us less than five seconds to answer. "If not, then we are good to go. Mike?"

CW4 Anthony didn't answer, at least not with words.

The whine of the motor and the rhythmic pulse of the rotors crescendoed as the ground beneath us pulled away. Katrina, who sat to my immediate right, grabbed my hand, her skin cool and clammy. I locked eyes with her in the near darkness and silently asked if she was okay. My only answer a squeeze of my fingers, I resigned myself to hold hands with the lovely young skiomancer for the duration of the flight. A glance revealed that she'd already taken L.J.'s hand as well, a fact I suspected the young technomancer didn't mind one bit.

And with that, we were off to Middle-of-Nowhere, Idaho on what I hoped wasn't a total wild goose chase. L.J. hadn't steered us wrong in Denver, but if this trip ended up a dead end, then the Cardinal would have almost a full day on us. Every minute mattered, and we were about to spend at least six hours completely out of touch with the world at large. I just hoped when we finally caught up to the Cardinal, wherever he was, that we weren't too late.

For all our sakes.

Patience, Rosemary, came Mother's voice, a pleasant memory from a training session several years gone that I'd never forgotten. *The early bird is not the only one who gets the worm.*

CHAPTER 29

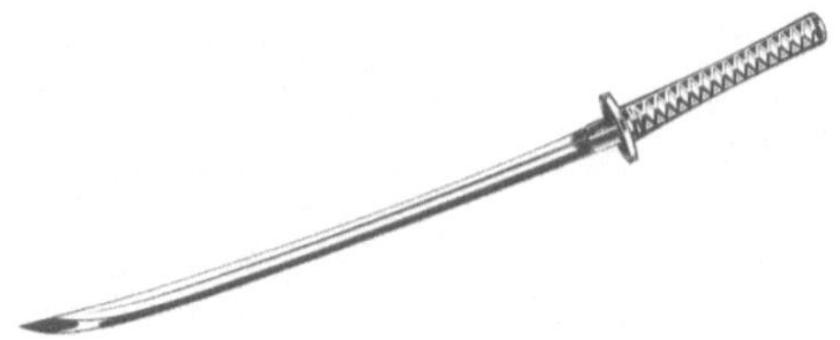

I KNOW YOU'RE OUT THERE SOMEWHERE

"If we make it out of this alive," Maddox whispered as we all piled out of the helicopter onto the tarmac at Challis's tiny airport, "some chiropractor is going to be able to put his kid through school when he's done with us."

I couldn't help but agree with the first words I'd heard without headphones since our brief stop in northwestern Nevada. Ethan and I had joked that we suspected some of the Spanish Inquisition's more effective torture devices were still more comfortable than standard issue passenger seats in a UH-60. But beggars, as the saying goes, can't be choosers.

Now, after three additional hours of sitting bolt upright and held in place by four-point restraints—we'd gotten quite the informative lecture on the safety features of the aircraft from our crew chief—my back ached like I'd been lying on a pile of broken concrete.

Still, we'd made it in one piece, and before sun up to boot.

We sent Maddox and Neko to quietly scout the area, but other than a few airport personnel, no one else was around. With the exception of a lone prop plane parked by a brick building that likely served more as storage than hangar, there were no other planes or helicopters present. Bradley used his connections to secure a brief chat with the on-site staff, but nothing came of that either, as they reported no aircraft in or out in the last six hours.

In other words, Square One and time to see if L.J. could pull yet another miracle out of his technological top hat.

"All right, Ethan," L.J. said as the two of them dragged the overloaded pack out of the Black Hawk, "let's see what you were able to find from my little shopping list."

Box after box of electronic gadgets spilled onto the still-warm tarmac: three identical boxes that contained a trio of smartphones, two larger boxes decorated with pictures of remote-control drones with rotor blades not that different from our helicopter, and a miscellany of various cables and batteries, all still in their various packages.

"Two drones, three phones, more cable than anyone could ever use." A mad glee flashed in L.J.'s eyes as he tore into the first drone like a kid at Christmas. "Let's do this."

"I was planning to get everything opened up and charged like you asked," Ethan said, politely deferring to L.J. as the resident expert, "but Rosemary called with some other last-minute preparations, and I ran out of time."

"It's all good," L.J. said as he ripped into the second of the two drones and assembled the various pieces as if he'd performed the task a thousand times. "Once I've got it all together, I can borrow a little electricity from those power lines over there and give everything a decent enough charge for our needs."

"Excuse me?" Falco muttered, suddenly interested. "You plan to 'borrow' the electricity from random power lines?"

L.J. looked up at the aeromancer, one eyebrow raised in amusement. "You can turn a gentle breeze into a cyclone, Mr. Falco. You're impressed that I can charge a battery?"

Falco's chin jutted forward as if he were about to say something snide, but then he turned away with a quiet "humph" and walked back over to lean against the helicopter and resume his conversation with the pilots.

Katrina, who'd been studying L.J. and Ethan from a few feet away, knelt by L.J.'s side. "Anything I can do to help?"

"You can get these open and turned on." L.J. handed her the three smartphones, still in their boxes. "Thanks."

A little too curt. A furrowed brow and wide eyes communicated that Katrina didn't understand the shortness of the response, but she set to work unboxing the phones regardless.

Interesting. Though L.J. could play any piece of technology like a virtuoso violinist, his interpersonal skills, at least where girls were concerned, were clearly still a work in progress. The obvious crush he had on Katrina hadn't helped the situation either. Poor kid.

I flopped down next to Katrina, took another of the phone boxes, and ripped into it as Ethan helped L.J. get the two drones fully assembled. The pink at the edge of the eastern sky announced that morning was speeding our way, but for the moment, we performed our various tasks by the halogen light streaming in from the airport's periphery. All of it would have been easier by the light of day, not to mention a decent night or two of sleep, but we all made do. In less than twenty minutes, we had both drones assembled and a smartphone lashed securely to the top of each.

"I'm curious." Ethan asked. "What's the third phone for?"

"For our third flight-capable asset." L.J.'s eyes shot in Falco's direction where he continued to converse with the two warrant officers who'd flown us through the night to our current destination. "The one who doesn't require batteries."

"You haven't said a word this entire time about needing Falco." I knelt by L.J.'s side. "He came to fight, not perform reconnaissance. You think he'll do it?"

"Of course I will, Miss Delacroix." Falco, ever observant behind those mirrored shades, had already halved the distance to our makeshift tarmac assembly line. "In for a penny, in for a pound, as they say." He stood, imperious yet strangely respectful, over L.J. who sat on the tarmac adjusting the rotors on one of the drones. "Tell me, technomancer, what is it you need me to do?"

I wasn't certain who was most surprised by Falco's response: L.J., Ethan, or me.

"I'm hoping to triangulate the location of the Cardinal's particular dead zone signature to let us know where to start looking. In a city full of power lines, electrical wiring, and wi-fi everywhere, that doesn't present much of a challenge, but out here—"

"You're not working with much." Falco studied the tech surrounding L.J. "Let me guess. Three phones but only two drones. I'm your third flyer, correct?"

"That's what I need. I send one drone west and the other north…"

"And me straight up the middle." Falco's mouth quirked to one side. "What if they blow me out of the sky?"

"You're an aeromancer. Figure it out." L.J. looked northwest to the area in question. "In any case, I don't need you too far out. I'm hoping to get sufficient data from the two drones to give our pilots the grid coordinates we need. You, on the other hand, represent a third axis to confirm the information I get from the first two, not to mention a set of eyes the Cardinal's technomancer can't touch."

"There's one thing you haven't explained, though." Maddox, who'd been listening from a few feet away, joined our circle. "You're using mobile phones to figure out where Seph might be, but unless I'm missing something, there aren't too many cell towers out here to bounce information off of."

"Cell towers?" L.J. directed both of his thumbs at his chest. "I'm the only cell tower we're going to need."

"Really?" Katrina perked up, her pale form barely visible in the shadow of the Black Hawk. "You can do that?"

"We all have our talents." L.J. pushed a few buttons on the first drone and sent it flying west with only a slight tilt of his head. "Welcome to the wonderful world of technomancy."

～

The sun had peeked above the eastern horizon when L.J.'s free hand began to tap the ground excitedly.

"I've got something." He pulled in a quick breath. "Or, to be more precise, a whole lot of nothing, like back in Denver."

"Another null area?" Ethan asked.

"Precisely. Such precautions would seem a bit unnecessary in such a technological desert." The sight of L.J.'s wide-open eyes rolled back in their sockets so that only the whites showed was unnerving, and I, for one, was glad when he looked up at me again with those brown irises and dark pupils front and center. "Still, it's the same pattern as before."

"Then we start our search there." Father walked over with Bradley and one of the warrant officers in tow. "Do you have the coordinates?"

L.J. waved a hand over the tablet computer he'd been using like a clever mix of divining rod and technological ouija board. In answer, a satellite picture of a mountain with an eight-digit number at the bottom right corner appeared on the screen.

"The null area is centered here."

Far from any road or waterway, the craggy mountain appeared bare other than a scant few trees. As austere a location as I'd seen, I couldn't imagine why the Cardinal would select such an exposed area as a headquarters.

Assuming he was here at all.

As I studied the picture further, something struck me. Something...off.

"Hey, L.J.," I asked, "can you zoom in on the mountain?"

"How close?"

"As close as you can."

He manipulated the image until only a few trees showed.

"Now, zoom out a bit."

He did, the resulting picture strikingly similar to one before, but with more trees.

"Again."

Same thing. Same pattern.

"This image," L.J. said. "It isn't real. It's like—"

"A Mandelbrot set." Maddox watched from across my shoulder. "Which means—"

"Whatever is on that mountain is something someone with

serious tech abilities doesn't want us to see." Father knelt by L.J.'s side. "Good job, L.J."

"It was a group effort," he said with a pleased grin. "So, what's the plan?"

Father looked to me. "Call Falco in. We'll take the helicopter to the nearest safe drop off point, but I'd like to have some literal air support in case things get hairy."

I clicked on the field radio Bradley had left me in charge of, its companion sent ahead with Falco. "Eye in the Sky, this is Heavy Metal." L.J. had insisted we use call signs for all communication, and though we did it mainly to humor him, a part of me was glad we weren't throwing out our names into the ether at the moment. "Pull back. I repeat, pull back. Location acquired and we're—"

"Get that bird in the air and get up here now," came Falco's crackling voice from the radio before I could finish. "She's here..." His voice broke into static. "...all about to go down..." More static. "...hurry..." Then, nothing more.

"Well," I handed the radio back to Bradley, "looks like we've found the right spot."

"Hey!" Bradley shouted to Warrant Officers Anthony and Roth who worked with Specialist Shaw inspecting their aircraft. "How long to get us back in the air?"

"Ten," Anthony shouted, as all three stepped up their efforts. "Seven, if all goes well."

Father pulled everyone close. "All right, everyone. We'd hoped for the element of surprise, but something's happened up there. We could be flying into a brick wall. There is no shame for anyone who wants to stay behind." He looked to Katrina. "I know your abilities wane in the daytime. I'd understand if—"

"Shadows aren't nearly as dark in the daylight, I'll give you that, but I'm still in if you'll have me."

Father nodded. "Neko? Maddox?"

"If you think I'm staying behind after that hellacious six-hour helicopter ride," Maddox answered, "you've got another think coming."

"Ditto," Neko added. "We're not going home without Seph."

"L.J.?" Father asked.

"Of course." He closed up his laptop and rose from the ground. "If the Cardinal has his technomancer up there, you're going to need all the help you can get."

"Thank you." Father turned to me and Ethan. "Eight for eight. Load up."

With only eight of us plus the crew chief this time, the six more combat-oriented of us positioned ourselves in the outside seats, three on each side. Bradley sat up front between Father and Neko while L.J. stayed with the rest of us in the back, his equipment taking up most of the remaining seats. As promised, the crew had us off the ground in seven, and with the mountain in question around twenty miles west, Shaw said he could put us there in ten minutes tops.

I prayed those few minutes didn't represent the rest of all our lives.

Ethan readied Mother's blades as I did mine. L.J focused on the tablet on his lap as if trying to divine even an iota more about the situation we were about to fly into. Maddox sat silently at the back corner, eyes already coyote yellow, while Father inspected the duffel bag the crew chiefs had handed him at our last stop.

"Five minutes out," came Shaw's Alabama twang through the headphones. "We'll be touching down on whatever spot we can find that's even remotely flat. Keep your head down and take care as you exit, as the rotor wash will be significant. Once you're clear of the aircraft, go to ground and stay down until we pull away, understand?" After a quick run of nods and verbal affirmatives, Shaw continued. "We'll be dropping you off as close as we can to the area in question, but after that, we're going to have to bug out, especially if the target's tech is as advanced as you all say. Can't risk the aircraft or crew."

"I'll stay with the helicopter," Bradley added. "We'll circle at a safe range until you're ready for extraction."

I stared straight ahead at Ethan, his eyes wide in the relative dim.

"We got this," I mouthed. "Don't worry."

"Who?" he mouthed back with a grin, one eyebrow disappearing beneath the forward edge of his aviation helmet. "Me?"

I snorted a laugh, my response earning an exasperated shake of

Maddox's head. I tried to catch his eye in an effort to make right whatever had upset him, but he quickly became preoccupied with the scenery below and ignored me completely.

Perfect. An ex-lovers' tiff mere minutes before we were about to dive into a life-or-death situation.

Katrina, the fifth and final one of us in the back, simply stared into space. As Father had alluded, her abilities would be severely hampered by the rising sun and would diminish with every passing minute. And yet, she'd stayed.

For all my negative self-talk about being nothing but a girl with a sword, at least my abilities didn't wax and wane with the time of day.

We spent the following minutes reviewing the pieces of our plan that still made sense considering the development. Once on site with boots on the ground, our two theriodans were to split up and search for any sign of Seph; L.J. was to counter any potential aggression from the enemy technomancer; Falco and Katrina were to run interference for any threat that might pop up, Ascendant or otherwise; and Father, Ethan, and I were going after the Cardinal.

All that being said, we had no idea if our enemy was actually here, and if so, whether he was alone, accompanied by this technomancer we'd been hearing so much about, or even with a small army backing him up. And even if we had somehow managed to locate our enemy, there was no guarantee that Seph was with him or whether she was still alive.

Mother always taught me not to fly into any situation blind, but in this case, it seemed we had no choice.

"Two minutes. Get ready to..."

Shaw's words over the comms descended into static. I shot L.J. a worried look and he answered with one of his own. Our shared premonition was confirmed seconds later when the helicopter engine began to skip, a sound I hadn't noticed once during our entire trip from Santa Barbara. L.J.'s eyes went wide for half a second, then closed tightly as if he were focusing every bit of his concentration on keeping us aloft. The helicopter's odd skipping sound diminished, though the new rhythmic grinding noise that replaced it did nothing to inspire confidence that we'd survive the next few moments.

"...Attempt a landing..." came a frantic CW4 Anthony's garbled voice over the broken comms. "Prepare...exit quickly...do our best..." And with that, the comms cut out completely.

L.J.'s face twisted with concentration, as if his will were all that kept the helicopter from falling out of the sky. The engine continued to buck like a wild horse, but somehow, we remained in the air. The jagged mountaintops below us grew closer and closer, and I hadn't a clue whether that meant we were coming in for a landing or about to crash.

Ethan reached across and grabbed my knee. "Ready?" he mouthed.

"Always," I shouted back, though there was no way he could hear me.

No sooner had I said the word than the helicopter went into a tailspin, the tree-lined mountaintops beneath us becoming a grey and green circular blur. Instinctively, I reached out for Ethan and instantly found his fingers intertwined with mine. My entire body tensed for the end as the helicopter dropped to the naked rock below us.

And then, mere seconds before impact, the helicopter stopped its mad spin as a hurricane gust of wind buffeted the fuselage from below. The Black Hawk's right wheel impacted the mountaintop and the continued blast of air from below kept us somehow steady.

"Out, out, out!" came Shaw's voice across the comms as the crew chief forced open the helicopter's right door. I quickly turned the release on my seatbelt, dove across to free Ethan, and then pushed him out the side of the helicopter and onto the rocky mountaintop. Without waiting to check on Ethan, I went to L.J. next only to have him open his eyes just long enough to lock gazes with me.

"Leave me here," he silently screamed. "Go."

Without understanding L.J.'s sudden suicidal streak, I looked over at Maddox, who was already out of his seat and working to coax Katrina out of hers. Wide-eyed, she stared terrified out the side of the aircraft at what appeared to be open air.

"Help me," I screamed to Maddox.

Together, the two of us managed to secure Katrina's flailing hands and undo her seatbelt. Then, as if rehearsed, we each grabbed her under an arm, dragged her to the opposite side of the Black Hawk, and dove as one to the bare rock below. Father was already there, crouched over a stuffed duffel bag between Neko and Ethan with his pistol drawn. All three kept their heads down, and Maddox and I covered Katrina to shield her body in case the helicopter crashed.

Before I could formulate another thought, a renewed gust of wind—so powerful, it threatened to hurl me off the mountain and into oblivion—rushed up from beneath us and pushed the helicopter into the sky. Its tailspin for the moment corrected, the Black Hawk flew east in the direction we'd come and quickly disappeared around the next mountain over, leaving the six of us alone in the wilderness. Neither Bradley nor L.J. had exited the aircraft and I prayed the helicopter crew would see them to safety. For now, however, they were beyond my help, and we were well beyond theirs.

"What just happened?" Ethan removed his helmet and stared around at all of us, his amazed gaze mirrored on all our faces. "I thought we were dead."

Before any of us could offer a theory, a lone form floated down from above. His hair pulled back in its usual silver ponytail, his mirrored shades reflecting the Idaho morning sky, and his immaculate white Chuck Taylors setting off his ivory suit, Dietrich Falco descended to the center of our circle in a slow spiral, his lips somewhere between smirk and smile as he took in each of our astonished gazes and muttered a quiet, "You're welcome."

CHAPTER 30

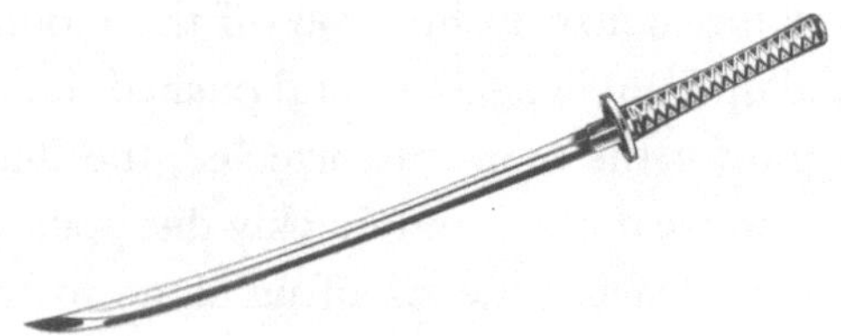

PROVE YOUR LOVE

Before I could catch my breath, a plume of flame jetted into the sky from atop a ridge a few hundred feet away. Only a single steep valley separated us from whoever or whatever had sent up the column of fire, but the few trees that littered both mountaintops obscured our view.

"What was that?" Maddox shouted.

"That, theriodan," Falco answered, "would be Ada."

"Ada?" I asked. "Your pyromancer? What's she doing here?"

"Avenging the death of her lover, I would imagine." Falco delivered the answer so matter-of-factly that I was left dumbfounded, searching for any hint of understanding among the faces of our team but finding only confusion.

"Her lover?" Ethan asked. "What the hell are you talking about?"

"You don't know, yet you were there the day they met." He met each of our gazes like a magician waiting to unveil his latest feat of

286

prestidigitation. "I'm speaking of your savior from Denver, the Greyhound."

"The Greyhound?" I asked.

"May he rest in peace." Falco cracked his neck. "Their introduction was fiery indeed, and their chemistry equally so."

"Wait." Maddox stalked over to where Falco floated midair and glared up into the man's mirrored shades. "You've known this entire time that Ada was after the same bastard we're searching for, and you never bothered to tell us?"

"To be honest," Falco breathed, lighting in front of Maddox, "I had no idea exactly where she'd gone or what she was doing."

"But I'm guessing you had a hunch." Maddox seethed, his yellow coyote eyes narrow and angry. "An important piece of information to lay on the table, don't you think?"

"Ascendant are a clandestine lot. Over the years, I've found that minding my own business unless a paycheck is involved tends to keep me out of hot water." A second column of fire erupted from the next mountain over, again drawing all our attention. "Trust me, when you spend most of your time around someone who can melt steel simply by thinking about it, you become a bit circumspect."

"Now's not the time for arguing." Ethan stepped between Falco and Maddox. "We may be down a technomancer, but it looks like we just got a major boost to our firepower. What say we get over there and finish this thing?"

"I couldn't agree more, Harkreader." Falco's pursed lips spread into a smile. "Nice to see that you're learning a thing or two along the way."

"But how do we get there?" Father asked as he peered down into the valley between our ridge and the next. "As a straight shot, it's not that far, but a hike down and back up will take at least an hour."

"If only there were a means for the lot of you to fly from one mountaintop to the other." Falco spun a finger in the air as he waited for all of us to catch on.

"You want us to let you fling us through the sky at an armored psychopath who has already nearly killed us all a couple times over?" Maddox asked.

"Do you have a better idea?" Falco stepped back. "Look, I understand you all may be upset that I kept my suspicions about Ada's whereabouts from you—"

"Upset?" Maddox growled.

"—but Ascendant business is their own. The sooner you all learn that, the better." His gaze shot to a third plume of orange flame, the largest yet, as it rocketed skyward. "Now, shall we join the battle against our shared enemy, a man who poses an existential threat to every Ascendant alive, or would you prefer to stand here and continue to quibble?"

Before Maddox could come back with another rejoinder, I broke into the discussion. "How do you suggest we all get there?" I asked. "Not to mention in one piece?"

"If you send us tumbling like you did Seph back in Denver," Ethan added, "we'll all be too drunk to fight."

"Agreed." Falco considered for a moment. "All right. Circle up, all of you, and take the forearm of whoever is to your left and your right." His eyes shot to our target location. "I should be able to control the lot of you better if you're one mass instead of six."

"Like skydivers." Neko, who'd been uncharacteristically quiet throughout, spoke up. "Yeah, that might work."

Sheer nervousness stole the vigor from our tiger friend's voice, though it was nothing compared to the abject terror that played across Katrina's features. Not a word had passed her lips since diving from a crashing helicopter onto a barren mountaintop, though the green in her otherwise pale skin told the story well enough.

Now we were asking her to allow a relative stranger to hurl her off the top of one mountain with a gale force wind at the broad side of another.

Funny. Put that way, Katrina seemed the only sane one of the bunch.

"I'm in." Ethan slung Mother's swords to his back and took my hand. "Let's do this."

"Me too." Maddox took my other hand, his eyes still firmly coyote but his features far less enraged than they'd been moments before. "Let's go get this bastard."

"From your lips to God's ears." Father slung the duffel bag across his shoulder and took Ethan's free hand and then extended his own to Neko. "Ready?"

Neko paused for half a second before joining the circle. "Like I'm going to let Maddox hog all the glory?"

Only Katrina remained, the lone outlier, her arms crossed before her chest, her brow knitted together, and her lips trembling with fear.

"I won't drop you, girl," Falco said, his words a whisper. "Let's go." I truly believed he was trying to reassure Katrina, but as with almost everything that fell from the aeromancer's lips, the words hit my ears and likely Katrina's as caustic.

"There's no shame for anyone who doesn't want to go." I shot Katrina an understanding glance. "None of this comes with a guarantee, and—"

"No." Before I could finish, she stepped to the space between Neko and Maddox and held out both her hands. "If I let you go on without me, I'll never be able to face Madame Midnight—or myself in the mirror—again." She looked to Falco. "Besides, Falco already said it best back at the airport." She dropped into her best German accent. "In for a penny, in for a pound." She grasped the forearms of the theriodans to her left and right. "Let's do this."

Falco smiled. "That's the spirit." He rose in the air at the center of our circle. "Now, for us to get started, I'll need you all to take, shall we say, a leap of faith?"

"Just tell us what to do," Father said as yet another localized inferno exploded on the next ridge. "The clock is ticking."

"Simple." Falco performed a slow spin. "I will count down from three, and then all of you are going to jump into the air like a circle of children playing a game." He let out a lone chuckle. "The difference being this time, your feet won't be returning to the earth."

"At least not until we reach the other side," Katrina asked, her voice quiet and tremulous, "right?"

"Of course." Falco levitated upwards another few feet. "So, without further ado, three..."

"Wait," Katrina shouted. "Do we jump on one or after?"

"After," Falco said, in as kind a voice as he could likely manage.

"You've got this, Katrina," Neko shouted, as much to convince himself as the terrified young skiomancer.

"Two…"

"Get ready, everyone." Ethan crouched into a stance I taught him for kicks, centering his mass and preparing for the big jump.

"One…"

I pulled in a deep breath and visualized myself floating on the wind currents like a bird, wings spread wide and eyes focused on the horizon.

"Jump!"

Our circle of six leaped into the air as a gust of wind from everywhere and nowhere at once billowed up beneath us. My ears popped as if I were aboard a jumbo jet headed straight for the stratosphere as we rose into the sky. Our six bodies began a slow ascending spin, our circle remaining level throughout.

"And," Falco shouted, his voice barely visible above the sudden wind, "here we go."

In seconds, we were flying over the valley separating us from Ada and whoever it was she fought. Halfway across, our rotation brought the mountaintop battle into view.

A three-way fight, I recognized but two of the combatants. Ada, all fire and brimstone as I remembered her, stood against the Cardinal who was currently on the defensive, his armor still bearing the marks of our fight back in Montecito. The third individual, a slender Asian woman wearing a skin-tight black bodysuit, appeared to be in her late twenties, though with Ascendant, one never really knew.

Surrounded by a variety of floating machines that orbited her body like tiny satellites, this new player crouched by our crimson-armored foe. With every bolt of flame Ada sent flying at the woman, the swarm of mechanical devices would converge upon the fiery blast and deflect the attack skyward. We'd all seen L.J. perform similar feats of technical wizardry, albeit on a smaller scale, though while his talents required significant focus and will, the host of machines defending the woman seemed to function independently.

The Cardinal's so-far-invincible armor was one thing, but Ada's fireballs weren't getting anywhere near his technomancer. In the movements of her machines, both individual and collective, I recognized defensive principles that Mother had ingrained in me from an early age and that I'd spent years training to perfect.

We'd be lucky to even land a blow on this chick, much less one that counted.

Still, no defense was impenetrable. Another pearl from the woman who taught me everything. I had a sneaking suspicion it wouldn't be long before I'd be putting that particular wisdom to the test.

"There," Ethan shouted, as he jerked his head in the direction of a bare spot half a football field from the three-way melee. "Put us down there."

Falco stretched out his arm in the direction of the open area of rock, and the wind sent us flying in that direction. Unfortunately, the sight of seven amateur skydivers without parachutes dropping from the sky caught the attention of all three combatants before we touched ground. As each looked skyward, their battle paused for a single heartbeat. Then, while pyromancer and technomancer resumed their stalemated melee, the Cardinal disengaged from the fight and disappeared into a nearby copse of trees.

Great. More hide-and-seek. As if the Cardinal had any need to hide. The bastard had already proven himself unstoppable in multiple fights against everything we could throw at him. I prayed the element of surprise and the addition of Ada to our ranks might be enough to avoid another defeat, but in my mind, I prepared for the worst.

Seconds that felt like an eternity later, Falco allowed his winds to dissipate and dropped us atop the mountain. Katrina immediately fell to all fours and all but kissed the bare rock beneath her trembling palms, a feeling I understood well. I'd never been so glad to feel solid ground beneath my feet and wasn't the only one to breathe an audible sigh of relief at returning to good old terra firma.

"All right, everyone," Ethan shouted, "get into position." He directed us into a spearhead formation as we'd discussed during the flight up, with him at the tip and us forming up on either side. "We've come all this way, and we're not going to let this guy get the drop on any of us."

"If we stick together and watch each other's backs," Father added, "we can end this today."

With a nod, I stepped to Ethan's right with Father behind me and Neko off Father's rear right flank. Maddox and Katrina fell in on Ethan's left while Falco continued to hover ten feet above the center of our hastily assembled formation. No sooner had we assumed a variation of the classic combat wedge I'd passed on from Mother's teachings to Ethan than an amplified voice split the relative quiet.

"I wondered who might have chartered a Black Hawk helicopter to take them to such a forlorn location." The Cardinal appeared several yards away as if from thin air. "Do any of you have the first idea how difficult it is to find a truly remote place to get away from it all?"

"Glad to know you're continuing to perfect your comic-book-villain banter." Ethan drew both of Mother's swords and directed the longer blade at the approaching Cardinal's chest. "Only chance. Surrender before this gets ugly."

"You're looking surprisingly well, Harkreader. Didn't I leave you gutted and bleeding in Montecito last evening?"

"You're not the only one with a few tricks up his sleeve," Ethan answered with a cold scowl. "Now, stand down and give us Seph, or all of this is going to go very badly for you."

"Seven against one, Cardinal, and no hostages this time to keep us from giving you everything we've got." I directed my katana at the Cardinal's hidden face. "Even with all your tech and stolen power, are you sure you're prepared to face all of us at once?"

"Children," the Cardinal taunted, "I faced the lot of you yesterday and, as I recall, won handily. For all the great effort you've put into executing this almost-surprise attack, understand that you now fight an enemy on their home turf." He shot a glance across his shoulder to where Ada and the Cardinal's technomancer continued their battle, neither gaining nor losing ground nor showing even the first sign of fatigue. "As for those ridiculous flight helmets, you may remove them." A single chirp of his sonic weapon through the same speakers we'd used to speak over the roar of the helicopter nearly blew my head off. "Not that I'll need to resort to my sonic bludgeon to defeat the lot of you, but my technomancer gave me full access to your communication equipment the moment she saw the Blackhawk approach." As we all removed the flight helmets we'd counted on to protect us from the Cardinal's sonic onslaught, our shared enemy crossed his arms and studied us. "Now, allow me to counter your *kind* offer." I could all but feel the smug grin behind his avian facade. "Call off your pyromancer and leave immediately, and I agree to spare all your lives."

"So you can hunt us down later?" Maddox shouted. "Not a chance."

"With all due respect," the Cardinal answered, "I have already acquired Snow. While the rest of you have proven yourselves both resourceful and formidable, I have no need of any of your talents, as I hope I've already made eminently clear." He tilted his head forward in a subtle bow. "Consider yourselves fortunate."

"Enough grandstanding." Ethan stepped forward, silently willing the Light into the paired blades in his grip. "What have you done with Seph?"

"You think I'm the one grandstanding?" The Cardinal laughed as he studied the forces gathered against him. "Pots and kettles, boy. Pots and kettles."

Ethan drew back at the words as if he'd been punched in the face.

"Enough." I stepped forward. "Like the man asked, where is Persephone Snow?"

"Miss Snow is quite safe, I assure you." The Cardinal took a step forward as well. "Though why you think I would bring such an exquisite woman with me to this barren wilderness is beyond me."

"She isn't here?" Ethan asked.

"You're welcome to look around—if you can get past me, that is." He held up a fist as if bringing the conversation to a close. "But enough cat-and-mouse. Since you all came prepared to fight, I'm happy to oblige, though I'm not certain why you think the outcome will be different this time." His razor wings slid into place, and his feet assumed a wide-based stance. "One at a time or all of you at once, it doesn't matter. Let's get this over with."

Ethan and I led the attack, him charging the Cardinal's right flank and me his left. Our crimson foe easily countered our first few blows, but then, as we'd planned during the flight up, the first phase of our actual assault began.

Ethan and I dove to either side with the remainder of our wedge following suit. This left a wide-open corridor between Falco and the Cardinal. Our aeromancer wasted no time sending a gale force wind at our armored enemy in hopes of knocking him off his feet or at least bringing him to his knees. For one hopeful moment, the Cardinal staggered, and it seemed our plan might work, but before the gust could finish toppling him, metallic talons shot from his feet and dug into the rock at his feet, keeping him upright.

No sooner had he stabilized his position than he raised an arm at Falco and fired half a dozen projectiles the color of fresh blood at our aeromancer. The blasting wind batted most of them away, but one of the six struck home, sending a flash of crimson from Falco's upper thigh. He managed to stay aloft, but the pain shook his concentration enough that the wind settled briefly. The scant seconds proved long enough, unfortunately, for the Cardinal to raise his other arm and send another half-dozen scarlet flechettes flying Falco's way. At least three of the second round found their mark, embedding themselves in Falco's chest, abdomen, and shoulder. The triple impact sent our aeromancer fluttering to the ground.

And with that, our most powerful player, aside from an already-occupied Ada, had been removed from play.

Time for blades and theriodans, though this part of the plan had seemed much more feasible with a technomancer of our own in the mix.

Ethan and I charged the Cardinal from opposite sides while Maddox and Neko rushed him from the front. The theriodan team of tiger and coyote had proven more than formidable in a multitude of fights over the years, and I'd been there for my share. Against such a foe, however, with his impenetrable armor, theriodan strength and speed, skiomancy, and God only knew how many other stolen powers and abilities, it was all hands on deck.

The two of us with swords continued to probe the Cardinal's defenses, aiming our jabs at the likely weak points in his armor, all the while taking care to avoid hitting Maddox or Neko, who worked together to pin the Cardinal's arms at his sides without taking a razor wing to the gut or losing any fingers. Their combined efforts kept him occupied enough that Ethan and I could press our attack. Ethan's blades, empowered by the Light, chipped away at our enemy's armor. My katana, however, didn't make so much as a dent, and despite my concentrated efforts at probing the seams of his crimson suit, I wasn't slowing him down a bit. From the corner of my eye, I kept track of Father, who had taken up a position at Falco's side and now rooted in the military duffel bag for something to help turn the tide.

And that left Katrina. We'd hoped to attack by night when her powers would be strongest, but as the sun continued its slow path across the morning sky, she appeared to grow weaker by the minute. Huddled next to Father, I couldn't help but recognize that we'd dragged her all this way for nothing and that her returning home alive and unhurt had become the best-case scenario.

We should have planned better. More weapons, better tactics...something.

It's funny. Mother's idea of battle planning had usually consisted of simply "right place, right time, right weapons," and everything had always seemed to work itself out. If she were here, she'd have known exactly what to do, not to mention would have had the power and skill to back it up. But then again, she was a true Daughter of Neith, while I was just a girl, albeit well-trained, with a sharp sword and sharper mind. Today, I wasn't sure if any of that was going to prove enough, a sentiment that doubled as the constant roar of Ada's fiery barrage faded into nothingness.

The Cardinal laughed. "Against me alone, you had no hope of winning this day," his amplified voice boomed, "but now your cause, I regret to inform you, is truly lost."

My eyes stole to one side and bore witness as an unconscious Ada slumped to the ground before the nameless technomancer. My mind went into overdrive, working to recalibrate our strategy now that we faced two enemies rather than one, but before I could as much as formulate a thought, a jagged pain ripped at my left shoulder. A tiny spinning pyramid fashioned of razors, wire, and circuitry jetted up and away into the sky only to return seconds later to hover before my face as if mocking me.

And it brought company.

In a blink, the air around us filled with dozens of floating machines, each more deadly in appearance than the one before: some bladed, some sporting jets of flame, and others crackling with electricity. As the queen of this technological swarm of angry hornets stalked toward us, a notable swagger in her step, the Cardinal swept his bladed arms wide.

"You all came prepared to fight, did you not?" he taunted as the four of us stood stock-still surrounded by the technomancer's deadly legion of flying tech, afraid any sudden movement might start an attack against which we had no hope of defense. "I do have many things to accomplish today, though, so if it's all the same to you, let's get this unpleasantness over with." He crossed his razor wings before his chest. "My apologies. I'm afraid this is going to hurt."

CHAPTER 31

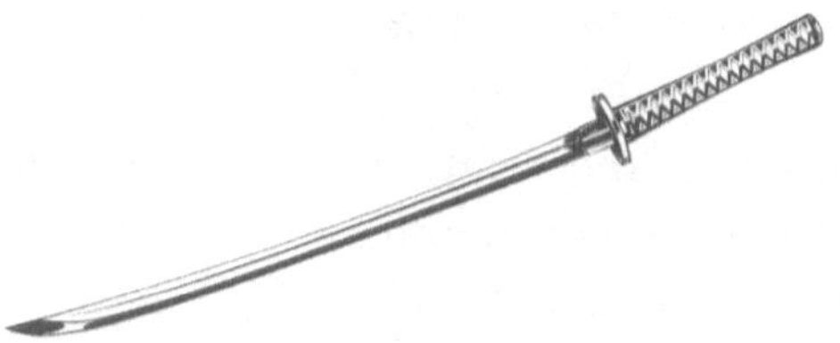

FIGHT FIRE WITH FIRE

The myriad of technological torture implements whirled around the four of us like a cyclone of steel, wire, and circuitry. Slow at first but gaining speed quickly, the horde of floating machines drew closer and closer with each deadly rotation, forcing us to converge at the center of our formation and dividing our attention. Meanwhile, the Cardinal looked on and simply bided his time.

To be besieged from every side at once, to defend against multiple simultaneous assailants, to face impossible odds and not just survive but win: such were the moments Mother trained me for since I was barely able to speak.

I feared, however, that the countless hours of preparation under her tutelage were about to prove woefully inadequate.

The technomancer went for Ethan first. With a casual wave of her hand, she sent a dozen of the swarm of attack widgets flying at him. Ethan successfully struck down three of his tiny attackers with an intricate series of paired slashes, sending them to the ground in pieces. The remainder, however, flew at him from every side, drawing blood from each limb while the largest struck him from behind and drove him to his knees. The shorter of Mother's two swords went flying, its steel clanging along the bare rock far too close to the edge of a long drop. Ethan managed to hang on to the longer blade, though the steel's inner Light faded as he struggled to rise from the ground.

With Ethan down, the technomancer turned her attention on Maddox and Neko. At her command, one of the tiny levitating gadgets flew at our tiger only to split apart less than a foot from his chest with an almost invisible fiber stretched between its two halves. Like a high-tech version of the bolas once used for hunting by indigenous people in South America, the pair of flying machines orbited Neko in opposite directions at blinding speed. In seconds, his arms suddenly lashed to his sides and his legs tethered tightly together, he fell to one side. His shoulder impacted a small boulder with a nauseating crack.

Maddox fared a little better against the quartet of hovering contraptions the techno-witch sent for him. The first fired a pair of barbed wires that lodged in his chest taser-style and lit him up with sufficient electricity to send his every hair standing on end. Fortunately, Maddox wasn't just any man; I'd had opportunity during our time together to see him shrug off far worse punishment and walk away.

A matching pair of different machines flanked him on either side, each firing a series of projectiles like tiny darts, catching him in a crossfire. I could only guess these must be drugged or poisoned, but as Maddox fought on, he seemed to shrug off their effects as effortlessly as he had the taser-bot.

Frustration lining her features, the technomancer sent the fourth and largest of the flying machines flying straight at Maddox's head. My experience with Maddox, however, went far beyond the battlefield. The summer we'd spent more or less every spare moment together, he'd played community league baseball several nights a week. With his coyote reflexes, he could practically catch a line drive with his eyes closed.

Dodging to one side, Maddox snagged the flying sphere mid-air, spun around like an Olympic discus thrower, and hurled the device straight at the technomancer. Clearly unprepared for the counterattack, the woman unsuccessfully leaped to one side, her attempted dodge half a second too late. The flying bludgeon struck her center chest with a loud thud, knocking the air from her lungs and sending her sprawling to the ground.

"You'll pay for that," she spat between heaving breaths, righting herself and reassuming control of the floating sphere. Delivered with a heavy Mandarin accent, they were the first words the technomancer had spoken in our presence. "My orders may be to incapacitate rather than kill, but understand that such vague orders still leave me quite a bit of latitude."

Interesting. She was under orders, likely from our crimson-armored-friend, that at least some of us were to be kept alive. That was a plus, unless, of course, she was lying.

The technomancer sent the compact sphere flying again at Maddox, but rather than a straight bullet shot like before, this time it bobbed and weaved as it raced his way. With reflexes beyond any he'd shown during our time together, Maddox leaped backward into a reverse handspring and managed to evade this second attack as well. The evasive maneuver, however, left him off balance and open for attack, no doubt the witch's plan.

Without missing a beat, the technomancer sent in both the taser and projectile units along with an additional device that hovered at head level spraying a fine mist likely meant to blind. Maddox may be one of the more skilled fighters I've ever encountered, but none of his training could have prepared him for such a fight.

It was over in an instant. Blinded as the irritating yellow mist hit him full in the face, struck by a good dozen more of the tiny darts, tased with electrical current so strong that the smell of charred flesh filled the air, and bludgeoned about the head and shoulders repeatedly by the floating sphere, Maddox couldn't do much but cover his face and wait for it to be over.

And that left me against the technomancer and our basically invincible armored foe who'd done nothing but watch, wait, and rest as his lieutenant took out our entire assembled strike force in less than two minutes. With Falco down, Katrina's abilities at an ebb, and everyone else incapacitated, it was up to me.

"Let's do this, then."

I'd drawn my katana high above my head, ready to fight to the last, when a shout from behind me sent my pulse racing even faster.

"Rosemary," came Father's insistent voice, "down!"

Without a second thought, I dove to the unforgiving earth just before an explosion like a thunderclap split the air. A loud whoosh sounded above my head accompanied by a flash of heat. A glance back revealed father discarding a smoking U.S. Army rocket launcher and pulling another from the green duffel bag. A moment later, the rocket exploded into the next mountain over with another deafening crash.

"Close, Mr. Delacroix," the Cardinal spoke through his amplification system. "Happy to see you didn't bring a knife to yet another gun fight." He looked to his technomancer. "That said, my dear, do take care of his little bag of tricks."

Another wave of the technomancer's hand, and a loud series of clicks sounded from the duffel bag.

"Father," I screamed, "run!"

I'd barely spoken the second word when Father grabbed Katrina, sprinted forward with her until they'd reached a low boulder, and dove across it, hurling his body atop hers. A moment later, the remaining munitions detonated all at once with a sound like the gates of hell opening wide, making me wish I'd left the stupid earplugs in.

And that left me, as before, all alone against the Cardinal and his technomancer.

Without wasting another breath, I rolled to my feet, raised my blade before me anew, and prepared myself for whatever punishment awaited.

If this was my time, I'd face it sword in hand, just as Mother had.

The world slowed as I focused my every sense on my pair of

opponents, vigilant for the first hint of attack or movement. As I waited for the two to start their final play, a maelstrom of thoughts spiraled in my head, a different face occupying my mind's eye with each passing breath.

How I'd never had a chance to tell Mother, the woman who made me into the person I'd become as surely as a blacksmith forges a shining blade from the crudest of iron, goodbye.

How I wished for the chance to tell Father one last time that I loved him and how much he meant to me. The same for Maddox, if I was being completely honest.

How I'd never once taken the chance, despite the cruel circumstances and the million reasons to keep my silence, to tell Ethan—

"Get away from my daughter."

Father came up on my side, his approach swift and quiet, and rushed the technomancer. Compared to the armored madman to her left, she appeared the softer target, but as I'd guessed earlier, he'd barely closed the distance between them before one of her bolo-bots tied his legs together and secured his arms to his sides. His momentum sent him falling head first onto bare rock, and the moment of Mother's death flashed across my memory.

"Father!" I cried as the man who raised me twisted to one side so his shoulder would take the brunt of the fall.

"Don't worry, girl." The technomancer spun her finger in the air and countless floating hunks of blinking, whirring tech surrounded me on every side. "You'll be joining him soon enough."

I shot a glance at Katrina, who watched from her position behind the low boulder. Catching her gaze, I shook my head, hoping she would stay put as I faced my fate.

"And now," the technomancer whispered, "for the last and the least." Her eyes narrowed even as her lips spread wide in a wicked grin. "If you pray to any gods, girl, now would be the time to—"

The last words were stolen from her lips by the rotor wash of the Black Hawk helicopter that rose silently behind her from the valley below. The gust of wind as strong as anything Falco might summon, the blast of debris-filled air flung both me and the nameless technomancer to the ground while the myriad floating torture devices were sent flying in every direction. Even the thus-far-unstoppable Cardinal dropped to one knee as the brutal downwash flung wood and rock in every direction.

Our aeromancer, on the other hand, found himself quite literally back in his element.

Through eyes clenched against wind and rock and dust, I looked on with newfound hope as Falco rose from the ground like a wounded jaguar, his jungle cat spots the blood of his many wounds seeping through his trademark white suit. The shattered remnants of his mirrored shades no longer obscured the fire in his furious gaze.

In seconds, the whipping winds in my vicinity subsided, leaving an eerie radius of calm around our strike force even as the windstorm around the Cardinal and his technomancer intensified into a full-blown cyclone.

Falco was right. He'd been holding back a month ago when he was our adversary rather than our ally. I wasn't certain how comforting I found that particular realization.

Taking full advantage of the respite, I rushed to Neko's side and severed the cables holding him tight, crunching one end of the bolo-bot beneath my heel.

"Help Ethan and Maddox," I shouted over the roar of the wind, the sound deafening despite the eerie stillness of the air where we stood. "I'll free Father."

I rushed to Father's side and slid my katana between his body and the cables binding him. No sooner had I severed his bonds, however, than the tornado surrounding our enemies dissipated. Falco fell gracelessly back to the ground, clearly having expended all he had left to buy us the few seconds we needed to regroup. The helicopter's blinding rotor wash immediately came rushing back, and I had to squint to keep a visual lock on our foes.

Recovering more quickly than I would have dreamed possible, the technomancer came to a low crouch and raised an arm at the silent Black Hawk, clearly in an effort to bring her powers to bear against the technological marvel that had turned the tide of battle. My heart froze in fear for L.J.'s and Bradley's lives, not to mention those of the brave Army crew that currently fought a battle that wasn't theirs.

Despite her efforts, however, the helicopter didn't budge an inch. Continuing its low hover, the Black Hawk scoured the mountaintop with cyclonic force winds making life difficult for friend and foe alike.

Through the flying debris, I could just make out the Cardinal's silhouette as he raised an arm and fired a rocket from his wrist at the helicopter. His effort no more effective than his partner's, the tiny missile exploded midair before it had traveled more than a few feet. The explosion rocked the Cardinal's armored form and sent the technomancer, who had nearly regained her footing despite the rotor wash, flying backward onto jagged rock. An instant later, the technomancer's multitude of devices returned en masse from their temporary banishment like a swarm of bees returning to their queen, and I thought it was over for all of us.

This time, however, the tiny battalion of flying lethal weapons appeared to be under the control of another.

Taser-bots, bolo-bots, bludgeons, dart-throwers: they all attacked their mistress at once in a tightly coordinated strike. Utter shock and disbelief overtook her panicked features as she reaped the whirlwind of her own inventions. In mere seconds, the vicious assault along with the continued hammering winds of the helicopter's rotor wash proved more than she could withstand.

No sooner had the technomancer succumbed to the finest example of poetic justice I'd ever seen than the Black Hawk took off, leaving us alone on the mountaintop facing a vengeful Cardinal. His abject anger manifested in clenched fists and a hunched stance, his face remained, as always, hidden behind the angular eyes and jet-black shield of his avian helmet.

"You petulant children," came the Cardinal's amplified voice. "You have no idea what I'm trying to accomplish or what you leave this world to face by standing against me." He directed a gauntleted finger in my direction. "If you knew what was coming, you'd be standing shoulder-to-shoulder with me against the darkness instead of getting in my way."

"Again with this bullshit?" Father appeared at my shoulder.

"Perhaps you should have led with something besides assault and kidnapping if you wanted people to greet you with something other than raised fists."

"Not to mention your cross-continental murder streak." Maddox pulled himself into a low crouch. "Don't forget, I've been on your trail for months, and what you did to the Greyhound alone lands you firmly in the bad guy column."

"In other words," Ethan said as he came up on my other side, "if you're looking for allies, you've got a strange way of asking."

"Oh, Mr. Harkreader, my currently indisposed associate notwithstanding, I need no allies. I stand before you prepared to face the coming reckoning all on my own, and I become more so with the acquisition of each new ability, each Ascendant soul." The Cardinal surveyed the unconscious technomancer sprawled at his feet. "That being said, I'm impressed that your little strikeforce was able to bring down Minako." The quiet chuckle, amplified by the speakers in the Cardinal's armor, echoed across the mountaintop. "She's a notoriously tough cookie."

Ethan's brow again furrowed, as if something in the Cardinal's voice and laugh had struck a chord. But the time to explore that was later. For the moment, we had a so-far-undefeated adversary to bring down and a missing pop star to find.

"We stopped her." I stepped forward, my sword directed at the Cardinal's breastplate. "We'll stop you."

"Not on your best day, Delacroix, but since all you lot wish to do is fight, I'm happy to oblige." His razor wings slid into place with a metallic click as he dropped into a martial stance. "Someday when I am proven right, however, remember that you all were warned."

"Give me one minute alone with you outside of that fucking armor," Neko growled, his eyes full tiger and his lips stretched in a bestial snarl, "and you'll be talking out the other side of your mouth."

"No, Neko." Katrina, all but forgotten in the moment, stepped through our ranks and approached the Cardinal, a renewed boldness in her step. "Allow me."

"You, shadow-girl?" The Cardinal laughed. "The sun beats down upon your pale skin even now from a cloudless sky. What can you possibly hope to do besides beg for mercy?"

"The sunlight may weaken me," she murmured with new confidence, "but I am far from powerless."

"Don't forget, girl." The Cardinal gestured to his own shadow stretching westward and summoned the winged silhouette up from the ground to stand by his side. "I have already taken one skiomancer's power for my own. I don't require a second shadow dealer's essence, but I'll gladly take such from you should you force my hand."

"And that's the thing," Katrina whispered. "You may have taken that poor skiomancer's talent, but you don't possess their skill, experience, control, or finesse." The dark faces of horror's elite along Katrina's crossed arms all narrowed their gazes at the Cardinal. "The first thing Midnight taught me was that merely having the power to control shadows doesn't make you their master."

"Doesn't it?" the Cardinal asked, his amplified voice smug and dismissive.

"In your rabid quest to attain abilities like playing cards, I suspect you haven't put in the time to learn even the most fundamental basics." Katrina's arms dropped to her sides. "You haven't honed your stolen talents, and instead wield them with only the crudest understanding of what wonders you can now perform. I, on the other hand, can make shadows dance at my whim." The various faces along her flesh mirrored their mistress's focused mien. "I'm giving you one warning before I—"

"I understand more than you can possibly imagine, girl." The Cardinal lowered his head. "And my resolve surpasses anything you can match."

"We shall see." She raised a finger and rested it on the Cardinal's breastplate. "Funny thing? As I stood here atop this mountain, the sun beating down inescapably bright and leaving any sort of shadow at its lowest ebb, I asked myself where the nearest source of darkness might be." Her voice went deep, husky. "Do you know what I came up with?"

"No, girl." The Cardinal's amplified voice dripped with impatient sarcasm. "What?"

"The interior of an impenetrable suit of armor is as dark a place as I can imagine." Katrina raised a hand, and the Cardinal arms shot out to either side like a puppet's. As his crimson-clad form rose in the air before Katrina, she continued. "And not just that. As my mistress taught me, all of us are filled with shadow. No hint of light ever touches our heart, our brain, our entrails until our souls have departed and our husk rests beneath the mortician's knife. I have spent years refining control of the shadows that reside within my own body." She stepped back to survey her victory. "Have you done the same?"

The Cardinal groaned in agony, as his arms and legs both stretched backward as if he were tied to a rack.

"Now," Katrina said, her voice cool and even, "where is Persephone Snow?" She raised one clawed hand, her fingers curling into a fist. "Instead of simply manipulating the shadows within your suit, I could always chat with the ones that reside within your skull."

Damn. I made a mental note to do whatever it took to stay on Katrina's good side.

"She..." the Cardinal got out between pained grunts.

"Yes?" Katrina tilted the levitating Cardinal forward in the air until they were eye-to-eye and his form almost horizontal. "You were saying?"

"She...will never...return to you."

That's when a terrible realization hit me. The Cardinal could fly, and Katrina's power now held him before her like a battering ram.

"Katrina!" I shouted. "Look out!"

The silent jets on the Cardinal's boots fired, shooting him forward like a missile. His helmeted head struck Katrina square in the face, rocking her head back with a horrifying snap and leaving her sprawled unconscious on the rocky ground. No longer shackled by our skiomancer's shadowy assault, the Cardinal flew a victory lap of the mountaintop before returning to mock us from ten feet above all our heads.

"Your gambit is over, would-be Daughter of Neith." He gestured to the horizon. "Your juvenile technomancer proved formidable indeed, but unless I miss my guess, he has expended all his energies for the day as your Black Hawk continues its retreat to the east." He peered around at the bodies littering our mountaintop battlefield. "I've defeated your pyromancer and aeromancer, and now, your skiomancer, however brave, lies unconscious at your feet." He extended his razor wings to either side in a show of dominance. "What chance have you now? Not one of you left standing has so much as slowed me down."

"Mother taught me that surrender is never an option." I raised my katana above my head. "One last time, Cardinal. Surrender, or face the consequences."

"You are brave, girl. I'll give you that." He surveyed the five of us remaining with a sweep of his helmet's avian eyes. "All of you, in fact." He turned his attention to Ethan with a short but notable pause in his soliloquy. "Still, you've created a truly regrettable situation. I'd planned to let you all walk away from this despite your continued interference, but you've made it clear that you intend to keep coming until you're either victorious or dead." He crossed his bladed wings before his chest and dropped from the sky, landing before us in a defensive posture, and extended a hand, beckoning any of us to be the first to attack. "Trust that the outcome will not be the former."

CHAPTER 32

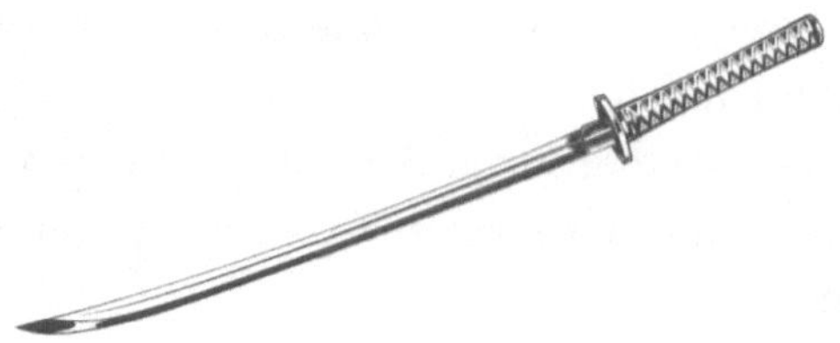

ETERNAL FLAME

"Say the word, Rosemary." Ethan stood to my right, the longer of Mother's two blades in his double grip, the blade glowing with its inner silver light. "It's now or never."

"I'm in," Maddox said as he pulled up on my left. "Whatever it takes."

"Me too." Neko crouched before me like the tiger that burned bright at his core, prepared to pounce upon the Cardinal at my command. "As one."

"Rosemary." The tenor of Father's voice raised the hairs on my neck. "Are you certain this is the best course of action?"

I cursed under my breath. I'd learned from an early age to defer to Mother's teachings and Father's wisdom in all things, but if we entered the next thirty seconds on anything but the exact same page, none of us were going to leave the mountain alive.

"There is no other course of action."

"I just wanted to hear you say it." Father sprinted right to flank the

Cardinal, firing round after round into our opponent's crimson armor. "Take him down!"

Neko sprung like a jungle cat for the Cardinal's left arm while Maddox went for his right. As soon as both theriodans were clear, Ethan swept his blade downward in a full cross-body slash that skimmed the Cardinal's armor from his left shoulder to his right hip. Not wasting an instant, I leaped forward and jabbed at the Cardinal's neck, attempting to get the tip of my blade beneath his bulky helmet, if not to wound, at least in hopes I might dislodge his head protection or disrupt the control of his suit.

All our efforts were for nothing. Ethan's blade, even empowered with the Light, did little more than superficial damage to the Cardinal's armor, my own blow ricocheted off his thick breastplate, and Neko and Maddox quickly realized that perhaps it was they who had the tiger by the tail and not the other way around.

With stolen strength augmented by technomancer genius, the Cardinal brought his theriodan-pinned arms together like a pair of cymbals, hurling tiger and coyote into each other with concussive force. Maddox and Neko both slumped unconscious to the ground at our enemy's feet.

That left Father, Ethan, and me still up and ready to fight.

Father continued to engage from a relatively safe distance with the only weapon he had remaining, though I feared his bullets had a greater chance of injuring one of us than the Cardinal, be it a direct shot or a ricochet. Meanwhile, Ethan and I continued to probe our opponent's defenses for any weakness. Ethan's blows might have had the power needed to eventually win the fight and mine the necessary precision, but as the fight wore on, one thing became clear: the Cardinal, having dispatched anyone who could actually do him harm, was merely playing with us. I struggled to keep that realization from provoking me to the point of making a stupid mistake as the fight was dangerous enough already. We'd seen what the Cardinal's razor wings could do, and Ethan had nearly paid the ultimate price.

"I must say, Harkreader," the Cardinal mocked, as if reading my mind, "you've bounced back quite well from the wound I inflicted in Montecito." He slashed at Ethan's neck with one crimson wing before sending the other flying at his solar plexus, the move almost identical to his previous near-fatal attack. Though Ethan managed to parry the blow this time, the razor tip missed his midsection by less than an inch. "I'd apologize in advance for what is inevitably to come, but I suspect both of us know all too well I wouldn't mean it."

"If only you fought as well as you talked," Ethan grunted, his blade flashing with silver electricity as it struck a weak point along the Cardinal's gauntlet and separated one razor wing from our enemy's armor. As the crimson blade of razor-sharp steel feathers clattered to the rocks at our feet, I wasn't sure who was more surprised, Ethan or the Cardinal.

"One down," Ethan grunted as he again swung Mother's sword, shining with the Light of Neith, at his enemy, "one to go."

The Cardinal shot out his hand, caught the blade mid-arc in a gauntleted fist, and yanked it from Ethan's grasp. "Two can play at that game, boy." He hurled Mother's sword for the edge of the rocky outcropping and raised his razor-winged arm at Ethan. "What now, Harkreader?"

"Ethan!" I cried. "Catch!" I tossed him my katana and then ducked beneath a sweep of the Cardinal's remaining razor wing as I raced to retrieve Mother's blades, the longer sword lying not far from where the shorter one had landed earlier. I hated leaving Ethan alone to face our shared enemy, but we were going to need every weapon possible if we were to survive the next sixty seconds.

Not to mention, without a sword, I was pretty much useless in this fight.

Father joined me halfway to the line of scrub trees. "We need to move," he said between breaths. "Ethan is all alone."

I worked to restrain my withering look. "I'm well aware."

A flash of silver caught my eye. Mother's longer blade, its inner Light all but faded, lay resting, wedged between two stones. I yanked it free and glanced up as Father discovered Mother's short sword resting precariously at the edge of the long drop I'd spotted earlier.

Mission accomplished. Now to get back to Ethan before it was too—

"Rosemary!" Father screamed, his eyes suddenly wide with terror. "Look out!"

I jerked my head to the right in time to catch a blur of crimson out of the corner of my vision half a second before a pain beyond anything I'd ever experienced erupted along my lower back. A glance down revealed a metallic feather jutting out next to my navel, the deep red of its razor edge complemented by the blood dripping from its tip.

"Rosemary!" Ethan cried out from somewhere very far away. "No!"

"You bastard!" Father's voice, somehow near and distant at the same time. "Get away from her!"

The agony along my flank flared, the pain accompanied by a wet sound like a boot being pulled out of mud. I fell to the ground, somehow landing on my hands and knees despite the fact that every ounce of strength had left my body at once. I stared at the bare rock between my bloodied hands as angry shouts and the clang of metal on metal filled the air, the disparate sounds growing fainter and fainter as a low roar grew in my ears like the repeating rumble of an oncoming steamroller. The bizarre realization that the ever-accelerating pounding in my head was my heart fighting to keep me alive brought a strange mix of panic and peace.

I'd always said I would go down fighting and found myself strangely relieved to know I'd been right about at least one thing in my life.

If only I had one more minute, though.

I'd tell Ethan everything.

I'd tell him...

❧

*B*reathe, Rosemary. Mother's voice. *Breathe.*

I pulled in a single sweet gulp of air, and for the first time in what felt like an eternity, it didn't hurt.

Though my body felt cold as a corpse, a comforting warmth rolled up my arms, across my belly, and down my legs. My mind flirted with the sweet oblivion of sleep as both the stabbing pain and the diffuse chill faded into the background, but that was not to be, as a pair of gunshots and the sound of shouting yanked me back to full consciousness.

That's when I noticed the unmistakable sensation of warm lips upon mine.

I opened my eyes to find Ethan hunched over me. My lower back rested crosswise atop his thighs. His muscular arms encircled my shoulders and held me tight to his chest. His head hovered above mine as his lips and mine danced for the very first time. Every inch of both our bodies shimmered, both of us engulfed in silver-white flame.

It felt like a dream.

I prayed it wasn't.

"Rosemary?" Ethan pulled away. His sudden absence stung worse than the Cardinal's blade. "Are you okay?"

"I'm alive." My eyes shot left and right and then down to my blood-soaked top, the exact level of danger we found ourselves in flooding back all at once. "Father?"

"He's giving the Cardinal all he's got."

"He's going to die." I did everything in my power to sit up, but the stabbing pain of the Cardinal's through-and-through assault returned with a vengeance.

"Hold on," Ethan said, "you're still healing."

"But Father..."

"I wouldn't worry too much," Ethan said with a grim smile. "The Cardinal is currently facing a side of your Father I hope I never experience."

Bracing myself for the pain, I pulled myself up Ethan's torso far enough that I could turn my head in the direction of the staccato metallic clangs filling the air. Father, armed only with my katana, and the Cardinal, now deprived of both his razor wings, battled at the edge of the rocky drop-off, and for once, our crimson enemy was on the defense.

Despite his lack of any special power, weaponry, or armor, Father fought with a mix of smart tactics, trained muscle, honed reflexes, and unqualified rage, no doubt thinking he'd just witnessed his only daughter's final moments. To see him not only stand firm against such an enemy but to know that he was actually winning filled me with renewed hope.

He shifted quickly and often from one technique to another, doing his best to keep the Cardinal off balance. His careful sword strikes landed true time and again, reminding me unequivocally that while Mother was born to be a Daughter of Neith, Father's skills with a sword were a force to reckoned with as well.

Continuing his brutal offensive, Father pushed the Cardinal farther and farther back until his opponent's heels rested at the edge of the drop-off.

But the Cardinal could fly. Surely Father hadn't forgotten as well.

"Father!" I shouted, the single word sending a tearing pain through my abdomen. "Remember! He can—"

I cursed myself, wishing the words back into my mouth. Stupid girl. Never distract someone mid-fight.

Father glanced across his shoulder, the rage in his features breaking into relief as he met my gaze like the sun coming out from behind a cloud.

The moment lasted just that, however, as the Cardinal took full advantage of Father's momentary distraction and seized his sword arm.

"You fight well for one of ordinary stock." The Cardinal pulled Father face-to-face with his crimson-and-black avian visage. "What a shame to end such a fine specimen of humanity..." He hurled Father from the edge of the rocky cliff and stalked in our direction. "...and so ignominiously at that."

"You bastard!" I forced my way to my feet despite Ethan's best efforts to keep me still. The simple act of standing hurt like hell, but I pushed through the agony. Fortunately, with every moment within our shared cocoon of flame, I felt my body knitting back together, the pain dissipating, my strength returning.

That last part was important, because Ethan and I would have to be at the top of our game in about five seconds if we were to survive the day.

Ethan came shoulder to shoulder with me and handed me the longer of Mother's blades. "You all right?"

"For the moment," I answered, trying to keep any bitterness from what was possibly the last thing I'd ever say to him. "Father..."

"I sense the Flame has done all it can for you." Ethan's eyes slid closed. "If we make it through this, I'll do what I can for him, for everyone, but for now, it's time to—"

"Do not extinguish the Flame, Harkreader."

This voice, unheard since a month ago when we stood at the center of the biggest arena in Los Angeles, cut the tense air, and even the Cardinal stopped in his tracks at the words, delivered in their strong Ethiopian accent.

"Let it grow within you." Ada, gravely injured but again conscious, pulled herself to her feet. "Let it burn away all that you do not need and leave behind only that which serves you."

"I've patched up Rosemary all I can," Ethan shouted as the Cardinal continued his inexorable approach. "For better or for worse, now we've got to fight."

"The inferno that burns within you does far more than simply heal wounds, Harkreader. Fire can warm, fire can light your way..." Ada's eyes grew cold even as the air around her shimmered with heat. "And fire can *burn*." She raised a hand in our direction, her fingers curled upward as a sliver of the same silver flame danced above her palm. "Here. Allow me to stoke the flame that rages in your heart."

In an instant, the silver-white flames surrounding Ethan and me flared into a full-fledged conflagration, so impossibly bright that it became all but impossible to see. I reached out a hand, my searching fingers blindly finding Ethan's, our digits intertwining as the eldritch fire swept over us, burning but not consuming, terrible yet fascinating, and above all, empowering.

"Focus on the Flame, Harkreader," Ada shouted. "You as well, Delacroix." Her words struck our hearing from every direction at once. "Bring it near to your core. Use it as you will." Her subvocal chuckle filled our ears, as if coming from the fire rather than the woman herself. "And then, end this."

Time slowed to a crawl. My eyes slid closed as I turned my

consciousness inward, focusing on the first thing Mother ever taught me.

To breathe.

In.

Focus on the Flame.

Out.

Bring it near to your core.

In.

Use it as you will.

Out.

End this.

My eyes opened on the Cardinal bearing down on us. Shoulder-to-shoulder with Ethan, we each held half of Mother's inheritance of steel. Not wasting a second, I leaped forward to defend Ethan, who continued to wrestle with the silver-white inferno that raged around him.

I brandished the longer of Mother's swords, its blade burning with a Light beyond anything it had ever known. Raging fire that augmented rather than melted the razor-sharp steel blazed from the sword's tip to its tang, engulfing my hands, my arms, my entire body.

The Cardinal rushed at me, one of his razor wings now held in his gauntleted hands like some bizarre feathered sword. A single swing of Mother's blade, aflame with Ethan's Fire, left the Cardinal's weapon so much ruined slag. Our enemy let out a furious cry and let the destroyed remnants of his weapon fall to the ground.

An instant later, the cyclone of silver-white flame circling Ethan exploded into the sky only to return to him a moment later, the fire and light and energy flowing into his eyes, his nostrils, his mouth, his very flesh.

"Whoa," he said, shaking off the influx of raw power with a confident smile, "that felt...incredible."

I shifted my weight onto my rear leg in preparation for whatever the Cardinal might throw next.

"You ready?" I asked.

"You heard Ada," Ethan answered. "This guy's ass isn't going to kick itself."

Ethan and I attacked as one, my overhead strike in concert with his short-bladed lunge. The Cardinal's arm shot up instinctively to block my slash, his amplified cry of pain blasting my ears as my blazing blade cut through his gauntlet and wedged itself just above his wrist. Ethan's blade simultaneously found its mark, piercing our opponent's crimson breastplate on the side opposite his cruel heart. With a pained grunt, the Cardinal immediately withdrew and assumed a rare defensive posture. He stared at the two of us in disbelief for several seconds before the near-silent jets in his boots flared to life, sending him upward and away from us until he hovered beyond the drop-off a full story above our heads.

"So, you have finally come fully into your power, Harkreader, and you've even allowed its rightful owner a taste of what your desperate action a month back, however noble, denied her. How...poetic."

"Come down here," Ethan directed the blazing sword skyward, "and I'll show you poetic, you bastard."

"Outnumbered and deprived of my weaponry to face two children suddenly imbued with power beyond their understanding? I think not." He paused, an ironic chuckle emanating from his helmet as he focused his attention on Ethan. "I have little doubt I could still take you both, but discretion is sometimes the better part of valor, as the saying goes, and my mother didn't raise fools." He hovered in silence for a moment, studying Ethan as if taking his full measure. "Fear not, Harkreader. Our fight is far from over."

"You're just going to take off," I shouted after him, "and leave your techno-witch to face the music for all you've done?"

"Minako is loyal to me and me alone," he uttered dismissively. "She won't talk."

"She won't have you to back her up," Ethan proclaimed. I half-imagined that his glare might set the Cardinal aflame. "Everyone has their limits. Even you, it would seem."

The Cardinal chuckled from his low hover. "Your threats are laughable and empty on more levels than you know. My technomancer has been doing this far longer than either of you have been alive. She's been interrogated and tortured by the best—or, I suppose, the worst—and held her tongue." He directed a gauntleted finger at Ethan. "As if any of you lot—aside from Alba's people and possibly the coyote—have the stomach to inflict even the barest minimum of unpleasantness toward one you view as helpless." Another amplified laugh reverberated down. "I fully trust that Minako will be quite safe in your care until such time that she decides she's bored of your company, at which point I wish you *all* the best of luck."

"But wait," Ethan shouted, a new vulnerability in his voice, "you never told us where Seph is."

The Cardinal shook his head sadly. "And this, Mr. Harkreader, is why you will ultimately lose. Even in your moment of temporary victory, you still plead with a superior adversary to concede a fight they'd won before the first punch landed. It's pitiable, really. For all your admirable bluster and effort today, you accomplished nothing. Snow is mine, and regardless of today's temporary setback, everything continues to proceed exactly as I require."

"I won't stop until I've found her." Ethan seethed, the fire returning to his voice matching the white flame surrounding both our forms. "And until I've made you pay for all of this."

"That's the spirit, kid. Keep telling yourself there's hope, and don't be too hard on yourself. You were never going to win this day."

Ethan blanched yet again at the Cardinal's words, his words catching in his throat.

"Harm Persephone Snow," I filled the sudden silence, "and there is no place on this planet so remote that I won't find and end you."

"Clearly," the Cardinal conceded as he motioned to the bare mountaintop, "though trust that you aren't the only one who's learned a thing or two in this fight." His hands balled into fists at his sides. "Should we meet again, Rosemary Delacroix, understand that no quarter will be asked or given."

"The truest statement you've made all day."

The Cardinal returned his attention to Ethan. "A piece of advice, Mr. Harkreader? Stay out of my way, and perhaps you and the lovely Miss Snow may be reunited someday. Interfere again, though—"

"Don't you dare harm her," Ethan answered.

"Harm *her*?" The Cardinal laughed midair. "Perish the thought."

Understand a few things, boy: I have need of Snow and her unique abilities. You don't want to admit it, but she is far safer in my care than under your protection. Until she plays her part in my plans, trust that no harm will befall her, a promise I cannot extend to you and your friends. Cross me again, and you will find out exactly how much restraint I've shown thus far." With that, he spun in the air to leave, only to address us one last time across his shoulder. "The day will come when you all will understand what truly happened today, what I am trying to accomplish, and why it must be this way, but for now, rest well knowing that you survived the first few skirmishes of a war unlike any the world has known for centuries."

Without another word, he circled the mountain in what Seph would call a "flex" and then disappeared into the valley below the drop-off where Father disappeared. Without a single word to Ethan, I rushed to the cliff edge only to find the rocky outcropping below empty.

"Father," I groaned as Ethan, close behind, extinguished the flames surrounding both our forms. "Not you too..."

"Rosemary," came a strained voice from a few feet away. I inched forward on hands and knees until I could see the crown of Father's head shifting left and right below an outcropping, his tanned fingers white-knuckled around a tree root that protruded from otherwise bare rock.

"Ethan!" I shouted. "It's Father! He's alive!"

Ethan was at my side in an instant, shimmying himself forward along the rocky outcrop until he could see Father as well. "Hang on, Mr. Delacroix. We'll get you out of there."

Father didn't waste any breath on responding, though his huffing breaths let me know that he was holding on with all he had. How much longer he could continue to hang on was anybody's guess.

"What do we do?" I asked. "I don't think we brought any rope, Neko and Maddox are still down for the count, and I don't think either of us can get to him with the overhang." I peered downward at the tree-covered mountainside below, dropping my voice to a low whisper. "Even if we can get down there before he lets go, what are we supposed to do? Catch him?"

"Allow me," came a familiar voice, the words almost pleasant despite the snide German tones. "And then, consider us even."

A bloodied Falco rose from beneath Father, borne by billowing winds, and caught him beneath his arms as the last strength in Father's fingers gave way. I let out a tiny scream, and then, like a scene out of a storybook, the wounded aeromancer rose like a guardian angel with my exhausted father held in his arms.

"Mr. Harkreader, Clan Delacroix," Falco said, "understand that any debt I may have incurred by my actions during the unfortunate circumstances a month ago are now considered paid in full."

"Now, now, Dietrich," Ada said from across our shoulders, her voice filled with subtle mirth, "no need for such formalities." Limping, she joined our circle. "We may not all be the best of friends, but I must admit a newfound closeness with this young couple, having helped them in some way achieve their shared destiny, not to mention survive this latest encounter with their sworn enemy."

"I'm sorry, Ada, but I don't think you understand," I interjected before Ethan could say a word. "Ethan and I aren't together. In fact, we're here searching for the woman he loves."

"Truly?" Ada's wise brown eyes cut from me to Ethan and back. "My apologies for making such an *obviously* incorrect assumption."

"I thought you knew," Ethan said. "We're here for Persephone Snow." He hung his head and sighed. "That bastard has her, and after everything we've done and sacrificed to get to this spot, today's fight amounted to nothing."

"I don't know, Ethan. We managed to stop the Cardinal, at least for the time being, not to mention we have his technomancer." I offered him a hopeful smile. "That's not totally nothing."

"Tell that to Seph," Ethan muttered.

"I know this must be difficult to accept, young man," Ada said, compassion coloring her tone, "but you've done all you can for Miss Snow, at least for now."

"Wait. You tracked the Cardinal here without the help of a technomancer." Ethan sucked in a breath. "Do you have any idea where Seph might be?" Desperation poured from his every syllable. "Any idea at all?"

"I do not," Ada said, "and trust that I speak the truth. While Dietrich has made it clear that any obligation he owed you has been expunged, it would seem that I now owe you and Miss Delacroix, and you in particular, Mr. Harkreader, a sincere debt."

"Me?" Ethan asked.

"Us?" I stammered almost simultaneously.

"A debt?" we asked together, the pair of syllables in perfect sync.

"Not only do I owe you my life this day, I understand that the two of you did everything you could to save the Greyhound, my precious Dugan, from this madman, even going so far as to pour your fire into him in an effort to keep him this side of the veil, and all for a stranger. If only I'd been there to help you stoke the flames of your newfound ability as I did today, perhaps he'd still be with us rather than dead at the hands of that crimson monster."

"We learned only recently that you and the Greyhound were... you know..." Ethan tipped his head forward, unable to meet Ada's gaze any longer, and massaged his neck. "I'm...so sorry."

"As I explained before," Falco interjected, "Ascendant tend to mind their own business, particularly in matters of love."

"We all keep secrets, Mr. Harkreader, and often for good reasons." Ada took Ethan's hand. "Sometimes even from ourselves." Her gaze shot to mine and then back to Ethan. "Know that from this day on, you can call upon me if and when you have need of a pyromancer's aid, and I will do all that I can to aid you in whatever way you require."

"To be honest, you could start by explaining something," Ethan said without missing a beat. "I don't understand what you did today. How you helped us win."

"I do not possess your ability, Mr. Harkreader. Your healing flame is unique to you and your current status as vessel for the power inherent in the line of Neith." Her lips quirked to one side in thought. "That being said, your power manifests as fire, and while I may not be able to duplicate your particular flame, my abilities are more than able to augment the already impressive inferno that burns even now at your core and magnify your power into a blinding white conflagration to be reckoned with."

Ethan considered her words. "In that case, Ada, I'd like to call in your debt, effective immediately."

"Would you, then?" Ada raised a brow. "I'm intrigued."

Ethan peered boldly into the pyromancer's smug smile. "Like it or not, I'm Neith's agent until such time that...something happens that leads to the Light passing to its next vessel. I'm learning all that I can about how to think, fight, and survive. So far, Rosemary has been there for me at every turn, helping me figure all this out."

"I'm quite certain," Ada murmured with another cut of her eyes in my direction.

"That being said, this flame that burns in me is nothing she's ever seen and a complete mystery to me." Ethan pulled in a deep breath. "As a mistress of all things fire, I was wondering if you could...show me a thing or two?"

A part of me hated that Ethan was seeking another teacher, and right in front of me to boot, but he was right. Nothing Mother ever taught me about the Daughters of Neith referenced anything about magical flame, healing abilities, or whatever it was that just happened that allowed Ethan and me to share a magical fire and fend off the Cardinal, who had just flown away almost certainly to fight another day.

"You desire instruction to better yourself and to prepare for what is to come. A noble request, Mr. Harkreader." Ada squeezed Ethan's fingers. "It is done."

"Thank you," Ethan said with a humble bow of his head.

Impressive. That's a move Mother would have used.

"Now, Mr. Harkreader, go check on your friends. Some or all may have need of your healing touch."

As Ethan took off with Falco to help the rest of our crew, Ada held me back.

"Miss Delacroix, I would have words with you."

"With me?"

She beckoned me closer. "Woman to woman."

I did as she asked, my scalp crawling the way it did when Mother used to take me into her confidence about truly important matters. "Yes?"

"Tell me that you know," Ada whispered. "That you understand."

"Know?" My brows bunched together. "Know what?"

"Oh, you poor girl." She shook her head. "You're as deluded as Harkreader."

My cheeks blossomed with a completely different fire. "What are you talking about?"

"Do you understand what happened here today?" The pyromancer's eyes burned with intensity. "You nearly died."

A gallow's laugh parted my lips. "How could I forget?"

"Hold your sarcasm." Ada raised a finger. "Today, I witnessed you bleed for Harkreader while he quested for another woman, this one whom he states he loves above all others. And yet, when it was you who was struck down, he gave of his own light and life to keep you from crossing the veil, all at great risk to his own safety."

"And I'd do the same for him in an instant." The words were out of my mouth before I could stop them. "I mean—"

Ada rested a hand on my wrist. "I know you would." She pulled in a deep breath through her nostrils. "I envy you, girl. This is the exciting part, the part where you don't know, but you hope and pray that maybe, just maybe..."

"Ethan and I are friends. Partners. Teacher and student." I looked away. "Anyway, he's with Seph. I don't dare intrude."

"I saw that kiss, Miss Delacroix. Poems have been written about kisses like that. Ships have sailed. Wars started and battles ended. Hide from your feelings all you want, but the truth is just that, the truth."

The warmth in my cheeks went white hot. "Ethan was simply doing what he needed to do to help me. That's all it was."

Ada laughed. "Keep telling yourself that for as long as you need to, girl, but trust a pyromancer when I tell you I know fire when I see it."

"Speaking of fire," I quickly changed the subject, "how is it that Ethan can do things neither Mother nor any of our ancestors could do, at least to the best of my knowledge? Mother could call the Light, but this Flame? It's new."

"Would that I could tell you," Ada answered. "Just because I recognize the fire in Mr. Harkreader doesn't mean I understand from where it comes."

Both our eyes followed Ethan as he moved from a dazed-but-sitting-up Neko to a still-sprawled Maddox. The burning in my cheeks doubled as the man with whom I'd spent the majority of my waking minutes for a month bent to aid a man I once gave all my love, not to mention something else quite precious.

"If I may wax a bit poetic," Ada added with a whimsical smile, "I'd say the passion that burns at Harkreader's core has let itself be known without any shred of doubt." She scrunched her nose thoughtfully. "The heart knows what it wants, Miss Delacroix, even when the mind hasn't quite caught up."

"Maybe."

Ethan knelt by Maddox, the two of them enveloped in white flame for what seemed like a year. Maddox eventually sat up, the effort clearly winding him as Ethan supported his upper body not that differently than he had mine before. The two shared a look of relief and gratitude, the moment between them bordering on friendly. The whole interaction sent the hairs on my neck on end more than when they'd been at each other's throats.

"It's funny." I continued to steer the conversation away from the topic that had left my intestines in knots. "Watching Ethan and Seph this month has reminded me of what it was like when Maddox and I were figuring everything out at the beginning."

"Wait." Ada asked. "You...and the coyote?"

"He's not all bad." I forced a smile. "I'm just glad that he and Ethan finally look like they're getting along."

"You think those two are destined to be friends?" Ada let out a lone chuckle. "And I thought I liked playing with fire."

"What are you trying to say?"

Any mirth left Ada's features. "Simply that I posited already that Mr. Harkreader's newfound talents are but a manifestation of an emotional fire that burns at his core, a flame that simply will not be denied." Her dark eyes burned through me. "The boy is clearly in love. The only question remaining, I suppose, is with whom?"

CODA
TAINTED LOVE

"So, you've earned their trust." The woman, her lustrous hair a deep brown with red highlights cascading down her exposed back and past her waist, whispered seductively to the man kneeling shirtless before her.

"I have, Mistress." The man tilted his head forward in deference to the woman in her sheer dress dyed the color of the brightest poppy of the field. "With more than my fair share of bruises, cuts, and hits to head."

"Then you have performed admirably." The woman stroked the man's hair as she would the fur of a favorite pet. "But the real question: have you won your way back into *her* heart?"

"Not yet." The man gazed into the woman's golden eyes. "She was slow to allow me into her life the first time, and given our recent history, it will take more than a few days for her to trust me in that way again."

"But you've made progress, I assume?"

The man offered a simple nod. "I've seen her looking my way a few times, sometimes in question, often in exasperation, but always with at least a hint of longing. That's a scent I know all too well."

"Longing?" the woman purred. "For what was, or for what could be?"

The man sniffed the air. "The yearning for love couldn't waft off her any more if she were a bitch in heat, be it for me or for this other she's found. For all her insistence on maintaining the illusion of indifference about being alone in the world, all she really wants is to *be* with someone, to *belong* with someone. I gave her that before, and as her current infatuation remains far too wrapped around the finger of another woman for him to see the bird he holds in his hand..."

"The Snow woman is indeed a beauty for the ages." The woman drew the man's head to her waist and pressed his temple to her supple midriff. "And Ascendant or not, such a voice is the stuff of legend."

"The Cardinal has her, though I actually believe him when he says his intent is not to harm her but to keep her as his ace against whoever or whatever he believes is coming."

The woman tensed. "Having one of such talents at his disposal would indeed represent a prudent strategy, I suppose."

"Do you know what is coming?" The man furrowed his brow. "Who or what it is the Cardinal fears?"

"Perhaps," the woman answered, her voice trembling with a mix of fear, anger, and passion. "But like the Cardinal, I believe I shall keep my own counsel on such matters, at least for the moment."

"Shall I return to them, then, Mistress?" the man asked. "Tonight, they celebrate surviving their latest hardship, if not victory. I managed to slip away long enough to offer you my report, but I should probably get back soon lest my absence arouse suspicion."

"You've fought for them, bled for them, and sacrificed for a cause that was not your own. They will believe whatever story you tell them." She pulled him up from the ground, drawing his chest to hers. "And I have been oh so lonely in the days since you left my side." She drew his mouth close to her own and softly bit his lower lip between her gleaming white incisors. "Did you miss me as well?"

"Of course, Mistress." The man pulled the woman into his body, his hands roaming the nape of her neck, the small of her back, the curve of her hip. His eyes golden in their own way, he studied her as an animal studies a mate, and the rest of the world faded into the background as he kissed her with a passion bordering on obsession.

"Take me, Coyote," the woman whispered as the man scooped her up from the floor and carried her to the softly lit bed in the next room. "Show me, Maddox Trainor. Show me who owns you, heart and soul, and who it is you truly love."

Author's Note

HELLO AGAIN

October 2023

As I sit in a coffee shop on Friday the 13th, the night before a new moon in October 2023 and smack in the middle of spooky season, having just completed my (God willing) last edit pass on Book II of Songs of the Ascendant, I find myself eager to turn my attention back to Book III—the first 70,000 words or so are done, though I sense an extensive rewrite in my near future—but before I jump ship, I wanted to record a few thoughts.

Writing *All Fired Up* was both very similar to and very different from writing *Shadows of the Night*. The same world, the same characters, the same tense and person: all of these commonalities greased the skids for the creative process for this particular book. Switching to Rosemary's point of view, however, proved challenging, as the trained-since-birth Daughter of Neith speaks, acts, and sees the same world very differently from our still relatively green Mr. Harkreader, and yet remains more naive than Ethan in many aspects of her life. Also, I hadn't switched POVs mid-series since the last book of *Fugue & Fable* either, so that was new and exciting as well. I had initially planned for the entire series to be told through Ethan's point of view, but as I started thinking about what happened in this particular part of the series, it became clear very quickly that we'd have to hang with Rosemary if we wanted to see most of the action. Throw in a bit of a time jump (more on that at the end of Book III, I suspect) and some new romantic complications, and we were off to the races.

I must say, I enjoyed trying on Rosemary for almost 110,000 words. Like Mira Tejedor and Carol Davis, writing a female character as a man is both challenging but also fun and rewarding. Learning page by page her place in this world and how she connects so many different characters from so many different corners was a ton of fun, particularly her interactions with the other two main characters. I look forward to spending more time in her head, but Book III is going to be all Persephone, so get ready for another shift, because the point of view is about to change again.

Time again for some acknowledgements.

To my first/alpha reader, Joelle Reizes, AKA J.D. Blackrose, thank you yet again for not only reading all my stuff first to make sure all my brain jigsaw puzzles aren't missing pieces, but also for letting me be the first to read your stories and trusting me with your words. This book and this series wouldn't be the same without you.

To Sarah Sover, my second/beta reader, thank you so much for burning through this book and for your excellent observations. You definitely helped sharpen the edge of this blade.

To Robyn Huss, my editor, thank you for another outstanding job in finding all the little peccadillos as well as the enormous gaffes in my story and taking my figurative little road full of plotholes and speed bumps transforming it into a nice smooth avenue fit for driving.

To Ivan Zann, your depiction of Purple Rain Rosemary couldn't have been more perfect if you'd reached into my head and poured my thoughts directly onto the screen. Thank you so much for working with me. I hope I have opportunity to work with you again in the future. Credit to Laura LiPuma, Ed Thrasher, and Ron Slenzak for the original image from Prince's album, *Purple Rain*.

To Natania Barron, my trusted book cover designer, I always appreciate not only the beauty, but the attention to detail you put into not only every cover you create, but pretty much everything you do. So glad to have you on board as this series moves forward.

A shout out to Amy Saatzer, the store manager of my local and favorite Starbucks, whose sleeve tattoos of all the iconic horror figures inspired our favorite young skiomancer, Katrina.

The last acknowledgement in each book in my *Songs of the Ascendant* series will be to the Queen of Rock and Roll and my muse for this series, Pat Benatar, and the song for which the particular volume is named.

"All Fired Up" was written by Kerryn Tolhurst and was initially performed and released by Rattling Sabres, an Australian country rock group, in 1987. A year later, Pat Benatar covered the song and released it as the lead single on her seventh studio album, *Wide Awake in Dreamland*. This song became Pat's last top 40 single in the US and charted high in the UK, Canada, South Africa, and hit number two in Australia. This song was nominated for Best Female Rock Vocal Performance at the 1989 Grammys and is still played daily across the globe three decades later. This song never fails to get my heart pumping and my blood flowing.

And what more can I say about Pat Benatar? She did make it to North Carolina this year, though it happened to be on a weekend I was away and the closest she came other than that weekend was Washington D.C. Of the big acts I've always wanted to see live, she and her husband, Neil Giraldo, are at the top of the list. God willing, it's going to happen someday, but for now, I will have to keep rocking out to Ms. Benatar from the comfort of my home here in Charlotte, NC, and continue to dream.

ABOUT THE AUTHOR

Darin Kennedy, born and raised in Winston-Salem, NC, is a graduate of Wake Forest University and Bowman Gray School of Medicine. After completing family medicine residency in the mountains of Virginia, he served eight years as a United States Army physician and wrote his first novel in the sands of northern Iraq.

His first published novel, *The Mussorgsky Riddle,* was born from a fusion of two of his lifelong loves: classical music and world mythology. *The Stravinsky Intrigue* continues those same themes, and his **Fugue & Fable** trilogy culminates in *The Tchaikovsky Finale*. **The Pawn Stratagem**, his contemporary fantasy trilogy of *Pawn's Gambit*, *Queen's Peril*, and *King's Crisis* combines contemporary fantasy, superheroics, and the ancient game of chess. His young adult novel is *Carol*, a modern-day retelling of *A Christmas Carol* billed as Scrooge meets *Mean Girls*.

His latest series, **Songs of the Ascendant**, falls at the intersection of *Highlander*, *X-Men*, *Buffy the Vampire Slayer*, and *Chuck*, all told through a filter of 80s pop music and specifically the oeuvre of Pat Benatar. Comprised thus far of *Shadows of the Night*, *All Fired Up*, and *You Better Run*, this story is just getting started.

His short stories can be found in numerous anthologies and magazines, and the best, particularly those about a certain *Necromancer for Hire*, are collected for your reading pleasure under Darin's imprint, 64Square Publishing.

Doctor-by-day and novelist-by-night, he writes and practices medicine in Charlotte, NC. When not engaged in either of the above activities, he has been known to strum the guitar, enjoy a bite of sushi, and rumor has it he even sleeps on occasion. Find him online at darinkennedy.com.

THE BAND
Rosemary Delacroix – Daughter of Neith
Ethan Harkreader – Agent of Neith
Persephone Snow – Siren
Luc Delacroix

SKIOMANCERS
Katrina Wellen

ELEMENTALISTS
Dietrich Falco – Aeromancer
Ada Abebe – Pyromancer

THERIODANS
Maddox Trainor - Coyote
Neko – Tiger

TECHNOMANCERS
L.J.
Minako

OTHERS
The Driver
The Greyhound
Madame Midnight / The Midnight Angel
El Ángel del Alba / The Angel of the Morning
Lady Day / The Angel of Harlem
The Cardinal

All Fired Up - Pat Benatar
The Glamorous Life - Sheila E.
Out of the Blue - Debbie Gibson
Cruel to Be Kind - Nick Lowe
Goodbye to You - Scandal
Breaking the Law - Judas Priest
Under Pressure - Queen & David Bowie
Spy in the House of Love - Was (Not Was)
Father Figure - George Michael
Every Breath You Take - The Police
Can't Fight this Feeling - REO Speedwagon
Together in Electric Dreams - Philip Oakey/Giorgio Moroder
Wanna Be Startin' Somethin' - Michael Jackson
Mystery Lady - Billy Ocean
Night Moves - Marilyn Martin
Let's Dance - David Bowie
Electric Avenue - Eddy Grant
Centerfield - John Fogerty
The Unforgettable Fire - U2
Flirtin' with Disaster - Molly Hatchet
Passengers - Elton John
Midnight at the Lost and Found - Meat Loaf
Devil Inside - INXS
Nite and Day - Al B. Sure!
We're Ready - Boston
Come Go With Me - Exposé
It's a Miracle - Culture Club
I Won't Back Down - Tom Petty
Patience - Guns N' Roses
I Know You're Out There Somewhere - The Moody Blues
Prove Your Love - Taylor Dayne
Fight Fire with Fire - Kansas
Eternal Flame - The Bangles
Tainted Love - Soft Cell
Hello Again - The Cars

KICKSTARTER BACKERS

A special thank you to our 227 Kickstarter Backers!
You helped make this happen, and these books are for you!

Sheryl R. Hayes, Kiersten Keipper, Bill Feero, Chuck Teal, Beth
Wojiski, Kerney Williams, Dino Hicks, Jessica Bay, Rowan Stone, Josh
Minchew, V. Hartman DiSanto, Hope Griffin Diaz, April Baker,
Princess Donut, Allison Charlesworth, Shanda, maileguy, Joelle
Reizes, Alexandra Corrsin, Joseph Procopio, Kevin A. Davis, Robert S.
Evans, Eric P. Kurniawan, Amber Derpinghaus, Andy Bartalone, R.
David Grimes, Patti & Joan Holland, Scott Casey, Asha Jade Goodwin,
Chuck & Colleen Parker, Jessica Nettles, Sarah J. Sover, Joe Compton,
Brendan Lonehawk, Tera, James & Hannah Fulbright, Chris
Fletemier, Carol B, A. L. Kaplan, Joey & Matt Starnes, Wanda
Harward, Dennis M. Myers, Evelyn M, Nick Crook, Bob!, Bill Bibo Jr.,
Karen Palmer, Dina Barron, Charlie "Kaiju Mapping" Kaufman,
Nancy E. Dunne, Rachel A. Brune, Noella Handley, Sara T. Bond, SM
Hillman, C Keeley, John L. French, Anthony Martin, Lynn K, Fay
Shlanda, Cristov Russell, Candice N. Carp, Samuel Montgomery-
Blinn, Susan Griffith, Vee Luvian, Randy Cantrell, Gail Z. Martin,
Tawni Muon, Caryn S, Jimmy Liang, Preacher Todd, Casey & Travis
Schilling, The King of Rhye, Ruth Brazell, Melisa Todd, Vic Chase,
Tom Sink, Nicholas Ahlhelm, Donna Berryman, Richard Novak, Liz
Lamb, Angie Ross, Jonathan Casas, Christy Wilhelm, Robert Claney,
Carol Gyzander, Ollie Oxxenfree, Ángel González, Caitlin Wright,
Michelle Botwinick, Ashley & Cody, Amelia Sides, Nicole Rich,
Ardinzul, Scott Valeri, Richard Dansky, Josh Bluestein, K.H. DeNeen,
David Price, Mair Clan, Leonard Rosenthol, Vikki Perry, RHR,
Jennifer & Benjamin Adelman, Everette Beach, Charlie Hawkins, Zeb
Berryman, Julia Benson-Slaughter, Jesse Adams, Ash Peeples, Susan

Ragsdale, Tina Hoffmann, Robert Osborne, A.M. Giddings, Michelle LeBlanc, Amanda, Ken St Clair, J. T. Arralle, Alec Christensen, hemisphire, Marian Gosling, Zack Keedy, Dee Kennedy, Andrea Fornero, Allison Finch, Sandy Reece, Maya Barb, Shirley Kohl, Ronald H. Miller, Adrianne McDonald, James Ball III, Louise K, Elyse M Grasso, Steve Ryder, Debbie Yerkes, Brendon Towle, LB Clark, Jenn Huerta, Emily L, Eric Guy, Reverend Trevor Curtis, Jim Reader, Shauna Kantes, Stephanie Taylor, Kyla M, Micah Cash, Eric R. Asher, Cindy & Scott Kuntzelman, Avery Wild, Wes "nothing clever to say" Smith, Tamsin Silver, Steve Saffel, phoenix17, Mike Dubost, M.C. Jordan, Sarah Thompson, Cursed Dragon Ship Publishing, Venessa Giunta, Drew Bailey, Sue Phillips, LaZrus66, Scott M. Williams, William C. Tracy, Larissa Lichty, David Scoggins, Mari Mancusi, Jim Ryan, Seth Keipper, Marc Alan Edelheit, Dr. William Alexander Graham IV, Perry Harward, Liam Fisher, Jessica Glanville, Susan Roddey, Regina Kirby, Jeremy Bredeson & Leon Moses, Misty Massey, Janet Iannantuono, Regis Murphy, "Yes That Mark" Wilcox, Berta Platas, Kristen Clark, Matt, B. Y., Theresa Glover, Carol Malcolm, Dr. Keith Hunter Nelson, Adam, Leigh A. Boros & Robert A. Hilliard Jr., Aysha Rehm, Gary Phillips, Tom Savola, Audrey Hackett, Michael J. Sullivan, Annarose Mitchell, Karen M, Patrick J. Blanchard, Kayleigh Osborne, Chris Oakley, Andrea Judy, Casey, Helen Gassaway, J. Matthew Saunders, Carol Mammano, Danielle Ackley-McPhail & eSpec Books, Jared Nelson, and The Creative Fund by BackerKit

SONGS OF THE ASCENDANT

Shadows of the Night

All Fired Up

You Better Run

ALSO BY DARIN KENNEDY

<u>FUGUE & FABLE</u>

The Mussorgsky Riddle

The Stravinsky Intrigue

The Tchaikovsky Finale

<u>THE PAWN STRATAGEM</u>

Pawn's Gambit

Queen's Peril

King's Crisis

Carol: Being a Ghost Story of Christmas

The April Sullivan Chronicles: Necromancer for Hire

www.ingramcontent.com/pod-product-compliance
Lightning Source LLC
Chambersburg PA
CBHW031313210726
48287CB00005B/1535